WORK

"An endless significance lies in work ; in idleness alone is there perpetual despair." — CARLYLE.

WORK

A STORY OF EXPERIENCE

Louisa May Alcott

Introduction by Sarah Elbert

SCHOCKEN BOOKS · NEW YORK

First published by SCHOCKEN BOOKS 1977

10 9 8 7 6 5 4 3   79 80 81 82 83 84

Introduction copyright © 1977 by Schocken Books Inc.

Library of Congress Cataloging in Publication Data

Alcott, Louisa May, 1832–1888.
  Work.

   I. Title.

[PZ3.A355Wo4] [PS1017]   813'.4   76-48849

Manufactured in the United States of America

TO

MY MOTHER,

WHOSE LIFE HAS BEEN A LONG LABOR OF LOVE,
THIS BOOK IS GRATEFULLY INSCRIBED

BY

HER DAUGHTER.

CONTENTS.

LIST OF ILLUSTRATIONS,

FROM DRAWINGS BY SOL EYTINGE.

INTRODUCTION

LOUISA MAY ALCOTT is best known as the author of *Little Women,* an enormously popular novel for adolescent girls in the late nineteenth century. It has remained lively reading for a twentieth century audience. Its first generation of readers assumed correctly that the characters and many of the events in the book were modeled on the author's childhood and domestic experiences. Her father, Bronson Alcott, was a philosopher and educator, but outside of his family and the Transcendentalist circle of Alcott friends contemporaries frequently identified him as the grandfather of the little women. Louisa Alcott's life differed in many respects from that of ordinary nineteenth century American women. Her family was active in public life, she remained a spinster in an age when marriage and motherhood were the central events in women's lives, and she had a successful literary career. But her unique ability to enter into the lives of women and children through her writings rested on her sympathy and personal sharing of the burdens of nineteenth century womanhood. *Work: A Story of Experience,* like all of her fiction, evoked her own life experience and the historical circumstances of womanhood in America.

At the height of Alcott's career she was exhausted by housekeeping and nursing chores coupled with the demands of writing. An experienced housekeeper appeared at her front door, announcing that she had read Louisa's novel *Work* and had come to see if its author lived up to her principles as an employer.[1] The housekeeper's appreciation of the novel reflects the trust Louisa Alcott's readers felt in her lucid portrayal of their lives. *Work* is an expression of Alcott's feminist principles and a major effort toward synthesizing in popular, readable form the broad set of beliefs encompassing family, education, suffrage, labor and the moral reform of social life that defined feminist ideology in the nineteenth century. In addressing these concerns, she broadened the scope of her fiction from the domestic relations she excelled in portraying, to an urgent, passionate portrait of the female life cycle in all its complexity.

For modern readers, an understanding of *Work* is enhanced by the analysis of events, problems, and characters drawn from Alcott's own life and times. The novel develops a definition of womanhood shaped by the changes and the continuity of woman's experience from 1833 through 1873. In that time, women's lives were marked by an awareness of the democratic potential liberated through the rise of individualism. But they also felt deeply about the loss of harmony and balance in a world divided into separate male and female spheres, social classes, ethnic and racial groups. The proper relationship of the individual to society was being questioned by Transcendentalists, who believed in the principle of individual self-reliance but also in the need to maintain a balanced and harmonious society. The search for answers to the problems of a fragmented and divided society defined Alcott's personal history and *Work*. The integrity of her writing reaches across a hundred years to readers who will find the search to be their own.

Bronson Alcott, the son of an impoverished Connecticut farm family, was a largely self-educated peddler before he became a philosophic school master.[2] Her mother, Abigail May Alcott, called Abba by her family and friends, was the youngest daughter of a distinguished and well-to-do New England family; her brother Samuel became a Unitarian minister dedicated to social reform.[3] In 1830, when the Alcotts married, they joined forces in support of a nineteenth century reform movement that included abolitionism, women's rights, domestic reform, and education as important issues in the creation of a just society. Anna Bronson Alcott was born in 1831, and her sister Louisa May Alcott was born on her father's birthday, November 29, 1832. Two more girls, Elizabeth and May, completed the family by 1840, when Bronson declared that a fourth female child obviously manifested God's will that the Alcotts be content to "rear women for the future world." So, the Alcotts acknowledged an end to Abba's childbearing role with May's birth. Bronson had publicly urged that husbands restrain their sexual impulses in favor of their wives' health and well-being. Such attitudes reflected the domestic reform movement that included not only Bronson and Abba Alcott but Bronson's cousin, William Alcott, the author of many advice pamphlets to spouses and parents, and some of the Alcotts' lifelong friends, Lydia Maria Child, the Horace Manns, and Elizabeth Peabody. The movement's goal was to "create a new family ideal, a strong conservative pattern for the American people, conventionally grounded in Christian morality and yet varied enough in its design to meet the many social needs of an expanding culture."[4]

Bronson's most interesting educational experiment, however, was carried out, with his wife's somewhat reluctant cooperation, on their two older daughters. He observed their development and kept a record that would inform his determined guidance of their steps toward Christian perfection. A consciousness of their individual gifts and flaws would be an invaluable scientific aid to discipline. Love was to be the key to that discipline, for familial love led to love of God. Bronson's journals, the family's letters and diaries, and Louisa's novels constitute a record of childhood, adolescence and family life designed to support and develop young people in the Transcendental ideal of perfection, an ideal that moves beyond material gratification to a union with divine Goodness and Harmony. It is an ideal critical of nineteenth century competitive materialism and at the same time supportive of individualism. The society's limitations on women's fulfillment as individual human beings were obvious to the Alcotts, and while their household mirrored the larger world's sexual division of tasks, it also encouraged the development of their daughters' impressive talents.

Louisa and her sisters had very little institutional schooling but an excellent tutorial education by their parents and friends. One family acquaintance recalled that Sophia Hawthorne helped teach Louisa her alphabet and that Henry David Thoreau taught her botany. In some ways, despite the poverty and anxiety which she recorded in her early journals, Louisa's childhood was a delightful departure from the genteel restrictions of most girls her age. Her childhood was spent in the country or in suburbs still rural in tone. The sisters were each other's best playmates, and all were encouraged to exercise their minds and bodies freely. The entire family's cultural environment was astonishingly rich by any standards. The girls read Plato, Thucydides, and Shakespeare, as well as Dickens, Scott, and a variety of popular literature. Louisa was identified by her parents and sisters as possessing literary talents when she was very young; her earliest poem was copied carefully by her mother when she was five years old. Abba presented her with writing materials and a desk, and the whole family listened to her stories and acted in her original plays. Ralph Waldo Emerson gave Louisa access to his library, and she made good use of it. In gratitude, her first collection of tales, *Flower Fables* published in 1855, was originally written for his daughter, Ellen Emerson. For sixteen hundred copies of the first edition, Louisa received a total of thirty-two dollars.

But this admittedly unusual and stimulating environment was not without serious tensions, which Louisa felt and often recorded. Her mother, at the end of her life, recalled that the family had moved more than twenty times, an unusual pattern even in a highly mobile society. The moves were largely dictated by financial constraints, for the Alcotts never owned a home of their own until Louisa's adolescence, when Abba inherited a modest sum of money. Louisa resolved at a very early age to earn enough money to free her family from the constant worries and real deprivation she experienced as a child. Bronson refused to seek conventional employment, and neither his lectures nor his books ever brought in a living for the family. He arrived home one night after a Western lecture tour with one dollar in his pocket and a shawl around his shoulders because his overcoat had been stolen. Abba uttered not one word of reproof but only rejoiced that he was home safe and sound.

The Transcendentalist circle supported a famous experiment in communal living, Brook Farm, and Bronson was moved to start such an experiment of his own with several English friends who had founded a school based upon Alcott's principles of education. Louisa later described the experiment, Fruitlands, hilariously in her essay, "Transcendental Wild Oats," but she was quite old enough in 1842 to have been aware of the cold, hunger and incredible burdens laid upon her mother and sisters during the experience at a run-down farm incapable of providing the self-sufficient economy and spiritually exalted life envisioned by Bronson.[5] When a visitor asked if there were any beasts of burden at Fruitlands, Mrs. Alcott replied, "only one woman."[6]

The failure of Fruitlands threw the burden of supporting the family on Abba Alcott and their friends, and by the age of thirteen Louisa was already contributing to the family income as a dressmaker for the neighbor children's dolls.

The Hillside House in Concord, purchased with Mrs. Alcott's small inheritance, was the scene of the Alcott girls' exploits, while the physical surroundings of the more spacious Orchard House are actually described in *Little Women*. But Concord, while an idyllic setting for domestic life, did not present opportunities for the Alcotts to sustain a living. The Boston South End Friendly Society asked Abba Alcott to be its City Missionary. She accepted and became a sort of social worker, urging her employers not to make her a "substitute for our own private charities" but "to give me the honor of being your pioneer to the worthy sufferer, to the destitute, the despairing and the hopeless."[7] So, by the age of sixteen Louisa Alcott found herself in Boston accepting waged work as her means of contributing to her family's survival. She tried school teaching in her sister Anna's small primary school but was frustrated and exhausted by it. The family fun of producing and acting Louisa's plays seemed a source of employment more congenial to her tastes, and friends tried to get Louisa's plays produced in Roxbury and Boston with little success. Abba Alcott's employment office gave Louisa one of the typical jobs open to young women in mid-nineteenth century, domestic service. But the promised work as "companion" turned out to be that of "galley slave," and a humiliating experience with her employer taught her very quickly that domestic work in one's family and domestic service were quite different things.

Her first published story in 1850 did not magically open a literary career, and she had to continue housework, laundering, and sewing for a living while her mother took in boarders. But in 1855 after a summer in Walpole, New Hampshire, with family and friends the tide began to turn, not in terms of cash income—for she recorded her winter's earnings that year as "School, one quarter . . . $50, Sewing . . . $50, Stories . . . $20,"[8]—but, as she put it, "I do seem to be getting on a little, and that encourages me." By 1856 *The Saturday Evening Gazette* was paying for Alcott's stories, and while sewing could not make her fortune it did leave her imagination free to plan the stories she wrote on Sundays.

A few years later the Alcotts purchased Orchard House in Concord, and it was there that two significant events in the family's history took place, both eventually immortalized by

Louisa. In January of 1858 Beth Alcott died, and Louisa wrote, "So the first break comes, and I know what Death means—a liberator for her, a teacher for us."[9] Then, in April, Anna became engaged to John Pratt, and with that engagement Louisa lost the close companionship of two of her sisters and really began her commitment to aiding May's self-actualization. From then on Louisa's earnings went not only to support her mother and father but also to May's education and artistic training.

She went to Boston to find work once again, sending most of her wages home. In 1859 Anna was married, and Louisa began her novel *Moods,* the first attempt to deal with the problem of the Lady as a fictional stereotype posed against the necessities of True Womanhood. In fact, she had briefly attempted to pose her ideal woman in a short story "The Lady and the Woman" when she said of the Woman:

> "I would have her strong enough to stand alone and give, not ask, support. Brave enough to think and act as well as feel. Keen-eyed enough to see her own and other faults, and wise enough to find a cure for them. I would have her humble, self-reliant; gentle though strong; man's companion, not his plaything; able and willing to face storm as well as sunshine and share life's burdens as they come."[10]

Alcott's task in *Moods* was to convince her readers of the necessity of nurturing just such a woman; it was a task she undertook over and over again in her fiction. The problem with American individualism, as reflected in Transcendental thought, was that it required experience and self-reliance, two preconditions denied young women in the nineteenth century.

Marriages based upon inequality of experience and female dependency would founder as Sylvia Yule's marriage in *Moods* foundered. But the experiences of independence and selfhood which could contribute to women's domestic competence and to equality in marriage might also lead women to challenge male authority in the home and outside in the marketplace. *Moods* was only a beginning in the development of Alcott's exploration of the problem. Yet the fact that she eventually completed the book for publication in 1865 and then, undaunted by Henry James' dismissal of it as "her version of the old story of the husband, the wife and the lover,"[11] rewrote the end and republished it in 1882 attests to her determination not to lose the original purpose of the story.

Before her completion of the first edition of *Moods,* a "war in what has been called the housewife's front yard could not leave Louisa Alcott out."[12] She decided to go to Washington as a nurse and at the age of twenty boarded the train with May and Julian Hawthorne as her escorts, feeling, she said, "as if I was the son of the house going to war."[13] This theme also echoed throughout her work—the need to expend her energies in direct confrontation with the world and to realize experiences traditionally reserved to "the son of the house."

Her experience in the Civil War was brief but intense. Within three months typhoid fever had discharged her and sent her back to Concord to recuperate. But the experience enabled her to write *Hospital Sketches,* "The Brothers," and "M.L.," and with their publication in *Atlantic Monthly* her status as a serious writer was sufficiently established to enable her to make writing a full time career. Encouraged by the "commendations bestowed on *Hospital Sketches,*" she completed *Moods* and was not deterred by James' criticism of it as trivial. *Work* was begun in this same period, in 1861, and the emotional differences between the struggling young woman who sewed, taught, washed, and cleaned for a living and the determined author are summed up in a letter in which Alcott recalled, "At twenty-five I supported myself by pen and needle; at thirty-five I supported myself and family by pen alone."[14] In 1865 Louisa went abroad as a paid companion, and her romantic encounter there with a young Pole, Ladislas Wisnewsky, who appears as Laurie in *Little Women,* was at least partly tarnished by her employment status. Louisa was thirty-three and Ladislas was twelve or thirteen years younger, and while they seemed to enjoy each other's company in a thoroughly open and affectionate way, there is no indication that it was ever a romantic attachment.

The central fact of woman's life in this period was marriage and motherhood. Both were experiences which, to Louisa's generation, generally precluded careers. Louisa's determination to support her family was both typical of the self-sacrifice idealized in conventional views of true womanhood and an atypical example of strivings toward individual achievement usually denied women. The fact that Louisa continued to hold herself responsible for the domestic chores associated with women's role even as she pursued a serious literary career is important to understand. In 1867, the year Thomas Niles of Roberts Brothers asked Louisa to write a girls' book and *Merry's Museum,* a children's magazine, asked her to assume editorial responsibility, she was still writing her stories as she nursed her ailing mother and sewed for the family.

But it was the editorial job and the promise of five hundred dollars a year that enabled Louisa to move to Boston, though it was not a permanent move. Until the end of her life, Louisa's room of her own was only a temporary one in which to escape family pressures and labor for their support. She wrote to her mother from her room at 6 Hayward Place in Boston, "Keep all the money I send; pay up every bill; get comforts and enjoy yourselves."[15]

Her love of plays and acting never diminished, and she continued to watch Charlotte Cushman and Fanny Kemble perform and to act herself in charity performances; but her talents and the need for a steady income for her family prevented any serious career in the theater. Theater and visits to family and friends combined with her increasing success as an author made her write that "perhaps we are to win after all, and conquer poverty, neglect, pain and debt, and march on with flags flying into the new world with the new year."[16] But there was a price to be paid for voluntary spinsterhood and literary success, for most of nineteenth century American society regarded the family as the only serious source of love and support for women. As Louisa played with her sister Anna's children she wrote, "She is a happy woman! I sell *my* children, and though they feed me, they don't love me as hers do."[17]

Between February and June of 1868 the first twelve chapters of *Little Women* were done while writing three other tales, and by July 15th the book was completed. In October the first edition was sold out. She was commissioned to write a second volume for spring, and despite the insistence of readers that its heroine "Jo" marry "Laurie," Louisa said, "As if that was the only end and aim of woman's life. I won't marry Jo to Laurie to please anyone."[18] The reviews were unanimously approving. Alcott had provided a means of preserving the family as the foundation of the Republic, of making female adolescence an important life stage, and of presenting a portrait of loving self-sacrifice that still recognized young women's dreams of human fulfillment. Yet Alcott never really acknowledged *Little Women* as a literary success, and as she developed the domestic formula for children's fiction she referred to herself as "the golden goose who can sell her eggs for a good price if she isn't killed by too much driving."[19]

An Old Fashioned Girl enabled her to go to Europe with May and their friend Alice Bartlett. The trip was a great success. Louisa enjoyed revisiting the sights she had seen as the paid companion of a more fortunate woman years earlier. She celebrated the entire trip in *Shawl Straps* and *Aunt Jo's Scrap Bag*,[20] and much of the comedy in these tales concerns the juxtaposition of independent American spinsters with imprisoned European girls. The latter are forever planning trousseaus or shopping with their watchful mammas, and the sight moved Louisa to sign letters "Spinsterhood Forever."

Finally, Louisa worked on *Little Men* early in 1871 while still abroad. John Pratt's death gave Louisa another family to support, and so her European holiday was not totally a self-indulgence. May was allowed to remain in London to receive art training, but Louisa returned home to deal with the family crises. In 1872, in the midst of literary success which brought no dimunition of domestic responsibilities, she wrote in her journal:

> "Work is my salvation . . . got out the old manuscript of "Success" and called it "Work!" Fired up the engine and plunged into a vortex, with many doubts about getting out. Can't work slowly; the thing possesses me and I must obey till it's done."[21]

Alcott marshalled incredible energy on behalf of her family and social causes, but for herself she had almost none. Neuralgia, headaches, and rheumatism led to the habitual use of morphine to gain the sanctuary of sleep in this period. She worried about her mother's health, her father's lack of public recognition, and her sister Anna's widowhood. Her journal records the shuttling back and forth between domestic duties and writing that characterized the year *Work* was finally completed:

February and March 1873

Anna very ill with pneumonia; home to nurse. Father telegraphed to come home, as we thought her dying. She gave me her boys, but the dear saint got well and kept the lads for herself. Thank God! Back to my work with what wits nursing left me. Had Johnny for a week to keep all quiet at home. . . . Finished *Work*—twenty chapters. Not what it should be—too many interruptions. Should like to do one book in peace and see if it wouldn't be good.

April 1873

The job being done I went home to take May's place. Gave her $1,000 and sent her to London for a year of study. . . . I felt that she needed it, and was glad to be able to help her.

May 1873

D. F. wanted a dozen little tales and agreed to pay $50 apiece, if I give up other things for this. Said I would, as I can do two a day and keep house between times. Cleaned and grubbed and didn't mind the change. Let head rest, and hands and feet do the work. . . . Cold and dull but the thought of May free and happy was my comfort as I messed about.

January 1874

Father disappointed, and rather sad to be left out of so much that he would enjoy and should be asked to help and adorn. A little more money, a pleasant house and time to attend to it, and I'll bring all the best people to see and entertain *him*.[22]

The title page of *Work: A Story of Experience* quoted Thomas Carlyle. "An endless significance lies in work; in idleness alone is there perpetual despair." It was dedicated "To My Mother, Whose Life has Been a Long Labor of Love."

Just four years later in 1877, with May in Paris enjoying her first artistic successes and a life freed from conventional domestic responsibilities, Abba Alcott died. May's letters home had been full of pride in her accomplishments, and both sides of the Atlantic resonated with protestations of self-sacrifice. While Abba said, "I think she has realized what a sacrifice to me it has been to have her gone so far,"[23] May replied to Louisa that "perhaps this sacrifice I have freely chosen to make in losing one year of Marmee's life may make me work better."[24] Four months after Abba's death May married a handsome, young Swiss businessman fourteen years younger than herself. May went to Europe, thereby achieving some physical and psychic distance from family ties and inhibitions and from the example of Louisa's spinsterhood as the only means of resolving the conflict between woman's domestic role and her larger aspirations. After Abba's death the youngest Alcott sister was finally free to claim the rights of a "new woman," marriage and a career. It seemed for a while that May really could break through to a new kind of life, as she wrote to Louisa that "it is the perfection of living; the wife so free from household cares, so busy and so happy. I never mean to have a house or many belongings, but lead the delightfully free life I do now with no society to bother me, and nothing to prevent my carrying out my aims."[25] Louisa compared May's life to her own. "How different our lives are just now—I so lonely, sad and sick, she so happy, well and blest. She always had the cream of things and deserved it. My time is yet to come. . . . I dawdle about and wait to see if I am to live or die. If I live it will be for some new work. . . . I wonder what?"[26]

But Louisa recovered, and by some strange irony it was May who died a few weeks after the birth of her child, Louisa May Neiriker. May's death left her sister unable to write for some time but also with the additional joy and responsibility of caring for Lulu, who arrived in America in 1880. Many of the children's tales completed in the 1880s speak to Louisa's hope for this new child. In an unpublished fragment of a novel about two female artists, Alcott explored the possibilities of career and marriage May's life suggested, but her sister's death left her unable to solve the puzzle. Still, in 1886, *Jo's Boys and How They Turned Out: A Sequel to Little Men* completed the March family trilogy with a depiction of coeducation, marriage and careers for women, and a resounding thump at separate spheres. Jo says:

"Now if you young people don't want England to get ahead of us in many ways, you must bestir yourselves and keep abreast, for our sisters are in earnest, you see, and don't waste time worrying about their sphere, but make it wherever duty calls them.

"'We will do our best, ma'am,' answered the girls heartily, and trooped away with their work baskets, feeling that though they might never be Harriet Martineaus, Elizabeth Barrett Brownings, or George Eliots, they might become noble, useful, and independent women, and earn for themselves some sweet

title from the grateful lips of the poor, better than any queen
could bestow."[27]

While self-sacrifice remained an important principle in all
of Alcott's work and one that was repeatedly praised in
contemporary reviews, one must be careful not to accuse
Alcott of claiming that domesticity was "natural" to women.
On the contrary she thought it a skill that must be taught
and practiced like any other. Her devotion to the women's
movement was a major commitment in her life and work; she
signed the Seneca Falls Principles in a public call to the first
meeting of the New England Women's Suffrage Association.
But while she shared speakers' platforms, earnestly canvassed
the women of Concord, and traveled to women in prison as
well as to women at Vassar College to read her stories, the
major expression of her feminist principles lies in the body of
her writings. When she died on March 6, 1888, in Roxbury,
Massachusetts, she had stories still unfinished on her writing
table. She was attended by Dr. Rhoda Lawrence, a women's
physician and friend, and by her nephew John, whom she had
adopted and made one of her heirs. The family was taken care
of and Lulu provided with an income, and when Bronson
Alcott died saying, "I am going up. Come with me," Duty's
child replied, "Oh, I wish I could,"[28] and did not survive him
by a week. She had lived for others and yet had managed to
create in her writings a vision of self-sacrifice that did not
preclude the realization of women's human potential.

In *Work: A Story of Experience* Louisa May Alcott created
her most complex and sustained heroine, Christie Devon, "one
of that large class of women, who moderately endowed with
talents, earnest and true-hearted, are driven by necessity,
temperament, or principle out into the world to find support,
happiness, and homes for themselves." In the ante-bellum
period, Harriet Martineau, a British social critic and traveler
in America, had listed governess, seamstress, and teacher as
genteel female employments in America. Out of her own

experiences and those of her contemporaries Alcott added domestic service, factory-workshop labor, nursing, and the stage as possibilities. The portraits of single and married women forced to work under circumstances of limited skills, education, and experience soon became familiar to Alcott's readers in *Work*. Women who knew their worth in terms of domestic responsibilities and skills found out that their experience was worthless in terms of jobs. Women's secondary job status reflected the pervasive notion that their primary status was as unwaged housewives and mothers.

The years between 1861, when Louisa began *Success,* and 1873, when the novel was finally completed as *Work,* included her most productive literary efforts and also her liveliest involvement in active social reforms. Her struggle to achieve security and to define her own life as an independent woman also sharpened her awareness that many of the problems of her personal life were embedded in the contradictions of woman's role in American society. Her mother's reminiscences and Grandmother Alcott's story-telling informed Louisa that womanhood had changed drastically. In *Work* the reader confronts those changes in mid-nineteenth century which relegated women to a separate domestic sphere within a larger society that no longer produced its goods and services in the home. Men were moving out into the business world, the factory, and workshop and earning wages as industrialization and urbanization transformed society. In the seventeenth and eighteenth centuries, when households produced most of what families needed for subsistence, women were not defined purely by their housewifely functions; they contributed directly to the family economy. Certainly their position within the household replicated the hierarchical nature of the larger society. But in such an ordered world nearly everyone was dependent upon another, and the sexes, while unequal, were still in the broadest sense interdependent through the family's intimate involvement in daily production.

The American Revolution had been part of a new spirit of

individualism, but daughters and granddaughters of the American Revolution were asked to transmit its democratic ideology of individual opportunity to their sons while they were denied the benefits of that opportunity themselves. The dominant society put forth the promise of a compensatory role for females and institutionalized a separate sphere for them. It idealized self-sacrifice, domesticity, and a loving service for true women who were expected to wield whatever power their purity justified through moral persuasion. Men's power was exercised directly through their ability to earn wages, to vote, and to hold property. Women's power was indirect; their primary function was reproductive, the care of husbands and families. While marriage and child rearing were the central facts of women's life cycle in the nineteenth century, Alcott's earlier books reasoned that sheltered young women were incapable of choosing husbands wisely and still more incapable of sensible child care if they were excluded from education and employment in the larger society. Moreover, the principles of true womanhood were not, for Alcott as for many women, simply an internalization of the ideal set forth in popular fiction, sermons, and editorials. The principles of loving service, compassion, and sisterhood were surely threatened by the impersonal atmosphere of the marketplace. But it was in the contradictions between the promise of individual fulfillment and the awareness of domestic social relationships as both limiting and fulfilling of human beings' deepest needs that Alcott struggled to define nineteenth century womanhood for her readers.

Alcott's first task was to find a satisfactory definition of the status and role of women, one which would lend itself to the heroine's story as a personal search for meaning, and one that could make that meaning universal to readers. She was inspired by Theodore Parker's sermon, "The Public Function of Woman."[29] Ednah Cheney, Alcott's friend and the editor of letters and diaries, recalled that Louisa once said, "Christie's adventures are many of them my own; Mr. Power is Mr.

Parker."[30] Parker assumed that the function of women "begins at home, then, like charity, goes everywhere." Women were not to abandon homemaking for waged labor but were to have the home work transformed through the "progress of mankind, and the application of masculine science to what was once only feminine work."[31] If a woman could buy her flour ready-ground and her cloth ready-woven, she could cut her housework in half and spend the other half of her time in a combination of philanthropy and waged labor as her class position allowed. There was, he noted, a sorry historical transition period in his lifetime in which spinsterhood was on the rise, but it would pass if only men would recognize that women were their equals mentally and morally. Marriage, he felt, must be based upon sexual equality even though he hardly envisioned the sharing of domestic tasks in the home.

Christie Devon is an orphan and so is freed from her natural obligations as the daughter of a farm household to seek her fortune in the broader experience of the waged world. In fact, she uses the language of the Seneca Falls Convention to claim her rights. "There's going to be a new Declaration of Independence," and "emphasized her speech by energetic demonstration in the bread trough, kneading dough as if it was her destiny, and she was shaping it to suit herself." The conversation is, naturally enough, carried on in the large farm kitchen, her Aunt Betsey replying in the form of a recipe. Though humorously done, the scene is really a farewell to rural life with its timeless pattern and prescribed stages of women's work and life. The Civil War had given many women the opportunity to participate in voluntary nursing and social service through the Sanitary Commission; it had disrupted family life sufficiently to turn housewives into heads of households temporarily. Secondary schools for girls were beginning to be commonplace at least in New England, and Christie's longing for the larger world was reflected in her desire to explain to Aunt Betsey that it was now possible to choose a pattern of life different from her aunt's. Christie's farewell statements are an indictment of the conventional choices for women.

Her experience has been a domestic one; all of her skills have been learned either at a village school or at home where she has received a thorough training in housewifery. She goes off knowing that "work was always to be found in the city." The wage system, then, is initially seen by Christie in mid-nineteenth century as the means to independence. At first the boarding house where she begins her round of job hunting frees her from the endless round of tasks that define domesticity and dependence. Abba Alcott had opened an employment office when her city missionary experience dramatized the need to find places for "good girls." Christie goes to just such an office, "the purgatory of the poor." But the combination of skills she associates with housewifery does not seem to be what is wanted. She must define herself by one particular skill and, unable to do so, she goes out into service as a maid, just as Louisa Alcott did.

When her fashionable employer denies her the use of her own name, Christie is beset by her first experience with the anonymity of the waged world. Her new employer is pleased that, unlike the Irish servant girls previously employed, Christie does not object to working with a black cook. It is the cook, Hepsey, who gives Christie a lesson in humility, kindness and patience. Directed to pull off her master's boots and clean them, Christie is horrified, regarding the order as a direct humiliation. In fact, Louisa, in the ordeal of her own few weeks in domestic service, was asked to perform just such a task, and her humiliation led her to quit the job. Hepsey, however, offers to perform the bootblacking for Christie:

> "Dere's more 'gradin works dan dat, chile, and dem dat's bin bliged to do 'em find dis sort bery easy. You's paid for it, honey . . . I's shore I'd never ask it of any woman if I was a man, 'less I was sick or ole. But folks don't seem to 'member dat we've got feelins."

Domesticity produced a consciousness of work not only as "craft" but also as a process quite apart from a wage and hours definition of service. This awareness made domestic service alienating and exploitative, and many servant "girls" openly preferred waged, factory work to the long hours and endless tasks set by household employers. Lucy Maynard Salmon, in discussing the "social disadvantages of domestic service," found the lack of "home privileges" to be a serious source of distress to female servants. "Board and lodging do not constitute a home, and the domestic can never be a part of the family whose external life she shares." As one girl reported, "One must remember that there is a difference between a house, a place of shelter, and a home, a place where all our affections are centered."[32] Domesticity was quite different from domestic service, and it was the substitution of a wage for affection and interdependency that made the one a house and the other a home. This consciousness of work as distinct from job was to cause some confusion in Alcott's heroine and in her own life. In her first twenty-four hours of domestic service Christie learns that she is expected to do the tasks asked of her with the devotion of a family member but with none of the kindness or even closeness of a family relationship to reward her. Actually, it is the pretensions of upwardly mobile social climbers that get Christie fired within a few months; for her elegant mistress, forgetting genteel pretensions, screams at her servant like a fishwife and, having lost her refined manner, is too embarrassed to keep the servant "Jane," who has, of course, seen through the "lady" long ago.

Christie is on her own once again, though she retains both the friendship of Hepsey Johnson and the commitment to abolition and racial integration. Hepsey's loyalty to her enslaved family, whom she hopes to free with her wages, had its real counterpart in many black families, and we know that such evidence in the form of slave narrative later reached Louisa Alcott. Winnie Beale, a freed slave, gratefully acknowledged the receipt of Abba Alcott's clothing and sent a message through Sally Holley to Louisa. "I wish I had something to send the lady. Why! She is a mammy to me. I shall be warm now."[33] Winnie did send something more valuable than clothes to the Alcotts—the long and sad tale of her struggles to reunite her family. Holley promised, "I will not forget to write out more stories as our colored folks tell us—and send you." Louisa had wanted to teach in Port Royal before her illness forced her retirement as a nurse in the Civil War. Hepsey is the first link in the chain of sisterhood that Christie Devon, like Alcott, forges as she discovers that jobs do not fulfill the promise of independence for women, though wages might buy freedom from chattel slavery.

Female friendship in her boarding house brings Christie the opportunity to try Alcott's own long cherished dream of a stage career. The work was tempting, exciting, and romantic enough to fulfill some of the farm girl's dreams; but the life offered unwholesome temptations too, and Christie found that an actress could rarely be a true woman. Sexual familiarities were commonplace, rivalries between actresses prevented real companionship, and Chrisite left this form of employment of her own volition. Having been warned that the stage was an impediment to "genteel" employment, she refrained from mentioning her experience and went off to the seashore with a mother, two children, and the bachelor brother of her employer.

The bachelor, Philip Fletcher, is a wealthy, snobbish invalid, hardly attractive to novelist or reader. But it is plain that Alcott knew enough of the world of fashion to make him a "catch" to husband-hunting maidens at the resort. The observation is clear; the alternative to waged work or slavery is "to marry for a living." Christie believes, as any true woman does, that marriage must be for love alone, yet she is briefly tempted not only by the prospect of luxury but also by the promise of ending her lonely struggle for independence. Family security with Fletcher, however, can only mean subordination and dependency. Christie, recalling that she left the stage of her own will and that honest work of any sort is honorable, refuses the offer of marriage.

At the end of three jobs it is clear to Christie that personal service occupations are humiliating not for the tasks done, or the wages paid, but for the social relations prescribed. Later on in the novel, a mature Christie sums up this experience. "Even in democratic America, the hand that earns its daily bread must wear some talent, name, or honor as an ornament before it is very cordially shaken by those who wear white gloves."

A pervasive social malaise is evidenced in the homes served by Christie and her working sisters. The homes are troubled, insecure, part of an endless round of upward striving for social status. Individualism, which requires the home as a refuge in "a cruel and heartless world," prevents the ideal from being realized. There are no true women in these scenes of genteel family life; for as husbands and fathers participated in the "freedom" of a competitive, speculative marketplace, they needed wives and daughters who could maneuver in the social marketplace to the advantage of their menfolk's businesses and careers. Philip Fletcher's sister was a parody of the fashionable woman; her husband traveled abroad on business and she only wrote to him for spending money.

Christie's experience as the companion of a young, mad woman indicated that even inherited insanity could have its link to the drive for social status. Mrs. Carroll married and bore children knowing of her husband's fatal flaw because she came from a poor, humble home, and marriage offered a wealthy and socially prominent one. So these women were not really outside or even elevated from their husbands' world, and, unable to achieve independence, they were similarly unable to achieve true womanhood, as ordinary women, waged and unwaged, understood it.

There are no faithful family retainers among the female servants in *Work*, even though their labor gives integrity to their lives, because the workers' insecurity is part and parcel of their employers' insecure status and anxiety. Theodore Parker remarked that it was not work which crushed the spirit of the laboring people but rather:

> "the tacit confession on the part of the employer, that he has wronged and subjugated the person who serves him; for when these same actions are performed by the mother for her child, or the son for his father, they are done for love and not money; they are counted not as low but rather ennobling."

The gulf between Christie and her employers is never bridged by love, but warmth and sympathy develop between the workers, especially when the domestic world of women's relationships makes communication and shared tasks possible. Hepsey cooks because she is saving to buy her aged mother's freedom. As an illiterate, runaway slave, Hepsey's job opportunities are doubly limited by sex and race. Still, she makes very clear to Christie and to the reader that a wage is a very definite gain over slavery. The job brings wages, and wages buy freedom from slavery. Further, the status of a free wage earner gives Hepsey the opportunity to become literate and so to progress further along the continuum to independence. Knowledge is power of a real sort in *Work,* and not only Hepsey but Christie and all of her sisters hunger for it, strive to acquire it and understand it to lead to some sort of control over their lives. The genteel ladies, on the other hand, carry velvet covered Bibles and only pretend to "culture."

The turning point of the novel is Christie's employment as a seamstress in a factory-like workroom. The details of Louisa Alcott's life in the 1860s and 1870s were enough like Christie Devon's to make the cautionary tale of the seamstress one of the best and most touching episodes in *Work.* Louisa had a momentary impulse to suicide during a period of unemployment and family mourning over the death of Elizabeth Alcott. She heard Parker's sermon on "Laborious Young Women" and pronounced it "just what I needed; for it said: Trust your fellow beings, and let them help you. Don't be too proud to ask, and accept the humblest work till you can find the task you want."[34] Just as she was about to sew ten hours a day at the Girl's Reform School at Lancaster, her old place as a governess came open and she took it. "Fixed for the winter. . . thank the Lord."

She had already experienced what it meant to be a part of the "putting out" system when she sewed for a Mr. G "a dozen pillow cases, six fine cambric neckties, and two dozen handkerchiefs, at which I had to work all one night to get them done. . . . I got only four dollars."[35] There were other times when genteel customers "forgot" or delayed payments that meant a humiliation for Alcott she never forgot.

Christie held herself aloof from all but one quiet, romantic girl, Rachel. Rachel is clearly fallen gentry and is hired as a trimmer because her taste is "superior" (or more precisely her taste is more like that of the prospective customers) despite the forewoman's lack of information about her personal background. It is almost a case of "how did a nice girl like you wind up in a place like this?" The respectable workshop manager must be intent not only on production but also on maintaining the legitimacy of such a system by hiring only girls of good character. In a dramatic confrontation between the necessities of production and the maintenance of social order, Rachel is fired as an undesirable influence on the workers, and the contradictions between true womanhood and waged work are made explicit.

Rachel is the first real friend in Christie's long search, a true heart's companion. Louisa met Rebecca Harding, author of a widely read novel about a fallen woman, *Margaret Howth,* in 1861 and commented, "She never had any troubles though she writes about woes. I told her I had lots of troubles, so I write jolly tales; and we wondered why each did so."[36] The importance of Rachel and Christie's affection for one another involves the difficult problem of woman's status in nineteenth century American society, a status that made marriage the

most serious event in a woman's life. Such a conventiona
truth meant that for those women who chose to remain single
like Louisa Alcott, the means of gaining subsistence, love, an
recognition were very limited. Female friendships were dou
bly important for spinsters. Although married women re
tained their female friends, they had prior commitments tha
could not easily be laid aside. Alcott also observes that "ε
brief but most sincere affection between two women was ε
viable experience which could open the heart to happines
that was its right." It makes perfect sense that, given all the
shared experiences of women in that "large class," relation
ships could and did develop that aroused a female conscious
ness of the heart's potential. We may have assumed tha
young women's experience of romantic love was limited to
novels unless we pause to notice the possibilities of direct and
affectionate experience between female friends. The power of
friendship was strong enough in *Work* to redeem a fallen
woman, and this conviction foreshadows Harriet Beecher
Stowe's similar belief in *We and Our Neighbors,* published in
1875. Since *Work* was serially published in Beecher's *The
Christian Union* during 1872 and 1873, it was certain tha
Mrs. Stowe read it.[37] Rachel's plight, like that of Stowe's
heroine, points to the inadequacy of the conventional institu
tions for fallen women; the Christian's duty is to stretch out
the hand of friendship directly to the unfortunate. Rachel's
dismissal heralds the beginning of Christie's conscious search
for religious faith as a means of joining with others to directly
affect the organization of a society that promised opportunity
and delivered oppression to that large class of women defined
at the beginning of *Work*.

The full contradiction of individualism is now evidenced in
the betrayal of all that ideology had promised to Christie. The
waged job invalidates the principles of true women. Profit
supersedes moral responsibility and charity must be mea
sured by its price. Even the manager of the factory is not a
free woman but must choose only what the laws of supply and

demand allow. The solution of an extended sphere for women
when "charity goes everywhere" are blown apart in this
scene. Private, personalized solutions to the injustices of de-
veloping industrialism are now presented as impossible.

Still, a personal, moral witness is called for, and Christie
must maintain her humanity at the cost of leaving her job.
Alone, ill, and reduced to piecework, she finds herself in debt.
The contradictions between job and work have collapsed before a new spectre—the experience of unemployment. In the
first half of *Work* the only alternative to the family was a job
for Christie, the promise of independence held out by the age
of individualism. But if her independence was based upon
either family support or job, how could she survive when
confronted with absence of both? Her Aunt Betsey was dead,
and she was unemployed. It is the lowest point in the
heroine's life and also the amazing beginning of Alcott's
alternative proposal to the dominant society's values. Individualism and women's acceptance of it either by entrance
into the waged world or by acceptance of the compensatory
separate sphere are part of the development of an ideology
that sought hegemony in the nineteenth century. But that
hegemony was complete, or nearly so, *only* if women consented to it. To the extent that they became aware, as Christie did, that patriarchy prevented independence for women
and that unchecked competitive, private enterprise prevented
true womanhood, the personal problems of women in the
nineteenth century became social problems. As a reformer,
Alcott finally accepted the responsibility to her female readers of presenting a feminist consciousness that implied a new
relationship between men and women. She speaks of it quite
openly throughout the rest of the book.

This new, open relationship between the sexes is ushered
into the novel by Rachel. She sends Christie to stay with
Cynthie Wilkins, a humble laundress, whose greatness of
heart resembles Peggotty in *David Copperfield*. Cynthie is the
voice of the working woman who manages to preserve com-

plete dedication to the family as she raises a brood of children
and props up a husband whose wages cannot support them.
Cynthie's awareness of true womanhood is the result of a natural disaster that transformed her from a runaway wife-
mother to a paragon of domestic social relations. But this
personal transformation is not enough; she joins a band of
reformers, led by the Reverend Mr. Power and assisted by
David Sterling, in order to extend her domestic compassion
to the entire society.

Cynthie plays the part of the mother Christie scarcely
knew. She advertises her services by a sign, "Cynthie Wilkins, Clear Starcher," and her vision of the world is as clear
as her starching: social change will come through liberal
Christianity in which Christ washes whitest of all. Alcott's
favorite childhood book was *The Pilgrim's Progress*,[38] and she
used it for many of the chapter headings in *Little Women* and
much of the moral message of *Work*. Cynthie, David Sterling,
and Reverend Power together embody the path through which
nineteenth century Christians could find salvation. As
Cynthie describes Power, "He starts the dirt and gits the
stains out, and leaves em ready for other folks to finish off."
His sermons give heart to his battered congregation, and he
does not stop at exhortation but goes on to criticize the
institutions and social relations that damage the souls and
bodies in his charge. He spends much of his time listening to
the problems of his congregation and finding companions to
help them on their way, much as the pilgrims in Bunyan's
morality tale are helped by the band of angels.

Christie's own feet are set on the path to redemption by her
experiences in the households of Cynthie Wilkins and later of
David Sterling. In Cynthie's kitchen she helps with the laun-
dry and the cooking, but the real easing of her heart's pain
comes when Cynthie sets her infant daughter in Christie's
lap. Transcendentalism expressed the conviction that material reality was the expression of the ideal: divinity lay within
each human being, and the spirit could transcend the prison

of the flesh through an original relationship with Nature. Nature was the symbol of the spirit, and insofar as women cherished children they were closer to nature and closer to the spirit, the essence of life that transcended material appearances. Christie was battered in body but more seriously damaged spiritually by her combat with the waged world. It was her spirit that was restored in Cynthie's kitchen, and the domestic relations of that woman's world gave her a model to extend the process of individual salvation to social reform.

Christie's relationship to David Sterling, who runs a greenhouse and a half-way shelter for wayward pilgrims, is informed by Thoreau's essay on "Friendship."[39] It is not too presumptuous to say that David Sterling is Alcott's idealized portrait of Henry David Thoreau. "Friendship," said Thoreau, "is evanescent in every man's experience and remembered like heat lightning in past summers."[40] It is through friendship, and the growing recognition of equality, mutuality, and commitment to a democratic society that Christie and David fall in love. But, like Thoreau's description of summer lightning, the incandescent relationship between Christie and David is brief; while culminating in a new sort of companionate marriage based upon equality, it is ended by David's death. As a fallen hero in the Civil War, his spirit both vitalizes Christie's commitment to carry on his reform efforts and, paradoxically, frees her to return to the world of women's work and companionship.

It had been safe to speculate on Thoreau as a mate since he was dead by the time Louisa created David Sterling, and she had already written a lovely poem "Thoreau's Flute" for *Atlantic Monthly,* reminding friends that Thoreau's music could be heard in Concord long after his death.[41] Thoreau himself had said that "the only danger in friendship is that it will end," and in compensation "even the death of friends will inspire us as much as their lives." The nineteenth century feminists, including Thoreau and the Alcotts, believed that harmony in marriage depended upon sexual equality and, most importantly, on openness and truth in relationships; where inequality made males dominant over females, tyranny and fear could destroy open communication. "Between whom there is hearty truth there is love; and in proportion to our truthfulness and confidence in one another, our lives are divine and miraculous, and answer to our ideal," said Thoreau.[42] But Alcott's own spinsterhood and the examples of her friends and associates may have led to a certain amount of skepticism as to the possibilities of perfect equality in nineteenth century marriage. She felt surer of women's work and companionship or at least of her own ability to write about it.

Christie's daughter, Pansy, becomes the center of her hopes and expectations for a new generation of women, but Christie does not retire on her widow's pension to do good works. She takes over her husband's greenhouse business, runs it not only efficiently but collectively, and proposes a new set of property relations. To her Uncle Enos, financial success is the only real measure of achievement, and when he questions the "bargain" in which Christie does the major work and receives the minor share of profits, she replies, "Ah, but we don't make bargains, sir: we work for one another and share every thing together." "So like women," grumbled Uncle Enos.

In joining an association of working women and making her first public speech, Christie's vision of the new women's movement after the Civil War is not only exciting but informative in its recognition of the problems evidenced by the gaps between their specific, personal experiences and their common experiences as women. The meeting is marked by familiar difficulties. "There were speeches of course, and of the most unparliamentary sort, for the meeting was composed almost entirely of women, each eager to tell her special grievance or theory . . . how difficult it was for the two classes to meet and help one another in spite of the utmost need on the one side and the sincerest good will on the other."

Finally, when Christie stops at the bottom step of the

speaker's platform and says, "I am better here, thank you; for I have been and mean to be a working woman all my life," she joins forces with her creator. Louisa May Alcott, like Christie Devon, was a working woman all her life, moving through the experiences of domesticity, jobs, and unemployment. Her awareness of these experiences as shaping women's responses to the expectations raised by the dominant ideology of individualism enabled her to write more vividly and with a greater sense of urgency in *Work* than in any of her more commercially successful novels.[43] Her accomplishment is the more remarkable because she was able to present both the common sensibility of women and their individual experiences in a way that exhibited the conflict of interests manifest in their lives.

Work, then, describes Alcott's sense of the formation of women's consciousness in the nineteenth century; true womanhood clearly meant different things to women than to men. Excluded from direct social power, women found it difficult to affect a society that attempted to destroy their experience of true womanhood. Alcott's heroine moved through a period of adolescent struggle, demanding that the principles of the American Revolution be applied to women and naively assuming that her domestic virtues could remain intact and were not in conflict with the promise of individualism. But here awareness did not remain limited by a passive acceptance of ideology. The ideological promise had to be fulfilled in terms of real material rewards in order to be accepted by women. For many women, then, the choices presented were lonely, impoverished spinsterhood or "marrying for a living." True womanhood, as Christie defined it and as it was struggled out in the Working Womens Association, transcended the individualist sensibility.[44]

But many women were aware of themselves as a group for the first time—a group at home, isolated from a productive process that had moved away from the domestic scene. All the absent husbands and fathers in Alcott's novel attested to the existence of a separate sphere. That sphere contained nega-tive implications for women's development of their full, human potential. But it is also true that "women's sphere provided them with companionship, a sense of self-worth, and most important, independence from men in a patriarchal world."[45] The differences between work and job were increas-ingly manifest to that half of the population still occupied with loving service and intimate social relationships, and they were able to criticize the alienation and inhumanities of the competitive society.

When Alcott finished *Work* it was with the usual pressures of caring for her mother and for Anna's boys when her sister fell ill. As success brought increasing demands from pub-lishers, she actually had to write three pages at once on "impression paper as Beecher, Roberts and Low of London all want copy at once."[46] She added several years later that "this was the cause of the paralysis of my thumb, which disabled me for the rest of my life." It was not a great novel as literary works go, and Alcott was well aware of it when she noted, "Not what it should be—too many interruptions. Should like to do one book in peace, and see if it wouldn't be good."

The publication brought two sorts of results, the first exemplified by the housekeeper who came to find a job with the author of *Work*. Her employer "was curious how she came to us. She had taught and sewed, and was tired, and wanted something else; decided to try for a housekeeper's place, but happened to read *Work,* and thought she'd do as Christie did—take anything that came." What came, of course, was Alcott and finding that Miss Alcott really did practice what she preached. The author remarked that "we had a good time together."[47]

The money earned with the sales of *Work* was distributed in ways quite reflective of Alcott's sense of family and social responsibility. One thousand dollars went to May to help her study art abroad. Part of the money was invested for the family's security, and some went as "a thank offering for my success" to the class of what she called "the silent poor to which we belonged for so many years—needy, but respectable, and forgotten because too proud to beg. Work difficult to find for such people, and life made very hard for want of a little money to ease the necessary need."[48] Another thousand dollars went to Ladislas Wisniewsky, the Laurie of *Little Women*, living in France in poverty.

If ordinary women found truth and compassion in *Work,* the reviewers were somewhat cynical about its depiction of woman's life and labor. "*The Lakeside Monthly* condemned the book as an immoderate apotheosis of Madam Work, pointing out to the author that slavery had been abolished and with it the necessity of cant on the subject of Negro rights."[49]

Harper's New Monthly Magazine was even more disturbing when it called *Work* "Miss Alcott's first *real* novel" and then went on to say that her name "will give this pleasant story a circulation and a celebrity which otherwise it would not attain. The book would not have made her reputation, but her reputation will make the book."[50] The problem, thought the reviewer, was that it was not a novel at all, "but a serious, didactic essay on the subject of woman's work."[51] Where the pictures described were pretty, the reviewers praised the book, and all agreed that Alcott was at her best in describing Cynthie Wilkins' children. "With them Miss Alcott is definitely in her element."[52] The same reviewer observed that the "story may have been too serious, but the bright cheeriness of a woman's 'trusting and loving heart' gave the reader a spiritual lift."[53]

No better example of the differences between male and female interpretations of true womanhood can exist than the record of Alcott's novel *Work* and the remarks of its critics and their colleagues. In 1869 at a meeting of working and middle class women to protest the degraded condition of women, Miss Phelps got up and said:

"We do not think the men of Massachusetts know how the women live. We do not think if they did they would allow such a state of things to exist. Some of us who signed the petition

have had to work for less than twenty-five cents a day, and we
know that many others have had to do the same. . . . They have
a little aid, to be sure, from the State, but it is only a little, and
they have today to live in miserable garrets without fire; and
during cold winters, with scanty food and insufficient clothing,
they go out daily to labor along these beautiful streets. Do you
not think that they feel the difference between their condition
and that of rich, well-dressed ladies who pass them. If they did
not they would be less than human. . . . Only help us to earn a
home that we can attach ourselves to, that will make us feel
that we have a country. . . . It has been said that we can go
anywhere and be at home. Women cannot. It is because they
have no homes. They have a husband's or a father's home, none
of their own. . . . I am met often with the objection that these
women can go to California or Nevada. But our mothers live
here. We know not these distant places. . . . Girls love independence, girls love society, just as much as men do. A woman
must have some intellectual society or she goes down. I am no
speechmaker—only a worker."[54]

It was for these women and millions more like them that
Louisa May Alcott spoke when she wrote *Work*. Nineteenth
century fiction for and by women was often oblivious to the
fact that "there are substantial heartfelt interests for women
of all ages, and under ordinary circumstances, quite apart
from love. . . ." *Work* was not, as *Harper's* supposed, Alcott's
first real novel, but it was a substantial attempt to break
through conventional plot lines to inform her audience that
the real lives of women were more complex and more deserving of attention than the idealization of woman as the
spiritual helpmate of man could portray. A modern reading of
Alcott's *Work* is substantively different from either the in-
terpretation of her contemporary audience or the literary
critics' appreciation. "It is well to remember that although
literature reflects an age it also illuminates it."[55] Alcott was a
faithful social secretary, and she did shed light on what she
saw and felt; the development of her own consciousness was
interwoven with the process she located in the lives of other

women. The strength of her vision is revealed in the authenticity of *Work;* the facts of women's lives in mid-nineteenth century, as well as we can reconstruct them, are vivid and true in Alcott's novel. And women still struggle today with the contradictions between the promise of individuality and the restrictions of individualism, between commitment to family and the impersonality of the wage system. The contradictions have taken new historical forms that often obscure their roots. *Work* deserves a modern audience, not only as an historical document and a minor literary achievement, but also as a key to understanding the commonality of our daily struggles with those of our mothers and grandmothers.

                                                              Sarah Elbert

NOTES

1. Louisa May Alcott, *Life, Letters and Journals,* ed. Ednah D. Cheney (Boston: Roberts Brothers, 1889), p. 297.

2. Sources for Bronson Alcott's life and work include Odell Shepard, ed., *The Journals of Bronson Alcott;* Shepard, *Pedlars Progress;* Dorothy McCuskey, Bronson Alcott, *Teacher.*

3. Sandford Salyer, *Marmee: The Mother of Little Women* (Norman, Okla.: University of Oklahoma Press, 1949).

4. Anne L. Kuhn, *The Mother's Role in Childhood Education: New England Concepts 1830–1860* (New Haven: Yale University Press, 1947), p. 40. I am grateful to William Leach of the Department of History, University of Rochester, for sharing his analysis of the broad scope of nineteenth century feminist ideology with me.

5. Louisa May Alcott, "Transcendental Wild Oats," *The Independent*, 18 December 1873.

6. Marjorie Worthington, *Miss Alcott of Concord* (New York: Doubleday & Co., 1958), p. 32.

7. *Ibid.,* p. 60.

8. Alcott, *Life, Letters, Journals,* p. 80.

9. *Ibid.,* p. 98.

10. Louisa May Alcott, "The Lady and the Woman," *Saturday Evening Gazette,* 4 October 1856.

11. Henry James, "Miss Alcott's Moods," *North American Review,* July 1865. Reprinted in *Henry James, Notes & Reviews* (New York: Dunsterhouse, 1968), p. 49.

12. Bessie Z. Jones, "Introduction to Louisa May Alcott," in Alcott, *Hospital Sketches* (Cambridge, Mass.: Harvard University Press, 1960), p. 17.

13. *Ibid.*

14. Louisa May Alcott to John Hart, September 13, 1872. Courtesy of Cornell University Regional History Archives, Ithaca, New York.

15. Alcott, *Life, Letters, Journals,* p. 187.

16. *Ibid,* p. 194.

17. *Ibid.,* p. 195.

18. *Ibid.,* p. 201.

19. Ticknor, Caroline, *May Alcott: A Memoir* (Boston: Little, Brown, 1927).

20. Louisa May Alcott, "Shawl Straps," *The Christian Union,* 13, 20, 27 March and 3 April 1872. *My Boys, Aunt Jo's Scrap Bag,* I (Boston: Roberts Brothers, 1872).

21. Alcott, *Life, Letters, Journals,* p. 267.

22. *Ibid.,* p. 270–272.

23. Ticknor, p. 127.

24. Alcott, *Life, Letters, Journals,* p. 271. I am indebted to Prof. Ellen DuBois for the simple but profound insight that the same words can mean very different things to different people.

25. Ticknor, p. 258–261.

26. Alcott, *Life, Letters, Journals,* p. 317.

27. Louisa May Alcott, *Jo's Boys: A Sequel to Little Men* (New York: Collier Books Edition, Fourth Printing, 1973), p. 232.

28. Madeleine B. Stern, *Louisa May Alcott* (London & New York: Peter Nevill Ltd. 1957), pp. 340–341.

29. Theodore Parker, "The Public Function of Woman," reprinted in Theodore Parker, *Sins and Safeguards of Society* (Boston: American Unitarian Association, 1907), 9: 178–206.

30. Alcott, *Life, Letters, Journals,* p. 265.

31. Parker, pp. 178–206.

32. Lucy Maynard Salmon, *Domestic Service* (New York: Macmillan Co., 1911), pp. 141–150.

33. Letter to Louisa May Alcott from Sally Holley, Alcott Family

Papers, Houghton Library, Harvard University, Cambridge, Mass., January 1882.

34. Alcott, *Life, Letters, Journals,* p. 102–103.

35. *Ibid.*

36. Alcott, *Life, Letters, Journals,* p. 131.

37. "Work: Or Christie's Experiment," *The Christian Union,* December 1872–June 1873. The first chapter was reprinted in *The Independent,* January 1873, and *Hearth and Home,* 18 January 1873.

Madeleine B. Stern's biography *Louisa May Alcott* contains the most reliable and comprehensive bibliography, and I have relied on it for dates of publication.

38. John Bunyan, *The Pilgrim's Progress.*

39. Henry David Thoreau, *Friendship* (New York: Thomas Y. Crowell & Co. 1906), excerpted from "A Week on the Concord & Merrimack Rivers." For more details on the Thoreau-Alcott friendship see Madeleine B. Stern, *Louisa May Alcott.*

40. *Ibid.*

41. Louisa May Alcott, "Thoreau's Flute," *Atlantic Monthly* 12, (September 1863).

42. Thoreau, *Friendship.*

43. In 1881 in a letter to Thomas Niles, her publisher, she said, "I can remember when antislavery was in just the same state that suffrage is now, and take more pride in the very small help we Alcotts could give than in all the books I ever wrote or ever shall write." Quoted in Alcott, *Life, Letters, Journals,* p. 341.

44. Louisa Alcott attended the Women's Congress at Syracuse, N.Y., in October 1873 where Antoinette Brown Blackwell spoke on the rights of married women to combine domestic life and waged work.

45. Jessie Bernard, "Historical & Structural Barriers to Occupational Desegregation," *Signs* I, no. 3 part 2 (Spring 1976), p. 89.

46. Alcott, *Life, Letters, Journals,* p. 268.

47. *Ibid.,* p. 271.

48. *Ibid.*

49. Madeleine B. Stern, *Louisa May Alcott,* p. 232.

50. *Harper's New Monthly Magazine,* 47 (September 1873), pp. 614–615.

51. *Ibid.*

52. *Ibid.*

53. *Ibid.*

54. Miss Phelps, "Address to Working Women," quoted in Rosalyn Baxandall, Linda Gordon, Susan Reverby, *America's Working Women: A Documentary History, 1600 to the Present* (New York: Vintage, 1976). I would like to thank Susan Reverby for sharing this document with me.

55. F. O. Matthiessen, *American Renaissance* (New York: Oxford University Press, 1941), p. x.

ACKNOWLEDGMENTS

A number of people shared in my appreciation of *Work* and in the task of explicating the novel for a modern audience. I would like to thank Gerda Lerner, William Leach, Elizabeth Fox Genovese, Heidi Hartmann, Ellen DuBois, Ann and Ira Brous, Sander Kelman, Carrie Kartman, Adam Kartman, and Madeleine B. Stern.

WORK

CHAPTER I.

CHRISTIE.

CHRISTIE.

" AUNT BETSEY, there's going to be a new Declaration of Independence."

"Bless and save us, what do you mean, child?" And the startled old lady precipitated a pie into the oven with destructive haste.

"I mean that, being of age, I'm going to take care

of myself, and not be a burden any longer. Uncle
wishes me out of the way; thinks I ought to go, and,
sooner or later, will tell me so. I don't intend to wait
for that, but, like the people in fairy tales, travel away
into the world and seek my fortune. I know I can
find it."

Christie emphasized her speech by energetic demonstrations in the bread-trough, kneading the dough as if
it was her destiny, and she was shaping it to suit herself; while Aunt Betsey stood listening, with uplifted
pie-fork, and as much astonishment as her placid face
was capable of expressing. As the girl paused, with a
decided thump, the old lady exclaimed:

" What crazy idee you got into your head now?"

"A very sane and sensible one that's got to be
worked out, so please listen to it, ma'am. I've had it a
good while, I've thought it over thoroughly, and I'm
sure it's the right thing for me to do. I'm old enough
to take care of myself; and if I'd been a boy, I should
have been told to do it long ago. I hate to be dependent; and now there's no need of it, I can't bear it any
longer. If you were poor, I wouldn't leave you; for I
never forget how kind *you* have been to me. But
Uncle doesn't love or understand me; I *am* a burden to
him, and I must go where I can take care of myself. I
can't be happy till I do, for there's nothing here for me.
I'm sick of this dull town, where the one idea is eat,
drink, and get rich; I don't find any friends to help me
as I want to be helped, or any work that I can do well;
so let me go, Aunty, and find my place, wherever it is."

"But I do need you, deary; and you mustn't think
Uncle don't like you. He does, only he don't show it;

and when your odd ways fret him, he ain't pleasant, I know. I don't see why you can't be contented; I've lived here all my days, and never found the place lonesome, or the folks unneighborly." And Aunt Betsey looked perplexed by the new idea.

"You and I are very different, ma'am. There was more yeast put into my composition, I guess; and, after standing quiet in a warm corner so long, I begin to ferment, and ought to be kneaded up in time, so that I may turn out a wholesome loaf. You can't do this; so let me go where it can be done, else I shall turn sour and good for nothing. Does that make the matter any clearer?" And Christie's serious face relaxed into a smile as her aunt's eye went from her to the nicely moulded loaf offered as an illustration.

"I see what you mean, Kitty; but I never thought on't before. You be better riz than me; though, let me tell you, too much emptins makes bread poor stuff, like baker's trash; and too much workin' up makes it hard and dry. Now fly 'round, for the big oven is most het, and this cake takes a sight of time in the mixin'."

"You haven't said I might go, Aunty," began the girl, after a long pause devoted by the old lady to the preparation of some compound which seemed to require great nicety of measurement in its ingredients; for when she replied, Aunt Betsey curiously interlarded her speech with audible directions to herself from the receipt-book before her.

"I ain't no right to keep you, dear, ef you choose to take (a pinch of salt). I'm sorry you ain't happy, and think you might be ef you'd only (beat six eggs, yolks and

AUNT BETSEY'S INTERLARDED SPEECH.

whites together). But ef you can't, and feel that you
need (two cups of sugar), only speak to Uncle, and ef
he says (a squeeze of fresh lemon), go, my dear, and
take my blessin' with you (not forgettin' to cover with
a piece of paper)."

Christie's laugh echoed through the kitchen; and the
old lady smiled benignly, quite unconscious of the
cause of the girl's merriment.

"I shall ask Uncle to-night, and I know he won't
object. Then I shall write to see if Mrs. Flint has a
room for me, where I can stay till I get something to

do. There is plenty of work in the world, and I 'm not afraid of it; so you 'll soon hear good news of me. Don't look sad, for you know I never could forget *you,* even if I should become the greatest lady in the land." And Christie left the prints of two floury but affectionate hands on the old lady's shoulders, as she kissed the wrinkled face that had never worn a frown to her.

Full of hopeful fancies, Christie salted the pans and buttered the dough in pleasant forgetfulness of all mundane affairs, and the ludicrous dismay of Aunt Betsey, who followed her about rectifying her mistakes, and watching over her as if this sudden absence of mind had roused suspicions of her sanity.

" Uncle, I want to go away, and get my own living, if you please," was Christie's abrupt beginning, as they sat round the evening fire.

" Hey! what 's that ? " said Uncle Enos, rousing from the doze he was enjoying, with a candle in perilous proximity to his newspaper and his nose.

Christie repeated her request, and was much relieved, when, after a meditative stare, the old man briefly answered:

" Wal, go ahead."

" I was afraid you might think it rash or silly, sir."

" I think it 's the best thing you could do ; and I like your good sense in pupposin' on't."

" Then I may really go ? "

" Soon 's ever you like. Don't pester me about it till you 're ready ; then I 'll give you a little suthing to start off with." And Uncle Enos returned to " The Farmer's Friend," as if cattle were more interesting than kindred.

Christie was accustomed to his curt speech and careless manner; had expected nothing more cordial; and, turning to her aunt, said, rather bitterly:

"Didn't I tell you he'd be glad to have me go? No matter! When I've done something to be proud of, he will be as glad to see me back again." Then her voice changed, her eyes kindled, and the firm lips softened with a smile. "Yes, I'll try my experiment; then I'll get rich; found a home for girls like myself; or, better still, be a Mrs. Fry, a Florence Nightingale, or" —

"How are you on't for stockin's, dear?"

Christie's castles in the air vanished at the prosaic question; but, after a blank look, she answered pleasantly:

"Thank you for bringing me down to my feet again, when I was soaring away too far and too fast. I'm poorly off, ma'am; but if you are knitting these for me, I shall certainly start on a firm foundation." And, leaning on Aunt Betsey's knee, she patiently discussed the wardrobe question from hose to head-gear.

"Don't you think you could be contented any way, Christie, ef I make the work lighter, and leave you more time for your books and things?" asked the old lady, loth to lose the one youthful element in her quiet life.

"No, ma'am, for I can't find what I want here," was the decided answer.

"What *do* you want, child?"

"Look in the fire, and I'll try to show you."

The old lady obediently turned her spectacles that way; and Christie said in a tone half serious, half playful:

"Do you see those two logs? Well that one smouldering dismally away in the corner is what my life is now; the other blazing and singing is what I want my life to be."

"Bless me, what an idee! They are both a-burnin' where they are put, and both will be ashes to-morrow; so what difference *doos* it make?"

Christie smiled at the literal old lady; but, following the fancy that pleased her, she added earnestly:

"I know the end is the same; but it *does* make a difference *how* they turn to ashes, and *how* I spend my life. That log, with its one dull spot of fire, gives neither light nor warmth, but lies sizzling despondently among the cinders. But the other glows from end to end with cheerful little flames that go singing up the chimney with a pleasant sound. Its light fills the room and shines out into the dark; its warmth draws us nearer, making the hearth the cosiest place in the house, and we shall all miss the friendly blaze when it dies. Yes," she added, as if to herself, "I hope my life may be like that, so that, whether it be long or short, it will be useful and cheerful while it lasts, will be missed when it ends, and leave something behind besides ashes."

Though she only half understood them, the girl's words touched the kind old lady, and made her look anxiously at the eager young face gazing so wistfully into the fire.

"A good smart blowin' up with the belluses would make the green stick burn most as well as the dry one after a spell. I guess contentedness is the best bellus for young folks, ef they would only think so."

"I dare say you are right, Aunty; but I want to try for myself; and if I fail, I 'll come back and follow your advice. Young folks always have discontented fits, you know. Didn't you when you were a girl?"

"Shouldn't wonder ef I did; but Enos came along, and I forgot 'em."

"My Enos has not come along yet, and never may; so I'm not going to sit and wait for any man to give me independence, if I can earn it for myself." And a quick glance at the gruff, gray old man in the corner plainly betrayed that, in Christie's opinion, Aunt Betsey made a bad bargain when she exchanged her girlish aspirations for a man whose soul was in his pocket.

"Jest like her mother, full of hifalutin notions, discontented, and sot in her own idees. Poor capital to start a fortin' on."

Christie's eye met that of her uncle peering over the top of his paper with an expression that always tried her patience. Now it was like a dash of cold water on her enthusiasm, and her face fell as she asked quickly:

"How do you mean, sir?"

"I mean that you are startin' all wrong; your redic'lus notions about independence and self-cultur won't come to nothin' in the long run, and you'll make as bad a failure of your life as your mother did of her'n."

"Please, don't say that to me; I can't bear it, for *I* shall never think her life a failure, because she tried to help herself, and married a good man in spite of poverty, when she loved him! You call that folly; but I'll do the same if I can; and I'd rather have what my father and mother left me, than all the money you are piling up, just for the pleasure of being richer than your neighbors."

"Never mind, dear, he don't mean no harm!" whispered Aunt Betsey, fearing a storm.

But though Christie's eyes had kindled and her color deepened, her voice was low and steady, and her indignation was of the inward sort.

"Uncle likes to try me by saying such things, and this is one reason why I want to go away before I get sharp and bitter and distrustful as he is. I don't suppose I can make you understand my feeling, but I'd like to try, and then I'll never speak of it again;" and, carefully controlling voice and face, Christie slowly added, with a look that would have been pathetically eloquent to one who could have understood the instincts of a strong nature for light and freedom: "You say I am discontented, proud and ambitious; that's true, and I'm glad of it. I am discontented, because I can't help feeling that there is a better sort of life than this dull one made up of everlasting work, with no object but money. I can't starve my soul for the sake of my body, and I mean to get out of the treadmill if I can. I'm proud, as you call it, because I hate dependence where there isn't any love to make it bearable. You don't say so in words, but I know you begrudge me a home, though you will call me ungrateful when I'm gone. I'm willing to work, but I want work that I can put my heart into, and feel that it does me good, no matter how hard it is. I only ask for a chance to be a useful, happy woman, and I don't think that is a bad ambition. Even if I only do what my dear mother did, earn my living honestly and happily, and leave a beautiful example behind me, to help one other woman as hers helps me, I shall be satisfied."

Christie's voice faltered over the last words, for the thoughts and feelings which had been working within

her during the last few days had stirred her deeply, and
the resolution to cut loose from the old life had not
been lightly made.   Mr. Devon had listened behind his
paper to this unusual outpouring with a sense of discomfort which was new to him.   But though the words
reproached and annoyed, they did not soften him, and
when Christie paused with tearful eyes, her uncle rose,
saying, slowly, as he lighted his candle :

"Ef I'd refused to let you go before, I'd agree to it
now ; for you need breakin' in, my girl, and you are
goin' where you'll get it, so the sooner you're off the
better for all on us.   Come, Betsey, we may as wal
leave, for we can't understand the wants of her higher
nater, as Christie calls it, and we've had lecterin' enough
for one night."   And with a grim laugh the old man
quitted the field, worsted but in good order.

"There, there, dear, hev a good cry, and forgit all
about it !" purred Aunt Betsey, as the heavy footsteps
creaked away, for the good soul had a most old-fashioned and dutiful awe of her lord and master.

"I shan't cry but act ; for it is high time I *was* off.
I've stayed for your sake ; now I'm more trouble than
comfort, and away I go.   Good-night, my dear old
Aunty, and don't look troubled, for I'll be a lamb while
I stay."

Having kissed the old lady, Christie swept her work
away, and sat down to write the letter which was the
first step toward freedom.   When it was done, she
drew nearer to her friendly *confidante* the fire, and till
late into the night sat thinking tenderly of the past,
bravely of the present, hopefully of the future.   Twenty-
one to-morrow, and her inheritance a head, a heart, a

pair of hands; also the dower of most New England girls, intelligence, courage, and common sense, many practical gifts, and, hidden under the reserve that soon melts in a genial atmosphere, much romance and enthusiasm, and the spirit which can rise to heroism when the great moment comes.

Christie was one of that large class of women who, moderately endowed with talents, earnest and true-hearted, are driven by necessity, temperament, or principle out into the world to find support, happiness, and homes for themselves. Many turn back discouraged; more accept shadow for substance, and discover their mistake too late; the weakest lose their purpose and themselves; but the strongest struggle on, and, after danger and defeat, earn at last the best success this world can give us, the possession of a brave and cheerful spirit, rich in self-knowledge, self-control, self-help. This was the real desire of Christie's heart; this was to be her lesson and reward, and to this happy end she was slowly yet surely brought by the long discipline of life and labor.

Sitting alone there in the night, she tried to strengthen herself with all the good and helpful memories she could recall, before she went away to find her place in the great unknown world. She thought of her mother, so like herself, who had borne the commonplace life of home till she could bear it no longer. Then had gone away to teach, as most country girls are forced to do. Had met, loved, and married a poor gentleman, and, after a few years of genuine happiness, untroubled even by much care and poverty, had followed him out of the world, leaving her little child to the protection of her brother.

Christie looked back over the long, lonely years she had spent in the old farm-house, plodding to school and church, and doing her tasks with kind Aunt Betsey while a child; and slowly growing into girlhood, with a world of romance locked up in a heart hungry for love and a larger, nobler life.

She had tried to appease this hunger in many ways, but found little help. Her father's old books were all she could command, and these she wore out with much reading. Inheriting his refined tastes, she found nothing to attract her in the society of the commonplace and often coarse people about her. She tried to like the buxom girls whose one ambition was to " get married," and whose only subjects of conversation were " smart bonnets" and " nice dresses." She tried to believe that the admiration and regard of the bluff young farmers was worth striving for; but when one well-to-do neighbor laid his acres at her feet, she found it impossible to accept for her life's companion a man whose soul was wrapped up in prize cattle and big turnips.

Uncle Enos never could forgive her for this piece of folly, and Christie plainly saw that one of three things would surely happen, if she lived on there with no vent for her full heart and busy mind. She would either marry Joe Butterfield in sheer desperation, and become a farmer's household drudge; settle down into a sour spinster, content to make butter, gossip, and lay up money all her days; or do what poor Matty Stone had done, try to crush and curb her needs and aspirations till the struggle grew too hard, and then in a fit of despair end her life, and leave a tragic story to haunt their quiet river.

To escape these fates but one way appeared; to break loose from this narrow life, go out into the world and see what she could do for herself. This idea was full of enchantment to the eager girl, and, after much earnest thought, she had resolved to try it.

"If I fail, I can come back," she said to herself, even while she scorned the thought of failure, for with all her shy pride she was both brave and ardent, and her dreams were of the rosiest sort.

"I won't marry Joe; I won't wear myself out in a district-school for the mean sum they give a woman; I won't delve away here where I'm not wanted; and I won't end my life like a coward, because it is dull and hard. I'll try my fate as mother did, and perhaps I may succeed as well." And Christie's thoughts went wandering away into the dim, sweet past when she, a happy child, lived with loving parents in a different world from that.

Lost in these tender memories, she sat till the old moon-faced clock behind the door struck twelve, then the visions vanished, leaving their benison behind them.

As she glanced backward at the smouldering fire, a slender spire of flame shot up from the log that had blazed so cheerily, and shone upon her as she went. A good omen, gratefully accepted then, and remembered often in the years to come.

CHAPTER II.

A FORTNIGHT later, and Christie was off. Mrs. Flint had briefly answered that she had a room, and that work was always to be found in the city. So the girl packed her one trunk, folding away splendid hopes among her plain gowns, and filling every corner with happy fancies, utterly impossible plans, and tender little dreams, so lovely at the time, so pathetic to remember, when contact with the hard realities of life has collapsed our bright bubbles, and the frost of disappointment nipped all our morning glories in their prime.

The old red stage stopped at Enos Devon's door, and his niece crossed the threshold after a cool handshake with the master of the house, and a close embrace with the mistress, who stood pouring out last words with spectacles too dim for seeing. Fat Ben swung up the trunk, slammed the door, mounted his perch, and the ancient vehicle swayed with premonitory symptoms of departure.

Then something smote Christie's heart. "Stop!" she cried, and springing out ran back into the dismal room where the old man sat. Straight up to him she went with outstretched hand, saying steadily, though her face was full of feeling:

"Uncle, I'm not satisfied with that good-bye. I don't mean to be sentimental, but I do want to say, 'Forgive me!' I see now that I might have made you sorry to part with me, if I had tried to make you love me more. It's too late now, but I'm not too proud to confess when I'm wrong. I want to part kindly; I ask your pardon; I thank you for all you've done for me, and I say good-bye affectionately now."

Mr. Devon had a heart somewhere, though it seldom troubled him; but it did make itself felt when the girl looked at him with his dead sister's eyes, and spoke in a tone whose unaccustomed tenderness was a reproach.

Conscience had pricked him more than once that week, and he was glad to own it now; his rough sense of honor was touched by her frank expression, and, as he answered, his hand was offered readily.

"I like that, Kitty, and think the better of you for 't. Let bygones be bygones. I gen'lly got as good as I give, and I guess I deserved some on 't. I wish you wal, my girl, I heartily wish you wal, and hope you won't forgit that the old house ain't never shet aginst you."

Christie astonished him with a cordial kiss; then bestowing another warm hug on Aunt Niobe, as she called the old lady in a tearful joke, she ran into the carriage, taking with her all the sunshine of the place.

Christie found Mrs. Flint a dreary woman, with "boarders" written all over her sour face and faded figure. Butcher's bills and house rent seemed to fill her eyes with sleepless anxiety; thriftless cooks and saucy housemaids to sharpen the tones of her shrill voice; and an incapable husband to burden her shoulders like a modern " Old man of the sea."

A little room far up in the tall house was at the girl's disposal for a reasonable sum, and she took possession, feeling very rich with the hundred dollars Uncle Enos gave her, and delightfully independent, with no milk-pans to scald; no heavy lover to elude; no humdrum district school to imprison her day after day.

For a week she enjoyed her liberty heartily, then set about finding something to do. Her wish was to be a governess, that being the usual refuge for respectable girls who have a living to get. But Christie soon found her want of accomplishments a barrier to success in that line, for the mammas thought less of the solid than of the ornamental branches, and wished their little darlings to learn French before English, music before grammar, and drawing before writing.

So, after several disappointments, Christie decided that her education was too old-fashioned for the city, and gave up the idea of teaching. Sewing she resolved not to try till every thing else failed; and, after a few more attempts to get writing to do, she said to herself, in a fit of humility and good sense: " I'll begin at the beginning, and work my way up. I'll put my pride in my pocket, and go out to service. Housework I like, and can do well, thanks to Aunt Betsey. I never thought it degradation to do it for her, so why should I mind doing it for others if they pay for it? It isn't what I want, but it's better than idleness, so I'll try it!"

Full of this wise resolution, she took to haunting that purgatory of the poor, an intelligence office. Mrs. Flint gave her a recommendation, and she hopefully took her place among the ranks of buxom German, incapable Irish, and " smart " American women; for in those days foreign help had not driven farmers' daughters out of the field, and made domestic comfort a lost art.

At first Christie enjoyed the novelty of the thing, and watched with interest the anxious housewives who flocked in demanding that *rara avis,* an angel at nine shillings a week; and not finding it, bewailed the degeneracy of the times. Being too honest to profess herself absolutely perfect in every known branch of house-work, it was some time before she suited herself. Meanwhile, she was questioned and lectured, half engaged and kept waiting, dismissed for a whim, and so worried that she began to regard herself as the incarnation of all human vanities and shortcomings.

" A desirable place in a small, genteel family," was at last offered her, and she posted away to secure it, having reached a state of desperation and resolved to go as a first-class cook rather than sit with her hands before her any longer.

A well-appointed house, good wages, and light duties seemed things to be grateful for, and Christie decided that going out to service was not the hardest fate in life, as she stood at the door of a handsome house in a sunny square waiting to be inspected.

Mrs. Stuart, having just returned from Italy, affected the artistic, and the new applicant found her with a Roman scarf about her head, a rosary like a string of small cannon balls at her side, and azure draperies which became her as well as they did the sea-green furniture of her marine boudoir, where unwary walkers

tripped over coral and shells, grew sea-sick looking at
pictures of tempestuous billows engulfing every sort of
craft, from a man-of-war to a hencoop with a ghostly
young lady clinging to it with one hand, and had their
appetites effectually taken away by a choice collection
of water-bugs and snakes in a glass globe, that looked
like a jar of mixed pickles in a state of agitation.

Mrs. Stuart.

Madame was intent on a water-color copy of Turner's " Rain, Wind, and Hail," that pleasing work which was sold upsidedown and no one found it out. Motioning Christie to a seat she finished some delicate sloppy process before speaking. In that little pause Christie examined her, and the impression then received was afterward confirmed.

Mrs. Stuart possessed some beauty and chose to think herself a queen of society. She assumed majestic manners in public and could not entirely divest herself of them in private, which often produced comic effects. Zenobia troubled about fish-sauce, or Aspasia indignant at the price of eggs will give some idea of this lady when she condescended to the cares of housekeeping.

Presently she looked up and inspected the girl as if a new servant were no more than a new bonnet, a necessary article to be ordered home for examination. Christie presented her recommendation, made her modest little speech, and awaited her doom.

Mrs. Stuart read, listened, and then demanded with queenly brevity:

" Your name? "

" Christie Devon."

" Too long; I should prefer to call you Jane as I am accustomed to the name."

" As you please, ma'am."

" Your age ? "

"Twenty-one."

" You are an American? "

" Yes, ma'am."

Mrs. Stuart gazed into space a moment, then delivered the following address with impressive solemnity.

" I wish a capable, intelligent, honest, neat, well-conducted person who knows her place and keeps it. The work is light, as there are but two in the family. I am very particular and so is Mr. Stuart. I pay two dollars and a half, allow one afternoon out, one service on Sunday, and no followers. My table-girl must understand her duties thoroughly, be extremely neat, and always wear white aprons."

"I think I can suit you, ma'am, when I have learned the ways of the house," meekly replied Christie.

Mrs. Stuart looked graciously satisfied and returned the paper with a gesture that Victoria might have used in restoring a granted petition, though her next words rather marred the effect of the regal act, " My cook is black."

" I have no objection to color, ma'am."

An expression of relief dawned upon Mrs. Stuart's countenance, for the black cook had been an insurmountable obstacle to all the Irish ladies who had applied. Thoughtfully tapping her Roman nose with the handle of her brush Madame took another survey of the new applicant, and seeing that she looked neat, intelligent, and respectful, gave a sigh of thankfulness and engaged her on the spot.

Much elated Christie rushed home, selected a bag of necessary articles, bundled the rest of her possessions into an empty closet (lent her rent-free owing to a profusion of cockroaches), paid up her board, and at two o'clock introduced herself to Hepsey Johnson, her fellow servant.

Hepsey was a tall, gaunt woman, bearing the tragedy of her race written in her face. with its melancholy eyes, subdued expression, and the pathetic patience of a wronged dumb animal. She received Christie with an air of resignation, and speedily bewildered her with an account of the duties she would be expected to perform.

A long and careful drill enabled Christie to set the table with but few mistakes, and to retain a tolerably clear recollection of the order of performances. She had just assumed her badge of servitude, as she called the white apron, when the bell rang violently and Hepsey, who was hurrying away to " dish up," said:

" It's de marster. You has to answer de bell, honey, and he likes it done bery spry."

Christie ran and admitted an impetuous, stout gentleman, who appeared to be incensed against the elements, for he burst in as if blown, shook himself like a Newfoundland dog, and said all in one breath:

" You're the new girl, are you? Well, take my umbrella and pull off my rubbers."

" Sir ? "

Mr. Stuart was struggling with his gloves, and, quite unconscious of the astonishment of his new maid, impatiently repeated his request.

" Take this wet thing away, and pull off my overshoes. Don't you see it's raining like the very deuce ! "

Christie folded her lips together in a peculiar manner as she knelt down and removed a pair of muddy overshoes, took the dripping umbrella, and was walking away with her agreeable burden when Mr. Stuart gave her another shock by calling over the banister:

" I'm going out again; so clean those rubbers, and

see that the boots I sent down this morning are in order."

"Yes, sir," answered Christie meekly, and immediately afterward startled Hepsey by casting overshoes and umbrella upon the kitchen floor, and indignantly demanding:

"Am I expected to be a boot-jack to that man?"

"I 'spects you is, honey."

"Am I also expected to clean his boots?"

"Yes, chile. Katy did, and de work ain't hard when you gits used to it."

"It isn't the work; it's the degradation; and I won't submit to it."

Christie looked fiercely determined; but Hepsey shook her head, saying quietly as she went on garnishing a dish:

"Dere's more 'gradin' works dan dat, chile, and dem dat's bin 'bliged to do um finds dis sort bery easy. You's paid for it, honey; and if you does it willin, it won't hurt you more dan washin' de marster's dishes, or sweepin' his rooms."

"There ought to be a boy to do this sort of thing. *Do* you think it's right to ask it of me?" cried Christie, feeling that being servant was not as pleasant a task as she had thought it.

"Dunno, chile. I'se shore I'd never ask it of any woman if I was a man, 'less I was sick or ole. But folks don't seem to 'member dat we've got feelin's, and de best way is not to mind dese ere little trubbles. You jes leave de boots to me; blackin' can't do dese ole hands no hurt, and dis ain't no deggydation to me now; I's a free woman."

" Why, Hepsey, were you ever a slave? " asked the girl, forgetting her own small injury at this suggestion of the greatest of all wrongs.

" All my life, till I run away five year ago. My ole folks, and eight brudders and sisters, is down dere in de pit now, waitin' for the Lord to set 'em free. And He's gwine to do it soon, *soon!* " As she uttered the last words, a sudden light chased the tragic shadow from Hepsey's face, and the solemn fervor of her voice thrilled Christie's heart. All her anger died out in a great pity, and she put her hand on the woman's shoulder, saying earnestly:

"I hope so; and I wish I could help to bring that happy day at once!"

For the first time Hepsey smiled, as she said gratefully, " De Lord bress you for dat wish, chile." Then, dropping suddenly into her old, quiet way, she added, turning to her work:

"Now you tote up de dinner, and I'll be handy by to 'fresh your mind 'bout how de dishes goes, for missis is bery 'ticular, and don't like no 'stakes in tendin'."

Thanks to her own neat-handed ways and Hepsey's prompting through the slide, Christie got on very well; managed her salver dexterously, only upset one glass, clashed one dish-cover, and forgot to sugar the pie before putting it on the table; an omission which was majestically pointed out, and graciously pardoned as a first offence.

By seven o'clock the ceremonial was fairly over, and Christie dropped into a chair quite tired out with frequent pacings to and fro. In the kitchen she found the table spread for one, and Hepsey busy with the boots.

"Aren't you coming to your dinner, Mrs. Johnson?" she asked, not pleased at the arrangement.

"When you's done, honey; dere's no hurry 'bout me. Katy liked dat way best, and I'se used ter waitin'."

"But *I* don't like that way, and I won't have it. I suppose Katy thought her white skin gave her a right to be disrespectful to a woman old enough to be her mother just because she was black. I don't; and while I'm here, there must be no difference made. If we can work together, we can eat together; and because you have been a slave is all the more reason I should be good to you now."

If Hepsey had been surprised by the new girl's protest against being made a boot-jack of, she was still more surprised at this sudden kindness, for she had set Christie down in her own mind as "one ob dem toppin' smart ones dat don't stay long nowheres." She changed her opinion now, and sat watching the girl with a new expression on her face, as Christie took boot and brush from her, and fell to work energetically, saying as she scrubbed:

"I'm ashamed of complaining about such a little thing as this, and don't mean to feel degraded by it, though I should by letting you do it for me. I never lived out before: that's the reason I made a fuss. There's a polish, for you, and I'm in a good humor again; so Mr. Stuart may call for his boots whenever he likes, and we'll go to dinner like fashionable people, as we are."

There was something so irresistible in the girl's hearty manner, that Hepsey submitted at once with a visible satisfaction, which gave a relish to Christie's dinner, though it was eaten at a kitchen table, with a bare-armed cook sitting opposite, and three rows of burnished dish-covers reflecting the dreadful spectacle.

After this, Christie got on excellently, for she did her best, and found both pleasure and profit in her new employment. It gave her real satisfaction to keep the handsome rooms in order, to polish plate, and spread bountiful meals. There was an atmosphere of ease and comfort about her which contrasted agreeably with the shabbiness of Mrs. Flint's boarding-house, and the bare simplicity of the old home. Like most young people, Christie loved luxury, and was sensible enough to see and value the comforts of her situation, and to wonder why more girls placed as she was did not choose a life like this rather than the confinements of a sewing-room, or the fatigue and publicity of a shop.

She did not learn to love her mistress, because Mrs. Stuart evidently considered herself as one belonging to a superior race of beings, and had no desire to establish any of the friendly relations that may become so helpful and pleasant to both mistress and maid. She made a royal progress through her dominions every morning, issued orders, found fault liberally, bestowed praise sparingly, and took no more personal interest in her servants than if they were clocks, to be wound up once a day, and sent away the moment they got out of repair.

Mr. Stuart was absent from morning till night, and all Christie ever knew about him was that he was a kind-hearted, hot-tempered, and very conceited man; fond of his wife, proud of the society they managed to draw about them, and bent on making his way in the world at any cost.

If masters and mistresses knew how skilfully they are studied, criticised, and imitated by their servants, they would take more heed to their ways, and set better examples, perhaps. Mrs. Stuart never dreamed that her quiet, respectful Jane kept a sharp eye on all her movements, smiled covertly at her affectations, envied her accomplishments, and practised certain little elegancies that struck her fancy.

Mr. Stuart would have become apoplectic with indignation if he had known that this too intelligent table-girl often contrasted her master with his guests, and dared to think him wanting in good breeding when he boasted of his money, flattered a great man, or laid plans to lure some lion into his house. When he lost his temper, she always wanted to laugh, he bounced and bumbled about so like an angry blue-bottle fly : and when he got himself up elaborately for a party, this disrespectful hussy confided to Hepsey her opinion that "master was a fat dandy, with nothing to be vain of but his clothes," — a sacrilegious remark which would have caused her to be summarily ejected from the house if it had reached the august ears of master or mistress.

"My father was a gentleman; and I shall never forget it, though I do go out to service. I've got no rich friends to help me up, but, sooner or later, I mean to find a place among cultivated people; and while I'm working and waiting, I can be fitting myself to fill that place like a gentlewoman, as I am."

With this ambition in her mind, Christie took notes of all that went on in the polite world, of which she got frequent glimpses while "living out." Mrs. Stuart received one evening of each week, and on these occasions Christie, with an extra frill on her white apron, served the company, and enjoyed herself more than they did, if the truth had been known.

While helping the ladies with their wraps, she observed what they wore, how they carried themselves, and what a vast amount of prinking they did, not to mention the flood of gossip they talked while shaking out their flounces and settling their topknots.

Later in the evening, when she passed cups and glasses, this demure-looking damsel heard much fine discourse, saw many famous beings, and improved her mind with surreptitious studies of the rich and great when on parade. But her best time was after supper, when, through the crack of the door of the little room where she was supposed to be clearing away the relics of the feast, she looked and listened at her ease; laughed at the wits, stared at the lions, heard the music, was impressed by the wisdom, and much edified by the gentility of the whole affair.

After a time, however, Christie got rather tired of it, for there was an elegant sameness about these evenings that became intensely wearisome to the uninitiated, but she fancied that as each had his part to play he managed to do it with spirit. Night after night the wag told his stories, the poet read his poems, the singers warbled, the pretty women simpered and dressed, the heavy scientific was duly discussed by the elect precious, and Mrs. Stuart, in amazing costumes, sailed to and fro in her most swan-like manner; while my lord stirred up the lions he had captured, till they roared their best, great and small.

"Good heavens! why don't they do or say something new and interesting, and not keep twaddling on about art, and music, and poetry, and cosmos? The papers are full of appeals for help for the poor, reforms of all sorts, and splendid work that others are doing; but these people seem to think it isn't genteel enough to be spoken of here. I suppose it is all very elegant to go on like a set of trained canaries, but it's very dull fun to watch them, and Hepsey's stories are a deal more interesting to me."

Having come to this conclusion, after studying dilettanteism through the crack of the door for some months, Christie left the "trained canaries" to twitter and hop about their gilded cage, and devoted herself to Hepsey, who gave her glimpses into another sort of life so bitterly real that she never could forget it.

HEPSEY.

Friendship had prospered in the lower regions, for Hepsey had a motherly heart, and Christie soon won her confidence by bestowing her own. Her story was like many another; yet, being the first Christie had ever heard, and told with the unconscious eloquence of one who had suffered and escaped, it made a deep impression on her, bringing home to her a sense of obligation so forcibly that she began at once to pay a little part of the great debt which the white race owes the black.

Christie loved books; and the attic next her own was full of them. To this store she found her way by a sort of instinct as sure as that which leads a fly to a honey-pot, and, finding many novels, she read her fill. This amusement lightened many heavy hours, peopled the silent house with troops of friends, and, for a time, was the joy of her life.

Hepsey used to watch her as she sat buried in her book when the day's work was done, and once a heavy sigh roused Christie from the most exciting crisis of "The Abbot."

" What's the matter? Are you very tired, Aunty?" she asked, using the name that came most readily to her lips.

" No, honey; I was only wishin' I could read fast like you does. I's berry slow 'bout readin' and I want to learn a heap," answered Hepsey, with such a wistful look in her soft eyes that Christie shut her book, saying briskly:

" Then I'll teach you. Bring out your primer and let's begin at once."

" Dear chile, it's orful hard work to put learnin' in my ole head, and I wouldn't 'cept such a ting from you only I needs dis sort of help so bad, and I can trust you to gib it to me as I wants it."

Then in a whisper that went straight to Christie's heart, Hepsey told her plan and showed what help she craved.

For five years she had worked hard, and saved her earnings for the purpose of her life. When a considerable sum had been hoarded up, she confided it to one whom she believed to be a friend, and sent him to buy her old mother. But he proved false, and she never saw either mother or money. It was a hard blow, but she took heart and went to work again, resolving this time to trust no one with the dangerous part of the affair, but when she had scraped together enough to pay her way she meant to go South and steal her mother at the risk of her life.

"I don't want much money, but I must know little 'bout readin' and countin' up, else I'll get lost and cheated. You'll help me do dis, honey, and I'll bless you all my days, and so will my old mammy, if I ever gets her safe away."

With tears of sympathy shining on her cheeks, and both hands stretched out to the poor soul who implored this small boon of her, Christie promised all the help that in her lay, and kept her word religiously.

From that time, Hepsey's cause was hers; she laid by a part of her wages for "ole mammy," she comforted Hepsey with happy prophecies of success, and taught with an energy and skill she had never known before. Novels lost their charms now, for Hepsey could give her a comedy and tragedy surpassing any thing she found in them, because truth stamped her tales with a power and pathos the most gifted fancy could but poorly imitate.

The select receptions upstairs seemed duller than
ever to her now, and her happiest evenings were spent
in the tidy kitchen, watching Hepsey laboriously shaping A's and B's, or counting up on her worn fingers the
wages they had earned by months of weary work, that
she might purchase one treasure, — a feeble, old woman,
worn out with seventy years of slavery far away there
in Virginia.

For a year Christie was a faithful servant to her
mistress, who appreciated her virtues, but did not
encourage them; a true friend to poor Hepsey, who
loved her dearly, and found in her sympathy and affection a solace for many griefs and wrongs. But Providence had other lessons for Christie, and when this one
was well learned she was sent away to learn another
phase of woman's life and labor.

While their domestics amused themselves with privy
conspiracy and rebellion at home, Mr. and Mrs. Stuart
spent their evenings in chasing that bright bubble
called social success, and usually came home rather
cross because they could not catch it.

On one of these occasions they received a warm
welcome, for, as they approached the house, smoke was
seen issuing from an attic window, and flames flickering
behind the half-drawn curtain. Bursting out of the
carriage with his usual impetuosity, Mr. Stuart let himself in and tore upstairs shouting "Fire!" like an
engine company.

In the attic Christie was discovered lying dressed
upon her bed, asleep or suffocated by the smoke that
filled the room. A book had slipped from her hand,
and in falling had upset the candle on a chair beside

her; the long wick leaned against a cotton gown hanging on the wall, and a greater part of Christie's wardrobe was burning brilliantly.

"I forbade her to keep the gas lighted so late, and
see what the deceitful creature has done with her private candle!" cried Mrs. Stuart with a shrillness that
roused the girl from her heavy sleep more effectually
than the anathemas Mr. Stuart was fulminating against
the fire.

Sitting up she looked dizzily about her. The smoke
was clearing fast, a window having been opened; and
the tableau was a striking one. Mr. Stuart with an
excited countenance was dancing frantically on a heap
of half-consumed clothes pulled from the wall. He had
not only drenched them with water from bowl and
pitcher, but had also cast those articles upon the pile
like extinguishers, and was skipping among the frag-
ments with an agility which contrasted with his stout
figure in full evening costume, and his besmirched face,
made the sight irresistibly ludicrous.

Mrs. Stuart, though in her most regal array, seemed
to have left her dignity downstairs with her opera
cloak, for with skirts gathered closely about her, tiara
all askew, and face full of fear and anger, she stood
upon a chair and scolded like any shrew.

The comic overpowered the tragic, and being a little
hysterical with the sudden alarm, Christie broke into a
peal of laughter that sealed her fate.

"Look at her! look at her!" cried Mrs. Stuart gesticulating on her perch as if about to fly. "She has been
at the wine, or lost her wits. She must go, Horatio,
she must go! I cannot have my nerves shattered by

such dreadful scenes. She is too fond of books, and it has turned her brain. Hepsey can watch her to-night, and at dawn she shall leave the house for ever."

"Not till after breakfast, my dear. Let us have that in comfort I beg, for upon my soul we shall need it," panted Mr. Stuart, sinking into a chair exhausted with the vigorous measures which had quenched the conflagration.

Christie checked her untimely mirth, explained the probable cause of the mischief, and penitently promised to be more careful for the future.

Mr. Stuart would have pardoned her on the spot, but Madame was inexorable, for she had so completely forgotten her dignity that she felt it would be impossible ever to recover it in the eyes of this disrespectful menial. Therefore she dismissed her with a lecture that made both mistress and maid glad to part.

She did not appear at breakfast, and after that meal Mr. Stuart paid Christie her wages with a solemnity which proved that he had taken a curtain lecture to heart. There was a twinkle in his eye, however, as he kindly added a recommendation, and after the door closed behind him Christie was sure that he exploded into a laugh at the recollection of his last night's performance.

This lightened her sense of disgrace very much, so, leaving a part of her money to repair damages, she packed up her dilapidated wardrobe, and, making Hepsey promise to report progress from time to time, Christie went back to Mrs. Flint's to compose her mind and be ready *à la* Micawber "for something to turn up."

CHAPTER III.

FEELING that she had all the world before her where to choose, and that her next step ought to take her up at least one round higher on the ladder she was climbing, Christie decided not to try going out to service again. She knew very well that she would never live with Irish mates, and could not expect to find another Hepsey. So she tried to get a place as companion to an invalid, but failed to secure the only situation of the sort that was offered her, because she mildly objected to waiting on a nervous cripple all day, and reading aloud half the night. The old lady called her an "impertinent baggage," and Christie retired in great disgust, resolving not to be a slave to anybody.

Things seldom turn out as we plan them, and after much waiting and hoping for other work Christie at last accepted about the only employment which had not entered her mind.

Among the boarders at Mrs. Flint's were an old lady and her pretty daughter, both actresses at a respectable theatre. Not stars by any means, but good second-rate players, doing their work creditably and earning an honest living. The mother had been kind to Christie in offering advice, and sympathizing with her disappointments. The daughter, a gay little lass, had taken Christie to the theatre several times, there to behold her in all the gauzy glories that surround the nymphs of spectacular romance.

To Christie this was a great delight, for, though she had pored over her father's Shakespeare till she knew many scenes by heart, she had never seen a play till Lucy led her into what seemed an enchanted world. Her interest and admiration pleased the little actress, and sundry lifts when she was hurried with her dresses made her grateful to Christie.

The girl's despondent face, as she came in day after day from her unsuccessful quest, told its own story, though she uttered no complaint, and these friendly souls laid their heads together, eager to help her in their own dramatic fashion.

"I've got it! I've got it! All hail to the queen!" was the cry that one day startled Christie as she sat thinking anxiously, while sewing mock-pearls on a crown for Mrs. Black.

Looking up she saw Lucy just home from rehearsal, going through a series of pantomimic evolutions suggestive of a warrior doing battle with incredible valor, and a very limited knowledge of the noble art of self-defence.

"What have you got? Who is the queen?" she asked, laughing, as the breathless hero lowered her umbrella, and laid her bonnet at Christie's feet.

"*You* are to be the Queen of the Amazons in our new spectacle, at half a dollar a night for six or eight weeks, if the piece goes well."

"No!" cried Christie, with a gasp.

"Yes!" cried Lucy, clapping her hands; and then she proceeded to tell her news with theatrical volubility. "Mr. Sharp, the manager, wants a lot of tallish girls, and I told him I knew of a perfect dear. He said: 'Bring her on, then,' and I flew home to tell you. Now, don't look wild, and say no. You 've only got to sing in one chorus, march in the grand procession, and lead your band in the terrific battle-scene. The dress is splendid! Red tunic, tiger-skin over shoulder, helmet, shield, lance, fleshings, sandals, hair down, and as much cork to your eyebrows as you like."

Christie certainly did look wild, for Lucy had burst into the room like a small hurricane, and her rapid words rattled about the listeners' ears as if a hail-storm had followed the gust. While Christie still sat with her mouth open, too bewildered to reply, Mrs. Black said in her cosey voice:

"Try it, me dear, it's just what you 'll enjoy, and a capital beginning I assure ye; for if you do well old Sharp will want you again, and then, when some one slips out of the company, you can slip in, and there you are quite comfortable. Try it, me dear, and if you don't like it drop it when the piece is over, and there's no harm done."

"It's much easier and jollier than any of the things you are after. We 'll stand by you like bricks, and in a week you 'll say it's the best lark you ever had in your life. Don't be prim, now, but say yes, like a trump, as you are," added Lucy, waving a pink satin train temptingly before her friend.

"I will try it!" said Christie, with sudden decision, feeling that something entirely new and absorbing was what she needed to expend the vigor, romance, and enthusiasm of her youth upon.

With a shriek of delight Lucy swept her off her chair, and twirled her about the room as excitable young ladies are fond of doing when their joyful emotions need a vent. When both were giddy they subsided into a corner and a breathless discussion of the important step.

Though she had consented, Christie had endless doubts and fears, but Lucy removed many of the former, and her own desire for pleasant employment conquered many of the latter. In her most despairing moods she had never thought of trying this. Uncle Enos considered "play-actin'" as the sum of all iniquity. What would he say if she went calmly to destruction by that road? Sad to relate, this recollection rather strengthened her purpose, for a delicious sense of freedom pervaded her soul, and the old defiant spirit seemed to rise up within her at the memory of her Uncle's grim prophecies and narrow views.

"Lucy is happy, virtuous, and independent, why can't I be so too if I have any talent? It isn't exactly what I should choose, but any thing honest is better than idleness. I'll try it any way, and get a little fun, even if I don't make much money or glory out of it."

So Christie held to her resolution in spite of many secret misgivings, and followed Mrs. Black's advice on all points with a docility which caused that sanguine lady to predict that she would be a star before she knew where she was.

"Is this the stage? How dusty and dull it is by daylight!" said Christie next day, as she stood by Lucy on the very spot where she had seen Hamlet die in great anguish two nights before.

"Bless you, child, it's in curl-papers now, as I am of a morning. Mr. Sharp, here's an Amazon for you."

As she spoke, Lucy hurried across the stage, followed by Christie, wearing any thing but an Amazonian expression just then.

"Ever on before?" abruptly asked a keen-faced, little man, glancing with an experienced eye at the young person who stood before him bathed in blushes.

"No, sir."

"Do you sing?"

"A little, sir."

"Dance, of course?"

"Yes, sir."

"Just take a turn across the stage, will you? Must walk well to lead a march."

As she went, Christie heard Mr. Sharp taking notes audibly:

"Good tread; capital figure; fine eye. She'll make up well, and behave herself, I fancy."

A strong desire to make off seized the girl; but, remembering that she had presented herself for inspection, she controlled the impulse, and returned to him with no demonstration of displeasure, but a little more fire in "the fine eye," and a more erect carriage of the "capital figure."

"All right, my dear. Give your name to Mr. Tripp, and your mind to the business, and consider yourself engaged," — with which satisfactory remark the little man vanished like a ghost.

"Lucy, did you hear that impertinent 'my dear'?"

asked Christie, whose sense of propriety had received its first shock.

"Lord, child, all managers do it. They don't mean any thing; so be resigned, and thank your stars he didn't say 'love' and 'darling,' and kiss you, as old Vining used to," was all the sympathy she got.

Having obeyed orders, Lucy initiated her into the mysteries of the place, and then put her in a corner to look over the scenes in which she was to appear. Christie soon caught the idea of her part, — not a difficult matter, as there were but few ideas in the whole piece, after which she sat watching the arrival of the troop she was to lead. A most forlorn band of warriors they seemed, huddled together, and looking as if afraid to speak, lest they should infringe some rule; or to move, lest they be swallowed up by some unsuspected trap-door.

Presently the ballet-master appeared, the orchestra struck up, and Christie found herself marching and counter-marching at word of command. At first, a most uncomfortable sense of the absurdity of her position oppressed and confused her; then the ludicrous contrast between the solemn anxiety of the troop and the fantastic evolutions they were performing amused her till the novelty wore off; the martial music excited her; the desire to please sharpened her wits; and natural grace made it easy for her to catch and copy the steps and poses given her to imitate. Soon she forgot herself, entered into the spirit of the thing, and exerted every sense to please, so successfully that Mr. Tripp praised her quickness at comprehension, Lucy applauded heartily from a fairy car, and Mr. Sharp popped his head out of a palace window to watch the Amazon's descent from the Mountains of the Moon.

When the regular company arrived, the troop was dismissed till the progress of the play demanded their reappearance. Much interested in the piece, Christie stood aside under a palm-tree, the foliage of which was strongly suggestive of a dilapidated green umbrella, enjoying the novel sights and sounds about her.

Yellow-faced gentlemen and sleepy-eyed ladies roamed languidly about with much incoherent jabbering of parts, and frequent explosions of laughter. Princes, with varnished boots and suppressed cigars, fought, bled, and died, without a change of countenance. Damsels of unparalleled beauty, according to the text, gaped in the faces of adoring lovers, and crocheted serenely on the brink of annihilation. Fairies, in rubber-boots and woollen head-gear, disported themselves on flowery barks of canvas, or were suspended aloft with hooks in their backs like young Hindoo devotees. Demons, guiltless of hoof or horn, clutched their victims with the inevitable "Ha! ha!" and vanished darkly, eating pea-nuts. The ubiquitous Mr. Sharp seemed to pervade the whole theatre; for his voice came shrilly from above or spectrally from below, and his active little figure darted to and fro like a critical will-o-the-wisp.

The grand march and chorus in the closing scene were easily accomplished; for, as Lucy bade her, Christie "sung with all her might," and kept step as she led her band with the dignity of a Boadicea. No one spoke to her; few observed her; all were intent on their own affairs; and when the final shriek and bang died away without lifting the roof by its din, she could hardly believe that the dreaded first rehearsal was safely over.

A visit to the wardrobe-room to see her dress came next; and here Christie had a slight skirmish with the mistress of that department relative to the length of her classical garments. As studies from the nude had not yet become one of the amusements of the *élite* of Little Babel, Christie was not required to appear in the severe simplicity of a costume consisting of a necklace, sandals, and a bit of gold fringe about the waist, but was allowed an extra inch or two on her tunic, and departed, much comforted by the assurance that her dress would not be "a shock to modesty," as Lucy expressed it.

"Now, look at yourself, and, for my sake, prove an honor to your country and a terror to the foe," said Lucy, as she led her *protégée* before the green-room mirror on the first night of "The Demon's Daughter, or The Castle of the Sun!! The most Magnificent Spectacle ever produced upon the American Stage!!!"

Christie looked, and saw a warlike figure with glittering helmet, shield and lance, streaming hair and savage cloak. She liked the picture, for there was much of the heroic spirit in the girl, and even this poor counterfeit pleased her eye and filled her fancy with martial memories of Joan of Arc, Zenobia, and Britomarte.

"Go to!" cried Lucy, who affected theatrical modes of speech. "Don't admire yourself any longer, but tie up your sandals and come on. Be sure you rush down the instant I cry, 'Demon, I defy thee!' Don't break your neck, or pick your way like a cat in wet weather, but come *with effect*, for I want that scene to make a hit."

CHRISTIE AS QUEEN OF THE AMAZONS.

Princess Caremfil swept away, and the Amazonian queen climbed to her perch among the painted mountains, where her troop already sat like a flock of pigeons shining in the sun. The gilded breast-plate rose and fell with the quick beating of her heart, the spear shook with the trembling of her hand, her lips were dry, her head dizzy, and more than once, as she waited for her cue, she was sorely tempted to run away and take the consequences.

But the thought of Lucy's good-will and confidence kept her, and when the cry came she answered with a ringing shout, rushed down the ten-foot precipice, and charged upon the foe with an energy that inspired her followers, and quite satisfied the princess struggling in the demon's grasp.

With clashing of arms and shrill war-cries the rescuers of innocence assailed the sooty fiends who fell before their unscientific blows with a rapidity which inspired in the minds of beholders a suspicion that the goblins' own voluminous tails tripped them up and gallantry kept them prostrate. As the last groan expired, the last agonized squirm subsided, the conquerors performed the intricate dance with which it appears the Amazons were wont to celebrate their victories. Then the scene closed with a glare of red light and a "grand tableau" of the martial queen standing in a bower of lances, the rescued princess gracefully fainting in her arms, and the vanquished demon scowling fiercely under her foot, while four-and-twenty dishevelled damsels sang a song of exultation, to the barbaric music of a tattoo on their shields.

All went well that night, and when at last the girls doffed crown and helmet, they confided to one another the firm opinion that the success of the piece was in a great measure owing to their talent, their exertions, and went gaily home predicting for themselves careers as brilliant as those of Siddons and Rachel.

It would be a pleasant task to paint the vicissitudes and victories of a successful actress; but Christie was no dramatic genius born to shine before the world and leave a name behind her. She had no talent except that which may be developed in any girl possessing the lively fancy, sympathetic nature, and ambitious spirit which make such girls naturally dramatic. This was to be only one of many experiences which were to show her her own weakness and strength, and through effort, pain, and disappointment fit her to play a nobler part on a wider stage.

For a few weeks Christie's illusions lasted; then she discovered that the new life was nearly as humdrum as the old, that her companions were ordinary men and women, and her bright hopes were growing as dim as her tarnished shield. She grew unutterably weary of "The Castle of the Sun," and found the "Demon's Daughter" an unmitigated bore. She was not tired of the profession, only dissatisfied with the place she held in it, and eager to attempt a part that gave some scope for power and passion.

Mrs. Black wisely reminded her that she must learn to use her wings before she tried to fly, and comforted her with stories of celebrities who had begun as she was beginning, yet who had suddenly burst from their grub-like obscurity to adorn the world as splendid butterflies.

"We'll stand by you, Kit; so keep up your courage, and do your best. Be clever to every one in general, old Sharp in particular, and when a chance comes, have your wits about you and grab it. That's the way to get on," said Lucy, as sagely as if she had been a star for years.

"If I had beauty I should stand a better chance," sighed Christie, surveying herself with great disfavor, quite unconscious that to a cultivated eye the soul of beauty was often visible in that face of hers, with its intelligent eyes, sensitive mouth, and fine lines about the forehead, making it a far more significant and attractive countenance than that of her friend, possessing only piquant prettiness.

" Never mind, child; you 've got a lovely figure, and an actress's best feature, — fine eyes and eyebrows. I heard old Kent say so, and he 's a judge. So make the best of what you 've got, as I do," answered Lucy, glancing at her own comely little person with an air of perfect resignation.

Christie laughed at the adviser, but wisely took the advice, and, though she fretted in private, was cheerful and alert in public. Always modest, attentive, and obliging, she soon became a favorite with her mates, and, thanks to Lucy's good offices with Mr. Sharp, whose favorite she was, Christie got promoted sooner than she otherwise would have been.

A great Christmas spectacle was brought out the next season, and Christie had a good part in it. When that was over she thought there was no hope for her, as the regular company was full and a different sort of performance was to begin. But just then her chance came, and she " grabbed it." The first soubrette died suddenly, and in the emergency Mr. Sharp offered the place to Christie till he could fill it to his mind. Lucy was second soubrette, and had hoped for this promotion; but Lucy did not sing well. Christie had a good voice, had taken lessons and much improved of late, so she had the preference and resolved to stand the test so well that this temporary elevation should become permanent.

She did her best, and though many of the parts were distasteful to her she got through them successfully, while now and then she had one which she thoroughly enjoyed. Her Tilly Slowboy was a hit, and a proud girl was Christie when Kent, the comedian, congratulated her on it, and told her he had seldom seen it better done.

To find favor in Kent's eyes was an honor indeed, for he belonged to the old school, and rarely condescended to praise modern actors. His own style was so admirable that he was justly considered the first comedian in the country, and was the pride and mainstay of the old theatre where he had played for years. Of course he possessed much influence in that little world, and being a kindly man used it generously to help up any young aspirant who seemed to him deserving.

He had observed Christie, attracted by her intelligent face and modest manners, for in spite of her youth there was a native refinement about her that made it impossible for her to romp and flirt as some of her mates did. But till she played Tilly he had not thought she possessed any talent. That pleased him, and seeing how mnch she valued his praise, and was flattered by his notice, he gave her the wise but unpalatable advice always offered young actors. Finding that she accepted it, was willing to study hard, work faithfully, and wait patiently, he predicted that in time she would make a clever actress, never a great one.

Of course Christie thought he was mistaken, and secretly resolved to prove him a false prophet by the triumphs of her career. But she meekly bowed to his opinion ; this docility pleased him, and he took a paternal sort of interest in her, which, coming from the powerful favorite, did her good service with the higher powers, and helped her on more rapidly than years of meritorious effort.

Toward the end of that second season several of Dickens's dramatized novels were played, and Christie earned fresh laurels. She loved those books, and seemed by instinct to understand and personate the humor and pathos of many of those grotesque creations. Believing she had little beauty to sacrifice, she dressed such parts to the life, and played them with a spirit and ease that surprised those who had considered her a dignified and rather dull young person.

" I 'll tell you what it is, Sharp, that girl is going to make a capital character actress. When her parts suit, she forgets herself entirely and does admirably well. Her Miggs was nearly the death of me to-night. She 's got that one gift, and it 's a good one. You 'd better give her a chance, for I think she 'll be a credit to the old concern."

Kent said that, — Christie heard it, and flew to Lucy, waving Miggs's cap for joy as she told the news.

" What did Mr. Sharp say ? " asked Lucy, turning round with her face half "made up."

" He merely said ' Hum,' and smiled. Wasn't that a good sign ? " said Christie, anxiously.

" Can't say," and Lucy touched up her eyebrows as if she took no interest in the affair.

Christie's face fell, and her heart sunk at the thought of failure ; but she kept up her spirits by working harder than ever, and soon had her reward. Mr. Sharp's " Hum " did mean yes, and the next season she was regularly engaged, with a salary of thirty dollars a week.

It was a grand step, and knowing that she owed it to Kent, Christie did her utmost to show that she deserved his good opinion. New trials and temptations beset her now, but hard work and an innocent nature kept her safe and busy. Obstacles only spurred her on to redoubled exertion, and whether she did well or ill, was praised or blamed, she found a never-failing excitement in her attempts to reach the standard of perfection she had set up for herself. Kent did not regret his patronage. Mr. Sharp was satisfied with the success of the experiment, and Christie soon became a favorite in a small way, because behind the actress the public always saw a woman who never " forgot the modesty of nature."

But as she grew prosperous in outward things, Christie found herself burdened with a private cross that tried her very much. Lucy was no longer her friend; something had come between them, and a steadily increasing coldness took the place of the confidence and affection which had once existed. Lucy was jealous for Christie had passed her in the race. She knew she could not fill the place Christie had gained by favor, and now held by her own exertions, still she was bitterly envious, though ashamed to own it.

Christie tried to be just and gentle, to prove her gratitude to her first friend, and to show that her heart was unchanged. But she failed to win Lucy back and felt herself injured by such unjust resentment. Mrs. Black took her daughter's part, and though they preserved the peace outwardly the old friendliness was quite gone.

Hoping to forget this trouble in excitement Christie

gave herself entirely to her profession, finding in it a satisfaction which for a time consoled her.

But gradually she underwent the sorrowful change which comes to strong natures when they wrong themselves through ignorance or wilfulness.

Pride and native integrity kept her from the worst temptations of such a life, but to the lesser ones she yielded, growing selfish, frivolous, and vain, — intent on her own advancement, and careless by what means she reached it. She had no thought now beyond her art, no desire beyond the commendation of those whose opinion was serviceable, no care for any one but herself.

Her love of admiration grew by what it fed on, till the sound of applause became the sweetest music to her ear. She rose with this hope, lay down with this satisfaction, and month after month passed in this feverish life, with no wish to change it, but a growing appetite for its unsatisfactory delights, an ever-increasing forgetfulness of any higher aspiration than dramatic fame.

"Give me joy, Lucy, I'm to have a benefit next week! Everybody else has had one, and I've played for them all, so no one seemed to begrudge me my turn when dear old Kent proposed it," said Christie, coming in one night still flushed and excited with the good news.

"What shall you have?" asked Lucy, trying to look pleased, and failing decidedly.

"'Masks and Faces.' I've always wanted to play Peg. and it has good parts for you and Kent, and St. George.

I chose it for that reason, for I shall need all the help I can get to pull me through, I dare say."

The smile vanished entirely at this speech, and Christie was suddenly seized with a suspicion that Lucy was not only jealous of her as an actress, but as a woman. St. George was a comely young actor who usually played lovers' parts with Christie, and played them very well, too, being possessed of much talent, and a gentleman. They had never thought of falling in love with each other, though St. George wooed and won Christie night after night in vaudeville and farce. But it was very easy to imagine that so much mock passion had a basis of truth, and Lucy evidently tormented herself with this belief.

"Why didn't you choose Juliet: St. George would do Romeo so well?" said Lucy, with a sneer.

"No, that is beyond me. Kent says Shakespeare will never be my line, and I believe him. I should think you'd be satisfied with 'Masks and Faces,' for you know Mabel gets her husband safely back in the end," answered Christie, watching the effect of her words.

"As if I wanted the man! No, thank you, other people's leavings won't suit me," cried Lucy, tossing her head, though her face belied her words.

"Not even though he has 'heavenly eyes,' 'distracting legs,' and 'a melting voice?'" asked Christie maliciously, quoting Lucy's own rapturous speeches when the new actor came.

"Come, come, girls, don't quarrel. I won't 'ave it in me room. Lucy's tired to death, and it's not nice of you, Kitty, to come and crow over her this way," said

Mamma Black, coming to the rescue, for Lucy was in tears, and Christie looking dangerous.

" It's impossible to please you, so I'll say good-night," and Christie went to her room with resentment burning hotly in her heart.

As she crossed the chamber her eye fell on her own figure reflected in the long glass, and with a sudden impulse she turned up the gas, wiped the rouge from her cheeks, pushed back her hair, and studied her own face intently for several moments. It was pale and jaded now, and all its freshness seemed gone; hard lines had come about the mouth, a feverish disquiet filled the eyes, and on the forehead seemed to lie the shadow of a discontent that saddened the whole face If one could believe the testimony of that countenance things were not going well with Christie, and she owned it with a regretful sigh, as she asked herself, " Am I what I hoped I should be? No, and it is my fault. If three years of this life have made me this, what shall I be in ten? A fine actress perhaps, but how good a woman?"

With gloomy eyes fixed on her altered face she stood a moment struggling with herself. Then the hard look returned, and she spoke out defiantly, as if in answer to some warning voice within herself. " No one cares what I am, so why care myself? Why not go on and get as much fame as I can? Success gives me power if it cannot give me happiness, and I must have some reward for my hard work. Yes! a gay life and a short one, then out with the lights and down with the curtain!"

But in spite of her reckless words Christie sobbed

herself to sleep that night like a child who knows it is astray, yet cannot see the right path or hear its mother's voice calling it home.

On the night of the benefit, Lucy was in a most exasperating mood, Christie in a very indignant one, and as they entered their dressing-room they looked as if they might have played the Rival Queens with great effect. Lucy offered no help and Christie asked none, but putting her vexation resolutely out of sight fixed her mind on the task before her.

As the pleasant stir began all about her, actress-like, she felt her spirits rise, her courage increase with every curl she fastened up, every gay garment she put on, and soon smiled approvingly at herself, for excitement lent her cheeks a better color than rouge, her eyes shone with satisfaction, and her heart beat high with the resolve to make a hit or die.

Christie needed encouragement that night, and found it in the hearty welcome that greeted her, and the full house, which proved how kind a regard was entertained for her by many who knew her only by a fictitious name. She felt this deeply, and it helped her much, for she was vexed with many trials those before the footlights knew nothing of.

The other players were full of kindly interest in her success, but Lucy took a naughty satisfaction in harassing her by all the small slights and unanswerable provocations which one actress has it in her power to inflict upon another.

Christie was fretted almost beyond endurance, and retaliated by an ominous frown when her position allowed, threatening asides when a moment's by-play favored their delivery, and angry protests whenever she met Lucy off the stage.

But in spite of all annoyances she had never played better in her life. She liked the part, and acted the warm-hearted, quick-witted, sharp-tongued Peg with a spirit and grace that surprised even those who knew her best. Especially good was she in the scenes with Triplet, for Kent played the part admirably, and cheered her on with many an encouraging look and word. Anxious to do honor to her patron and friend she threw her whole heart into the work; in the scene where she comes like a good angel to the home of the poor play-wright, she brought tears to the eyes of her audience; and when at her command Triplet strikes up a jig to amuse the children she "covered the buckle" in gallant style, dancing with all the frolicsome *abandon* of the Irish orange-girl who for a moment forgot her grandeur and her grief.

That scene was her best, for it is full of those touches of nature that need very little art to make them effective; and when a great bouquet fell with a thump at Christie's feet, as she paused to bow her thanks for an encore, she felt that she had reached the height of earthly bliss.

In the studio scene Lucy seemed suddenly gifted with unsuspected skill; for when Mabel kneels to the picture, praying her rival to give her back her husband's heart, Christie was amazed to see real tears roll down Lucy's cheeks, and to hear real love and longing thrill her trembling words with sudden power and passion.

"That is not acting. She does love St. George, and thinks I mean to keep him from her. Poor dear! I'll tell her all about it to-night, and set her heart at rest," thought Christie; and when Peg left the frame, her face expressed the genuine pity that she felt, and her voice was beautifully tender as she promised to restore the stolen treasure.

Lucy felt comforted without knowing why, and the piece went smoothly on to its last scene. Peg was just relinquishing the repentant husband to his forgiving wife with those brave words of hers, when a rending sound above their heads made all look up and start back; all but Lucy, who stood bewildered. Christie's quick eye saw the impending danger, and with a sudden spring she caught her friend from it. It was only a second's work, but it cost her much; for in the act, down crashed one of the mechanical contrivances used in a late spectacle, and in its fall stretched Christie stunned and senseless on the stage.

A swift uprising filled the house with tumult; a crowd of actors hurried forward, and the panic-stricken audience caught glimpses of poor Peg lying mute and pallid in Mabel's arms, while Vane wrung his hands, and Triplet audibly demanded, " Why the devil somebody didn't go for a doctor?"

Then a brilliant view of Mount Parnassus, with Apollo and the Nine Muses in full blast, shut the scene from sight, and soon Mr. Sharp appeared to ask their patience till the after-piece was ready, for Miss Douglas was too much injured to appear again. And with an unwonted expression of feeling, the little man alluded to " the generous act which perhaps had changed the comedy to a tragedy and robbed the beneficiary of her well-earned reward at their hands."

All had seen the impulsive spring toward, not from, the danger, and this unpremeditated action won heartier applause than Christie ever had received for her best rendering of more heroic deeds.

But she did not hear the cordial round they gave her. She had said she would " make a hit or die; " and just then it seemed as if she had done both, for she was deaf and blind to the admiration and the sympathy bestowed upon her as the curtain fell on the first, last benefit she ever was to have.

CHAPTER IV.

GOVERNESS.

Mr. Philip Fletcher.

DURING the next few weeks Christie learned the worth of many things which she had valued very lightly until then. Health became a boon too precious to be trifled with; life assumed a deeper significance when death's shadow fell upon its light, and she discovered that dependence might be made endurable by the sympathy of unsuspected friends.

Lucy waited upon her with a remorseful devotion

which touched her very much and won entire forgiveness for the past, long before it was repentantly implored. All her comrades came with offers of help and affectionate regrets. Several whom she had most disliked now earned her gratitude by the kindly thoughtfulness which filled her sick-room with fruit and flowers, supplied carriages for the convalescent, and paid her doctor's bill without her knowledge.

Thus Christie learned, like many another needy member of the gay profession, that though often extravagant and jovial in their way of life, these men and women give as freely as they spend, wear warm, true hearts under their motley, and make misfortune only another link in the bond of good-fellowship which binds them loyally together.

Slowly Christie gathered her energies after weeks of suffering, and took up her life again, grateful for the gift, and anxious to be more worthy of it. Looking back upon the past she felt that she had made a mistake and lost more than she had gained in those three years. Others might lead that life of alternate excitement and hard work unharmed, but she could not. The very ardor and insight which gave power to the actress made that mimic life unsatisfactory to the woman, for hers was an earnest nature that took fast hold of whatever task she gave herself to do, and lived in it heartily while duty made it right, or novelty lent it charms. But when she saw the error of a step, the emptiness of a belief, with a like earnestness she tried to retrieve the one and to replace the other with a better substitute.

In the silence of wakeful nights and the solitude of

quiet days, she took counsel with her better self, condemned the reckless spirit which had possessed her,
and came at last to the decision which conscience
prompted and much thought confirmed.

"The stage is not the place for me," she said. "I
have no genius to glorify the drudgery, keep me from
temptation, and repay me for any sacrifice I make.
Other women can lead this life safely and happily: I
cannot, and I must not go back to it, because, with all
my past-experience, and in spite of all my present good
resolutions, I should do no better, and I might do worse.
I'm not wise enough to keep steady there; I must
return to the old ways, dull but safe, and plod along
till I find my real place and work."

Great was the surprise of Lucy and her mother when
Christie told her resolution, adding, in a whisper, to the
girl, "I leave the field clear for you, dear, and will
dance at your wedding with all my heart when St.
George asks you to play the 'Honeymoon' with him,
as I'm sure he will before long."

Many entreaties from friends, as well as secret longings, tried and tempted Christie sorely, but she with-
stood them all, carried her point, and renounced the
profession she could not follow without self-injury and
self-reproach. The season was nearly over when she
was well enough to take her place again, but she
refused to return, relinquished her salary, sold her wardrobe, and never crossed the threshold of the theatre
after she had said good-bye.

Then she asked, "What next?" and was speedily
answered. An advertisement for a governess met her
eye, which seemed to combine the two things she

most needed just then, — employment and change of air.

"Mind you don't mention that you've been an actress or it will be all up with you, me dear," said Mrs. Black, as Christie prepared to investigate the matter, for since her last effort in that line she had increased her knowledge of music, and learned French enough to venture teaching it to very young pupils.

"I'd rather tell in the beginning, for if you keep any thing back it's sure to pop out when you least expect or want it. I don't believe these people will care as long as I'm respectable and teach well," returned Christie, wishing she looked stronger and rosier.

"You'll be sorry if you do tell," warned Mrs. Black, who knew the ways of the world.

"I shall be sorry if I don't," laughed Christie, and so she was, in the end.

"L. N. Saltonstall" was the name on the door, and L. N. Saltonstall's servant was so leisurely about answering Christie's meek solo on the bell, that she had time to pull out her bonnet-strings half-a-dozen times before a very black man in a very white jacket condescended to conduct her to his mistress.

A frail, tea-colored lady appeared, displaying such a small proportion of woman to such a large proportion of purple and fine linen, that she looked as if she was literally as well as figuratively "dressed to death."

Christie went to the point in a business-like manner that seemed to suit Mrs. Saltonstall, because it saved so much trouble, and she replied, with a languid affability:

"I wish some one to teach the children a little, for they are getting too old to be left entirely to nurse. I am anxious to get to the sea-shore as soon as possible, for they have been poorly all winter, and my own health has suffered. Do you feel inclined to try the place? And what compensation do you require?"

Christie had but a vague idea of what wages were usually paid to nursery governesses, and hesitatingly named a sum which seemed reasonable to her, but was so much less than any other applicant had asked, that Mrs. Saltonstall began to think she could not do better than secure this cheap young person, who looked firm enough to manage her rebellious son and heir, and well-bred enough to begin the education of a little fine lady. Her winter had been an extravagant one, and she could economize in the governess better perhaps than elsewhere; so she decided to try Christie, and get out of town at once.

"Your terms are quite satisfactory, Miss Devon, and if my brother approves, I think we will consider the matter settled. Perhaps you would like to see the children? They are little darlings, and you will soon be fond of them, I am sure."

A bell was rung, an order given, and presently appeared an eight-year old boy, so excessively Scotch in his costume that he looked like an animated checker-board; and a little girl, who presented the appearance of a miniature opera-dancer staggering under the weight of an immense sash.

"Go and speak prettily to Miss Devon, my pets, for she is coming to play with you, and you must mind what she says," commanded mamma.

The pale, fretful-looking little pair went solemnly to Christie's knee, and stood there staring at her with a dull composure that quite daunted her, it was so sadly unchildlike.

"What is your name, dear?" she asked, laying her hand on the young lady's head.

"Villamena Temmatina Taltentall. You mustn't touch my hair; it's just turled," was the somewhat embarrassing reply.

"Mine's Louy 'Poleon Thaltensthall, like papa's," volunteered the other young person, and Christie privately wondered if the possession of names nearly as long as themselves was not a burden to the poor dears.

Feeling that she must say something, she asked, in her most persuasive tone:

"Would you like to have me come and teach you some nice lessons out of your little books?"

If she had proposed corporal punishment on the spot it could not have caused greater dismay. Wilhelmina cast herself upon the floor passionately, declaring that she "touldn't tuddy," and Saltonstall, Jr., retreated precipitately to the door, and from that refuge defied the whole race of governesses and "nasty lessons" jointly.

"There, run away to Justine. They are sadly out of sorts, and quite pining for sea-air," said mamma, with both hands at her ears, for the war-cries of her darlings were piercing as they departed, proclaiming their wrongs while swarming up stairs, with a skirmish on each landing.

With a few more words Christie took leave and

scandalized the sable retainer by smiling all through the hall, and laughing audibly as the door closed. The contrast of the plaid boy and beruffled girl's irritability with their mother's languid affectation, and her own unfortunate efforts, was too much for her. In the middle of her merriment she paused suddenly, saying to herself:

"I never told about my acting. I must go back and have it settled." She retraced a few steps, then turned and went on again, thinking, "No; for once I'll be guided by other people's advice, and let well alone."

A note arrived soon after, bidding Miss Devon consider herself engaged, and desiring her to join the family at the boat on Monday next.

At the appointed time Christie was on board, and looked about for her party. Mrs. Saltonstall appeared in the distance with her family about her, and Christie took a survey before reporting herself. Madame looked more like a fashion-plate than ever, in a mass of green flounces, and an impressive bonnet flushed with poppies and bristling with wheat-ears. Beside her sat a gentleman, rapt in a newspaper, of course, for to an American man life is a burden till the daily news have been absorbed. Mrs. Saltonstall's brother was the possessor of a handsome eye without softness, thin lips without benevolence, but plenty of will; a face and figure which some thirty-five years of ease and pleasure had done their best to polish and spoil, and a costume without flaw, from his aristocratic boots to the summer hat on his head.

The little boy more checkered and the little girl

more operatic than before, sat on stools eating *bonbons*, while a French maid and the African footman hovered in the background.

Mrs. Saltonstall and Family.

Feeling very much like a meek gray moth among a flock of butterflies, Christie modestly presented herself.

"Good morning," said Madame with a nod, which,

slight as it was, caused a great commotion among the poppies and the wheat; " I began to be anxious about you. Miss Devon, my brother, Mr. Fletcher."

The gentleman bowed, and as Christie sat down he got up, saying, as he sauntered away with a bored expression :

" Will you have the paper, Charlotte? There's nothing in it."

As Mrs. Saltonstall seemed going to sleep and she felt delicate about addressing the irritable infants in public, Christie amused herself by watching Mr. Fletcher as he roamed listlessly about, and deciding, in her usual rash way, that she did not like him because he looked both lazy and cross, and *ennui* was evidently his bosom friend. Soon, however, she forgot every thing but the shimmer of the sunshine on the sea, the fresh wind that brought color to her pale cheeks, and the happy thoughts that left a smile upon her lips. Then Mr. Fletcher put up his glass and stared at her, shook his head, and said, as he lit a cigar :

" Poor little wretch, what a time she will have of it between Charlotte and the brats ! "

But Christie needed no pity, and thought herself a fortunate young woman when fairly established in her corner of the luxurious apartments occupied by the family. Her duties seemed light compared to those she had left, her dreams were almost as bright as of old, and the new life looked pleasant to her, for she was one of those who could find little bits of happiness for herself and enjoy them heartily in spite of loneliness or neglect.

One of her amusements was studying her companions,

and for a time this occupied her, for Christie possessed penetration and a feminine fancy for finding out people.

Mrs. Saltonstall's mission appeared to be the illustration of each new fashion as it came, and she performed it with a devotion worthy of a better cause. If a color reigned supreme she flushed herself with scarlet or faded into primrose, made herself pretty in the bluest of blue gowns, or turned livid under a gooseberry colored bonnet. Her hat-brims went up or down, were preposterously wide or dwindled to an inch, as the mode demanded. Her skirts were rampant with sixteen frills, or picturesque with landscapes down each side, and a Greek border or a plain hem. Her waists were as pointed as those of Queen Bess or as short as Diana's; and it was the opinion of those who knew her that if the autocrat who ruled her life decreed the wearing of black cats as well as of vegetables, bugs, and birds, the blackest, glossiest Puss procurable for money would have adorned her head in some way.

Her time was spent in dressing, driving, dining and dancing; in skimming novels, and embroidering muslin; going to church with a velvet prayer-book and a new bonnet; and writing to her husband when she wanted money, for she had a husband somewhere abroad, who so happily combined business with pleasure that he never found time to come home. Her children were inconvenient blessings, but she loved them with the love of a shallow heart, and took such good care of their little bodies that there was none left for their little souls. A few days' trial satisfied her as to Christie's capabilities, and, relieved of that anxiety, she gave herself up to her social duties, leaving the ocean and the governess to make the summer wholesome and agreeable to " the darlings."

Mr. Fletcher, having tried all sorts of pleasure and found that, like his newspaper, there was " nothing in it," was now paying the penalty for that unsatisfactory knowledge. Ill health soured his temper and made his life a burden to him. Having few resources within himself to fall back upon, he was very dependent upon other people, and other people were so busy amusing themselves, they seemed to find little time or inclination to amuse a man who had never troubled himself about them. He was rich, but while his money could hire a servant to supply each want, gratify each caprice, it could not buy a tender, faithful friend to serve for love, and ask no wages but his comfort.

He knew this, and felt the vain regret that inevitably comes to those who waste life and learn the value of good gifts by their loss. But he was not wise or brave enough to bear his punishment manfully, and lay the lesson honestly to heart. Fretful and imperious when in pain, listless and selfish when at ease, his one aim in life now was to kill time, and any thing that aided him in this was most gratefully welcomed.

For a long while he took no more notice of Christie than if she had been a shadow, seldom speaking beyond the necessary salutations, and merely carrying his finger to his hat-brim when he passed her on the beach with the children. Her first dislike was softened by pity when she found he was an invalid, but she troubled herself very little about him, and made no romances with him, for all her dreams were of younger, nobler lovers.

Busied with her own affairs, the days though monotonous were not unhappy. She prospered in her work
and the children soon believed in her as devoutly as
young Turks in their Prophet. She devised amusements for herself as well as for them; walked, bathed,
drove, and romped with the little people till her own
eyes shone like theirs, her cheek grew rosy, and her
thin figure rounded with the promise of vigorous health
again.

Christie was at her best that summer, physically
speaking, for sickness had refined her face, giving it
that indescribable expression which pain often leaves
upon a countenance as if in compensation for the bloom
it takes away. The frank eyes had a softer shadow in
their depths, the firm lips smiled less often, but when it
came the smile was the sweeter for the gravity that
went before, and in her voice there was a new undertone of that subtle music, called sympathy, which steals
into the heart and nestles there.

She was unconscious of this gracious change, but
others saw and felt it, and to some a face bright with
health, intelligence, and modesty was more attractive
than mere beauty. Thanks to this and her quiet, cordial
manners, she found friends here and there to add charms
to that summer by the sea.

The dashing young men took no more notice of her
than if she had been a little gray peep on the sands;
not so much, for they shot peeps now and then, but a
governess was not worth bringing down. The fashionable belles and beauties were not even aware of her
existence, being too entirely absorbed in their yearly
husband-hunt to think of any one but themselves and

their prey. The dowagers had more interesting topics to discuss, and found nothing in Christie's humble fortunes worthy of a thought, for they liked their gossip strong and highly flavored, like their tea.

But a kind-hearted girl or two found her out, several lively old maids, as full of the romance of the past as ancient novels, a bashful boy, three or four invalids, and *all* the children, for Christie had a motherly heart and could find charms in the plainest, crossest baby that ever squalled.

Of her old friends she saw nothing, as her theatrical ones were off on their vacations, Hepsey had left her place for one in another city, and Aunt Betsey seldom wrote.

But one day a letter came, telling her that the dear old lady would never write again, and Christie felt as if her nearest and dearest friend was lost. She had gone away to a quiet spot among the rocks to get over her first grief alone, but found it very hard to check her tears, as memory brought back the past, tenderly recalling every kind act, every loving word, and familiar scene. She seldom wept, but when any thing did unseal the fountains that lay so deep, she cried with all her heart, and felt the better for it.

With the letter crumpled in her hand, her head on her knees, and her hat at her feet, she was sobbing like a child, when steps startled her, and, looking up, she saw Mr. Fletcher regarding her with an astonished countenance from under his big sun umbrella.

Something in the flushed, wet face, with its tremulous lips and great tears rolling down, seemed to touch even lazy Mr. Fletcher, for he furled his umbrella with unusual rapidity, and came up, saying, anxiously :

"My dear Miss Devon, what's the matter? Are you hurt? Has Mrs. S. been scolding? Or have the children been too much for you?"

"No; oh, no! it's bad news from home," and Christie's head went down again, for a kind word was more than she could bear just then.

"Some one ill, I fancy? I'm sorry to hear it, but you must hope for the best, you know," replied Mr. Fletcher, really quite exerting himself to remember and present this well-worn consolation.

"There is no hope; Aunt Betsey's dead!"

"Dear me! that's very sad."

Mr. Fletcher tried not to smile as Christie sobbed out the old-fashioned name, but a minute afterward there were actually tears in his eyes, for, as if won by his sympathy, she poured out the homely little story of Aunt Betsey's life and love, unconsciously pronouncing the kind old lady's best epitaph in the unaffected grief that made her broken words so eloquent.

For a minute Mr. Fletcher forgot himself, and felt as he remembered feeling long ago, when, a warm-hearted boy, he had comforted his little sister for a lost kitten or a broken doll. It was a new sensation, therefore interesting and agreeable while it lasted, and when it vanished, which it speedily did, he sighed, then shrugged his shoulders and wished "the girl would stop crying like a water-spout."

"It's hard, but we all have to bear it, you know; and sometimes I fancy if half the pity we give the dead, who don't need it, was given to the living, who do, they'd bear their troubles more comfortably. I know *I* should," added Mr. Fletcher, returning to his own afflictions, and vaguely wondering if any one would cry like that when he departed this life.

Christie minded little what he said, for his voice was pitiful and it comforted her. She dried her tears, put back her hair, and thanked him with a grateful smile, · which gave him another pleasant sensation; for, though young ladies showered smiles upon him with midsummer radiance, they seemed cool and pale beside the sweet sincerity of this one given by a girl whose eyes were red with tender tears.

"That's right, cheer up, take a little run on the beach, and forget all about it," he said, with a heartiness that surprised himself as much as it did Christie.

"I will, thank you. Please don't speak of this; I'm used to bearing my troubles alone, and time will help me to do it cheerfully."

"That's brave! If I can do any thing, let me know; I shall be most happy." And Mr. Fletcher evidently meant what he said.

Christie gave him another grateful "Thank you," then picked up her hat and went away along the sands to try his prescription; while Mr. Fletcher walked the other way, so rapt in thought that he forgot to put up his umbrella till the end of his aristocratic nose was burnt a deep red.

That was the beginning of it; for when Mr. Fletcher found a new amusement, he usually pursued it regardless of consequences. Christie took his pity for what it was worth, and thought no more of that little interview, for her heart was very heavy. But he remembered it, and, when they met on the beach next day, wondered how the governess would behave. She was reading as she walked, and, with a mute acknowledgment of his nod, tranquilly turned a page and read on without a pause, a smile, or change of color.

Mr. Fletcher laughed as he strolled away; but Christie was all the more amusing for her want of coquetry, and soon after he tried her again. The great hotel was all astir one evening with bustle, light, and music; for the young people had a hop, as an appropriate entertainment for a melting July night. With no taste for such folly, even if health had not forbidden it, Mr. Fletcher lounged about the piazzas, tantalizing the fair fowlers who spread their nets for him, and goading sundry desperate spinsters to despair by his erratic movements. Coming to a quiet nook, where a long window gave a fine view of the brilliant scene, he found Christie leaning in, with a bright, wistful face, while her hand kept time to the enchanting music of a waltz.

"Wisely watching the lunatics, instead of joining in their antics," he said, sitting down with a sigh.

Christie looked around and answered, with the wistful look still in her eyes:

"I'm very fond of that sort of insanity; but there is no place for me in Bedlam at present."

"I daresay I can find you one, if you care to try it. I don't indulge myself." And Mr. Fletcher's eye went from the rose in Christie's brown hair to the silvery folds of her best gown, put on merely for the pleasure of wearing it because every one else was in festival array.

She shook her head. "No, thank you. Governesses are very kindly treated in America; but ball-rooms like that are not for them. I enjoy looking on, fortunately; so I have my share of fun after all."

"I shan't get any complaints out of her. Plucky little soul! I rather like that," said Mr. Fletcher to himself; and, finding his seat comfortable, the corner cool, and his companion pleasant to look at, with the moonlight doing its best for her, he went on talking for his own satisfaction.

Christie would rather have been left in peace; but fancying that he did it out of kindness to her, and that she had done him injustice before, she was grateful now, and exerted herself to seem so; in which endeavor she succeeded so well that Mr. Fletcher proved he could be a very agreeable companion when he chose. He talked well; and Christie was a good listener. Soon interest conquered her reserve, and she ventured to ask a question, make a criticism, or express an opinion in her own simple way. Unconsciously she piqued the curiosity of the man; for, though he knew many lovely, wise, and witty women, he had never chanced to meet with one like this before; and novelty was the desire of his life. Of course he did not find moonlight, music, and agreeable chat as delightful as she did; but there *was* something animating in the fresh face opposite, something flattering in the eager interest she showed, and something most attractive in the glimpses unconsciously given him of a nature genuine in its womanly sincerity and strength. Something about this girl seemed to appeal to the old self, so long neglected that he thought it dead. He could not analyze the feeling, but was conscious of a desire to seem better than he was as he looked into those honest eyes; to talk well, that he might bring that frank smile to the lips that grew either sad or scornful when he tried worldly gossip or bitter satire; and to prove himself a man under all the elegance and polish of the gentleman.

He was discovering then, what Christie learned when her turn came, that fine natures seldom fail to draw out the finer traits of those who approach them, as the little witch-hazel wand, even in the hand of a child, detects and points to hidden springs in unsuspected spots. Women often possess this gift, and when used worthily find it as powerful as beauty; for, if less alluring, it is more lasting and more helpful, since it appeals, not to the senses, but the souls of men.

Christie was one of these; and in proportion as her own nature was sound and sweet so was its power as a touchstone for the genuineness of others. It was this unconscious gift that made her wonder at the unexpected kindness she found in Mr. Fletcher, and this which made him, for an hour or two at least, heartily wish he could live his life over again and do it better.

After that evening Mr. Fletcher spoke to Christie when he met her, turned and joined her sometimes as she walked with the children, and fell into the way of lounging near when she sat reading aloud to an invalid friend on piazza or sea-shore. Christie much preferred to have no auditor but kind Miss Tudor; but finding the old lady enjoyed his chat she resigned herself, and when he brought them new books as well as himself, she became quite cordial.

Everybody sauntered and lounged, so no one minded the little group that met day after day among the rocks. Christie read aloud, while the children revelled in sand, shells, and puddles; Miss Tudor spun endless webs of gay silk and wool; and Mr. Fletcher, with his hat over his eyes, lay sunning himself like a luxurious lizard, as he watched the face that grew daily fairer in his sight, and listened to the pleasant voice that went reading on till all his ills and *ennui* seemed lulled to sleep as by a spell.

A week or two of this new caprice set Christie to thinking. She knew that Uncle Philip was not fond of "the darlings;" it was evident that good Miss Tudor, with her mild twaddle and eternal knitting, was not the attraction, so she was forced to believe that he came for her sake alone. She laughed at herself for this fancy at first; but not possessing the sweet unconsciousness of those heroines who can live through three volumes with a burning passion before their eyes, and never see it till the proper moment comes, and Eugene goes down upon his knees, she soon felt sure that Mr. Fletcher found her society agreeable, and wished her to know it.

Being a mortal woman, her vanity was flattered, and she found herself showing that she liked it by those small signs and symbols which lovers' eyes are so quick to see and understand, — an artful bow on her hat, a flower in her belt, fresh muslin gowns, and the most becoming arrangement of her hair.

"Poor man, he has so few pleasures I 'm sure I needn't grudge him such a small one as looking at and listening to me if he likes it," she said to herself one

day, as she was preparing for her daily stroll with unusual care. "But how will it end? If he only wants a
mild flirtation he is welcome to it; but if he really
cares for me, I must make up my mind about it, and
not deceive him. I don't believe he loves me: how
can he? such an insignificant creature as I am."

Here she looked in the glass, and as she looked the
color deepened in her cheek, her eyes shone, and a
smile would sit upon her lips, for the reflection showed
her a very winning face under the coquettish hat put
on to captivate.

"Don't be foolish, Christie! Mind what you do, and
be sure vanity doesn't delude you, for you are only a
woman, and in things of this sort we are so blind and
silly. I'll think of this possibility soberly, but I won't
flirt, and then which ever way I decide I shall have
nothing to reproach myself with."

Armed with this virtuous resolution, Christie sternly
replaced the pretty hat with her old brown one, fastened up a becoming curl, which of late she had worn
behind her ear, and put on a pair of stout, rusty boots,
much fitter for rocks and sand than the smart slippers
she was preparing to sacrifice. Then she trudged away
to Miss Tudor, bent on being very quiet and reserved,
as became a meek and lowly governess.

But, dear heart, how feeble are the resolutions of
womankind! When she found herself sitting in her
favorite nook, with the wide, blue sea glittering below,
the fresh wind making her blood dance in her veins,
and all the earth and sky so full of summer life and
loveliness, her heart *would* sing for joy, her face *would*
shine with the mere bliss of living, and underneath

all this natural content the new thought, half confessed, yet very sweet, *would* whisper, "Somebody
cares for me."

If she had doubted it, the expression of Mr. Fletcher's face that morning would have dispelled the doubt,
for, as she read, he was saying to himself: " Yes, this
healthful, cheery, helpful creature is what I want to
make life pleasant. Every thing else is used up ; why
not try this, and make the most of my last chance ?
She does me good, and I don't seem to get tired of her.
I can't have a long life, they tell me, nor an easy one,
with the devil to pay with my vitals generally ; so it
would be a wise thing to provide myself with a good-
tempered, faithful soul to take care of me. My fortune
would pay for loss of time, and my death leave her
a bonny widow. I won't be rash, but I think I'll
try it."

With this mixture of tender, selfish, and regretful
thoughts in his mind, it is no wonder Mr. Fletcher's
eyes betrayed him, as he lay looking at Christie. Never
had she read so badly, for she could not keep her mind
on her book. It *would* wander to that new and troublesome fancy of hers ; she could not help thinking that
Mr. Fletcher must have been a handsome man before
he was so ill ; wondering if his temper was *very* bad,
and fancying that he might prove both generous and
kind and true to one who loved and served him well.
At this point she was suddenly checked by a slip of the
tongue that covered her with confusion.

She was reading " John Halifax," and instead of saying " Phineas Fletcher" she said Philip, and then colored
to her forehead, and lost her place. Miss Tudor did

not mind it, but Mr. Fletcher laughed, and Christie thanked Heaven that her face was half hidden by the old brown hat.

Nothing was said, but she was much relieved to find that Mr. Fletcher had joined a yachting party next day and he would be away for a week. During that week Christie thought over the matter, and fancied she had made up her mind. She recalled certain speeches she had heard, and which had more weight with her than she suspected. One dowager had said to another: "P. F. intends to marry, I assure you, for his sister told me so, with tears in her eyes. Men who have been gay in their youth make very good husbands when their wild oats are sowed. Clara could not do better, and I should be quite content to give her to him."

"Well, dear, I should be sorry to see my Augusta his wife, for whoever he marries will be a perfect slave to him. His fortune would be a nice thing if he did not live long; but even for that my Augusta shall not be sacrificed," returned the other matron whose Augusta had vainly tried to captivate "P. F.," and revenged herself by calling him "a wreck, my dear, a perfect wreck."

At another time Christie heard some girls discussing the eligibility of several gentlemen, and Mr. Fletcher was considered the best match among them.

"You can do any thing you like with a husband a good deal older than yourself. He's happy with his business, his club, and his dinner, and leaves you to do what you please ; just keep him comfortable and he'll pay your bills without much fuss," said one young thing who had seen life at twenty.

"I'd take him if I had the chance, just because everybody wants him. Don't admire him a particle, but it will make a jolly stir whenever he does marry, and I wouldn't mind having a hand in it," said the second budding belle.

"I'd take him for the diamonds alone. Mamma says they are splendid, and have been in the family for ages. He won't let Mrs. S. wear them, for they always go to the eldest son's wife. Hope he'll choose a handsome woman who will show them off well," said a third sweet girl, glancing at her own fine neck.

"He won't; he'll take some poky old maid who will cuddle him when he is sick, and keep out of his way when he is well. See if he don't."

"I saw him dawdling round with old Tudor, perhaps he means to take her : she's a capital nurse, got ill herself taking care of her father, you know."

"Perhaps he's after the governess ; she's rather nice looking, though she hasn't a bit of style."

"Gracious, no ! she's a dowdy thing, always trailing round with a book and those horrid children. No danger of his marrying *her.*" And a derisive laugh seemed to settle that question beyond a doubt.

"Oh, indeed ! " said Christie, as the girls went trooping out of the bath-house, where this pleasing chatter had been carried on regardless of listeners. She called them "mercenary, worldly, unwomanly flirts," and felt herself much their superior. Yet the memory of their gossip haunted her, and had its influence upon her decision, though she thought she came to it through her own good judgment and discretion.

"If he really cares for me I will listen, and not refuse

till I know him well enough to decide. I 'm tired of being alone, and should enjoy ease and pleasure so much. He 's going abroad for the winter, and that would be charming. I 'll try not to be worldly-minded and marry without love, but it does look tempting to a poor soul like me."

So Christie made up her mind to accept, if this promotion was offered her; and while she waited, went through so many alternations of feeling, and was so harassed by doubts and fears that she sometimes found herself wishing it had never occurred to her.

Mr. Fletcher, meantime, with the help of many meditative cigars, was making up *his* mind. Absence only proved to him how much he needed a better time-killer than billiards, horses, or newspapers, for the long, listless days seemed endless without the cheerful governess to tone him up, like a new and agreeable sort of bitters. A gradually increasing desire to secure this satisfaction had taken possession of him, and the thought of always having a pleasant companion, with no nerves, nonsense, or affectation about her, was an inviting idea to a man tired of fashionable follies and tormented with the *ennui* of his own society.

The gossip, wonder, and chagrin such a step would cause rather pleased his fancy; the excitement of trying almost the only thing as yet untried allured him; and deeper than all the desire to forget the past in a better future led him to Christie by the nobler instincts that never wholly die in any soul. He wanted her as he had wanted many other things in his life, and had little doubt that he could have her for the asking. Even if love was not abounding, surely his fortune, which hitherto had procured him all he wished (except health and happiness) could buy him a wife, when his friends made better bargains every day. So, having settled the question, he came home again, and every one said the trip had done him a world of good.

Christie sat in her favorite nook one bright September morning, with the inevitable children hunting hapless crabs in a pool near by. A book lay on her knee, but she was not reading; her eyes were looking far across the blue waste before her with an eager gaze, and her face was bright with some happy thought. The sound of approaching steps disturbed her reverie, and, recognizing them, she plunged into the heart of the story, reading as if utterly absorbed, till a shadow fell athwart the page, and the voice she had expected to hear asked blandly:

" What book now, Miss Devon? "

" 'Jane Eyre,' sir."

Mr. Fletcher sat down just where her hat-brim was no screen, pulled off his gloves, and leisurely composed himself for a comfortable lounge.

" What is your opinion of Rochester? " he asked, presently.

" Not a very high one."

" Then you think Jane was a fool to love and try to make a saint of him, I suppose ? "

" I like Jane, but never can forgive her marrying that man, as I haven't much faith in the saints such sinners make."

" But don't you think a man who had only follies to regret might expect a good woman to lend him a hand and make him happy ? "

"If he has wasted his life he must take the consequences, and be content with pity and indifference, instead of respect and love. Many good women do 'lend a hand,' as you say, and it is quite Christian and amiable, I 've no doubt; but I cannot think it a fair bargain."

Mr. Fletcher liked to make Christie talk, for in the interest of the subject she forgot herself, and her chief charm for him was her earnestness. But just then the earnestness did not seem to suit him, and he said, rather sharply:

"What hard-hearted creatures you women are sometimes! Now, I fancied you were one of those who wouldn't leave a poor fellow to his fate, if his salvation lay in your hands."

"I can't say what I should do in such a case; but it always seemed to me that a man should have energy enough to save himself, and not expect the 'weaker vessel,' as he calls her, to do it for him," answered Christie, with a conscious look, for Mr. Fletcher's face made her feel as if something was going to happen.

Evidently anxious to know what she *would* do in aforesaid case, Mr. Fletcher decided to put one before her as speedily as possible, so he said, in a pensive tone, and with a wistful glance:

"You looked very happy just now when I came up. I wish I could believe that my return had any thing to do with it."

Christie wished she could control her tell-tale color, but finding she could not, looked hard at the sea, and, ignoring his tender insinuation, said, with suspicious enthusiasm:

"I was thinking of what Mrs. Saltonstall said this morning. She asked me if I would like to go to Paris with her for the winter. It has always been one of my dreams to go abroad, and I do hope I shall not be disappointed."

Christie's blush seemed to be a truer answer than her words, and, leaning a little nearer, Mr. Fletcher said, in his most persuasive tone:

"Will you go to Paris as *my* governess, instead of Charlotte's?"

Christie thought her reply was all ready; but when the moment came, she found it was not, and sat silent, feeling as if that "Yes" would promise far more than she could give. Mr. Fletcher had no doubt what the answer would be, and was in no haste to get it, for that was one of the moments that are so pleasant and so short-lived they should be enjoyed to the uttermost. He liked to watch her color come and go, to see the asters on her bosom tremble with the quickened beating of her heart, and tasted, in anticipation, the satisfaction of the moment when that pleasant voice of hers would falter out its grateful assent. Drawing yet nearer, he went on, still in the persuasive tone that would have been more lover-like if it had been less assured.

"I think I am not mistaken in believing that you care for me a little. You must know how fond I am of you, how much I need you, and how glad I should be to give all I have if I might keep you always to make my hard life happy. May I, Christie?"

"You would soon tire of me. I have no beauty, no accomplishments, no fortune, — nothing but my heart and my hand to give the man I marry. Is that enough?" asked Christie, looking at him with eyes that betrayed the hunger of an empty heart longing to be fed with genuine food.

But Mr. Fletcher did not understand its meaning; he saw the humility in her face, thought she was overcome by the weight of the honor he did her, and tried to reassure her with the gracious air of one who wishes to lighten the favor he confers.

"It might not be for some men, but it is for me, because I want you very much. Let people say what they will, if you say yes I am satisfied. You shall not regret it, Christie; I'll do my best to make you happy; you shall travel wherever I can go with you, have what you like, if possible, and when we come back by and by, you shall take your place in the world as my wife. You will fill it well, I fancy, and I shall be a happy man. I've had my own way all my life, and I mean to have it now, so smile, and say, 'Yes, Philip,' like a sweet soul, as you are."

But Christie did not smile, and felt no inclination to say "Yes, Philip," for that last speech of his jarred on her ear. The tone of unconscious condescension in it wounded the woman's sensitive pride; self was too apparent, and the most generous words seemed to her like bribes. This was not the lover she had dreamed of, the brave, true man who gave her all, and felt it could not half repay the treasure of her innocent, first love. This was not the happiness she had hoped for, the perfect faith, the glad surrender, the sweet content that made all things possible, and changed this work-a-day world into a heaven while the joy lasted.

She had decided to say " yes," but her heart said
" no " decidedly, and with instinctive loyalty she obeyed
it, even while she seemed to yield to the temptation
which appeals to three of the strongest foibles in most
women's nature, — vanity, ambition, and the love of
pleasure.

" You are very kind, but you may repent it, you
know so little of me," she began, trying to soften her
refusal, but sadly hindered by a feeling of contempt.

" I know more about you than you think; but it
makes no difference," interrupted Mr. Fletcher, with a
smile that irritated Christie, even before she understood
its significance. " I thought it would at first, but I
found I couldn't get on without you, so I made up my
mind to forgive and forget that my wife had ever been
an actress."

Christie had forgotten it, and it would have been
well for him if he had held his tongue. Now she
understood the tone that had chilled her, the smile that
angered her, and Mr. Fletcher's fate was settled in the
drawing of a breath.

" Who told you that? " she asked, quickly, while
every nerve tingled with the mortification of being
found out then and there in the one secret of her life.

" I saw you dancing on the beach with the children
one day, and it reminded me of an actress I had once
seen. I should not have remembered it but for the
accident which impressed it on my mind. Powder,
paint, and costume made 'Miss Douglas' a very different woman from Miss Devon, but a few cautious inquiries settled the matter, and I then understood where
you got that slight *soupçon* of dash and daring which

makes our demure governess so charming when with me."

As he spoke, Mr. Fletcher smiled again, and kissed his hand to her with a dramatic little gesture that exasperated Christie beyond measure. She would not make light of it, as he did, and submit to be forgiven for a past she was not ashamed of. Heartily wishing she had been frank at first, she resolved to have it out now, and accept nothing Mr. Fletcher offered her, not even silence.

"Yes," she said, as steadily as she could, "I *was* an actress for three years, and though it was a hard life it was an honest one, and I'm not ashamed of it. I ought to have told Mrs. Saltonstall, but I was warned that if I did it would be difficult to find a place, people are so prejudiced. I sincerely regret it now, and shall tell her at once, so you may save yourself the trouble."

"My dear girl, I never dreamed of telling any one!" cried Mr. Fletcher in an injured tone. "I beg you won't speak, but trust me, and let it be a little secret between us two. I assure you it makes no difference to me, for I should marry an opera dancer if I chose, so forget it, as I do, and set my mind at rest upon the other point. I'm still waiting for my answer, you know."

"It is ready."

"A kind one, I'm sure. What is it, Christie?"

"No, I thank you."

"But you are not in earnest?"

"Perfectly so."

Mr. Fletcher got up suddenly and set his back against

the rock, saying in a tone of such unaffected surprise and disappointment that her heart reproached her:

"No, I thank you."

"Am I to understand that as your final answer, Miss Devon?"

"Distinctly and decidedly my final answer, Mr Fletcher."

Christie tried to speak kindly, but she was angry with herself and him, and unconsciously showed it both in face and voice, for she was no actress off the stage, and wanted to be very true just then as a late atonement for that earlier want of candor.

A quick change passed over Mr. Fletcher's face ; his cold eyes kindled with an angry spark, his lips were pale with anger, and his voice was very bitter, as he slowly said :

" I 've made many blunders in my life, and this is one of the greatest ; for I believed in a woman, was fool enough to care for her with the sincerest love I ever knew, and fancied that she would be grateful for the sacrifice I made."

He got no further, for Christie rose straight up and answered him with all the indignation she felt burning in her face and stirring the voice she tried in vain to keep as steady as his own.

" The sacrifice would not have been *all* yours, for it is what we *are*, not what we *have*, that makes one human being superior to another. I am as well-born as you in spite of my poverty ; my life, I think, has been a better one than yours ; my heart, I know, is fresher, and my memory has fewer faults and follies to reproach me with. What can you give me but money and position in return for the youth and freedom I should sacrifice in marrying you ? Not love, for you count the cost of your bargain, as no true lover could, and you reproach me for deceit when in your heart you know you only cared for me because I can amuse and serve you. I too deceived myself, I too see my mistake, and I decline the honor you would do me, since it is so great in your eyes that you must remind me of it as you offer it."

In the excitement of the moment Christie unconsciously spoke with something of her old dramatic fervor in voice and gesture ; Mr. Fletcher saw. it, and, while he never had admired her so much, could not resist avenging himself for the words that angered him, the more deeply for their truth. Wounded vanity and baffled will can make an ungenerous man as spiteful as a woman; and Mr. Fletcher proved it then, for he saw where Christie's pride was sorest, and touched the wound with the skill of a resentful nature.

As she paused, he softly clapped his hands, saying, with a smile that made her eyes flash:

"Very well done! infinitely superior to your 'Woffington,' Miss Devon. I am disappointed in the woman, but I make my compliment to the actress, and leave the stage free for another and a more successful Romeo."

Still smiling, he bowed and went away apparently quite calm and much amused, but a more wrathful, disappointed man never crossed those sands than the one who kicked his dog and swore at himself for a fool that day when no one saw him.

For a minute Christie stood and watched him, then, feeling that she must either laugh or cry, wisely chose the former vent for her emotions, and sat down feeling inclined to look at the whole scene from a ludicrous point of view.

"My second love affair is a worse failure than my first, for I did pity poor Joe, but this man is detestable, and I never will forgive him that last insult. I dare say I *was* absurdly tragical, I'm apt to be when very angry, but what a temper he has got! The white, cold kind, that smoulders and stabs, instead of blazing up and being over in a minute. Thank Heaven, I'm not his wife! Well, I've made an enemy and lost my place, for of course Mrs. Saltonstall won't keep me

after this awful discovery. I'll tell her at once, for I
will have no 'little secrets' with him. No Paris either,
and that's the worst of it all! Never mind, I haven't
sold my liberty for the Fletcher diamonds, and that's
a comfort. Now a short scene with my lady and then
exit governess."

But though she laughed, Christie felt troubled at the
part she had played in this affair; repented of her
worldly aspirations; confessed her vanity; accepted
her mortification and disappointment as a just punishment for her sins; and yet at the bottom of her heart
she did enjoy it mightily.

She tried to spare Mr. Fletcher in her interview with
his sister, and only betrayed her own iniquities. But,
to her surprise, Mrs. Saltonstall, though much disturbed
at the discovery, valued Christie as a governess, and
respected her as a woman, so she was willing to bury
the past, she said, and still hoped Miss Devon would
remain.

Then Christie was forced to tell her why it was impossible for her to do so; and, in her secret soul, she
took a naughty satisfaction in demurely mentioning
that she had refused my lord.

Mrs. Saltonstall's consternation was comical, for she
had been so absorbed in her own affairs she had suspected nothing; and horror fell upon her when she
learned how near dear Philip had been to the fate from
which she jealously guarded him, that his property
might one day benefit the darlings.

In a moment every thing was changed; and it was
evident to Christie that the sooner she left the better it
would suit madame. The proprieties were preserved

to the end, and Mrs. Saltonstall treated her with unusual respect, for she had come to honor, and also con-
ducted herself in a most praiseworthy manner. How
she could refuse a Fletcher visibly amazed the lady;
but she forgave the slight, and gently insinuated that
" my brother" was, perhaps, only amusing himself.

Christie was but too glad to be off; and when Mrs.
Saltonstall asked when she would prefer to leave,
promptly replied, " To-morrow," received her salary,
which was forthcoming with unusual punctuality, and
packed her trunks with delightful rapidity.

As the family was to leave in a week, her sudden
departure caused no surprise to the few who knew her,
and with kind farewells to such of her summer friends
as still remained, she went to bed that night all ready
for an early start. She saw nothing more of Mr.
Fletcher that day, but the sound of excited voices in
the drawing-room assured her that madame was having
it out with her brother; and with truly feminine incon-
sistency Christie hoped that she would not be too hard
upon the poor man, for, after all, it was kind of him to
overlook the actress, and ask the governess to share his
good things with him.

She did not repent, but she got herself to sleep,
imagining a bridal trip to Paris, and dreamed so
delightfully of lost splendors that the awakening was
rather blank, the future rather cold and hard.

She was early astir, meaning to take the first boat
and so escape all disagreeable *rencontres*, and having
kissed the children in their little beds, with tender
promises not to forget them, she took a hasty breakfast
and stepped into the carriage waiting at the door. The

sleepy waiters stared, a friendly housemaid nodded, and Miss Walker, the hearty English lady who did her ten miles a day, cried out, as she tramped by, blooming and bedraggled :

"Bless me, are you off ?"

"Yes, thank Heaven !" answered Christie ; but as she spoke Mr. Fletcher came down the steps looking as wan and heavy-eyed as if a sleepless night had been added to his day's defeat. Leaning in at the window, he asked abruptly, but with a look she never could forget:

"Will nothing change your answer, Christie?"

"Nothing."

His eyes said, "Forgive me," but his lips only said, "Good-by," and the carriage rolled away.

Then, being a woman, two great tears fell on the hand still red with the lingering grasp he had given it, and Christie said, as pitifully as if she loved him :

"He *has* got a heart, after all, and perhaps I might have been glad to fill it if he had only shown it to me sooner. Now it is too late."

CHAPTER V.

COMPANION.

BEFORE she had time to find a new situation, Christie received a note from Miss Tudor, saying that hearing she had left Mrs. Saltonstall she wanted to offer her the place of companion to an invalid girl, where the duties were light and the compensation large.

"How kind of her to think of me," said Christie, gratefully. "I'll go at once and do my best to secure it, for it must be a good thing or she wouldn't recommend it."

Away went Christie to the address sent by Miss Tudor, and as she waited at the door she thought:

"What a happy family the Carrols must be!" for the house was one of an imposing block in a West End square, which had its own little park where a fountain sparkled in the autumn sunshine, and pretty children played among the fallen leaves.

Mrs. Carrol was a stately woman, still beautiful in spite of her fifty years. But though there were few lines on her forehead, few silver threads in the dark hair that lay smoothly over it, and a gracious smile showed the fine teeth, an indescribable expression of unsubmissive sorrow touched the whole face, betraying that life had brought some heavy cross, from which her wealth could purchase no release, for which her pride could find no effectual screen.

She looked at Christie with a searching eye, listened attentively when she spoke, and seemed testing her with covert care as if the place she was to fill demanded some unusual gift or skill.

" Miss Tudor tells me that you read aloud well, sing sweetly, possess a cheerful temper, and the quiet, patient ways which are peculiarly grateful to an invalid," began Mrs. Carrol, with that keen yet wistful gaze, and an anxious accent in her voice that went to Christie's heart.

" Miss Tudor is very kind to think so well of me and my few accomplishments. I have never been with an invalid, but I think I can promise to be patient, willing, and cheerful. My own experience of illness has taught me how to sympathize with others and love to lighten pain. I shall be very glad to try if you think I have any fitness for the place."

" I do," and Mrs. Carrol's face softened as she spoke, for something in Christie's words or manner seemed to please her. Then slowly, as if the task was a hard one, she added:

" My daughter has been very ill and is still weak and nervous. I must hint to you that the loss of one very dear to her was the cause of the illness and the melancholy which now oppresses her. Therefore we must avoid any thing that can suggest or recall this trouble. She cares for nothing as yet, will see no one, and prefers to live alone. She is still so feeble this is but natural; yet solitude is bad for her, and her physician thinks that a new face might rouse her, and the society of one in no way connected with the painful past might interest and do her good. You see it is a little difficult to find just what we want, for a young companion is best, yet must be discreet and firm, as few young people are."

Fancying from Mrs. Carrol's manner that Miss Tudor had said more in her favor than had been repeated to her, Christie in a few plain words told her little story, resolving to have no concealments here, and feeling that perhaps her experiences might have given her more firmness and discretion than many women of her age possessed. Mrs. Carrol seemed to find it so; the anxious look lifted a little as she listened, and when Christie ended she said, with a sigh of relief:

" Yes, I think Miss Tudor is right, and you *are* the one we want. Come and try it for a week and then we can decide. Can you begin to-day?" she added, as Christie rose. "Every hour is precious, for my poor girl's sad solitude weighs on my heart, and this is my one hope."

" I will stay with pleasure," answered Christie, thinking Mrs. Carrol's anxiety excessive, yet pitying the mother's pain, for something in her face suggested the idea that she reproached herself in some way for her daughter's state.

With secret gratitude that she had dressed with care, Christie took off her things and followed Mrs. Carrol upstairs. Entering a room in what seemed to be a wing of the great house, they found an old woman sewing.

"How is Helen to-day, Nurse?" asked Mrs. Carrol, pausing.

"Poorly, ma'am. I've been in every hour, but she only says: 'Let me be quiet,' and lies looking up at the picture till it's fit to break your heart to see her," answered the woman, with a shake of the head.

"I have brought Miss Devon to sit with her a little while. Doctor advises it, and I fancy the experiment may succeed if we can only amuse the dear child, and make her forget herself and her troubles."

"As you please, ma'am," said the old woman, looking with little favor at the new-comer, for the good soul was jealous of any interference between herself and the child she had tended for years.

"I won't disturb her, but you shall take Miss Devon in and tell Helen mamma sends her love, and hopes she will make an effort for all our sakes."

"Yes, ma'am."

"Go, my dear, and do your best." With these words Mrs. Carrol hastily left the room, and Christie followed Nurse.

A quick glance showed her that she was in the daintily furnished boudoir of a rich man's daughter, but before she could take a second look her eyes were arrested by the occupant of this pretty place, and she forgot all else. On a low luxurious couch lay a girl, so beautiful and pale and still, that for an instant Christie thought her dead or sleeping. She was neither, for at the sound of a voice the great eyes opened wide, darkening and dilating with a strange expression as they fell on the unfamiliar face.

"Nurse, who is that? I told you I would see no one. I'm too ill to be so worried," she said, in an imperious tone.

HELEN CARROL.

"Yes, dear, I know, but your mamma wished you to make an effort. Miss Devon is to sit with you and try to cheer you up a bit," said the old woman in a dissatisfied tone, that contrasted strangely with the tender way in which she stroked the beautiful disordered hair that hung about the girl's shoulders.

Helen knit her brows and looked most ungracious, but evidently tried to be civil, for with a courteous wave of her hand toward an easy chair in the sunny window she said, quietly:

"Please sit down, Miss Devon, and excuse me for a little while. I've had a bad night, and am too tired to talk just yet. There are books of all sorts, or the conservatory if you like it better."

"Thank you. I'll read quietly till you want me. Then I shall be very glad to do any thing I can for you."

With that Christie retired to the big chair, and fell to reading the first book she took up, a good deal embarrassed by her reception, and very curious to know what would come next.

The old woman went away after folding the down coverlet carefully over her darling's feet, and Helen seemed to go to sleep.

For a time the room was very still; the fire burned softly on the marble hearth, the sun shone warmly on velvet carpet and rich hangings, the delicate breath of flowers blew in through the half-open door that led to a gay little conservatory, and nothing but the roll of a distant carriage broke the silence now and then.

Christie's eyes soon wandered from her book to the lovely face and motionless figure on the couch. Just opposite, in a recess, hung the portrait of a young and handsome man, and below it stood a vase of flowers, a graceful Roman lamp, and several little relics, as if it were the shrine where some dead love was mourned and worshipped still.

As she looked from the living face, so pale and so pathetic in its quietude, to the painted one so full of color, strength, and happiness, her heart ached for poor Helen, and her eyes were wet with tears of pity. A sudden movement on the couch gave her no time to hide them, and as she hastily looked down upon her book a treacherous drop fell glittering on the page.

"What have you there so interesting?" asked Helen, in that softly imperious tone of hers.

"Don Quixote," answered Christie, too much abashed to have her wits about her.

Helen smiled a melancholy smile as she rose, saying wearily:

"They gave me that to make me laugh, but I did not find it funny; neither was it sad enough to make me cry as you do."

"I was not reading, I was" — there Christie broke down, and could have cried with vexation at the bad beginning she had made. But that involuntary tear was better balm to Helen than the most perfect tact, the most brilliant conversation. It touched and won her without words, for sympathy works miracles. Her whole face changed, and her mournful eyes grew soft as with the gentle freedom of a child she lifted Christie's downcast face and said, with a falter in her voice:

"I know you were pitying me. Well, I need pity, and from you I'll take it, because you don't force it on me. Have *you* been ill and wretched too? I think so, else you would never care to come and shut yourself up here with me!"

"I have been ill, and I know how hard it is to get one's spirits back again. I've had my troubles, too, but not heavier than I could bear, thank God."

"What made you ill? Would you mind telling me about it? I seem to fancy hearing other people's woes, though it can't make mine seem lighter."

"A piece of the Castle of the Sun fell on my head

and nearly killed me," and Christie laughed in spite of herself at the astonishment in Helen's face. " I was an actress once ; your mother knows and didn't mind," she added, quickly.

" I 'm glad of that. I used to wish I could be one, I was so fond of the theatre. They should have consented, it would have given me something to do, and, however hard it is, it couldn't be worse than this." Helen spoke vehemently and an excited flush rose to her white cheeks; then she checked herself and dropped into a chair, saying, hurriedly :

" Tell about it: don't let me think; it 's bad for me."

Glad to be set to work, and bent on retrieving her first mistake, Christie plunged into her theatrical experiences and talked away in her most lively style. People usually get eloquent when telling their own stories, and true tales are always the most interesting. Helen listened at first with a half-absent air, but presently grew more attentive, and when the catastrophe came sat erect, quite absorbed in the interest of this glimpse behind the curtain.

Charmed with her success, Christie branched off right and left, stimulated by questions, led on by suggestive incidents, and generously supplied by memory. Before she knew it, she was telling her whole history in the most expansive manner, for women soon get sociable together, and Helen's interest flattered her immensely. Once she made her laugh at some droll trifle, and as if the unaccustomed sound had startled her, old nurse popped in her head ; but seeing nothing amiss retired, wondering what on earth that girl could be doing to cheer up Miss Helen so.

"Tell about your lovers: you must have had some; actresses always do. Happy women, they can love as they like!" said Helen, with the inquisitive frankness of an invalid for whom etiquette has ceased to exist.

Remembering in time that this was a forbidden subject, Christie smiled and shook her head.

"I had a few, but one does not tell those secrets, you know."

Evidently disappointed, and a little displeased at being reminded of her want of good-breeding, Helen got up and began to wander restlessly about the room. Presently, as if wishing to atone for her impatience, she bade Christie come and see her flowers. Following her, the new companion found herself in a little world where perpetual summer reigned. Vines curtained the roof, slender shrubs and trees made leafy walls on either side, flowers bloomed above and below, birds carolled in half-hidden prisons, aquariums and ferneries stood all about, and the soft plash of a little fountain made pleasant music as it rose and fell.

Helen threw herself wearily down on a pile of cushions that lay beside the basin, and beckoning Christie to sit near, said, as she pressed her hands to her hot forehead and looked up with a distressful brightness in the haggard eyes that seemed to have no rest in them:

"Please sing to me; any humdrum air will do. I am so tired, and yet I cannot sleep. If my head would only stop this dreadful thinking and let me forget one hour it would do me so much good."

"I know the feeling, and I'll try what Lucy used to do to quiet me. Put your poor head in my lap, dear, and lie quite still while I cool and comfort it."

Obeying like a worn-out child, Helen lay motionless while Christie, dipping her fingers in the basin, passed the wet tips softly to and fro across the hot forehead, and the thin temples where the pulses throbbed so fast. And while she soothed she sang the "Land o' the Leal," and sang it well; for the tender words, the plaintive air were dear to her, because her mother loved and sang it to her years ago. Slowly the heavy eyelids drooped, slowly the lines of pain were smoothed away from the broad brow, slowly the restless hands grew still, and Helen lay asleep.

So intent upon her task was Christie, that she forgot herself till the discomfort of her position reminded her that she had a body. Fearing to wake the poor girl in her arms, she tried to lean against the basin, but could not reach a cushion to lay upon the cold stone ledge. An unseen hand supplied the want, and, looking round, she saw two young men standing behind her.

Helen's brothers, without doubt; for, though utterly unlike in expression, some of the family traits were strongly marked in both. The elder wore the dress of a priest, had a pale, ascetic face, with melancholy eyes, stern mouth, and the absent air of one who leads an inward life. The younger had a more attractive face, for, though bearing marks of dissipation, it betrayed a generous, ardent nature, proud and wilful, yet lovable in spite of all defects. He was very boyish still, and plainly showed how much he felt, as, with a hasty nod to Christie, he knelt down beside his sister, saying, in a whisper:

"Look at her, Augustine! so beautiful, so quiet! What a comfort it is to see her like herself again."

"Ah, yes; and but for the sin of it, I could find it in my heart to wish she might never wake!" returned the other, gloomily.

"Don't say that! How could we live without her?" Then, turning to Christie, the younger said, in a friendly tone:

"You must be very tired; let us lay her on the sofa. It is very damp here, and if she sleeps long you will faint from weariness."

Carefully lifting her, the brothers carried the sleeping girl into her room, and laid her down. She sighed as her head touched the pillow, and her arm clung to Harry's neck, as if she felt his nearness even in sleep. He put his cheek to hers, and lingered over her with an affectionate solicitude beautiful to see. Augustine stood silent, grave and cold as if he had done with human ties, yet found it hard to sever this one, for he stretched his hand above his sister as if he blessed her, then, with another grave bow to Christie, went away as noiselessly as he had come. But Harry kissed the sleeper tenderly, whispered, "Be kind to her," with an imploring voice, and hurried from the room as if to hide the feeling that he must not show.

A few minutes later the nurse brought in a note from Mrs. Carrol.

"My son tells me that Helen is asleep, and you look very tired. Leave her to Hester, now; you have done enough to-day, so let me thank you heartily, and send you home for a quiet night before you continue your good work to-morrow."

Christie went, found a carriage waiting for her, and drove home very happy at the success of her first attempt at companionship.

The next day she entered upon the new duties with interest and good-will, for this was work in which heart took part, as well as head and hand. Many things surprised, and some things perplexed her, as she came to know the family better. But she discreetly held her tongue, used her eyes, and did her best to please.

Mrs. Carrol seemed satisfied, often thanked her for her faithfulness to Helen, but seldom visited her daughter, never seemed surprised or grieved that the girl expressed no wish to see her; and, though her handsome face always wore its gracious smile, Christie soon felt very sure that it was a mask put on to hide some heavy sorrow from a curious world.

Augustine never came except when Helen was asleep: then, like a shadow, he passed in and out, always silent, cold, and grave, but in his eyes the gloom of some remorseful pain that prayers and penances seemed powerless to heal.

Harry came every day, and no matter how melancholy, listless, or irritable his sister might be, for him she always had a smile, an affectionate greeting, a word of praise, or a tender warning against the reckless spirit that seemed to possess him. The love between them was very strong, and Christie found a never-failing pleasure in watching them together, for then Helen showed what she once had been, and Harry was his best self. A boy still, in spite of his one-and-twenty years, he seemed to feel that Helen's room was a safe refuge from the temptations that beset one of his thoughtless and impetuous nature. Here he came to confess his faults and follies with the frankness which is half sad, half comical, and wholly charming in a good-hearted young scatter-brain. Here he brought gay gossip, lively descriptions, and masculine criticisms of the world he moved in. All his hopes and plans, joys and sorrows, successes and defeats, he told to Helen. And she, poor soul, in this one happy love of her sad life, forgot a little the burden of despair that darkened all the world to her. For his sake she smiled, to him she talked when others got no word from her, and Harry's salvation was the only duty that she owned or tried to fulfil.

A younger sister was away at school, but the others seldom spoke of her, and Christie tired herself with wondering why Bella never wrote to Helen, and why Harry seemed to have nothing but a gloomy sort of pity to bestow upon the blooming girl whose picture hung in the great drawing-room below.

It was a very quiet winter, yet a very pleasant one to Christie, for she felt herself loved and trusted, saw that she suited, and believed that she was doing good, as women best love to do it, by bestowing sympathy and care with generous devotion.

Helen and Harry loved her like an elder sister; Augustine showed that he was grateful, and Mrs. Carrol sometimes forgot to put on her mask before one who seemed fast becoming *confidante* as well as companion.

In the spring the family went to the fine old country-house just out of town, and here Christie and her charge led a freer, happier life. Walking and driving, boating and gardening, with pleasant days on the wide terrace, where Helen swung idly in her hammock, while Christie read or talked to her; and summer twilights beguiled with music, or the silent reveries more eloquent than speech, which real friends may enjoy together, and find the sweeter for the mute companionship.

Harry was with them, and devoted to his sister, who seemed slowly to be coming out of her sad gloom, won by patient tenderness and the cheerful influences all about her.

Christie's heart was full of pride and satisfaction, as she saw the altered face, heard the tone of interest in that once hopeless voice, and felt each day more sure that Helen had outlived the loss that seemed to have broken her heart.

Alas, for Christie's pride, for Harry's hope, and for poor Helen's bitter fate! When all was brightest, the black shadow came; when all looked safest, danger was at hand; and when the past seemed buried, the ghost which haunted it returned, for the punishment of a broken law is as inevitable as death.

When settled in town again Bella came home, a gay, young girl, who should have brought sunshine and happiness into her home. But from the hour she returned a strange anxiety seemed to possess the others. Mrs. Carrol watched over her with sleepless care, was evidently full of maternal pride in the lovely creature, and began to dream dreams about her future. She seemed to wish to keep the sisters apart, and said to Christie, as if to explain this wish :

" Bella was away when Helen's trouble and illness came, she knows very little of it, and I do not want her to be saddened by the knowledge. Helen cares only for Hal, and Bella is too young to be of any use to my poor girl; therefore the less they see of each other the better for both. I am sure you agree with me ?" she added, with that covert scrutiny which Christie had often felt before.

She could but acquiesce in the mother's decision, and devote herself more faithfully than ever to Helen, who soon needed all her care and patience, for a terrible unrest grew upon her, bringing sleepless nights again, moody days, and all the old afflictions with redoubled force.

Bella " came out " and began her career as a beauty and a belle most brilliantly. Harry was proud of her, but seemed jealous of other men's admiration for his charming sister, and would excite both Helen and himself over the flirtations into which " that child " as they called her, plunged with all the zest of a light-hearted girl whose head was a little turned with sudden and excessive adoration.

In vain Christie begged Harry not to report these things, in vain she hinted that Bella had better not come to show herself to Helen night after night in all the dainty splendor of her youth and beauty ; in vain she asked Mrs. Carrol to let her go away to some quieter place with Helen, since she never could be persuaded to join in any gayety at home or abroad. All seemed wilful, blind, or governed by the fear of the gossiping world. So the days rolled on till an event occurred which enlightened Christie, with startling abruptness, and showed her the skeleton that haunted this unhappy family.

Going in one morning to Helen she found her walking to and fro as she often walked of late, with hurried steps and excited face as if driven by some power beyond her control.

" Good morning, dear. I'm so sorry you had a restless night, and wish you had sent for me. Will you come out now for an early drive? It's a lovely day, and your mother thinks it would do you good," began Christie, troubled by the state in which she found the girl.

But as she spoke Helen turned on her, crying passionately :

" My mother! don't speak of her to me, I hate her!"

" Oh, Helen, don't say that. Forgive and forget if she has displeased you, and don't exhaust yourself by brooding over it. Come, dear, and let us soothe ourselves with a little music. I want to hear that new song again, though I can never hope to sing it as you do."

" Sing!" echoed Helen, with a shrill laugh, " you don't know what you ask. Could *you* sing when your heart was heavy with the knowledge of a sin about to be committed by those nearest to you? Don't try to quiet me, I *must* talk whether you listen or not; I shall go frantic if I don't tell some one; all the world will know it soon. Sit down, I'll not hurt you, but don't thwart me or you'll be sorry for it."

Speaking with a vehemence that left her breathless, Helen thrust Christie down upon a seat, and went on with an expression in her face that bereft the listener of power to move or speak.

" Harry has just told me of it ; he was very angry, and I saw it, and made him tell me. Poor boy, he can keep nothing from *me*. I've been dreading it, and now it's coming. You don't know it, then? Young Butler is in love with Bella, and no one has prevented it. Think how wicked when such a curse is on us all."

The question, "What curse?" rose involuntarily to Christie's lips, but did not pass them, for, as if she read the thought, Helen answered it in a whisper that made the blood tingle in the other's veins, so full of ominous suggestion was it.

"The curse of insanity I mean. We are all mad, or shall be; we come of a mad race, and for years we have gone recklessly on bequeathing this awful inheritance to our descendants. It should end with us, we are the last; none of us should marry; none dare think of it but Bella, and she knows nothing. She must be told, she must be kept from the sin of deceiving her lover, the agony of seeing her children become what I am, and what we all may be."

Here Helen wrung her hands and paced the room in such a paroxysm of impotent despair that Christie sat bewildered and aghast, wondering if this were true, or but the fancy of a troubled brain. Mrs. Carrol's face and manner returned to her with sudden vividness, so did Augustine's gloomy expression, and the strange wish uttered over his sleeping sister long ago. Harry's reckless, aimless life might be explained in this way; and all that had perplexed her through that year. Every thing confirmed the belief that this tragical assertion was true, and Christie covered up her face, murmuring, with an involuntary shiver:

"My God, how terrible!"

Helen came and stood before her with such grief and penitence in her countenance that for a moment it conquered the despair that had broken bounds.

" We should have told you this at first ; I longed to
do it, but I was afraid you 'd go and leave me. I was
so lonely, so miserable, Christie. I could not give you
up when I had learned to love you ; and I did learn
very soon, for no wretched creature ever needed help
and comfort more than I. For your sake I tried to be
quiet, to control my shattered nerves, and hide my
desperate thoughts. You helped me very much, and
your unconsciousness made me doubly watchful. Forgive me ; don't desert me now, for the old horror may
be coming back, and I want you more than ever."

Too much moved to speak, Christie held out her
hands, with a face full of pity, love, and grief. Poor
Helen clung to them as if her only help lay there, and
for a moment was quite still. But not long ; the old
anguish was too sharp to be borne in silence ; the relief
of confidence once tasted was too great to be denied ;
and, breaking loose, she went to and fro again, pouring
out the bitter secret which had been weighing upon
heart and conscience for a year.

" You wonder that I hate my mother ; let me tell
you why. When she was beautiful and young she
married, knowing the sad history of my father's family.
He was rich, she poor and proud ; ambition made her
wicked, and she did it after being warned that, though
he might escape, his children were sure to inherit the
curse, for when one generation goes free it falls more
heavily upon the rest. She knew it all, and yet she
married him. I have her to thank for all I suffer, and
I cannot love her though she is my mother. It may be
wrong to say these things, but they are true ; they
burn in my heart, and I must speak out ; for I tell you

there comes a time when children judge their parents as men and women, in spite of filial duty, and woe to those whose actions change affection and respect to hatred or contempt."

The bitter grief, the solemn fervor of her words, both touched and awed Christie too much for speech. Helen had passed beyond the bounds of ceremony, fear, or shame : her hard lot, her dark experience, set her apart, and gave her the right to utter the bare truth. To her heart's core Christie felt that warning; and for the first time saw what many never see or wilfully deny, — the awful responsibility that lies on every man and woman's soul forbidding them to entail upon the innocent the burden of their own infirmities, the curse that surely follows their own sins.

Sad and stern, as an accusing angel, that most unhappy daughter spoke :

" If ever a woman had cause to repent, it is my mother; but she will not, and till she does, God has forsaken us. Nothing can subdue her pride, not even an affliction like mine. She hides the truth; she hides me, and lets the world believe I am dying of consumption; not a word about insanity, and no one knows the secret beyond ourselves, but doctor, nurse, and you. This is why I was not sent away, but for a year was shut up in that room yonder where the door is always locked. If you look in, you 'll see barred windows, guarded fire, muffled walls, and other sights to chill your blood, when you remember all those dreadful things were meant for me."

" Don't speak, don't think of them ! Don't talk any more; let me do something to comfort you, for my heart is broken with all this," cried Christie, panic-stricken at the picture Helen's words had conjured up.

"I *must* go on ! There is no rest for me till I have tried to lighten this burden by sharing it with you. Let me talk, let me wear myself out, then you shall help and comfort me, if there is any help and comfort for such as I. Now I can tell you all about my Edward, and you 'll listen, though mamma forbade it. Three years ago my father died, and we came here. I was well then, and oh, how happy ! "

Clasping her hands above her head, she stood like a beautiful, pale image of despair ; tearless and mute, but with such a world of anguish in the eyes lifted to the smiling picture opposite that it needed no words to tell the story of a broken heart.

" How I loved him ! " she said, softly, while her whole face glowed for an instant with the light and warmth of a deathless passion. " How I loved him, and how he loved me ! Too well to let me darken both our lives with a remorse which would come too late for a just atonement. I thought him cruel then, — I bless him for it now. I had far rather be the innocent suf-ferer I am, than a wretched woman like my mother. I shall never see him any more, but I know he thinks of me far away in India, and when I die one faithful heart will remember me."

There her voice faltered and failed, and for a moment the fire of her eyes was quenched in tears. Christie thought the reaction had come, and rose to go and com-fort her. But instantly Helen's hand was on her shoul-der, and pressing her back into her seat, she said, almost fiercely :

"I'm not done yet; you must hear the whole, and help me to save Bella. We knew nothing of the blight that hung over us till father told Augustine upon his death-bed. August, urged by mother, kept it to himself, and went away to bear it as he could. He should have spoken out and saved me in time. But not till he came home and found me engaged did he have courage to warn me of the fate in store for us. So Edward tore himself away, although it broke his heart, and I — do you see that?"

With a quick gesture she rent open her dress, and on her bosom Christie saw a scar that made her turn yet paler than before.

"Yes, I tried to kill myself; but they would not let me die, so the old tragedy of our house begins again. August became a priest, hoping to hide his calamity and expiate his father's sin by endless penances and prayers. Harry turned reckless; for what had he to look forward to? A short life, and a gay one, he says, and when his turn comes he will spare himself long suffering, as I tried to do it. Bella was never told; she was so young they kept her ignorant of all they could, even the knowledge of my state. She was long away at school, but now she has come home, now she has learned to love, and is going blindly as I went, because no one tells her what she *must* know soon or late. Mamma will not. August hesitates, remembering me. Harry swears he will speak out, but I implore him not to do it, for he will be too violent; and I am powerless. I never knew about this man till Hal told me to-day. Bella only comes in for a moment, and I have no chance to tell her she must *not* love him."

Pressing her hands to her temples, Helen resumed her restless march again, but suddenly broke out more violently than before :

"Now do you wonder why I am half frantic ? Now will you ask me to sing and smile, and sit calmly by while this wrong goes on ? You have done much for me, and God will bless you for it, but you cannot keep me sane. Death is the only cure for a mad Carrol, and I 'm so young, so strong, it will be long in coming unless I hurry it."

She clenched her hands, set her teeth, and looked about her as if ready for any desperate act that should set her free from the dark and dreadful future that lay before her.

For a moment Christie feared and trembled ; then pity conquered fear. She forgot herself, and only remembered this poor girl, so hopeless, helpless, and afflicted. Led by a sudden impulse, she put both arms about her, and held her close with a strong but silent tenderness better than any bonds. At first, Helen seemed unconscious of it, as she stood rigid and motionless, with her wild eyes dumbly imploring help of earth and heaven. Suddenly both strength and excitement seemed to leave her, and she would have fallen but for the living, loving prop that sustained her.

Still silent, Christie laid her down, kissed her white lips, and busied herself about her till she looked up quite herself again, but so wan and weak, it was pitiful to see her.

"It 's over now," she whispered, with a desolate sigh. 'Sing to me, and keep the evil spirit quiet for a little while. To-morrow, if I'm strong enough, we'll talk about poor little Bella."

And Christie sang, with tears dropping fast upon the keys, that made a soft accompaniment to the sweet old hymns which soothed this troubled soul as David's music brought repose to Saul.

When Helen slept at last from sheer exhaustion, Christie executed the resolution she had made as soon as the excitement of that stormy scene was over. She went straight to Mrs. Carrol's room, and, undeterred by the presence of her sons, told all that had passed. They were evidently not unprepared for it, thanks to old Hester, who had overheard enough of Helen's wild words to know that something was amiss, and had reported accordingly; but none of them had ventured to interrupt the interview, lest Helen should be driven to desperation as before.

" Mother, Helen is right; we should speak out, and not hide this bitter fact any longer. The world will pity us, and we must bear the pity, but it would condemn us for deceit, and we should deserve the condemnation if we let this misery go on. Living a lie will ruin us all. Bella will be destroyed as Helen was; I am only the shadow of a man now, and Hal is killing himself as fast as he can, to avoid the fate we all dread."

Augustine spoke first, for Mrs. Carrol sat speechless with her trouble as Christie paused.

" Keep to your prayers, and let me go my own way, it's the shortest," muttered Harry, with his face hidden, and his head down on his folded arms.

" Boys, boys, you'll kill me if you say such things! I have more now than I can bear. Don't drive me wild with your reproaches to each other!" cried their mother, her heart rent with the remorse that came too late.

"No fear of that; *you* are not a Carrol," answered Harry, with the pitiless bluntness of a resentful and rebellious boy.

Augustine turned on him with a wrathful flash of the eye, and a warning ring in his stern voice, as he pointed to the door.

"You shall not insult your mother! Ask her pardon, or go!"

"She should ask mine! I'll go. When you want me, you'll know where to find me." And, with a reckless laugh, Harry stormed out of the room.

Augustine's indignant face grew full of a new trouble as the door banged below, and he pressed his thin hands tightly together, saying, as if to himself:

"Heaven help me! Yes, I do know; for, night after night, I find and bring the poor lad home from gambling-tables and the hells where souls like his are lost."

Here Christie thought to slip away, feeling that it was no place for her now that her errand was done. But Mrs. Carrol called her back.

"Miss Devon — Christie — forgive me that I did not trust you sooner. It was so hard to tell; I hoped so much from time; I never could believe that my poor children would be made the victims of my mistake. Do not forsake us: Helen loves you so. Stay with her, I implore you, and let a most unhappy mother plead for a most unhappy child." Then Christie went to the poor woman, and earnestly assured her of her love and loyalty; for now she felt doubly bound to them because they trusted her.

" What shall we do ? " they said to her, with pathetic submission, turning like sick people to a healthful soul for help and comfort.

" Tell Bella all the truth, and help her to refuse her lover. Do this just thing, and God will strengthen you to bear the consequences," was her answer, though she trembled at the responsibility they put upon her.

" Not yet," cried Mrs. Carrol. " Let the poor child enjoy the holidays with a light heart, — then we will tell her ; and then Heaven help us all ! "

So it was decided ; for only a week or two of the old year remained, and no one had the heart to rob poor Bella of the little span of blissful ignorance that now remained to her.

A terrible time was that to Christie ; for, while one sister, blessed with beauty, youth, love, and pleasure, tasted life at its sweetest, the other sat in the black shadow of a growing dread, and wearied Heaven with piteous prayers for her relief.

" The old horror is coming back ; I feel it creeping over me. Don't let it come, Christie ! Stay by me ! Help me ! Keep me sane ! And if you cannot, ask God to take me quickly ! "

With words like these, poor Helen clung to Christie ; and, soul and body, Christie devoted herself to the afflicted girl. She would not see her mother ; and the unhappy woman haunted that closed door, hungering for the look, the word, that never came to her. Augustine was her consolation, and, during those troublous days, the priest was forgotten in the son. But Harry was all in all to Helen then ; and it was touching to see how these unfortunate young creatures clung to one another, she tenderly trying to keep him from the wild life that was surely hastening the fate he might otherwise escape for years, and he patiently bearing all her moods, eager to cheer and soothe the sad captivity from which he could not save her.

. These tender ministrations seemed to be blessed at last; and Christie began to hope the haunting terror would pass by, as quiet gloom succeeded to wild excitement. The cheerful spirit of the season seemed to reach even that sad room; and, in preparing gifts for others, Helen seemed to find a little of that best of all gifts, — peace for herself.

On New Year's morning, Christie found her garlanding her lover's picture with white roses and the myrtle sprays brides wear.

" These were his favorite flowers, and I meant to make my wedding wreath of this sweet-scented myrtle, because he gave it to me," she said, with a look that made Christie's eyes grow dim. " Don't grieve for me, dear; we shall surely meet hereafter, though so far asunder here. Nothing can part us there, I devoutly believe; for we leave our burdens all behind us when we go." Then, in a lighter tone, she said, with her arm on Christie's neck :

" This day is to be a happy one, no matter what comes after it. I 'm going to be my old self for a little while, and forget there 's such a word as sorrow. Help me to dress, so that when the boys come up they may find the sister Nell they have not seen for two long years."

" Will you wear this, my darling? Your mother sends it, and she tried to have it dainty and beautiful enough to please you. See, your own colors, though the bows are only laid on that they may be changed for others if you like."

As she spoke Christie lifted the cover of the box old Hester had just brought in, and displayed a cashmere wrapper, creamy-white, silk-lined, down-trimmed, and delicately relieved by rosy knots, like holly berries lying upon snow. Helen looked at it without a word for several minutes, then gathering up the ribbons, with a strange smile, she said:

" I like it better so; but I 'll not wear it yet."

" Bless and save us, deary; it *must* have a bit of color somewhere, else it looks just like a shroud," cried Hester, and then wrung her hands in dismay as Helen answered, quietly:

"Ah, well, keep it for me, then. I shall be happier when I wear it so than in the gayest gown I own, for when you put it on, this poor head and heart of mine will be quiet at last."

Motioning Hester to remove the box, Christie tried to banish the cloud her unlucky words had brought to Helen's face, by chatting cheerfully as she helped her make herself " pretty for the boys."

All that day she was unusually calm and sweet, and seemed to yield herself wholly to the happy influences of the hour, gave and received her gifts so cheerfully that her brothers watched her with delight; and unconscious Bella said, as she hung about her sister, with loving admiration in her eyes:

" I always thought you would get well, and now I 'm sure of it, for you look as you used before I went away to school, and seem just like our own dear Nell."

"I'm glad of that; I wanted you to feel so, my Bella. I'll accept your happy prophecy, and hope I may get well soon, very soon."

So cheerfully she spoke, so tranquilly she smiled, that all rejoiced over her believing, with love's blindness, that she might yet conquer her malady in spite of their forebodings.

It was a very happy day to Christie, not only that she was generously remembered and made one of them by all the family, but because this change for the better in Helen made her heart sing for joy. She had given time, health, and much love to the task, and ventured now to hope they had not been given in vain. One thing only marred her happiness, the sad estrangement of the daughter from her mother, and that evening she resolved to take advantage of Helen's tender mood, and plead for the poor soul who dared not plead for herself.

As the brothers and sisters said good-night, Helen clung to them as if loth to part, saying, with each embrace:

"Keep hoping for me, Bella; kiss me, Harry; bless me, Augustine, and all wish for me a happier New Year than the last."

When they were gone she wandered slowly round the room, stood long before the picture with its fading garland, sung a little softly to herself, and came at last to Christie, saying, like a tired child:

"I have been good all day; now let me rest."

"One thing has been forgotten, dear," began Christie, fearing to disturb the quietude that seemed to have been so dearly bought.

Helen understood her, and looked up with a sane sweet face, out of which all resentful bitterness had passed.

"No, Christie, not forgotten, only kept until the last. To-day is a good day to forgive, as we would be forgiven, and I mean to do it before I sleep." Then holding Christie close, she added, with a quiver of emotion in her voice: "I have no words warm enough to thank you, my good angel, for all you have been to me, but I know it will give you a great pleasure to do one thing more. Give dear mamma my love, and tell her that when I am quiet for the night I want her to come and get me to sleep with the old lullaby she used to sing when I was a little child."

No gift bestowed that day was so precious to Christie as the joy of carrying this loving message from daughter to mother. How Mrs. Carrol received it need not be told. She would have gone at once, but Christie begged her to wait till rest and quiet, after the efforts of the day, had prepared Helen for an interview which might undo all that had been done if too hastily attempted.

Hester always waited upon her child at night; so, feeling that she might be wanted later, Christie went to her own room to rest. Quite sure that Mrs. Carrol would come to tell her what had passed, she waited for an hour or two, then went to ask of Hester how the visit had sped.

"Her mamma came up long ago, but the dear thing was fast asleep, so I wouldn't let her be disturbed, and Mrs. Carrol went away again," said the old woman, rousing from a nap.

Grieved at the mother's disappointment, Christie stole in, hoping that Helen might rouse. She did not, and Christie was about to leave her, when, as she bent to smooth the tumbled coverlet, something dropped at her feet. Only a little pearl-handled penknife of Harry's; but her heart stood still with fear, for it was open, and, as she took it up, a red stain came off upon her hand.

Helen's face was turned away, and, bending nearer, Christie saw how deathly pale it looked in the shadow of the darkened room. She listened at her lips; only a faint flutter of breath parted them; she lifted up the averted head, and on the white throat saw a little wound, from which the blood still flowed. Then, like a flash of light, the meaning of the sudden change which came over her grew clear, — her brave efforts to make the last day happy, her tender good-night partings, her wish to be at peace with every one, the tragic death she had chosen rather than live out the tragic life that lay before her.

Christie's nerves had been tried to the uttermost; the shock of this discovery was too much for her, and, in the act of calling for help, she fainted, for the first time in her life.

When she was herself again, the room was full of people; terror-stricken faces passed before her; broken voices whispered, "It is too late," and, as she saw the group about the bed, she wished for unconsciousness again.

Helen lay in her mother's arms at last, quietly breathing her life away, for though every thing that love and skill could devise had been tried to save her, the little knife in that desperate hand had done its work, and this world held no more suffering for her. Harry was down upon his knees beside her, trying to stifle his passionate grief. Augustine prayed audibly above her, and the fervor of his broken words comforted all hearts but one. Bella was clinging, panic-stricken, to the kind old doctor, who was sobbing like a boy, for he had loved and served poor Helen as faithfully as if she had been his own.

" Can nothing save her ? " Christie whispered, as the prayer ended, and a sound of bitter weeping filled the room.

" Nothing ; she is sane and safe at last, thank God ! "

Christie could not but echo his thanksgiving, for the blessed tranquillity of the girl's countenance was such as none but death, the great healer, can bring ; and, as they looked, her eyes opened, beautifully clear and calm before they closed for ever. From face to face they passed, as if they looked for some one, and her lips moved in vain efforts to speak.

Christie went to her, but still the wide, wistful eyes searched the room as if unsatisfied ; and, with a longing that conquered the mortal weakness of the body, the heart sent forth one tender cry:

" My mother — I want my mother ! "

There was no need to repeat the piteous call, for, as it left her lips, she saw her mother's face bending over her, and felt her mother's arms gathering her in an embrace which held her close even after death had set its seal upon the voiceless prayers for pardon which passed between those reunited hearts.

When she was asleep at last, Christie and her mother

made her ready for her grave; weeping tender tears as they folded her in the soft, white garment she had put by for that sad hour; and on her breast they laid the flowers she had hung about her lover as a farewell gift. So beautiful she looked when all was done, that in the early dawn they called her brothers, that they might not lose the memory of the blessed peace that shone upon her face, a mute assurance that for her the new year had happily begun.

" Now my work here is done, and I must go," thought Christie, when the waves of life closed over the spot where another tired swimmer had gone down. But she found that one more task remained for her before she left the family which, on her coming, she had thought so happy.

Mrs. Carrol, worn out with the long effort to conceal her secret cross, broke down entirely under this last blow, and besought Christie to tell Bella all that she must know. It was a hard task, but Christie accepted it, and, when the time came, found that there was very little to be told, for at the death-bed of the elder sister, the younger had learned much of the sad truth. Thus prepared, she listened to all that was most carefully and tenderly confided to her, and, when the heavy tale was done, she surprised Christie by the unsuspected strength she showed. No tears, no lamentations, for she was her mother's daughter, and inherited the pride that can bear heavy burdens, if they are borne unseen.

" Tell me what I must do, and I will do it," she said, with the quiet despair of one who submits to the inevitable, but will not complain.

When Christie with difficulty told her that she should

give up her lover, Bella bowed her head, and for a moment could not speak, then lifted it as if defying her own weakness, and spoke out bravely :

"It shall be done, for it is right. It is very hard for *me*, because I love him ; he will not suffer much, for he can love again. I should be glad of that, and I'll try to wish it for his sake. He is young, and if, as Harry says, he cares more for my fortune than myself, so much the better. What next, Christie ? "

Amazed and touched at the courage of the creature she had fancied a sort of lovely butterfly to be crushed by a single blow, Christie took heart, and, instead of soothing sympathy, gave her the solace best fitted for strong natures, something to do for others. What inspired her, Christie never knew ; perhaps it was the year of self-denying service she had rendered for pity's sake ; such devotion is its own reward, and now, in herself, she discovered unsuspected powers.

"Live for your mother and your brothers, Bella ; they need you sorely, and in time I know you will find true consolation in it, although you must relinquish much. Sustain your mother, cheer Augustine, watch over Harry, and be to them what Helen longed to be."

"And fail to do it, as she failed ! " cried Bella, with a shudder.

"Listen, and let me give you this hope, for I sincerely do believe it. Since I came here, I have read many books, thought much, and talked often with Dr. Shirley about this sad affliction. He thinks you and Harry may escape it, if you will. You are like your mother in temperament and temper ; you have self-control, strong wills, good nerves, and cheerful spirits.

Poor Harry is willfully spoiling all his chances now; but you may save him, and, in the endeavor, save yourself."

"Oh, Christie, may I hope it? Give me one chance of escape, and I will suffer any hardship to keep it. Let me see any thing before me but a life and death like Helen's, and I'll bless you for ever!" cried Bella, welcoming this ray of light as a prisoner welcomes sunshine in his cell.

Christie trembled at the power of her words, yet, honestly believing them, she let them uplift this disconsolate soul, trusting that they might be in time fulfilled through God's mercy and the saving grace of sincere endeavor.

Holding fast to this frail spar, Bella bravely took up arms against her sea of troubles, and rode out the storm. When her lover came to know his fate, she hid her heart, and answered "no," finding a bitter satisfaction in the end, for Harry was right, and, when the fortune was denied him, young Butler did not mourn the woman long. Pride helped Bella to bear it; but it needed all her courage to look down the coming years so bare of all that makes life sweet to youthful souls, so desolate and dark, with duty alone to cheer the thorny way, and the haunting shadow of her race lurking in the background.

Submission and self-sacrifice are stern, sad angels, but in time one learns to know and love them, for when they have chastened, they uplift and bless. Dimly discerning this, poor Bella put her hands in theirs, saying, "Lead me, teach me; I will follow and obey you."

All soon felt that they could not stay in a house so

full of heavy memories, and decided to return to their old home. They begged Christie to go with them, using every argument and entreaty their affection could suggest. But Christie needed rest, longed for freedom, and felt that in spite of their regard it would be very hard for her to live among them any longer. Her healthy nature needed brighter influences, stronger comrades, and the memory of Helen weighed so heavily upon her heart that she was eager to forget it for a time in other scenes and other work.

So they parted, very sadly, very tenderly, and laden with good gifts Christie went on her way weary, but well satisfied, for she had earned her rest.

CHAPTER VI.

FOR some weeks Christie rested and refreshed herself by making her room gay and comfortable with the gifts lavished on her by the Carrols, and by sharing with others the money which Harry had smuggled into her possession after she had steadily refused to take one penny more than the sum agreed upon when she first went to them.

She took infinite satisfaction in sending one hundred dollars to Uncle Enos, for she had accepted what he gave her as a loan, and set her heart on repaying every fraction of it. Another hundred she gave to Hepsey, who found her out and came to report her trials and tribulations. The good soul had ventured South and tried to buy her mother. But " ole missis " would not let her go at any price, and the faithful chattel would not run away. Sorely disappointed, Hepsey had been obliged to submit; but her trip was not a failure, for she liberated several brothers and sent them triumphantly to Canada.

" You *must* take it, Hepsey, for I could not rest happy if I put it away to lie idle while you can save men and women from torment with it. I 'd give it if it was my last penny, for I can help in no other way; and if I need money, I can always earn it, thank God!" said Christie, as Hepsey hesitated to take so much from a fellow-worker.

The thought of that investment lay warm at Christie's heart, and never woke a regret, for well she knew that every dollar of it would be blessed, since shares in the Underground Railroad pay splendid dividends that never fail.

Another portion of her fortune, as she called Harry's gift, was bestowed in wedding presents upon Lucy, who at length succeeded in winning the heart of the owner of the " heavenly eyes " and " distracting legs; " and, having gained her point, married him with dramatic celerity, and went West to follow the fortunes of her lord.

The old theatre was to be demolished and the company scattered, so a farewell festival was held, and Christie went to it, feeling more solitary than ever as she bade her old friends a long good-bye.

The rest of the money burned in her pocket, but she prudently put it by for a rainy day, and fell to work again when her brief vacation was over.

Hearing of a chance for a good needle-woman in a large and well-conducted mantua-making establishment, she secured it as a temporary thing, for she wanted to divert her mind from that last sad experience by entirely different employment and surroundings. She liked to return at night to her own little home, solitary and simple as it was, and felt a great repugnance to accept any place where she would be mixed up with family affairs again.

So day after day she went to her seat in the work-room where a dozen other young women sat sewing busily on gay garments, with as much lively gossip to beguile the time as Miss Cotton, the forewoman, would allow.

For a while it diverted Christie, as she had a feminine love for pretty things, and enjoyed seeing delicate silks, costly lace, and all the indescribable fantasies of fashion. But as spring came on, the old desire for something fresh and free began to haunt her, and she had both waking and sleeping dreams of a home in the country somewhere, with cows and flowers, clothes bleaching on green grass, bob-o'-links making rapturous music by the river, and the smell of new-mown hay, all lending their charms to the picture she painted for herself.

Most assuredly she would have gone to find these things, led by the instincts of a healthful nature, had not one slender tie held her till it grew into a bond so strong she could not break it.

Among her companions was one, and one only, who attracted her. The others were well-meaning girls, but full of the frivolous purposes and pleasures which their tastes prompted and their dull life fostered. Dress, gossip, and wages were the three topics which absorbed them. Christie soon tired of the innumerable changes rung upon these themes, and took refuge in her own thoughts, soon learning to enjoy them undisturbed by the clack of many tongues about her. Her evenings at home were devoted to books, for she had the true New England woman's desire for education, and read or studied for the love of it. Thus she had much to

think of as her needle flew, and was rapidly becoming
a sort of sewing-machine when life was brightened for
her by the finding of a friend.

Among the girls was one quiet, skilful creature,
whose black dress, peculiar face, and silent ways
attracted Christie. Her evident desire to be let alone
amused the new comer at first, and she made no effort
to know her. But presently she became aware that
Rachel watched her with covert interest, stealing quick,
shy glances at her as she sat musing over her work.
Christie smiled at her when she caught these glances,
as if to reassure the looker of her good-will. But
Rachel only colored, kept her eyes fixed on her work,
and was more reserved than ever.

This interested Christie, and she fell to studying this
young woman with some curiosity, for she was different
from the others. Though evidently younger than she
looked, Rachel's face was that of one who had known
some great sorrow, some deep experience; for there
were lines on the forehead that contrasted strongly
with the bright, abundant hair above it; in repose, the
youthfully red, soft lips had a mournful droop, and the
eyes were old with that indescribable expression which
comes to those who count their lives by emotions, not
by years.

Strangely haunting eyes to Christie, for they seemed
to appeal to her with a mute eloquence she could not
resist. In vain did Rachel answer her with quiet coldness, nod silently when she wished her a cheery "good
morning," and keep resolutely in her own somewhat
isolated corner, though invited to share the sunny
window where the other sat. Her eyes belied her

words, and those fugitive glances betrayed the longing of a lonely heart that dared not yield itself to the genial companionship so freely offered it.

Christie was sure of this, and would not be repulsed; for her own heart was very solitary. She missed Helen, and longed to fill the empty place. She wooed this shy, cold girl as patiently and as gently as a lover might, determined to win her confidence, because all the others had failed to do it. Sometimes she left a flower in Rachel's basket, always smiled and nodded as she entered, and often stopped to admire the work of her tasteful fingers. It was impossible to resist such friendly overtures, and slowly Rachel's coldness melted; into the beseeching eyes came a look of gratitude, the more touching for its wordlessness, and an irrepressible smile broke over her face in answer to the cordial ones that made the sunshine of her day.

Emboldened by these demonstrations, Christie changed her seat, and quietly established between them a daily interchange of something beside needles, pins, and spools. Then, as Rachel did not draw back offended, she went a step farther, and, one day when they chanced to be left alone to finish off a delicate bit of work, she spoke out frankly :

" Why can't we be friends ? I want one sadly, and so do you, unless your looks deceive me. We both seem to be alone in the world, to have had trouble, and to like one another. I won't annoy you by any impertinent curiosity, nor burden you with uninteresting confidences ; I only want to feel that you like me a little and don't mind my liking you a great deal. Will you be my friend, and let me be yours ? "

A great tear rolled down upon the shining silk in
Rachel's hands as she looked into Christie's earnest
face, and answered with an almost passionate gratitude
in her own:

"You can never need a friend as much as I do, or
know what a blessed thing it is to find such an one as
you are."

"Then I may love you, and not be afraid of offending?" cried Christie, much touched.

"Yes. But remember *I* didn't ask it first," said
Rachel, half dropping the hand she had held in both
her own.

"You proud creature! I'll remember; and when
we quarrel, I'll take all the blame upon myself."

Then Christie kissed her warmly, whisked away the
tear, and began to paint the delights in store for them
in her most enthusiastic way, being much elated with
her victory; while Rachel listened with a newly kindled
light in her lovely eyes, and a smile that showed how
winsome her face had been before many tears washed
its bloom away, and much trouble made it old too soon.

Christie kept her word, — asked no questions, volunteered no confidences, but heartily enjoyed the new
friendship, and found that it gave to life the zest which
it had lacked before. Now some one cared for her,
and, better still, she could make some one happy, and
in the act of lavishing the affection of her generous nature on a creature sadder and more solitary than herself, she found a satisfaction that never lost its charm.
There was nothing in her possession that she did not
offer Rachel, from the whole of her heart to the larger
half of her little room.

" I 'm tired of thinking only of myself. It makes me selfish and low-spirited; for I 'm not a bit interesting. I must love somebody, and 'love them hard,' as children say; so why can't you come and stay with me? There 's room enough, and we could be so cosy evenings with our books and work. I know you need some one to look after you, and I love dearly to take care of people. Do come," she would say, with most persuasive hospitality.

But Rachel always answered steadily: " Not yet, Christie, not yet. I 've got something to do before I can think of doing any thing so beautiful as that. Only love me, dear, and some day I 'll show you all my heart, and thank you as I ought."

So Christie was content to wait, and, meantime, enjoyed much; for, with Rachel as a friend, she ceased to care for country pleasures, found happiness in the work that gave her better food than mere daily bread, and never thought of change; for love can make a home for itself anywhere.

A very bright and happy time was this in Christie's life; but, like most happy times, it was very brief. Only one summer allowed for the blossoming of the friendship that budded so slowly in the spring; then the frost came and killed the flowers; but the root lived long underneath the snows of suffering, doubt, and absence.

Coming to her work late one morning, she found the usually orderly room in confusion. Some of the girls were crying; some whispering together, — all looking excited and dismayed. Mrs. King sat majestically at her table, with an ominous frown upon her face. Miss

Cotton stood beside her, looking unusually sour and stern, for the ancient virgin's temper was not of the best. Alone, before them all, with her face hidden in her hands, and despair in every line of her drooping figure, stood Rachel, — a meek culprit at the stern bar of justice, where women try a sister woman.

"What's the matter?" cried Christie, pausing on the threshold.

MRS. KING AND MISS COTTON.

Rachel shivered, as if the sound of that familiar voice was a fresh wound, but she did not lift her head ; and Mrs. King answered, with a nervous emphasis that made the bugles of her head-dress rattle dismally:

" A very sad thing, Miss Devon, — *very* sad, indeed ; a thing which *never* occurred in my establishment before, and *never* shall again. It appears that Rachel, whom we all considered a most respectable and worthy girl, has been quite the reverse. I shudder to think what the consequences of my taking her without a character (a thing I never do, and was only tempted by her superior taste as a trimmer) might have been if Miss Cotton, having suspicions, had not made strict inquiry and confirmed them."

" That was a kind and generous act, and Miss Cotton must feel proud of it," said Christie, with an indignant recollection of Mr. Fletcher's " cautious inquiries " about herself.

" It was perfectly right and proper, Miss Devon ; and I thank her for her care of my interests." And Mrs. King bowed her acknowledgment of the service with a perfect castanet accompaniment, whereat Miss Cotton bridled with malicious complacency.

" Mrs. King, are you sure of this ? " said Christie. " Miss Cotton does not like Rachel because her work is so much praised. May not her jealousy make her unjust, or her zeal for you mislead her ? "

" I thank you for your polite insinuations, miss," returned the irate forewoman. "*I* never make mistakes ; but you will find that *you* have made a very great one in choosing Rachel for your bosom friend instead of some one who would be a credit to you. Ask the creature herself if all I've said of her isn't true. She can't deny it."

With the same indefinable misgiving which had held her aloof, Christie turned to Rachel, lifted up the hidden face with gentle force, and looked into it imploringly, as she whispered: "Is it true?"

The woful countenance she saw made any other answer needless. Involuntarily her hands fell away, and she hid her own face, uttering the one reproach, which, tender and tearful though it was, seemed harder to be borne than the stern condemnation gone before.

"Oh, Rachel, I so loved and trusted you!"

The grief, affection, and regret that trembled in her voice roused Rachel from her state of passive endurance and gave her courage to plead for herself. But it was Christie whom she addressed, Christie whose pardon she implored, Christie's sorrowful reproach that she most keenly felt.

"Yes, it *is* true," she said, looking only at the woman who had been the first to befriend and now was the last to desert her. "It is true that I once went astray, but God knows I have repented; that for years I've tried to be an honest girl again, and that but for His help I should be a far sadder creature than I am this day. Christie, you can never know how bitter hard it is to outlive a sin like mine, and struggle up again from such a fall. It clings to me; it won't be shaken off or buried out of sight. No sooner do I find a safe place like this, and try to forget the past, than some one reads my secret in my face and hunts me down. It seems very cruel, very hard, yet it is my punishment, so I try to bear it, and begin again. What hurts me now more than all the rest, what breaks my heart, is that I deceived *you.* I never meant to do it. I did not seek you, did I? I tried to be cold and stiff; never asked for love, though starving for it, till you came to me, so kind, so generous, so dear, — how could I help it? Oh, how could I help it then?"

Christie had watched Rachel while she spoke, and spoke to her alone; her heart yearned toward this one friend, for she still loved her, and, loving, she believed in her.

"I don't reproach you, dear: I don't despise or desert you, and though I'm grieved and disappointed, I'll stand by you still, because you need me more than ever now, and I want to prove that I am a true friend. Mrs. King, please forgive and let poor Rachel stay here, safe among us."

"Miss Devon, I'm surprised at you! By no means; it would be the ruin of my establishment; not a girl would remain, and the character of my rooms would be lost for ever," replied Mrs. King, goaded on by the relentless Cotton.

"But where will she go if you send her away? Who will employ her if you inform against her? What stranger will believe in her if we, who have known her so long, fail to befriend her now? Mrs. King, think of your own daughters, and be a mother to this poor girl for their sake."

That last stroke touched the woman's heart; her cold eye softened, her hard mouth relaxed, and pity was about to win the day, when prudence, in the shape of Miss Cotton, turned the scale, for that spiteful spinster suddenly cried out, in a burst of righteous wrath:

"If that hussy stays, *I* leave this establishment for ever!" and followed up the blow by putting on her bonnet with a flourish.

At this spectacle, self-interest got the better of sympathy in Mrs. King's worldly mind. To lose Cotton was to lose her right hand, and charity at that price was too expensive a luxury to be indulged in; so she hardened her heart, composed her features, and said, impressively:

"Take off your bonnet, Cotton; I have no intention of offending you, or any one else, by such a step. I forgive you, Rachel, and I pity you; but I can't think of allowing you to stay. There are proper institutions for such as you, and I advise you to go to one and repent. You were paid Saturday night, so nothing prevents your leaving at once. Time is money here, and we are wasting it. Young ladies, take your seats."

All but Christie obeyed, yet no one touched a needle, and Mrs. King sat, hurriedly stabbing pins into the fat cushion on her breast, as if testing the hardness of her heart.

Rachel's eye went round the room; saw pity, aversion, or contempt, on every face, but met no answering glance, for even Christie's eyes were bent thoughtfully on the ground, and Christie's heart seemed closed against her. As she looked her whole manner changed; her tears ceased to fall, her face grew hard, and a reckless mood seemed to take possession of her, as if finding herself deserted by womankind, she would desert her own womanhood.

"I might have known it would be so," she said abruptly, with a bitter smile, sadder to see than her most hopeless tears. "It's no use for such as me to try; better go back to the old life, for there are kinder hearts among the sinners than among the saints, and no one can live without a bit of love. Your Magdalen Asylums are penitentiaries, not homes; I won't go to any of them. Your piety isn't worth much, for though you read in your Bible how the Lord treated a poor soul like me, yet when I stretch out my hand to you for help, not one of all you virtuous, Christian women dare take it and keep me from a life that's worse than hell."

As she spoke Rachel flung out her hand with a half-defiant gesture, and Christie took it. That touch, full of womanly compassion, seemed to exorcise the desperate spirit that possessed the poor girl in her despair, for, with a stifled exclamation, she sunk down at Christie's feet, and lay there weeping in all the passionate abandonment of love and gratitude, remorse and shame. Never had human voice sounded so heavenly sweet to her as that which broke the silence of the room, as this one friend said, with the earnestness of a true and tender heart:

"Mrs. King, if you send her away, I must take her in; for if she does go back to the old life, the sin of it will lie at our door, and God will remember it against us in the end. Some one must trust her, help her, love her, and so save her, as nothing else will. Perhaps I can do this better than you,— at least, I'll try; for even if I risk the loss of my good name, I could bear that better than the thought that Rachel had lost the work of these hard years for want of upholding now. She shall come home with me; no one there need know of this discovery, and I will take any work to her that you will give me, to keep her from want and its temptations. Will you do this, and let me sew for less, if I can pay you for the kindness in no other way?"

Poor Mrs. King was "much tumbled up and down in her own mind;" she longed to consent, but Cotton's eye was upon her, and Cotton's departure would be an irreparable loss, so she decided to end the matter in the most summary manner. Plunging a particularly large pin into her cushioned breast, as if it was a relief to inflict that mock torture upon herself, she said sharply:

"It is impossible. You can do as you please, Miss Devon, but I prefer to wash my hands of the affair at once and entirely."

Christie's eye went from the figure at her feet to the hard-featured woman who had been a kind and just mistress until now, and she asked, anxiously:

"Do you mean that you wash your hands of me also, if I stand by Rachel?"

"I do. I'm very sorry, but my young ladies *must* keep respectable company, or leave my service," was the brief reply, for Mrs. King grew grimmer externally as the mental rebellion increased internally.

"Then I *will* leave it!" cried Christie, with an indignant voice and eye. "Come, dear, we'll go together." And without a look or word for any in the room, she raised the prostrate girl, and led her out into the little hall.

There she essayed to comfort her, but before many words had passed her lips Rachel looked up, and she was silent with surprise, for the face she saw was neither despairing nor defiant, but beautifully sweet and clear, as the unfallen spirit of the woman shone through the grateful eyes, and blessed her for her loyalty.

"Christie, you have done enough for me," she said. "Go back, and keep the good place you need, for such are hard to find. I can get on alone; I'm used to this, and the pain will soon be over."

"I'll not go back!" cried Christie, hotly. I'll do slop-work and starve, before I'll stay with such a narrow-minded, cold-hearted woman. Come home with me at once, and let us lay our plans together."

"No, dear; if I wouldn't go when you first asked me, much less will I go now, for I've done you harm enough already. I never can thank you for your great goodness to me, never tell you what it has been to me. We must part now; but some day I'll come back and show you that I've not forgotten how you loved and helped and trusted me, when all the others cast me off."

Vain were Christie's arguments and appeals. Rachel was immovable, and all her friend could win from her was a promise to send word, now and then, how things prospered with her.

"And, Rachel, I charge you to come to me in any strait, no matter what it is, no matter where I am; for if any thing could break my heart, it would be to know that you had gone back to the old life, because there was no one to help and hold you up."

"I *never* can go back; you have saved me, Christie, for you love me, you have faith in me, and that will keep me strong and safe when you are gone. Oh, my dear, my dear, God bless you for ever and for ever!"

Then Christie, remembering only that they were two

loving women, alone in a world of sin and sorrow, took Rachel in her arms, kissed and cried over her with sisterly affection, and watched her prayerfully, as she went away to begin her hard task anew, with nothing but the touch of innocent lips upon her cheek, the baptism of tender tears upon her forehead to keep her from despair.

Still cherishing the hope that Rachel would come back to her, Christie neither returned to Mrs. King nor sought another place of any sort, but took home work from a larger establishment, and sat sewing diligently in her little room, waiting, hoping, longing for her friend. But month after month went by, and no word, no sign came to comfort her. She would not doubt, yet she could not help fearing, and in her nightly prayer no petition was more fervently made than that which asked the Father of both saint and sinner to keep poor Rachel safe, and bring her back in his good time.

Never had she been so lonely as now, for Christie had a social heart, and, having known the joy of a cordial friendship even for a little while, life seemed very barren to her when she lost it. No new friend took Rachel's place, for none came to her, and a feeling of loyalty kept her from seeking one. But she suffered for the want of genial society, for all the tenderness of her nature seemed to have been roused by that brief but most sincere affection. Her hungry heart clamored for the happiness that was its right, and grew very heavy as she watched friends or lovers walking in the summer twilight when she took her evening stroll. Often her eyes followed some humble pair, longing to bless and to be blessed by the divine passion whose magic beautifies the little milliner and her lad with the same tender grace as the poet and the mistress whom he makes immortal in a song. But neither friend nor lover came to Christie, and she said to herself, with a sad sort of courage:

"I shall be solitary all my life, perhaps; so the sooner I make up my mind to it, the easier it will be to bear."

At Christmas-tide she made a little festival for herself, by giving to each of the household drudges the most generous gift she could afford, for no one else thought of them, and having known some of the hardships of servitude herself, she had much sympathy with those in like case.

Then, with the pleasant recollection of two plain faces, brightened by gratitude, surprise, and joy, she went out into the busy streets to forget the solitude she left behind her.

Very gay they were with snow and sleigh-bells, holly-boughs, and garlands, below, and Christmas sunshine in the winter sky above. All faces shone, all voices had a cheery ring, and everybody stepped briskly on errands of good-will. Up and down went Christie, making herself happy in the happiness of others. Looking in at the shop-windows, she watched, with interest, the purchases of busy parents, calculating how best to fill the little socks hung up at home, with a childish faith that never must be disappointed, no matter how hard the times might be. She was glad to see so many turkeys on their way to garnish hospitable tables, and hoped that all the dear home circles might be found unbroken, though she had place in none. No Christmas-tree went by leaving a whiff of piny sweetness behind, that she did not wish it all success, and picture to herself the merry little people dancing in its light. And whenever she saw a ragged child eying a window full of goodies, smiling even while it shivered, she could not resist playing Santa Claus till her purse was empty, sending the poor little souls enraptured home with oranges and apples in either hand, and splendid sweeties in their pockets, for the babies.

No envy mingled with the melancholy that would not be dispelled even by these gentle acts, for her heart was very tender that night, and if any one had asked what gifts she desired most, she would have answered with a look more pathetic than any shivering child had given her:

" I want the sound of a loving voice; the touch of a friendly hand."

Going home, at last, to the lonely little room where no Christmas fire burned, no tree shone, no household group awaited her, she climbed the long, dark stairs, with drops on her cheeks, warmer than any melted snow-flake could have left, and opening her door paused on the threshold, smiling with wonder and delight, for in her absence some gentle spirit *had* remembered her. A fire burned cheerily upon the hearth, her lamp was lighted, a lovely rose-tree, in full bloom, filled the air with its delicate breath, and in its shadow lay a note from Rachel.

" A merry Christmas and a happy New Year, Christie! Long ago you gave me your little rose; I have watched and tended it for your sake, dear, and now when I want to show my love and thankfulness, I give it back again as my one treasure. I crept in while you were gone, because I feared I might harm you in some way if you saw me. I longed to stay and tell you that I am safe and well, and busy, with your good face looking into mine, but I don't deserve that yet. Only love me, trust me, pray for me, and some day you shall know what you have done for me. Till then, God bless and keep you, dearest friend, your   RACHEL."

Never had sweeter tears fallen than those that dropped upon the little tree as Christie took it in her arms, and all the rosy clusters leaned toward her as if eager to deliver tender messages. Surely her wish was granted now, for friendly hands had been at work for her. Warm against her heart lay words as precious as if uttered by a loving voice, and nowhere, on that happy night, stood a fairer Christmas tree than that which bloomed so beautifully from the heart of a Magdalen who loved much and was forgiven.

CHAPTER VII.

THROUGH THE MIST.

THE year that followed was the saddest Christie had ever known, for she suffered a sort of poverty which is more difficult to bear than actual want, since money cannot lighten it, and the rarest charity alone can minister to it. Her heart was empty and she could not fill it; her soul was hungry and she could not feed it; life was cold and dark and she could not warm and brighten it, for she knew not where to go.

She tried to help herself by all the means in her power, and when effort after effort failed she said: " I am not good enough yet to deserve happiness. I think too much of human love, too little of divine. When I have made God my friend perhaps He will let me find and keep one heart to make life happy with. How shall I know God? Who will tell me where to find Him, and help me to love and lean upon Him as I ought?"

In all sincerity she asked these questions, in all sincerity she began her search, and with pathetic patience waited for an answer. She read many books, some wise, some vague, some full of superstition, all unsatisfactory to one who wanted a living God. She went to many churches, studied many creeds, and watched their fruits as well as she could; but still remained unsatisfied. Some were cold and narrow, some seemed theatrical and superficial, some stern and terrible, none simple, sweet, and strong enough for humanity's many needs. There was too much machinery, too many walls, laws, and penalties between the Father and His children. Too much fear, too little love; too many saints and intercessors; too little faith in the instincts of the soul which turns to God as flowers to the sun. Too much idle strife about names and creeds; too little knowledge of the natural religion which has no name but godliness, whose creed is boundless and benignant as the sunshine, whose faith is as the tender trust of little children in their mother's love.

Nowhere did Christie find this all-sustaining power, this paternal friend, and comforter, and after months of patient searching she gave up her quest, saying, despondently:

" I'm afraid I never shall get religion, for all that's offered me seems so poor, so narrow, or so hard that I cannot take it for my stay. A God of wrath I cannot love; a God that must be propitiated, adorned, and adored like an idol I cannot respect; and a God who can be blinded to men's iniquities through the week by a little beating of the breast and bowing down on the seventh day, I cannot serve. I want a Father to whom I can go with all my sins and sorrows, all my hopes and joys, as freely and fearlessly as I used to go to my human father, sure of help and sympathy and love. Shall I ever find Him?"

Alas, poor Christie! she was going through the sorrowful perplexity that comes to so many before they learn that religion cannot be given or bought, but must grow as trees grow, needing frost and snow, rain and wind to strengthen it before it is deep-rooted in the soul; that God is in the hearts of all, and they that seek shall surely find Him when they need Him most.

So Christie waited for religion to reveal itself to her, and while she waited worked with an almost desperate industry, trying to buy a little happiness for herself by giving a part of her earnings to those whose needs money could supply. She clung to her little room, for there she could live her own life undisturbed, and preferred to stint herself in other ways rather than give up this liberty. Day after day she sat there sewing health of mind and body into the long seams or dainty stitching that passed through her busy hands, and while she sewed she thought sad, bitter, oftentimes rebellious thoughts.

It was the worst life she could have led just then, for, deprived of the active, cheerful influences she most needed, her mind preyed on itself, slowly and surely, preparing her for the dark experience to come. She knew that there was fitter work for her somewhere, but how to find it was a problem which wiser women have often failed to solve. She was no pauper, yet was one of those whom poverty sets at odds with the world, for favors burden and dependence makes the bread bitter unless love brightens the one and sweetens the other.

There are many Christies, willing to work, yet unable to bear the contact with coarser natures which makes labor seem degrading, or to endure the hard struggle for the bare necessities of life when life has lost all that makes it beautiful. People wonder when such as she say they can find little to do ; but to those who know nothing of the pangs of pride, the sacrifices of feeling, the martyrdoms of youth, love, hope, and ambition that go on under the faded cloaks of these poor gentle-women, who tell them to go into factories, or scrub in kitchens, for there is work enough for all, the most convincing answer would be, " Try it."

Christie kept up bravely till a wearisome low fever broke both strength and spirit, and brought the weight of debt upon her when least fitted to bear or cast it off. For the first time she began to feel that she had nerves which would rebel, and a heart that could not long endure isolation from its kind without losing the cheerful courage which hitherto had been her staunchest friend. Perfect rest, kind care, and genial society were the medicines she needed, but there was no one to minister to her, and she went blindly on along the road so many women tread.

She left her bed too soon, fearing to ask too much of the busy people who had done their best to be neighborly. She returned to her work when it felt heavy in her feeble hands, for debt made idleness seem wicked to her conscientious mind. And, worst of all, she fell back into the bitter, brooding mood which had become habitual to her since she lived alone. While the tired hands slowly worked, the weary brain ached and burned with heavy thoughts, vain longings, and feverish fancies, till things about her sometimes seemed as strange and spectral as the phantoms that had haunted her half-delirious sleep. Inexpressibly wretched were the dreary days, the restless nights, with only pain and labor for companions. The world looked very dark to her, life seemed an utter failure, God a delusion, and the long, lonely years before her too hard to be endured.

It is not always want, insanity, or sin that drives women to desperate deaths; often it is a dreadful loneliness of heart, a hunger for home and friends, worse than starvation, a bitter sense of wrong in being denied the tender ties, the pleasant duties, the sweet rewards that can make the humblest life happy; a rebellious protest against God, who, when they cry for bread, seems to offer them a stone. Some of these impatient souls throw life away, and learn too late how rich it might have been with a stronger faith, a more submissive spirit. Others are kept, and slowly taught to stand and wait, till blest with a happiness the sweeter for the doubt that went before.

There came a time to Christie when the mist about her was so thick she would have stumbled and fallen had not the little candle, kept alight by her own hand, showed her how far " a good deed shines in a naughty world ; " and when God seemed utterly forgetful of her He sent a friend to save and comfort her.

March winds were whistling among the house-tops, and the sky was darkening with a rainy twilight as Christie folded up her finished work, stretched her weary limbs, and made ready for her daily walk. Even this was turned to profit, for then she took home her work, went in search of more, and did her own small marketing. As late hours and unhealthy labor destroyed appetite, and unpaid debts made each mouthful difficult to swallow with Mrs. Flint's hard eye upon her, she had undertaken to supply her own food, and so lessen the obligation that burdened her. An unwise retrenchment, for, busied with the tasks that must be done, she too often neglected or deferred the meals to which no society lent interest, no appetite gave flavor; and when the fuel was withheld the fire began to die out spark by spark.

As she stood before the little mirror, smoothing the hair upon her forehead, she watched the face reflected there, wondering if it could be the same she used to see so full of youth and hope and energy.

"Yes, I'm growing old; my youth is nearly over, and at thirty I shall be a faded, dreary woman, like so many I see and pity. It's hard to come to this after trying so long to find my place, and do my duty. I'm a failure after all, and might as well have stayed with Aunt Betsey or married Joe."

"Miss Devon, to-day is Saturday, and I'm makin' up my bills, so I'll trouble you for your month's board, and as much on the old account as you can let me have."

Mrs. Flint spoke, and her sharp voice rasped the silence like a file, for she had entered without knocking, and her demand was the first intimation of her presence.

Christie turned slowly round, for there was no elasticity in her motions now; through the melancholy anxiety her face always wore of late, there came the worried look of one driven almost beyond endurance, and her hands began to tremble nervously as she tied on her bonnet. Mrs. Flint was a hard woman, and dunned her debtors relentlessly; Christie dreaded the

sight of her, and would have left the house had she
been free of debt.

"I am just going to take these things home and get
more work. I am sure of being paid, and you shall
have all I get. But, for Heaven's sake, give me time."

Two days and a night of almost uninterrupted labor
had given a severe strain to her nerves, and left her in
a dangerous state. Something in her face arrested
Mrs. Flint's attention; she observed that Christie was
putting on her best cloak and hat, and to her suspicious
eye the bundle of work looked unduly large.

It had been a hard day for the poor woman, for the
cook had gone off in a huff; the chamber girl been
detected in petty larceny; two desirable boarders had
disappointed her; and the incapable husband had fallen
ill, so it was little wonder that her soul was tried, her
sharp voice sharper, and her sour temper sourer than
ever.

"I *have* heard of folks putting on their best things
and going out, but never coming back again, when
they owed money. It's a mean trick, but it's sometimes done by them you wouldn't think it of," she said,
with an aggravating sniff of intelligence.

To be suspected of dishonesty was the last drop in
Christie's full cup. She looked at the woman with a
strong desire to do something violent, for every nerve
was tingling with irritation and anger. But she controlled herself, though her face was colorless and her
hands were more tremulous than before. Unfastening
her comfortable cloak she replaced it with a shabby
shawl; took off her neat bonnet and put on a hood,
unfolded six linen shirts, and shook them out before her

landlady's eyes; then retied the parcel, and, pausing on the threshold of the door, looked back with an expression that haunted the woman long afterward, as she said, with the quiver of strong excitement in her voice:

" Mrs. Flint, I have always dealt honorably by you; I always mean to do it, and don't deserve to be suspected of dishonesty like that. I leave every thing I own behind me, and if I don't come back, you can sell them all and pay yourself, for I feel now as if I *never* wanted to see you or this room again."

Then she went rapidly away, supported by her indignation, for she had done her best to pay her debts; had sold the few trinkets she possessed, and several treasures given by the Carrols, to settle her doctor's bill, and had been half killing herself to satisfy Mrs. Flint's demands. The consciousness that she had been too lavish in her generosity when fortune smiled upon her, made the present want all the harder to bear. But she would neither beg nor borrow, though she knew Harry would delight to give, and Uncle Enos lend her money, with a lecture on extravagance, gratis.

" I 'll paddle my own canoe as long as I can," she said, sternly; " and when I must ask help I 'll turn to strangers for it, or scuttle my boat, and go down without troubling any one."

When she came to her employer's door, the servant said: " Missis was out;" then seeing Christie's disappointed face, she added, confidentially:

" If it 's any comfort to know it, I can tell you that missis wouldn't have paid you if she had a been to home. There 's been three other women here with work, and she 's put 'em all off. She always does, and beats 'em down into the bargain, which ain't genteel to my thinkin'."

"She promised me I should be well paid for these, because I undertook to get them done without fail. I 've worked day and night rather than disappoint her, and felt sure of my money," said Christie, despondently.

"I 'm sorry, but you won't get it. She told me to tell you your prices was too high, and she could find folks to work cheaper."

"She did not object to the price when I took the work, and I have half-ruined my eyes over the fine stitching. See if it isn't nicely done." And Christie displayed her exquisite needlework with pride.

The girl admired it, and, having a grievance of her own, took satisfaction in berating her mistress.

"It 's a shame! These things are part of a present the ladies are going to give the minister; but I don't believe he 'll feel easy in 'em if poor folks is wronged to get 'em. Missis won't pay what they are worth, I know; for, don't you see, the cheaper the work is done, the more money she has to make a spread with her share of the present? It 's my opinion you 'd better hold on to these shirts till she pays for 'em handsome."

"No; I 'll keep *my* promise, and I hope she will keep hers. Tell her I need the money very much, and have worked very hard to please her. I 'll come again on Monday, if I 'm able."

Christie's lips trembled as she spoke, for she was feeble still, and the thought of that hard-earned money had been her sustaining hope through the weary hours spent over that ill-paid work. The girl said " Good-bye," with a look of mingled pity and respect, for in her eyes the seamstress was more of a lady than the mistress in this transaction.

Christie hurried to another place, and asked eagerly if the young ladies had any work for her. "Not a stitch," was the reply, and the door closed. She stood a moment looking down upon the passers-by wondering what answer she would get if she accosted any one; and had any especially benevolent face looked back at her she would have been tempted to do it, so heart-sick and forlorn did she feel just then.

She knocked at several other doors, to receive the same reply. She even tried a slop-shop, but it was full, and her pale face was against her. Her long illness had lost her many patrons, and if one steps out from the ranks of needle-women it is very hard to press in again, so crowded are they, and so desperate the need of money.

One hope remained, and, though the way was long, and a foggy drizzle had set in, she minded neither distance nor the chilly rain, but hurried away with anxious thoughts still dogging her steps. Across a long bridge, through muddy roads and up a stately avenue she went, pausing, at last, spent and breathless at another door.

A servant with a wedding-favor in his button-hole opened to her, and, while he went to deliver her urgent message, she peered in wistfully from the dreary world without, catching glimpses of home-love and happiness that made her heart ache for very pity of its own loneliness.

A wedding was evidently afoot, for hall and staircase

blazed with light and bloomed with flowers. Smiling men and maids ran to and fro; opening doors showed tables beautiful with bridal white and silver; savory odors filled the air; gay voices echoed above and below; and once she caught a brief glance at the bonny bride, standing with her father's arm about her, while her mother gave some last, loving touch to her array; and a group of young sisters with April faces clustered round her.

The pretty picture vanished all too soon; the man returned with a hurried " No " for answer, and Christie went out into the deepening twilight with a strange sense of desperation at her heart. It was not the refusal, not the fear of want, nor the reaction of over-taxed nerves alone; it was the sharpness of the contrast between that other woman's fate and her own that made her wring her hands together, and cry out, bitterly:

" Oh, it isn't fair, it isn't right, that she should have so much and I so little! What have I ever done to be so desolate and miserable, and never to find any happiness, however hard I try to do what seems my duty ? "

There was no answer, and she went slowly down the long avenue, feeling that there was no cause for hurry now, and even night and rain and wind were better than her lonely room or Mrs. Flint's complaints. Afar off the city lights shone faintly through the fog, like pale lamps seen in dreams; the damp air cooled her feverish cheeks; the road was dark and still, and she longed to lie down and rest among the sodden leaves.

When she reached the bridge she saw the draw was up, and a spectral ship was slowly passing through.

With no desire to mingle in the crowd that waited on either side, she paused, and, leaning on the railing, let her thoughts wander where they would. As she stood there the heavy air seemed to clog her breath and wrap her in its chilly arms. She felt as if the springs of life were running down, and presently would stop; for, even when the old question, "What shall I do?" came haunting her, she no longer cared even to try to answer it, and had no feeling but one of utter weari⁴ ness. She tried to shake off the strange mood that was stealing over her, but spent body and spent brain were not strong enough to obey her will, and, in spite of her efforts to control it, the impulse that had seized her grew more intense each moment.

"Why should I work and suffer any longer for myself alone?" she thought; "why wear out my life struggling for the bread I have no heart to eat? I am not wise enough to find my place, nor patient enough to wait until it comes to me. Better give up trying, and leave room for those who have something to live for."

Many a stronger soul has known a dark hour when the importunate wish has risen that it were possible and right to lay down the burdens that oppress, the perplexities that harass, and hasten the coming of the long sleep that needs no lullaby. Such an hour was this to Christie, for, as she stood there, that sorrowful bewilderment which we call despair came over her, and ruled her with a power she could not resist.

A flight of steps close by led to a lumber wharf, and, scarcely knowing why, she went down there, with a vague desire to sit still somewhere, and think her way out of the mist that seemed to obscure her mind. A single tall lamp shone at the farther end of the platform, and presently she found herself leaning her hot forehead against the iron pillar, while she watched with curious interest the black water rolling sluggishly below.

She knew it was no place for her, yet no one waited for her, no one would care if she staid for ever, and, yielding to the perilous fascination that drew her there, she lingered with a heavy throbbing in her temples, and a troop of wild fancies whirling through her brain. Something white swept by below, — only a broken oar — but she began to wonder how a human body would look floating through the night. It was an awesome fancy, but it took possession of her, and, as it grew, her eyes dilated, her breath came fast, and her lips fell apart, for she seemed to see the phantom she had conjured up, and it wore the likeness of herself.

With an ominous chill creeping through her blood, and a growing tumult in her mind, she thought, "I *must* go," but still stood motionless, leaning over the wide gulf, eager to see where that dead thing would pass away. So plainly did she see it, so peaceful was the white face, so full of rest the folded hands, so strangely like, and yet unlike, herself, that she seemed to lose her identity, and wondered which was the real and which the imaginary Christie. Lower and lower she bent; looser and looser grew her hold upon the pillar; faster and faster beat the pulses in her temples, and the rush of some blind impulse was swiftly coming on, when a hand seized and caught her back.

For an instant every thing grew black before her

eyes, and the earth seemed to slip away from underneath her feet. Then she was herself again, and found
that she was sitting on a pile of lumber, with her head
uncovered, and a woman's arm about her.

THE RESCUE.

"Was I going to drown myself?" she asked, slowly,
with a fancy that she had been dreaming frightfully,
and some one had wakened her.

"You were most gone; but I came in time, thank God! O Christie! don't you know me?"

Ah! no fear of that; for with one bewildered look, one glad cry of recognition, Christie found her friend again, and was gathered close to Rachel's heart.

"My dear, my dear, what drove you to it? Tell me all, and let me help you in your trouble, as you helped me in mine," she said, as she tenderly laid the poor, white face upon her breast, and wrapped her shawl about the trembling figure clinging to her with such passionate delight.

"I have been ill; I worked too hard; I'm not myself to-night. I owe money. People disappoint and worry me; and I was so worn out, and weak, and wicked, I think I meant to take my life."

"No, dear; it was not you that meant to do it, but the weakness and the trouble that bewildered you. Forget it all, and rest a little, safe with me; then we'll talk again."

Rachel spoke soothingly, for Christie shivered and sighed as if her own thoughts frightened her. For a moment they sat silent, while the mist trailed its white shroud above them, as if death had paused to beckon a tired child away, but, finding her so gently cradled on a warm, human heart, had relented and passed on, leaving no waif but the broken oar for the river to carry toward the sea.

"Tell me about yourself, Rachel. Where have you been so long? I've looked and waited for you ever since the second little note you sent me on last Christmas; but you never came."

"I've been away, dear heart, hard at work in another

city, larger and wickeder than this. I tried to get work
here, that I might be near you; but that cruel Cotton
always found me out; and I was so afraid I should get
desperate that I went away where I was not known.
There it came into my mind to do for others more
wretched than I what you had done for me. God put
the thought into my heart, and He helped me in my
work, for it has prospered wonderfully. All this year
I have been busy with it, and almost happy; for I felt
that your love made me strong to do it, and that, in
time, I might grow good enough to be your friend."

"See what I am, Rachel, and never say that any
more!"

"Hush, my poor dear, and let me talk. You are not
able to do any thing, but rest, and listen. I knew how
many poor souls went wrong when the devil tempted
them; and I gave all my strength to saving those who
were going the way I went. I had no fear, no shame
to overcome, for I was one of them. They would listen
to me, for I knew what I spoke; they could believe in
salvation, for I was saved; they did not feel so outcast
and forlorn when I told them you had taken me into
your innocent arms, and loved me like a sister. With
every one I helped my power increased, and I felt as if
I had washed away a little of my own great sin. O
Christie! never think it's time to die till you are called;
for the Lord leaves us till we have done our work, and
never sends more sin and sorrow than we can bear and
be the better for, if we hold fast by Him."

So beautiful and brave she looked, so full of strength
and yet of meek submission was her voice, that Christie's heart was thrilled; for it was plain that Rachel

had learned how to distil balm from the bitterness of
life, and, groping in the mire to save lost souls, had
found her own salvation there.

" Show me how to grow pious, strong, and useful, as
you are," she said. " I am all wrong, and feel as if I
never could get right again, for I haven't energy
enough to care what becomes of me."

" I know the state, Christie : I 've been through it all!
but when *I* stood where you stand now, there was no
hand to pull me back, and I fell into a blacker river
than this underneath our feet. Thank God, I came in
time to save you from either death ! "

" How did you find me ? " asked Christie, when she
had echoed in her heart the thanksgiving that came
with such fervor from the other's lips.

" I passed you on the bridge. I did not see your face,
but you stood leaning there so wearily, and looking
down into the water, as I used to look, that I wanted to
speak, but did not; and I went on to comfort a poor
girl who is dying yonder. Something turned me back,
however; and when I saw you down here I knew why
I was sent. You were almost gone, but I kept you ;
and when I had you in my arms I knew you, though
it nearly broke my heart to find you here. Now, dear,
come home.

" Home! ah, Rachel, I 've got no home, and for want
of one I shall be lost ! "

The lament that broke from her was more pathetic
than the tears that streamed down, hot and heavy,
melting from her heart the frost of her despair. Her
friend let her weep, knowing well the worth of tears,
and while Christie sobbed herself quiet, Rachel took
thought for her as tenderly as any mother.

When she had heard the story of Christie's troubles, she stood up as if inspired with a happy thought, and stretching both hands to her friend, said, with an air of cheerful assurance most comforting to see:

"I'll take care of you; come with me, my poor Christie, and I'll give you a home, very humble, but honest and happy."

"With you, Rachel?"

"No, dear, I must go back to my work, and you are not fit for that. Neither must you go again to your own room, because for you it is haunted, and the worst place you could be in. You want change, and I'll give you one. It will seem queer at first, but it is a wholesome place, and just what you need."

"I'll do any thing you tell me. I'm past thinking for myself to-night, and only want to be taken care of till I find strength and courage enough to stand alone," said Christie, rising slowly and looking about her with an aspect as helpless and hopeless as if the cloud of mist was a wall of iron.

Rachel put on her bonnet for her and wrapped her shawl about her, saying, in a tender voice, that warmed the other's heart:

"Close by lives a dear, good woman who often befriends such as you and I. She will take you in without a question, and love to do it, for she is the most hospitable soul I know. Just tell her you want work, that I sent you, and there will be no trouble. Then, when you know her a little, confide in her, and you will never come to such a pass as this again. Keep up your heart, dear; I'll not leave you till you are safe."

So cheerily she spoke, so confident she looked, that

the lost expression passed from Christie's face, and hand in hand they went away together, — two types of the sad sisterhood standing on either shore of the dark river that is spanned by a Bridge of Sighs.

Rachel led her friend toward the city, and, coming to the mechanics' quarter, stopped before the door of a small, old house.

"Just knock, say 'Rachel sent me,' and you'll find yourself at home."

"Stay with me, or let me go with you. I can't lose you again, for I need you very much," pleaded Christie, clinging to her friend.

"Not so much as that poor girl dying all alone. She's waiting for me, and I must go. But I'll write soon ; and remember, Christie, I shall feel as if I had only paid a very little of my debt if you go back to the sad old life, and lose your faith and hope again. God bless and keep you, and when we meet next time let me find a happier face than this."

Rachel kissed it with her heart on her lips, smiled her brave sweet smile, and vanished in the mist.

Pausing a moment to collect herself, Christie recollected that she had not asked the name of the new friend whose help she was about to ask. A little sign on the door caught her eye, and, bending down, she managed to read by the dim light of the street lamp these words :

"C. Wilkins, Clear-Starcher.
"Laces done up in the best style."

Too tired to care whether a laundress or a lady took her in, she knocked timidly, and, while she waited for an answer to her summons, stood listening to the noises within.

A swashing sound as of water was audible, likewise a scuffling as of flying feet; some one clapped hands, and a voice said, warningly, "Into your beds this instant minute or I'll come to you! Andrew Jackson, give Gusty a boost; Ann Lizy, don't you tech Wash's feet to tickle 'em. Set pretty in the tub, Victory, dear, while ma sees who's rappin'."

"C. Wilkins, Clear Starcher.'

Then heavy footsteps approached, the door opened wide, and a large woman appeared, with fuzzy red hair, no front teeth, and a plump, clean face, brightly illuminated by the lamp she carried.

"If you please, Rachel sent me. She thought you might be able" —

Christie got no further, for C. Wilkins put out a strong bare arm, still damp, and gently drew her in,

saying, with the same motherly tone as when addressing her children, "Come right in, dear, and don't mind
the clutter things is in. I'm givin' the children their
Sat'day scrubbin', and they will slop and kite 'round,
no matter ef I do spank 'em."

Talking all the way in such an easy, comfortable
voice that Christie felt as if she must have heard it
before, Mrs. Wilkins led her unexpected guest into a
small kitchen, smelling suggestively of soap-suds and
warm flat-irons. In the middle of this apartment was
a large tub; in the tub a chubby child sat, sucking a
sponge and staring calmly at the new-comer with a
pair of big blue eyes, while little drops shone in the
yellow curls and on the rosy shoulders.

"How pretty!" cried Christie, seeing nothing else
and stopping short to admire this innocent little Venus
rising from the sea.

"So she is! Ma's darlin' lamb! and ketchin' her
death a cold this blessed minnit. Set right down, my
dear, and tuck your wet feet into the oven. I'll have
a dish o' tea for you in less'n no time; and while it's
drawin' I'll clap Victory Adelaide into her bed."

Christie sank into a shabby but most hospitable old
chair, dropped her bonnet on the floor, put her feet in
the oven, and, leaning back, watched Mrs. Wilkins
wipe the baby as if she had come for that especial purpose. As Rachel predicted, she found herself at home
at once, and presently was startled to hear a laugh
from her own lips when several children in red and
yellow flannel night-gowns darted like meteors across
the open doorway of an adjoining room, with whoops
and howls, bursts of laughter, and antics of all sorts.

How pleasant it was ; that plain room, with no orna-
ments but the happy faces, no elegance, but cleanliness,
no wealth, but hospitality and lots of love. This latter blessing gave the place its charm, for, though Mrs.
Wilkins threatened to take her infants' noses off if they
got out of bed again, or "put 'em in the kettle and
bile 'em" they evidently knew no fear, but gambolled
all the nearer to her for the threat; and she beamed
upon them with such maternal tenderness and pride
that her homely face grew beautiful in Christie's eyes.

When the baby was bundled up in a blanket and
about to be set down before the stove to simmer a
trifle before being put to bed, Christie held out her
arms, saying with an irresistible longing in her eyes
and voice :

" Let me hold her ! I love babies dearly, and it seems
as if it would do me more good than quarts of tea to
cuddle her, if she 'll let me."

" There now, that 's real sensible ; and mother's bird 'll
set along with you as good as a kitten. Toast her
tootsies wal, for she 's croupy, and I have to be extra
choice of her."

" How good it feels ! " sighed Christie, half devouring
the warm and rosy little bunch in her lap, while baby
lay back luxuriously, spreading her pink toes to the
pleasant warmth and smiling sleepily up in the hungry
face that hung over her.

Mrs. Wilkins's quick eyes saw it all, and she said to
herself, in the closet, as she cut bread and rattled down
a cup and saucer :

" That 's what she wants, poor creeter ; I 'll let her
have a right nice time, and warm and feed and chirk

her up, and then I 'll see what 's to be done for her. She
ain't one of the common sort, and goodness only knows
what Rachel sent her here for. She 's poor and sick,
but she ain't bad. I can tell that by her face, and she 's
the sort I like to help. It 's a mercy I ain't eat my supper, so she can have that bit of meat and the pie."

Putting a tray on the little table, the good soul set
forth all she had to give, and offered it with such hospitable warmth that Christie ate and drank with unaccustomed appetite, finishing off deliciously with a
kiss from baby before she was borne away by her
mother to the back bedroom, where peace soon
reigned.

" Now let me tell you who I am, and how I came to
you in such an unceremonious way," began Christie,
when her hostess returned and found her warmed,
refreshed, and composed by a woman's three best com-
forters, — kind words, a baby, and a cup of tea.

" 'Pears to me, dear, I wouldn't rile myself up by
telling any werryments to-night, but git right warm
inter bed, and have a good long sleep," said Mrs. Wilkins, without a ray of curiosity in her wholesome red
face.

" But you don't know any thing about me, and I may
be the worst woman in the world," cried Christie,
anxious to prove herself worthy of such confidence.

" I know that you want takin' care of, child, or
Rachel wouldn't a sent you. Ef I can help any one, I
don't want no introduction ; and ef you be the wust
woman in the world (which you' ain't), I wouldn't shet
my door on you, for then you 'd need a lift more 'n you
do now."

Christie could only put out her hand, and mutely thank her new friend with full eyes.

"You're fairly tuckered out, you poor soul, so you jest come right up chamber and let me tuck you up, else you'll be down sick. It ain't a mite of inconvenience; the room is kep for company, and it's all ready, even to a clean night-cap. I'm goin' to clap this warm flat to your feet when you're fixed; it's amazin' comfortin' and keeps your head cool."

Up they went to a tidy little chamber, and Christie found herself laid down to rest none too soon, for she was quite worn out. Sleep began to steal over her the moment her head touched the pillow, in spite of the much beruffled cap which Mrs. Wilkins put on with visible pride in its stiffly crimped borders. She was dimly conscious of a kind hand tucking her up, a comfortable voice purring over her, and, best of all, a motherly good-night kiss, then the weary world faded quite away and she was at rest.

CHAPTER VIII.

A CURE FOR DESPAIR.

Lisha Wilkins.

WHEN Christie opened the eyes that had closed so wearily, afternoon sunshine streamed across the room, and seemed the herald of happier days. Refreshed by sleep, and comforted by grateful recollections of her kindly welcome, she lay tranquilly enjoying the friendly atmosphere about her, with so strong a feeling that a skilful hand had taken the rudder, that she felt very little anxiety or curiosity about the haven which was to receive her boat after this narrow escape from shipwreck.

Her eye wandered to and fro, and brightened as it went; for though a poor, plain room it was as neat as hands could make it, and so glorified with sunshine that she thought it a lovely place, in spite of the yellow paper with green cabbage roses on it, the gorgeous plaster statuary on the mantel-piece, and the fragrance of dough-nuts which pervaded the air. Every thing suggested home life, humble but happy, and Christie's solitary heart warmed at the sights and sounds about her.

A half open closet-door gave her glimpses of little frocks and jackets, stubby little shoes, and go-to-meeting hats all in a row. From below came up the sound of childish voices chattering, childish feet trotting to and fro, and childish laughter sounding sweetly through the Sabbath stillness of the place. From a room near by, came the soothing creak of a rocking-chair, the rustle of a newspaper, and now and then a scrap of conversation common-place enough, but pleasant to hear, because so full of domestic love and confidence; and, as she listened, Christie pictured Mrs. Wilkins and her husband taking their rest together after the week's hard work was done.

"I wish I could stay here; it's so comfortable and home-like. I wonder if they wouldn't let me have this room, and help me to find some better work than sewing? I'll get up and ask them," thought Christie, feeling an irresistible desire to stay, and strong repugnance to returning to the room she had left, for, as Rachel truly said, it *was* haunted for her.

When she opened the door to go down, Mrs. Wilkins

bounced out of her rocking-chair and hurried to meet
her with a smiling face, saying all in one breath :

"Good mornin', dear! Rested well, I hope? I 'm
proper glad to hear it. Now come right down and
have your dinner. I kep it hot, for I couldn't bear to
wake you up, you was sleepin' so beautiful."

"I was so worn out I slept like a baby, and feel like
a new creature. It was so kind of you to take me in,
and I 'm so grateful I don't know how to show it," said
Christie, warmly, as her hostess ponderously descended
the complaining stairs and ushered her into the tidy
kitchen from which tubs and flat-irons were banished
one day in the week.

"Lawful sakes, the' ain't nothing to be grateful for,
child, and you 're heartily welcome to the little I done.
We are country folks in our ways, though we be livin'
in the city, and we have a reg'lar country dinner Sundays. Hope you 'll relish it; my vittles is clean ef
they ain't rich."

As she spoke, Mrs. Wilkins dished up baked beans,
Indian-pudding, and brown bread enough for half a
dozen. Christie was hungry now, and ate with an
appetite that delighted the good lady who vibrated
between her guest and her children, shut up in the
" settin'-room."

"Now please let me tell you all about myself, for I
am afraid you think me something better than I am.
If I ask help from you, it is right that you should
know whom you are helping," said Christie, when the
table was cleared and her hostess came and sat down
beside her.

" Yes, my dear, free your mind, and then we 'll fix

things up right smart. Nothin' I like better, and Lisha says I have considerable of a knack that way," replied Mrs. Wilkins, with a smile, a nod, and an air of interest most reassuring.

So Christie told her story, won to entire confidence by the sympathetic face opposite, and the motherly pats so gently given by the big, rough hand that often met her own. When all was told, Christie said very earnestly:

" I am ready to go to work to-morrow, and will do any thing I can find, but I *should* love to stay here a little while, if I could; I do so dread to be alone. Is it possible? I mean to pay my board of course, and help you besides if you 'll let me."

Mrs. Wilkins glowed with pleasure at this compliment, and leaning toward Christie, looked into her face a moment in silence, as if to test the sincerity of the wish. In that moment Christie saw what steady, sagacious eyes the woman had; so clear, so honest that she looked through them into the great, warm heart below, and looking forgot the fuzzy, red hair, the paucity of teeth, the faded gown, and felt only the attraction of a nature genuine and genial as the sunshine dancing on the kitchen floor.

Beautiful souls often get put into plain bodies, but they cannot be hidden, and have a power all their own, the greater for the unconsciousness or the humility which gives it grace. Christie saw and felt this then, and when the homely woman spoke, listened to her with implicit confidence.

"My dear, I 'd no more send you away now than I would my Adelaide, for you need looking after for a

spell, most as much as she doos. You 've been thinkin'
and broodin' too much, and sewin' yourself to death.
We 'll stop all that, and keep you so busy there won't
be no time for the hypo. You 're one of them that
can't live alone without starvin' somehow, so I 'm jest
goin' to turn you in among them children to paster, so
to speak. That 's wholesome and fillin' for *you*, and
goodness knows it will be a puffect charity to *me*, for
I 'm goin' to be dreadful drove with gettin' up curtins
and all manner of things, as spring comes on. So it
ain't no favor on my part, and you can take out your
board in tendin' baby and putterin' over them little
tykes."

"I should like it *so* much! But I forgot my debt to
Mrs. Flint; perhaps she won't let me go," said Christie,
with an anxious cloud coming over her brightening
face.

"Merciful, suz! don't you be werried about her. I 'll
see to her, and ef she acts ugly Lisha 'll fetch her
round; men can always settle such things better 'n we
can, and he 's a dreadful smart man Lisha is. We 'll
go to-morrer and get your belongins, and then settle
right down for a spell; and by-an'-by when you git a
trifle more chipper we 'll find a nice place in the country
some'rs. That 's what you want; nothin' like green
grass and woodsy smells to right folks up. When I
was a gal, ef I got low in my mind, or riled in my
temper, I jest went out and grubbed in the gardin, or
made hay, or walked a good piece, and it fetched me
round beautiful. Never failed; so I come to see that
good fresh dirt is fust rate physic for folk's spirits as
it is for wounds, as they tell on."

" That sounds sensible and pleasant, and I like it. Oh, it is *so* beautiful to feel that somebody cares for you a little bit, and you ain't one too many in the world," sighed Christie.

" Don't you never feel that agin, my dear. What's the Lord for ef He ain't to hold on to in times of trouble. Faith ain't wuth much ef it's only lively in fair weather; you've got to believe hearty and stan' by the Lord through thick and thin, and He'll stan' by you as no one else begins to. I remember of havin' this bore in upon me by somethin' that happened to a man I knew. He got blowed up in a powder-mill, and when folks asked him what he thought when the bust come, he said, real sober and impressive: ' Wal, it come through me, like a flash, that I'd served the Lord as faithful as I knew how for a number a years, and I guessed He'd fetch me through somehow, and He did.' Sure enough the man warn't killed; I'm bound to confess he was shook dreadful, but his faith warn't."

Christie could not help smiling at the story, but she liked it, and sincerely wished she could imitate the hero of it in his piety, not his powder. She was about to say so when the sound of approaching steps announced the advent of her host. She had been rather impressed with the " smartness " of Lisha by his wife's praises, but when a small, sallow, sickly looking man came in she changed her mind; for not even an immensely stiff collar, nor a pair of boots that seemed composed entirely of what the boys call " creak leather," could inspire her with confidence.

Without a particle of expression in his yellow face, Mr. Wilkins nodded to the stranger over the picket fence of his collar, lighted his pipe, and clumped away to enjoy his afternoon promenade without compromising himself by a single word.

His wife looked after him with an admiring gaze as she said :

"Them boots is as good as an advertisement, for he made every stitch on 'em himself;" then she added, laughing like a girl: " It 's redick'lus my bein' so proud of Lisha, but ef a woman ain't a right to think wal of her own husband, I should like to know who has ! "

Christie was afraid that Mrs. Wilkins had seen her disappointment in her face, and tried, with wifely zeal, to defend her lord from even a disparaging thought. Wishing to atone for this transgression she was about to sing the praises of the wooden-faced Elisha, but was spared any polite fibs by the appearance of a small girl who delivered an urgent message to the effect, that " Mis Plumly was down sick and wanted Mis Wilkins to run over and set a spell."

As the good lady hesitated with an involuntary glance at her guest, Christie said quickly :

"Don't mind me ; I 'll take care of the house for you if you want to go. You may be sure I won't run off with the children or steal the spoons."

" I ain't a mite afraid of anybody wantin' to steal them little toads ; and as for spoons, I ain't got a silver one to bless myself with," laughed Mrs. Wilkins. " I guess I will go, then, ef you don't mind, as it 's only acrost the street. Like 's not settin' quiet will be better for you 'n talkin', for I 'm a dreadful hand to gab when I git started. Tell Mis Plumly I 'm a comin'."

Then, as the child ran off, the stout lady began to

rummage in her closet, saying, as she rattled and slammed:

"I'll jest take her a drawin' of tea and a couple of nut-cakes: mebby she'll relish 'em, for I shouldn't wonder ef she hadn't had a mouthful this blessed day. She's dreadful slack at the best of times, but no one can much wonder, seein' she's got nine children, and is jest up from a rheumatic fever. I'm sure I never grudge a meal of vittles or a hand's turn to such as she is, though she does beat all for dependin' on her neighbors. I'm a thousand times obleeged. You needn't werry about the children, only don't let 'em git lost, or burnt, or pitch out a winder; and when it's done give 'em the patty-cake that's bakin' for 'em."

With which maternal orders Mrs. Wilkins assumed a sky-blue bonnet, and went beaming away with several dishes genteelly hidden under her purple shawl.

Being irresistibly attracted toward the children Christie opened the door and took a survey of her responsibilities.

Six lively infants were congregated in the "settin'-room," and chaos seemed to have come again, for every sort of destructive amusement was in full operation. George Washington, the eldest blossom, was shearing a resigned kitten; Gusty and Ann Eliza were concocting mud pies in the ashes; Adelaide Victoria was studying the structure of lamp-wicks, while Daniel Webster and Andrew Jackson were dragging one another in a clothes-basket, to the great detriment of the old carpet and still older chariot.

Thinking that some employment more suited to the

day might be introduced, Christie soon made friends with these young persons, and, having rescued the kitten, banished the basket, lured the elder girls from their mud-piety, and quenched the curiosity of the Pickwickian Adelaide, she proposed teaching them some little hymns.

The idea was graciously received, and the class decorously seated in a row. But before a single verse was given out, Gusty, being of a house-wifely turn of mind, suggested that the patty-cake might burn. Instant alarm pervaded the party, and a precipitate rush was made for the cooking-stove, where Christie proved by ocular demonstration that the cake showed no signs of baking, much less of burning. The family pronounced themselves satisfied, after each member had poked a grimy little finger into the doughy delicacy, whereon one large raisin reposed in proud pre-eminence over the vulgar herd of caraways.

Order being with difficulty restored, Christie taught her flock an appropriate hymn, and was flattering herself that their youthful minds were receiving a devotional bent, when they volunteered a song, and incited thereunto by the irreverent Wash, burst forth with a gem from Mother Goose, closing with a smart skirmish of arms and legs that set all law and order at defiance.

Hoping to quell the insurrection Christie invited the breathless rioters to calm themselves by looking at the pictures in the big Bible. But, unfortunately, her explanations were so vivid that her audience were fired with a desire to enact some of the scenes portrayed, and no persuasions could keep them from playing Ark on the spot. The clothes-basket was elevated upon two chairs, and into it marched the birds of the air and the beasts of the field, to judge by the noise, and all set sail, with Washington at the helm, Jackson and Webster plying the clothes and pudding-sticks for oars, while the young ladies rescued their dolls from the flood, and waved their hands to imaginary friends who were not unmindful of the courtesies of life even in the act of drowning.

MRS. WILKINS' SIX LIVELY INFANTS.

Finding her authority defied Christie left the rebels to their own devices, and sitting in a corner, began to think about her own affairs. But before she had time to get anxious or perplexed the children diverted her mind, as if the little flibberty-gibbets knew that their pranks and perils were far wholesomer for her just then than brooding.

The much-enduring kitten being sent forth as a dove upon the waters failed to return with the olive-branch; of which peaceful emblem there was soon great need, for mutiny broke out, and spread with disastrous rapidity.

Ann Eliza slapped Gusty because she had the biggest bandbox; Andrew threatened to " chuck " Daniel overboard if he continued to trample on the fraternal toes, and in the midst of the fray, by some unguarded motion, Washington capsized the ship and precipitated the patriarchal family into the bosom of the deep.

Christie flew to the rescue, and, hydropathically treated, the anguish of bumps and bruises was soon assuaged. Then appeared the appropriate moment for a story, and gathering the dilapidated party about her she soon enraptured them by a recital of the immortal history of " Frank and the little dog Trusty." Charmed with her success she was about to tell another moral tale, but no sooner had she announced the name, " The Three Cakes," when, like an electric flash a sudden recollection seized the young Wilkinses, and with one voice they demanded their lawful prize, sure that now it must be done.

Christie had forgotten all about it, and was harassed with secret misgivings as she headed the investigating committee. With skipping of feet and clapping of hands the eager tribe surrounded the stove, and with fear and trembling Christie drew forth a melancholy cinder, where, like Casabianca, the lofty raisin still remained, blackened, but undaunted, at its post.

Then were six little vials of wrath poured out upon her devoted head, and sounds of lamentation filled the air, for the irate Wilkinses refused to be comforted till the rash vow to present each member of the outraged family with a private cake produced a lull, during which the younger ones were decoyed into the back yard, and the three elders solaced themselves with mischief.

Mounted on mettlesome broomsticks Andrew and Daniel were riding merrily away to the Banbury Cross, of blessed memory, and little Vic was erecting a pagoda of oyster-shells, under Christie's superintendence, when a shrill scream from within sent horsemen and architects flying to the rescue.

Gusty's pinafore was in a blaze ; Ann Eliza was dancing frantically about her sister as if bent on making a *suttee* of herself, while George Washington hung out of window, roaring, "Fire!" "water!" "engine!" "pa!" with a presence of mind worthy of his sex.

A speedy application of the hearth-rug quenched the conflagration, and when a minute burn had been enveloped in cotton-wool, like a gem, a coroner sat upon the pinafore and investigated the case.

It appeared that the ladies were "only playing paper dolls," when Wash, sighing for the enlightenment of his race, proposed to make a bonfire, and did so with an old book; but Gusty, with a firm belief in future punishment, tried to save it, and fell a victim to her principles, as the virtuous are very apt to do.

The book was brought into court, and proved to be an ancient volume of ballads, cut, torn, and half consumed. Several peculiarly developed paper dolls, branded here and there with large letters, like galley-slaves, were then produced by the accused, and the judge could with difficulty preserve her gravity when she found "John Gilpin" converted into a painted petticoat, "The Bay of Biscay, O," situated in the crown of a hat, and "Chevy Chase" issuing from the mouth of a triangular gentleman, who, like Dickens's cherub, probably sung it by ear, having no lungs to speak of.

It was further apparent from the agricultural appearance of the room that beans had been sowed broadcast by means of the apple-corer, which Wash had converted into a pop-gun with a mechanical ingenuity worthy of more general appreciation. He felt this deeply, and when Christie reproved him for leading his sisters astray, he resented the liberty she took, and retired in high dudgeon to the cellar, where he appeared to set up a menagerie, — for bears, lions, and unknown animals, endowed with great vocal powers, were heard to solicit patronage from below.

Somewhat exhausted by her labors, Christie rested, after clearing up the room, while the children found a solace for all afflictions in the consumption of relays of bread and molasses, which infantile restorative occurred like an inspiration to the mind of their guardian.

Peace reigned for fifteen minutes; then came a loud crash from the cellar, followed by a violent splashing, and wild cries of, "Oh, oh, oh, I 've fell into the pork barrel! I 'm drownin', I 'm drownin'!"

Down rushed Christie, and the sticky innocents ran screaming after, to behold their pickled brother fished up from the briny deep. A spectacle well calculated to impress upon their infant minds the awful consequences of straying from the paths of virtue.

At this crisis Mrs. Wilkins providentially appeared, breathless, but brisk and beaming, and in no wise dismayed by the plight of her luckless son, for a ten years' acquaintance with Wash's dauntless nature had inured his mother to " didoes " that would have appalled most women.

" Go right up chamber, and change every rag on you, and don't come down agin till I rap on the ceilin'; you dreadful boy, disgracin' your family by sech actions. I'm sorry I was kep' so long, but Mis Plumly got tellin' her werryments, and 'peared to take so much comfort in it I couldn't bear to stop her. Then I jest run round to your place and told that woman that you was safe and well, along 'r friends, and would call in to-morrer to get your things. She'd ben so scart by your not comin' home that she was as mild as milk, so you won't have no trouble with her, I expect."

" Thank you very much ! How kind you are, and how tired you must be ! Sit down and let me take your things," cried Christie, more relieved than she could express.

" Lor', no, I'm fond of walkin', but bein' ruther hefty it takes my breath away some to hurry. I'm afraid these children have tuckered you out though. They are proper good gen'lly, but when they do take to trainen they're a sight of care," said Mrs. Wilkins, as she surveyed her imposing bonnet with calm satisfaction.

" I 've enjoyed it very much, and it's done me good, for I haven't laughed so much for six months as I have this afternoon," answered Christie, and it was quite true, for she had been too busy to think of herself or her woes.

" Wal, I thought likely it would chirk you up some, or I shouldn't have went," and Mrs. Wilkins put away a contented smile with her cherished bonnet, for Christie's face had grown so much brighter since she saw it last, that the good woman felt sure her treatment was the right one.

At supper Lisha reappeared, and while his wife and children talked incessantly, he ate four slices of bread and butter, three pieces of pie, five dough-nuts, and drank a small ocean of tea out of his saucer. Then, evidently feeling that he had done his duty like a man, he gave Christie another nod, and disappeared again without a word.

When she had done up. her dishes Mrs. Wilkins brought out a few books and papers, and said to Christie, who sat apart by the window, with the old shadow creeping over her face :

"Now don't feel lonesome, my dear, but jest lop right down on the soffy and have a sociable kind of a time. Lisha's gone down street for the evenin'. I'll keep the children as quiet as one woman can, and you may read or rest, or talk, jest as you're a mind."

" Thank you; I'll sit here and rock little Vic to sleep for you. I don't care to read, but I'd like to have you talk to me, for it seems as if I'd known you a long time and it does me good," said Christie, as she settled herself and baby on the old settee which had served as a cradle for six young Wilkinses, and now received the honorable name of sofa in its old age.

Mrs. Wilkins looked gratified, as she settled her brood round the table with a pile of pictorial papers to amuse them. Then having laid herself out to be agreeable, she sat thoughtfully rubbing the bridge of her nose, at a loss how to begin. Presently Christie helped her by an involuntary sigh.

"What's the matter, dear? Is there any thing I can do to make you comfortable?" asked the kind soul, alert at once, and ready to offer sympathy.

"I'm very cosy, thank you, and I don't know why I sighed. It's a way I've got into when I think of my worries," explained Christie, in haste.

"Wal, dear, I wouldn't ef I was you. Don't keep turnin' your troubles over. Git atop of 'em somehow, and stay there ef you can," said Mrs. Wilkins, very earnestly.

"But that's just what I can't do. I've lost all my spirits and courage, and got into a dismal state of mind. You seem to be very cheerful, and yet you must have a good deal to try you sometimes. I wish you'd tell me how you do it;" and Christie looked wistfully into that other face, so plain, yet so placid, wondering to see how little poverty, hard work, and many cares had soured or saddened it.

"Really I don't know, unless it's jest doin' whatever comes along, and doin' of it hearty, sure that things is all right, though very often I don't see it at fust."

"Do you see it at last?"

"Gen'lly I do; and if I don't I take it on trust, same as children do what older folks tell 'em; and byme-by when I'm grown up in spiritual things I'll understan' as the dears do, when they git to be men and women."

That suited Christie, and she thought hopefully within herself:

"This woman has got the sort of religion I want, if it makes her what she is. Some day I'll get her to tell me where she found it." Then aloud she said :

"But it's *so* hard to be patient and contented when nothing happens as you want it to, and you don't get your share of happiness, no matter how much you try to deserve it."

"It ain't easy to bear, I know, but having tried my own way and made a dreadful mess on 't, I concluded that the Lord knows what's best for us, and things go better when He manages than when we go scratchin' round and can't wait."

"Tried your own way? How do you mean?" asked Christie, curiously; for she liked to hear her hostess talk, and found something besides amusement in the conversation, which seemed to possess a fresh country flavor as well as country phrases.

Mrs. Wilkins smiled all over her plump face, as if she liked to tell her experience, and having hunched sleepy little Andy more comfortably into her lap, and given a preparatory hem or two, she began with great good-will.

"It happened a number a years ago and ain't much of a story any way. But you're welcome to it, as some of it is rather humorsome, the laugh may do you good ef the story don't. We was livin' down to the east'ard at the time. It was a real pretty place; the house stood under a couple of maples and a gret brook come

foamin' down the rayvine and away through the med-
ders to the river. Dear sakes, seems as ef I see it now,
jest as I used to settin' on the doorsteps with the lay-
locks all in blow, the squirrels jabberin' on the wall,
and the saw-mill screekin' way off by the dam."

Pausing a moment, Mrs. Wilkins looked musingly at
the steam of the tea-kettle, as if through its silvery
haze she saw her early home again. Wash promptly
roused her from this reverie by tumbling off the boiler
with a crash. His mother picked him up and placidly
went on, falling more and more into the country dia-
lect which city life had not yet polished.

"I oughter hev been the contentedest woman alive,
but I warn't, for you see I'd worked at millineryin'
before I was married, and had an easy time on't,
Afterwards the children come along pretty fast, there
was sights of work to do, and no time for pleasurin',
so I got wore out, and used to hanker after old times
in a dreadful wicked way.

"Finally I got acquainted with a Mis Bascum, and
she done me a sight of harm. You see, havin' few pies
of her own to bake, she was fond of puttin' her fingers
into her neighborses, but she done it so neat that no
one mistrusted she was takin' all the sarce and leavin'
all the crust to them, as you may say. Wal, I told her
my werryments and she sympathized real hearty, and
said I didn't ought to stan' it, but have things to suit
me, and enjoy myself, as other folks did. So when she
put it into my head I thought it amazin' good advice,
and jest went and done as she told me.

"Lisha was the kindest man you ever see, so when I
up and said I warn't goin' to drudge round no more,

but must hev a girl, he got one, and goodness knows
what a trial *she* was. After she came I got dreadful
slack, and left the house and the children to Hen'retta,
and went pleasurin' frequent all in my best. I always
was a dressy woman in them days, and Lisha give me
his earnin's real lavish, bless his heart! and I went and
spent 'em on my sinful gowns and bunnets."

Here Mrs. Wilkins stopped to give a remorseful groan
and stroke her faded dress, as if she found great comfort in its dinginess.

"It ain't no use tellin' all I done, but I had full swing,
and at fust I thought luck was in my dish sure. But it
warn't, seein' I didn't deserve it, and I had to take my
mess of trouble, which was needful and nourishin,' ef
I'd had the grace to see it so.

"Lisha got into debt, and no wonder, with me a
wastin' of his substance; Hen'retta went off suddin',
with whatever she could lay her hands on, and every-
thing was at sixes and sevens. Lisha's patience give
out at last, for I was dreadful fractious, knowin' it was
all my fault. The children seemed to git out of sorts,
too, and acted like time in the primer, with croup and
pins, and whoopin'-cough and temper. I declare I
used to think the pots and kettles biled over to spite
each other and me too in them days.

"All this was nuts to Mis Bascum, and she kep'
advisin' and encouragin' of me, and I didn't see through
her a mite, or guess that settin' folks by the ears was
as relishin' to her as bitters is to some. Merciful, suz!
what a piece a work we did make betwixt us! I
scolded and moped 'cause I couldn't have my way;
Lisha swore and threatened to take to drinkin' ef I

didn't make home more comfortable; the children run wild, and the house was gittin' too hot to hold us, when we was brought up with a round turn, and I see the redicklousness of my doin's in time.

" One day Lisha come home tired and cross, for bills was pressin', work slack, and folks talkin' about us as ef they'd nothin' else to do. I was dishin' up dinner, feelin' as nervous as a witch, for a whole batch of bread had burnt to a cinder while I was trimmin' a new bunnet, Wash had scart me most to death swallerin' a cent, and the steak had been on the floor more'n once, owin' to my havin' babies, dogs, cats, or hens under my feet the whole blessed time.

" Lisha looked as black as thunder, throwed his hat into a corner, and came along to the sink where I was skinnin' pertaters. As he washed his hands, I asked what the matter was; but he only muttered and slopped, and I couldn't git nothin' out of him, for he ain't talkative at the best of times as you see, and when he's werried corkscrews wouldn't draw a word from him.

" Bein' riled myself didn't mend matters, and so we fell to hectorin' one another right smart. He said somethin' that dreened my last drop of patience; I give a sharp answer, and fust thing I knew he up with his hand and slapped me. It warn't a hard blow by no means, only a kind of a wet spat side of the head; but I thought I should have flew, and was as mad as ef I'd been knocked down. You never see a man look so 'shamed as Lisha did, and ef I'd been wise I should have made up the quarrel then. But I was a fool. I jest flung fork, dish, pertaters and all into the pot, and says, as ferce as you please:

"'Lisha Wilkins, when you can treat me decent you may come and fetch me back; you won't see me till then, and so I tell you.'

"Then I made a bee-line for Mis Bascum's; told her the whole story, had a good cry, and was all ready to go home in half an hour, but Lisha didn't come.

"Wal, that night passed, and what a long one it was to be sure! and me without a wink of sleep, thinkin' of Wash and the cent, my emptins and the baby. Next day come, but no Lisha, no message, no nuthin', and I began to think I'd got my match though I had a sight of grit in them days. I sewed, and Mis Bascum she clacked; but I didn't say much, and jest worked like sixty to pay for my keep, for I warn't goin' to be beholden to her for nothin'.

"The day dragged on terrible slow, and at last I begged her to go and git me a clean dress, for I'd come off jest as I was, and folks kep' droppin' in, for the story was all round, thanks to Mis Bascum's long tongue.

"Wal, she went, and ef you'll believe me Lisha wouldn't let her in! He handed my best things out a winder and told her to tell me they were gittin' along fust rate with Florindy Walch to do the work. He hoped I'd have a good time, and not expect him for a consider'ble spell, for he liked a quiet house, and now he'd got it.

"When I heard that, I knew he must be provoked the wust kind, for he ain't a hash man by nater. I could have crep' in at the winder ef he wouldn't open the door, I was so took down by that message. But Mis Bascum wouldn't hear of it, and kep' stirrin' of me up till I was ashamed to eat 'umble pie fust; so I waited to see how soon he'd come round. But he had the best on't you see, for he'd got the babies and lost a cross wife, while I'd lost every thing but Mis Bascum, who grew hatefuler to me every hour, for I begun to mistrust she was a mischief-maker, — widders most always is, — seein' how she pampered up my pride and 'peared to like the quarrel.

"I thought I should have died more'n once, for sure as you live it went on three mortal days, and of all miser'ble creeters I was the miser'blest. Then I see how wicked and ungrateful I'd been; how I'd shirked my bounden duty and scorned my best blessins. There warn't a hard job that ever I'd hated but what grew easy when I remembered who it was done for; there warn't a trouble or a care that I wouldn't have welcomed hearty, nor one hour of them dear fractious babies that didn't seem precious when I'd gone and left 'em. I'd got time to rest enough now, and might go pleasuring all day long; but I couldn't do it, and would have given a dozin bunnets trimmed to kill ef I could only have been back moilin' in my old kitchen with the children hangin' round me and Lisha a comin' in cheerful from his work as he used to 'fore I spoilt his home for him. How sing'lar it is folks never *do* know when they are wal off!"

"I know it now," said Christie, rocking lazily to and fro, with a face almost as tranquil as little Vic's, lying half asleep in her lap.

"Glad to hear it, my dear. As I was goin' on to say when Saturday come, a tremenjus storm set in, and it rained guns all day. I never shall forget it, for I was hankerin' after baby, and dreadful werried about the others, all bein' croupy, and Florindy with no more idee of nussin' than a baa lamb. The rain come down like a reg'lar deluge, but I didn't seem to have no ark to run to. As night come on things got wuss and wuss, for the wind blowed the roof off Mis Bascum's barn and stove in the butt'ry window; the brook riz and went ragin' every which way, and you never did see such a piece of work.

"My heart was most broke by that time, and I knew I should give in 'fore Monday. But I set and sewed and listened to the tinkle tankle of the drops in the pans set round to ketch 'em, for the house leaked like a sieve. Mis Bascum was down suller putterin' about, for every kag and sarce jar was afloat. Moses, her brother, was lookin' after his stock and tryin' to stop the damage. All of a sudden he bust in lookin' kinder wild, and settin' down the lantern, he sez, sez he: 'You're ruthern an unfortinate woman to-night, Mis Wilkins.' 'How so?' sez I, as ef nuthin' was the matter already.

"'Why,' sez he, 'the spilins have give way up in the rayvine, and the brook's come down like a river, upsot your lean-to, washed the mellion patch slap into the road, and while your husband was tryin' to git the pig out of the pen, the water took a turn and swep him away.'

"'Drownded?' sez I, with only breath enough for that one word. 'Shouldn't wonder,' sez Moses, 'nothin' ever did come up alive after goin' over them falls.'

"It come over me like a streak of lightenin'; every thin' kinder slewed round, and I dropped in the first faint I ever had in my life. Next I knew Lisha was holdin' of me and cryin' fit to kill himself. I thought I was dreamin', and only had wits enough to give a sort of permiscuous grab at him and call out:

"'Oh, Lisha! ain't you drownded?' He give a gret start at that, swallered down his sobbin', and sez as lovin' as ever a man did in this world:

"'Bless your dear heart, Cynthy, it warn't me it was the pig;' and then fell to kissin' of me, till betwixt laughin' and cryin' I was most choked. Deary me, it all comes back so livin' real it kinder takes my breath away."

And well it might, for the good soul entered so heartily into her story that she unconsciously embellished it with dramatic illustrations. At the slapping episode she flung an invisible "fork, dish, and pertaters" into an imaginary kettle, and glared; when the catastrophe arrived, she fell back upon her chair to express fainting; gave Christie's arm the "permiscuous grab" at the proper moment, and uttered the repentant Lisha's explanation with an incoherent pathos that forbid a laugh at the sudden introduction of the porcine martyr.

"What did you do then?" asked Christie in a most flattering state of interest.

"Oh, law! I went right home and hugged them children for a couple of hours stiddy," answered Mrs. Wilkins, as if but one conclusion was possible.

"Did all your troubles go down with the pig?" asked Christie, presently.

"Massy, no, we're all poor, feeble worms, and the best meanin' of us fails too often," sighed Mrs. Wilkins, as she tenderly adjusted the sleepy head of the young worm in her lap. "After that scrape I done my best; Lisha was as meek as a whole flock of sheep, and we give Mis Bascum a wide berth. Things went lovely for ever so long, and though, after a spell, we had our ups and downs, as is but natural to human creeters, we never come to such a pass agin. Both on us tried real hard; whenever I felt my temper risin' or discontent comin' on I remembered them days and kep' a taut rein; and as for Lisha he never said a raspin' word, or got sulky, but what he'd bust out laughin' after it and say: 'Bless you, Cynthy, it warn't me, it was the pig.'"

Mrs. Wilkins' hearty laugh fired a long train of lesser ones, for the children recognized a household word. Christie enjoyed the joke, and even the tea-kettle boiled over as if carried away by the fun.

"Tell some more, please," said Christie, when the merriment subsided, for she felt her spirits rising.

"There's nothin' more to tell, except one thing that prevented my ever forgittin' the lesson I got then. My little Almiry took cold that week and pined away rapid. She'd always been so ailin' I never expected to raise her, and more'n once in them sinful tempers of mine I'd thought it would be a mercy ef she was took out of her pain. But when I laid away that patient, sufferin' little creeter I found she was the dearest of 'em all. I most broke my heart to hev her back, and never, never forgive myself for leavin' her that time."

With trembling lips and full eyes Mrs. Wilkins stopped to wipe her features generally on Andrew Jackson's pinafore, and heave a remorseful sigh.

"And this is how you came to be the cheerful, con-

tented woman you are?" said Christie, hoping to
divert the mother's mind from that too tender memory.

"Yes," she answered, thoughtfully, "I told you Lisha
was a smart man; he give me a good lesson, and it set
me to thinkin' serious. 'Pears to me trouble is a kind
of mellerin' process, and ef you take it kindly it doos
you good, and you learn to be glad of it. I'm sure Lisha
and me is twice as fond of one another, twice as
willin' to work, and twice as patient with our trials
sense dear little Almiry died, and times was hard.
I ain't what I ought to be, not by a long chalk, but I
try to live up to my light, do my duty cheerful, love
my neighbors, and fetch up my family in the fear of
God. Ef I do this the best way I know how, I'm sure
I'll get my rest some day, and the good Lord won't
forgit Cynthy Wilkins. He ain't so fur, for I keep my
health wonderfle, Lisha is kind and stiddy, the children
flourishin', and I'm a happy woman though I be a humly
one."

There she was mistaken, for as her eye roved round
the narrow room from the old hat on the wall to the
curly heads bobbing here and there, contentment,
piety, and mother-love made her plain face beautiful.

"That story has done me ever so much good, and I
shall not forget it. Now, good-night, for I must be up
early to-morrow, and I don't want to drive Mr. Wilkins
away entirely," said Christie, after she had helped put
the little folk to bed, during which process she had
heard her host creaking about the kitchen as if afraid
to enter the sitting-room.

She laughed as she spoke, and ran up stairs, wondering if she could be the same forlorn creature who had
crept so wearily up only the night before.

It was a very humble little sermon that Mrs. Wilkins had preached to her, but she took it to heart and profited by it; for she was a pupil in the great charity school where the best teachers are often unknown, unhonored here, but who surely will receive commendation and reward from the head master when their long vacation comes.

CHAPTER IX.

MRS. WILKINS'S MINISTER.

MR. POWER.

NEXT day Christie braved the lion in his den, otherwise the flinty Flint, in her second-class boarding-house, and found that alarm and remorse had produced a softening effect upon her. She was unfeignedly glad to see her lost lodger safe, and finding that the new friends were likely to put her in the way of paying her debts, this much harassed matron permitted her to pack up her possessions, leaving one trunk as a sort of hostage. Then, with promises to redeem it as soon as possible, Christie said good-bye to the little room where she had hoped and suffered, lived and labored so long, and went joyfully back to the humble home she had found with the good laundress.

All the following week Christie " chored round," as Mrs. Wilkins called the miscellaneous light work she let her do. Much washing, combing, and clean pinaforing of children fell to her share, and she enjoyed it amazingly; then, when the elder ones were packed off to school she lent a hand to any of the numberless tasks housewives find to do from morning till night. In the afternoon, when other work was done, and little Vic asleep or happy 'with her playthings, Christie clapped laces, sprinkled muslins, and picked out edgings at the great table where Mrs. Wilkins stood ironing, fluting, and crimping till the kitchen bristled all over with immaculate frills and flounces.

It was pretty delicate work, and Christie liked it, for Mrs. Wilkins was an adept at her trade and took as much pride and pleasure in it as any French *blanchisseuse* tripping through the streets of Paris with a tree full of coquettish caps, capes, and petticoats borne before her by a half invisible boy.

Being women, of course they talked as industriously as they worked; fingers flew and tongues clacked with equal profit and pleasure, and, by Saturday, Christie had made up her mind that Mrs. Wilkins was the most sensible woman she ever knew. Her grammar was an outrage upon the memory of Lindley Murray, but the goodness of her heart would have done honor to any saint in the calendar. She was very plain, and her manners were by no means elegant, but good temper

made that homely face most lovable, and natural refinement of soul made mere external polish of small
account. Her shrewd ideas and odd sayings amused
Christie very much, while her good sense and bright
way of looking at things did the younger woman a
world of good.

Mr. Wilkins devoted himself to the making of shoes
and the consumption of food, with the silent regularity
of a placid animal. His one dissipation was tobacco,
and in a fragrant cloud of smoke he lived and moved
and had his being so entirely that he might have been
described as a pipe with a man somewhere behind it.
Christie once laughingly spoke of this habit and declared she would try it herself if she thought it would
make her as quiet and undemonstrative as Mr. Wilkins,
who, to tell the truth, made no more impression on her
than a fly.

"I don't approve on 't, but he might do wuss. We
all have to have our comfort somehow, so I let Lisha
smoke as much as he likes, and he lets me gab, so it 's
about fair, I reckon," answered Mrs. Wilkins, from the
suds.

She laughed as she spoke, but something in her face
made Christie suspect that at some period of his life
Lisha had done " wuss; " and subsequent observations
confirmed this suspicion and another one also, — that
his good wife had saved him, and was gently easing
him back to self-control and self-respect. But, as old
Fuller quaintly says, " She so gently folded up his
faults in silence that few guessed them," and loyally
paid him that respect which she desired others to
bestow. It was always " Lisha and me," " I 'll ask my

husband " or " Lisha 'll know ; he don't say much, but he 's a dreadful smart man," and she kept up the fiction so dear to her wifely soul by endowing him with her own virtues, and giving him the credit of her own intelligence.

Christie loved her all the better for this devotion, and for her sake treated Mr. Wilkins as if he possessed the strength of Samson and the wisdom of Solomon. He received her respect as if it was his due, and now and then graciously accorded her a few words beyond the usual scanty allowance of morning and evening greetings. At his shop all day, she only saw him at meals and sometimes of an evening, for Mrs. Wilkins tried to keep him at home safe from temptation, and Christie helped her by reading, talking, and frolicking with the children, so that he might find home attractive. He loved his babies and would even relinquish his precious pipe for a time to ride the little chaps on his foot, or amuse Vic with shadow rabbits on the wall.

At such times the entire content in Mrs. Wilkins's face made tobacco fumes endurable, and the burden of a dull man's presence less oppressive to Christie, who loved to pay her debts in something besides money.

As they sat together finishing off some delicate laces that Saturday afternoon, Mrs. Wilkins said, "Ef it 's fair to-morrow I want you to go to my meetin' and hear my minister. It 'll do you good."

" Who is he ? "

" Mr. Power."

Christie looked rather startled, for she had heard of Thomas Power as a rampant radical and infidel of the deepest dye, and been warned never to visit that den of iniquity called his free church.

"Why, Mrs. Wilkins, you don't mean it!" she said, leaving her lace to dry at the most critical stage.

"Yes, I do!" answered Mrs. Wilkins, setting down her flat-iron with emphasis, and evidently preparing to fight valiantly for her minister, as most women will.

"I beg your pardon; I was a little surprised, for I'd heard all sorts of things about him," Christie hastened to say.

"Did you ever hear *him*, or read any of his writins?" demanded Mrs. Wilkins, with a calmer air.

"Never."

"Then don't judge. You go hear and see that blessed man, and ef you don't say he's the shadder of a great rock in a desert land, I'll give up," cried the good woman, waxing poetical in her warmth.

"I will to please you, if nothing else. I did go once just because I was told not to; but he did not preach that day and every thing was so peculiar, I didn't know whether to like it or be shocked."

"It is kind of sing'lar at fust, I'm free to confess, and not as churchy as some folks like. But there ain't no place but that big enough to hold the crowds that want to go, for the more he's abused the more folks flock to see him. They git their money's wuth I do believe, for though there ain't no pulpits and pews, there's a sight of brotherly love round in them seats, and pious practice, as well as powerful preaching, in that shabby desk. *He* don't need no commandments painted up behind him to read on Sunday, for he keeps 'em in his heart and life all the week as honest as man can."

There Mrs. Wilkins paused, flushed and breathless with her defence, and Christie said, candidly : "I did like the freedom and good-will there, for people sat where they liked, and no one frowned over shut pew-doors, at me a stranger.   An old black woman sat next me, and said ' Amen ' when she liked what she heard, and a very shabby young man was on the other, listening as if his soul was as hungry as his body.   People read books, laughed and cried, clapped when pleased, and hissed when angry ; that I did *not* like."

" No more does Mr. Power ; he don't mind the cryin' and the smilin' as it's nat'ral, but noise and disrespect of no kind ain't pleasin' to him.   His own folks behave becomin', but strangers go and act as they like, thinkin' that there ain't no bounds to the word free.   Then we are picked at for their doin's, and Mr. Power has to carry other folkses' sins on his shoulders.   But, dear suz, it ain't much matter after all, ef the souls is well-meanin'.   Children always make a noise a strivin' after what they want most, and I shouldn't wonder ef the Lord forgive all our short-comin's of that sort, sense we are hankerin' and reachin' for the truth."

" I wish I *had* heard Mr. Power that day, for I was striving after peace with all my heart, and he might have given it to me," said Christie, interested and impressed with what she heard.

" Wal, no, dear, I guess not.   Peace ain't give to no one all of a suddin, it gen'lly comes through much tribulation, and the sort that comes hardest is best wuth havin'.   Mr. Power would a' ploughed and harrered you, so to speak, and sowed good seed liberal; then ef you warn't barren ground things would have throve, and the Lord give you a harvest accordin' to your labor. Who did you hear?" asked Mrs. Wilkins, pausing to starch and clap vigorously.

"A very young man who seemed to be airing his ideas and beliefs in the frankest manner. He belabored everybody and every thing, upset church and state, called names, arranged heaven and earth to suit himself, and evidently meant every word he said. Much of it would have been ridiculous if the boy had not been so thoroughly in earnest; sincerity always commands respect, and though people smiled, they liked his courage, and seemed to think he would make a man when his spiritual wild oats were sown."

"I ain't a doubt on 't. We often have such, and they ain't all empty talk, nuther;' some of 'em are surprisingly bright, and all mean so well I don't never reluct to hear 'em. They must blow off their steam somewheres, else they'd bust with the big idees a swellin' in 'em; Mr. Power knows it and gives 'em the chance they can't find nowheres else. 'Pears to me," added Mrs. Wilkins, ironing rapidly as she spoke, "that folks is very like clothes, and a sight has to be done to keep 'em clean and whole. All on us has to lend a hand in this dreadful mixed-up wash, and each do our part, same as you and me is now. There's scrubbin' and bilin', wrenchin' and bluein', dryin' and foldin', ironin' and polishin', before any of us is fit for wear a Sunday mornin'.'"

"What part does Mr. Power do?" asked Christie, much amused at this peculiarly appropriate simile.

"The scrubbin' and the bilin'; that's always the hardest and the hottest part. He starts the dirt and gits the stains out, and leaves 'em ready for other folks to finish off. It ain't such pleasant work as hangin' out, or such pretty work as doin' up, but some one's got to do it, and them that's strongest does it best, though they don't git half so much credit as them as polishes and crimps. That's showy work, but it wouldn't be no use ef the things warn't well washed fust," and Mrs. Wilkins thoughtfully surveyed the snowy muslin cap, with its border fluted like the petals of a prim white daisy, that hung on her hand.

"I'd like to be a washerwoman of that sort; but as I'm not one of the strong, I'll be a laundress, and try to make purity as attractive as you do," said Christie, soberly.

"Ah, my dear, it's warm and wearin' work I do assure you, and hard to give satisfaction, try as you may. Crowns of glory ain't wore in this world, but it's my 'pinion that them that does the hard jobs here will stand a good chance of havin' extra bright ones when they git through."

"I know *you* will," said Christie, warmly.

"Land alive, child! I warn't thinking of Cynthy Wilkins, but Mr. Power. I'll be satisfied ef I can set low down somewheres and see him git the meddle. He won't in this world, but I know there's rewards savin' up for him byme-by."

"I'll go to-morrow if it pours!" said Christie, with decision.

"Do, and I'll lend you my bunnit," cried Mrs. Wilkins, passing, with comical rapidity, from crowns of glory to her own cherished head-gear.

" Thank you, but I can't wear blue, I look as yellow as a dandelion in it. Mrs. Flint let me have my best things though I offered to leave them, so I shall be respectable and by-and-by blossom out."

On the morrow Christie went early, got a good seat, and for half an hour watched the gathering of the motley congregation that filled the great hall. Some came in timidly, as if doubtful of their welcome ; some noisily, as if, as Mrs. Wilkins said, they had not learned the wide difference between liberty and license ; many as if eager and curious ; and a large number with the look of children gathering round a family table ready to be fed, and sure that wholesome food would be bountifully provided for them.

Christie was struck by the large proportion of young people in the place, of all classes, both sexes, and strongly contrasting faces. Delicate girls looking with the sweet wistfulness of maidenly hearts for something strong to lean upon and love ; sad-eyed women turning to heaven for the consolations or the satisfactions earth could not give them ; anxious mothers perplexed with many cares, trying to find light and strength ; young men with ardent faces, restless, aspiring, and impetuous, longing to do and dare ; tired-looking students, with perplexed wrinkles on their foreheads, evidently come to see if this man had discovered the great secrets they were delving after ; and soul-sick people trying this new, and perhaps dangerous medicine, when others failed to cure. Many earnest, thoughtful men and women were there, some on the anxious seat, and some already at peace, having found the clew that leads safely through the labyrinth of life. Here and there a white head, a placid old face, or one of those fine countenances that tell, unconsciously, the beautiful story of a victorious soul.

Some read, some talked, some had flowers in their hands, and all sat at ease, rich and poor, black and white, young and old, waiting for the coming of the man who had power to attract and hold so many of his kind. Christie was so intent on watching those about her that she did not see him enter, and only knew it by the silence which began just in front of her, and seemed to flow backward like a wave, leaving a sea of expectant faces turning to one point. That point was a gray head, just visible above the little desk which stood in the middle of a great platform. A vase of lovely flowers was on the little shelf at one side, a great Bible reposed on the other, and a manuscript lay on the red slope between.

In a moment Christie forgot every thing else, and waited with a curious anxiety to see what manner of man this was. Presently he got up with an open book in his hand, saying, in a strong, cheerful voice: "Let us sing," and having read a hymn as if he had composed it, he sat down again.

Then everybody did sing; not harmoniously, but heartily, led by an organ, which the voices followed at their own sweet will. At first, Christie wanted to smile, for some shouted and some hummed, some sat silent, and others sung sweetly; but before the hymn ended she liked it, and thought that the natural praise of each individual soul was perhaps more grateful to the ear of God than masses by great masters, or psalms warbled tunefully by hired opera singers.

Then Mr. Power rose again, and laying his hands together, with a peculiarly soft and reverent gesture, lifted up his face and prayed. Christie had never heard a prayer like that before; so devout, so comprehensive, and so brief. A quiet talk with God, asking nothing but more love and duty toward Him and our fellow-men; thanking Him for many mercies, and confiding all things trustfully to the " dear father and mother of souls."

The sermon which followed was as peculiar as the prayer, and as effective. " One of Power's judgment-day sermons," as she heard one man say to another, when it was over. Christie certainly felt at first as if kingdoms and thrones were going down, and each man being sent to his own place. A powerful and popular wrong was arrested, tried, and sentenced then and there, with a courage and fidelity that made plain words eloquent, and stern justice beautiful. He did not take David of old for his text, but the strong, sinful, splendid Davids of our day, who had not fulfilled the promise of their youth, and whose seeming success was a delusion and a snare to themselves and others, sure to be followed by sorrowful abandonment, defeat, and shame. The ashes of the ancient hypocrites and Pharisees was left in peace, but those now living were heartily denounced; modern money-changers scourged out of the temple, and the everlasting truth set up therein.

As he spoke, not loudly nor vehemently, but with the indescribable effect of inward force and true inspiration, a curious stir went through the crowd at times, as a great wind sweeps over a corn field, lifting the broad leaves to the light and testing the strength of root and stem. People looked at one another with a roused expression; eyes kindled, heads nodded involuntary approval, and an emphatic, " that's so!" dropped from the lips of men who saw their own vague instincts and silent opinions strongly confirmed and nobly uttered. Consciences seemed to have been pricked to duty, eyes cleared to see that their golden idols had feet of clay, and wavering wills strengthened by the salutary courage and integrity of one indomitable man.

Another hymn, and a benediction that seemed like a fit grace after meat, and then the crowd poured out; not yawning, thinking of best clothes, or longing for dinner, but waked up, full of talk, and eager to do something to redeem the country and the world.

Christie went rapidly home because she could not help it, and burst in upon Mrs. Wilkins with a face full of enthusiasm, exclaiming, while she cast off her bonnet as if her head had outgrown it since she left:

" It was splendid! I never heard such a sermon before, and I'll never go to church anywhere else."

" I knew it! ain't it fillin'? don't it give you a kind of spiritual h'ist, and make things wuth more somehow?" cried Mrs. Wilkins, gesticulating with the pepper-pot in a way which did not improve the steak she was cooking, and caused great anguish to the noses of her offspring, who were watching the operation.

Quite deaf to the chorus of sneezes which accompanied her words, Christie answered, brushing back her hair, as if to get a better out-look at creation generally:

" Oh, yes, indeed! At first it was rather terrible,

and yet so true I wouldn't change a word of it. But I don't wonder he is misunderstood, belied, and abused. He tells the truth so plainly, and lets in the light so clearly, that hypocrites and sinners must fear and hate him. I think he *was* a little hard and unsparing, sometimes, though I don't know enough to judge the men and measures he condemned. I admire him very much, but I should be afraid of him if I ever saw him nearer."

"No, you wouldn't; not a grain. You hear him preach agin and you'll find him as gentle as a lamb. Strong folks is apt to be ruther ha'sh at times; they can't help it no more than this stove can help scorchin' the vittles when it gits red hot. Dinner's ready, so set right up and tell me all about it," said Mrs. Wilkins, slapping the steak on to the platter, and beginning to deal out fried potatoes all round with absent-minded lavishness.

Christie talked, and the good soul enjoyed that far more than her dinner, for she meant to ask Mr. Power to help her find the right sort of home for the stranger whose unfitness for her present place was every day made more apparent to the mind of her hostess.

"What took you there first?" asked Christie, still wondering at Mrs. Wilkins's choice of a minister.

"The Lord, my dear," answered the good woman, in a tone of calm conviction. "I'd heard of him, and I always have a leanin' towards them that's reviled; so one Sabbath I felt to go, and did. 'That's the gospel for me,' says I, 'my old church ain't big enough now, and I ain't goin' to set and nod there any longer,' and I didn't."

"Hadn't you any doubts about it, any fears of going

wrong or being sorry afterwards?" asked Christie, who believed, as many do, that religion could not be attained without much tribulation of some kind.

"In some things folks is led; I be frequent, and when them leadin's come I don't ask no questions but jest foller, and it always turns out right."

"I wish I could be led."

"You be, my dear, every day of your life only you don't see it. When you are doubtful, set still till the call comes, then git up and walk whichever way it says, and you won't fall. You 've had bread and water long enough, now you want meat and wine a spell; take it, and when it's time for milk and honey some one will fetch 'em ef you keep your table ready. The Lord feeds us right; it's we that quarrel with our vittles."

"I will," said Christie, and began at once to prepare her little board for the solid food of which she had had a taste that day.

That afternoon Mrs. Wilkins took her turn at church-going, saw Mr. Power, told Christie's story in her best style, and ended by saying:

"She's true grit, I do assure you, sir. Willin' to work, but she's seen the hard side of things and got kind of discouraged. Soul and body both wants tinkerin' up, and I don't know anybody who can do the job better 'n you can."

"Very well, I'll come and see her," answered Mr. Power, and Mrs. Wilkins went home well satisfied.

He kept his word, and about the middle of the week came walking in upon them as they were at work.

"Don't let the irons cool," he said, and sitting down

in the kitchen began to talk as comfortably as if in the best parlor ; more so, perhaps, for best parlors are apt to have a depressing effect upon the spirits, while the mere sight of labor is exhilarating to energetic minds.

He greeted Christie kindly, and then addressed himself to Mrs. Wilkins on various charitable matters, for he was a minister at large, and she one of his almoners. Christie could really see him now, for when he preached she forgot the man in the sermon, and thought of him only as a visible conscience.

A sturdy man of fifty, with a keen, brave face, penetrating eyes, and mouth a little grim ; but a voice so resonant and sweet it reminded one of silver trumpets, and stirred and won the hearer with irresistible power. Rough gray hair, and all the features rather rugged, as if the Great Sculptor had blocked out a grand statue, and left the man's own soul to finish it.

Had Christie known that he came to see *her* she would have been ill at ease ; but Mrs. Wilkins had kept her own counsel, so when Mr. Power turned to Christie, saying :

" My friend here tells me you want something to do. Would you like to help a Quaker lady with her housework, just out of town ? "

She answered readily : " Yes, sir, any thing that is honest."

" Not as a servant, exactly, but companion and helper. Mrs. Sterling is a dear old lady, and the place a pleasant little nest. It is good to be there, and I think you 'll say so if you go."

" It sounds pleasant. When shall I go ? "

Mr. Power smiled at her alacrity, but the longing look in her eyes explained it, for he saw at a glance that her place was not here.

"I will write at once and let you know how matters are settled. Then you shall try it, and if it is not what you want, we will find you something else. There's plenty to do, and nothing pleasanter than to put the right pair of hands to the right task. Good-by; come and see me if the spirit moves, and don't let go of Mrs. Wilkins till you lay hold of a better friend, if you can find one."

Then he shook hands cordially, and went walking out again into the wild March weather as if he liked it.

"Were you afraid of him?" asked Mrs. Wilkins.

"I forgot all about it: he looked so kind and friendly. But I shouldn't like to have those piercing eyes of his fixed on me long if I had any secret on my conscience," answered Christie.

"You ain't nothin' to fear. He liked your way of speakin' fust rate, I see that, and you'll be all right now he's took hold."

"Do you know Mrs. Sterling?"

"Only by sight, but she's a sweet appearin' woman, and I wouldn't ask nothin' better'n to see more of her," said Mrs. Wilkins, warmly, fearing Christie's heart might misgive her.

But it did not, and when a note came saying Mrs. Sterling would be ready for her the next week, she seemed quite content with every thing, for though the wages were not high she felt that country air and quiet were worth more to her just then than money, and that Wilkinses were better taken homœopathically.

The spirit did move her to go and see Mr. Power, but she could not make up her mind to pass that invisible barrier which stands between so many who could give one another genuine help if they only dared to ask it. But when Sunday came she went to church, eager for more, and thankful that she knew where to go for it.

This was a very different sermon from the other, and Christie felt as if he preached it for her alone. "Keep innocency and take heed to the thing that is right, for this will bring a man peace at the last," might have been the text, and Mr. Power treated it as if he had known all the trials and temptations that made it hard to live up to.

Justice and righteous wrath possessed him before, now mercy and tenderest sympathy for those who faltered in well-doing, and the stern judge seemed changed to a pitiful father. But better than the pity was the wise counsel, the cheering words, and the devout surrender of the soul to its best instincts; its close communion with its Maker, unchilled by fear, untrammelled by the narrowness of sect or superstition, but full and free and natural as the breath of life.

As she listened Christie felt as if she was climbing up from a solitary valley, through mist and shadow toward a mountain top, where, though the way might be rough and strong winds blow, she would get a wider outlook over the broad earth, and be nearer the serene blue sky. For the first time in her life religion seemed a visible and vital thing; a power that she could grasp and feel, take into her life and make her daily bread.

Not a vague, vast idea floating before her, now beautiful, now terrible, always undefined and far away.

She was strangely and powerfully moved that day, for the ploughing had begun; and when the rest stood up for the last hymn, Christie could only bow her head and let the uncontrollable tears flow down like summer rain, while her heart sang with new aspiration:

> "Nearer, my God, to thee,
> E'en though a cross it be
> That raiseth me,
> Still all my song shall be,
> Nearer, my God, to thee.
> Nearer to thee!"

Sitting with her hand before her eyes, she never stirred till the sound of many feet told her that service was done. Then she wiped her eyes, dropped her veil, and was about to rise when she saw a little bunch of flowers between the leaves of the hymn book lying open in her lap. Only a knot of violets set in their own broad leaves, but blue as friendly eyes looking into hers, and sweet as kind words whispered in her ear. She looked about her hoping to detect and thank the giver; but all faces were turned the other way, and all feet departing rapidly.

Christie followed with a very grateful thought in her heart for this little kindness from some unknown friend; and, anxious to recover herself entirely before she faced Mrs. Wilkins, she took a turn in the park.

The snow was gone, high winds had dried the walk, and a clear sky overhead made one forget sodden turf and chilly air. March was going out like a lamb, and Christie enjoyed an occasional vernal whiff from far-off fields and wakening woods, as she walked down the broad mall watching the buds on the boughs, and listening to the twitter of the sparrows, evidently discussing the passers-by as they sat at the doors of their little mansions.

Presently she turned to walk back again and saw Mr. Power coming toward her. She was glad, for all her fear had vanished now, and she wanted to thank him for the sermon that had moved her so deeply. He shook hands in his cordial way, and, turning, walked with her, beginning at once to talk of her affairs as if interested in them.

" Are you ready for the new experiment? " he asked.

" Quite ready, sir; very glad to go, and very much obliged to you for your kindness in providing for me."

" That is what we were put into the world for, to help one another. You can pass on the kindness 'by serving my good friends who, in return, will do their best for you."

" That 's so pleasant! I always knew there were plenty of good, friendly people in the world, only I did not seem to find them often, or be able to keep them long when I did. Is Mr. Sterling an agreeable old man? "

" Very agreeable, but not old. David is about thirty-one or two, I think. He is the son of my friend, the husband died some years ago. I thought I mentioned it."

" You said in your note that Mr. Sterling was a florist, and might like me to help in the green-house, if I was willing. It must be lovely work, and I *should* like it very much."

"Yes, David devotes himself to his flowers, and leads a very quiet life. You may think him rather grave and blunt at first, but you 'll soon find him out and get on comfortably, for he is a truly excellent fellow, and my right-hand man in good works."

A curious little change had passed over Christie's face during these last questions and answers, unconscious, but quite observable to keen eyes like Mr. Power's. Surprise and interest appeared first, then a shadow of reserve as if the young woman dropped a thin veil between herself and the young man, and at the last words a half smile and a slight raising of the brows seemed to express the queer mixture of pity and indifference with which we are all apt to regard "excellent fellows" and "amiable girls." Mr. Power understood the look, and went on more confidentially than he had at first intended, for he did not want Christie to go off with a prejudice in her mind which might do both David and herself injustice.

"People sometimes misjudge him, for he is rather old-fashioned in manner and plain in speech, and may seem unsocial, because he does not seek society. But those who know the cause of this forgive any little short-comings for the sake of the genuine goodness of the man. David had a great trouble some years ago and suffered much. He is learning to bear it bravely, and is the better for it, though the memory of it is still bitter, and the cross hard to bear even with pride to help him hide it, and principle to keep him from despair."

Mr. Power glanced at Christie as he paused, and was satisfied with the effect of his words, for interest, pity, and respect shone in her face, and proved that he had touched the right string. She seemed to feel that this little confidence was given for a purpose, and showed that she accepted it as a sort of gage for her own fidelity to her new employers.

"Thank you, sir, I shall remember," she said, with her frank eyes lifted gravely to his own. "I like to work for people whom I can respect," she added, "and will bear with any peculiarities of Mr. Sterling's without a thought of complaint. When a man has suffered through one woman, all women should be kind and patient with him, and try to atone for the wrong which lessens his respect and faith in them."

"There you are right; and in this case all women *should* be kind, for David pities and protects womankind as the only retaliation for the life-long grief one woman brought upon him. That's not a common revenge, is it?"

"It's beautiful!" cried Christie, and instantly David was a hero.

"At one time it was an even chance whether that trouble sent David to 'the devil,' as he expressed it, or made a man of him. That little saint of a mother kept him safe till the first desperation was over, and now he lives for her, as he ought. Not so romantic an ending as a pistol or Byronic scorn for the world in general and women in particular, but dutiful and brave, since it often takes more courage to live than to die."

"Yes, sir," said Christie, heartily, though her eyes fell, remembering how she had failed with far less cause for despair than David.

They were at the gate now, and Mr. Power left her, saying, with a vigorous hand-shake:

"Best wishes for a happy summer. I shall come sometimes to see how you prosper; and remember, if you tire of it and want to change, let me know, for I take great satisfaction in putting the right people in the right places. Good-by, and God be with you."

CHAPTER X.

BEGINNING AGAIN.

MRS. STERLING.

IT was an April day when Christie went to her new home. Warm rains had melted the last trace of snow, and every bank was full of pricking grass-blades, brave little pioneers and heralds of the Spring. The budding elm boughs swung in the wind; blue-jays screamed among the apple-trees; and robins chirped shrilly, as if rejoicing over winter hardships safely passed. Vernal freshness was in the air despite its chill, and lovely hints of summer time were everywhere.

These welcome sights and sounds met Christie, as she walked down the lane,. and, coming to a gate, paused there to look about her. An old-fashioned cottage stood in the midst of a garden just awakening from its winter sleep. One elm hung protectingly over the low roof, sunshine lay warmly on it, and at every window flowers' bright faces smiled at the passer-by invitingly.

On one side glittered a long green-house, and on the other stood a barn, with a sleek cow ruminating in the yard, and an inquiring horse poking his head out of his stall to view the world. Many comfortable gray hens were clucking and scratching about the hay-strewn floor, and a flock of doves sat cooing on the roof.

A quiet, friendly place it looked; for nothing marred its peace, and the hopeful, healthful spirit of the season seemed to haunt the spot. Snow-drops and crocuses were up in one secluded nook; a plump maltese cat sat purring in the porch; and a dignified old dog came marching down the walk to escort the stranger in. With a brightening face Christie went up the path, and tapped at the quaint knocker, hoping that the face she was about to see would be in keeping with the pleasant place.

She was not disappointed, for the dearest of little Quaker ladies opened to her, with such an air of peace and good-will that the veriest ruffian, coming to molest or make afraid, would have found it impossible to mar the tranquillity of that benign old face, or disturb one fold of the soft muslin crossed upon her breast.

"I come from Mr. Power, and I have a note for Mrs. Sterling," began Christie in her gentlest tone, as her last fear vanished at sight of that mild maternal figure.

" I am she ; come in, friend ; I am glad to see thee," said the old lady, smiling placidly, as she led the way into a room whose principal furniture seemed to be books, flowers, and sunshine.

The look, the tone, the gentle " thee," went straight to Christie's heart ; and, while Mrs. Sterling put on her spectacles and slowly read the note, she stroked the cat and said to herself : " Surely, I have fallen among a set of angels. I thought Mrs. Wilkins a sort of saint, Mr. Power was an improvement even upon that good soul, and if I am not mistaken this sweet little lady is the best and dearest of all. I do hope she will like me."

" It is quite right, my dear, and I am most glad to see thee ; for we need help at this season of the year, and have had none for several weeks. Step up to the room at the head of the stairs, and lay off thy things. Then, if thee is not tired, I will give thee a little job with me in the kitchen," said the old lady with a kindly directness which left no room for awkwardness on the new-comer's part.

Up went Christie, and after a hasty look round a room as plain and white and still as a nun's cell, she whisked on a working-apron and ran down again, feeling, as she fancied the children did in the fairy tale, when they first arrived at the house of the little old woman who lived in the wood.

Mrs. Wilkins's kitchen was as neat as a room could be, wherein six children came and went, but this kitchen was tidy with the immaculate order of which Shakers and Quakers alone seem to possess the secret, —

a fragrant, shining cleanliness, that made even black
kettles ornamental and dish-pans objects of interest.
Nothing burned or boiled over, though the stove was
full of dinner-pots and skillets. There was no litter or
hurry, though the baking of cake and pies was going
on, and when Mrs. Sterling put a pan of apples, and a
knife into her new assistant's hands, saying in a tone
that made the request a favor, "Will thee kindly pare
these for me?" Christie wondered what would happen
if she dropped a seed upon the floor, or did not cut the
apples into four exact quarters.

"I never shall suit this dear prim soul," she thought,
as her eye went from Puss, sedately perched on one
small mat, to the dog dozing upon another, and neither
offering to stir from their own dominions.

This dainty nicety amused her at first, but she liked
it, and very soon her thoughts went back to the old
times when she worked with Aunt Betsey, and learned
the good old-fashioned arts which now were to prove
her fitness for this pleasant place.

Mrs. Sterling saw the shadow that crept into Christie's face, and led the chat to cheerful things, not saying
much herself, but beguiling the other to talk, and listening with an interest that made it easy to go on.

Mr. Power and the Wilkinses made them friends
very soon; and in an hour or two Christie was moving
about the kitchen as if she had already taken possession of her new kingdom.

"Thee likes housework I think," said Mrs. Sterling,
as she watched her hang up a towel to dry, and rinse
her dish-cloth when the cleaning up was done.

"Oh, yes! if I need not do it with a shiftless Irish girl

to drive me distracted by pretending to help. I have lived out, and did not find it hard while I had my good Hepsey. I was second girl, and can set a table in style. Shall I try now?" she asked, as the old lady went into a little dining-room with fresh napkins in her hand.

"Yes, but we have no style here. I will show thee once, and hereafter it will be thy work, as thy feet are younger than mine."

A nice old-fashioned table was soon spread, and Christie kept smiling at the contrast between this and Mrs. Stuart's. Chubby little pitchers appeared, delicate old glass, queer china, and tiny tea-spoons; linen as smooth as satin, and a quaint tankard that might have come over in the "May-flower."

"Now, will thee take that pitcher of water to David's room? It is at the top of the house, and may need a little dusting. I have not been able to attend to it as I would like since I have been alone," said Mrs. Sterling.

Rooms usually betray something of the character and tastes of their occupants, and Christie paused a moment as she entered David's, to look about her with feminine interest.

It was the attic, and extended the whole length of the house. One end was curtained off as a bedroom, and she smiled at its austere simplicity.

A gable in the middle made a sunny recess, where were stored bags and boxes of seed, bunches of herbs, and shelves full of those tiny pots in which baby plants are born and nursed till they can grow alone.

The west end was evidently the study, and here Christie took a good look as she dusted tidily. The furniture was nothing, only an old sofa, with the horse-hair sticking out in tufts here and there; an antique secretary; and a table covered with books. As she whisked the duster down the front of the ancient piece of furniture, one of the doors in the upper half swung open, and Christie saw three objects that irresistibly riveted her eyes for a moment. A broken fan, a bundle of letters tied up with a black ribbon, and a little work-basket in which lay a fanciful needle-book with "Letty" embroidered on it in faded silk.

"Poor David, that is his little shrine, and I have no right to see it," thought Christie, shutting the door with self-reproachful haste.

At the table she paused again, for books always attracted her, and here she saw a goodly array whose names were like the faces of old friends, because she remembered them in her father's library.

Faust was full of ferns, Shakspeare, of rough sketches of the men and women whom he has made immortal. Saintly Herbert lay side by side with Saint Augustine's confessions. Milton and Montaigne stood socially together, and Andersen's lovely "Märchen" fluttered its pictured leaves in the middle of an open Plato; while several books in unknown tongues were half-hidden by volumes of Browning, Keats, and Coleridge.

In the middle of this fine society, slender and transparent as the spirit of a shape, stood a little vase holding one half-opened rose, fresh and fragrant as if just gathered.

Christie smiled as she saw it, and wondered if the dear, dead, or false woman had been fond of roses.

Then her eye went to the mantel-piece, just above

the table, and she laughed; for, on it stood three busts, idols evidently, but very shabby ones; for Göthe's nose was broken, Schiller's head cracked visibly, and the dust of ages seemed to have settled upon Linnæus in the middle. On the wall above them hung a curious old picture of a monk kneeling in a devout ecstasy, while the face of an angel is dimly seen through the radiance that floods the cell with divine light. Portraits of Mr. Power and Martin Luther stared thoughtfully at one another from either side, as if making up their minds to shake hands in spite of time and space.

"Melancholy, learned, and sentimental," said Christie to herself, as she settled David's character after these discoveries.

The sound of a bell made her hasten down, more curious than ever to see if this belief was true.

"Perhaps thee had better step out and call my son. Sometimes he does not hear the bell when he is busy. Thee will find my garden-hood and shawl behind the door," said Mrs. Sterling, presently; for punctuality was a great virtue in the old lady's eyes.

Christie demurely tied on the little pumpkin-hood, wrapped the gray shawl about her, and set out to find her "master," as she had a fancy to call this unknown David.

From the hints dropped by Mr. Power, and her late discoveries, she had made a hero for herself; a sort of melancholy Jaques; sad and pale and stern; retired from the world to nurse his wounds in solitude. She rather liked this picture; for romance dies hard in a woman, and, spite of her experiences, Christie still indulged in dreams and fancies. "It will be so interesting to see how he bears his secret sorrow. I am fond of woe; but I do hope he won't be too lackadaisical, for I never could abide that sort of blighted being."

Thinking thus, she peeped here and there, but saw no one in yard or barn, except a workman scraping the mould off his boots near the conservatory.

"This David is among the flowers, I fancy; I will just ask, and not bolt in, as he does not know me. "Where is Mr. Sterling?" added Christie aloud, as she approached.

The man looked up, and a smile came into his eyes, as he glanced from the old hood to the young face inside. Then he took off his hat, and held out his hand, saying with just his mother's simple directness:

"I am David; and this is Christie Devon, I know. How do you do?"

"Yes; dinner's ready," was all she could reply, for the discovery that this was the "master," nearly took her breath away. Not the faintest trace of the melancholy Jaques about him; nothing interesting, romantic, pensive, or even stern. Only a broad-shouldered, brown-bearded man, with an old hat and coat, trousers tucked into his boots, fresh mould on the hand he had given her to shake, and the cheeriest voice she had ever heard.

What a blow it was to be sure! Christie actually felt vexed with him for disappointing her so, and could not recover herself, but stood red and awkward, till, with a last scrape of his boots, David said with placid brevity:

"Well, shall we go in?"

Christie walked rapidly into the house, and by the

time she got there the absurdity of her fancy struck her, and she stifled a laugh in the depths of the little pumpkin-hood, as she hung it up. Then, assuming her gravest air, she went to give the finishing touches to dinner.

Ten minutes later she received another surprise; for David appeared washed, brushed, and in a suit of gray, — a personable gentleman, quite unlike the workman in the yard.

Christie gave one look, met a pair of keen yet kind eyes with a suppressed laugh in them, and dropped her own, to be no more lifted up till dinner was done.

It was a very quiet meal, for no one said much; and it was evidently the custom of the house to eat silently, only now and then saying a few friendly words, to show that the hearts were social if the tongues were not.

On the present occasion this suited Christie; and she ate her dinner without making any more discoveries, except that the earth-stained hands were very clean now, and skilfully supplied her wants before she could make them known.

As they rose from table, Mrs. Sterling said: "Davy, does thee want any help this afternoon?"

"I shall be very glad of some in about an hour if thee can spare it, mother."

"I can, dear."

"Do you care for flowers?" asked David, turning to Christie, "because if you do not, this will be a very trying place for you."

"I used to love them dearly; but I have not had any for so long I hardly remember how they look," answered Christie with a sigh, as she recalled Rachel's roses, dead long ago. "Shy, sick, and sad; poor soul, we must lend a hand and cheer her up a bit" thought David, as he watched her eyes turn toward the green things in the windows with a bright, soft look, he liked to see.

"Come to the conservatory in an hour, and I'll show you the best part of a 'German,'" he said, with a nod and a smile, as he went away, beginning to whistle like a boy when the door was shut behind him.

"What did he mean?" thought Christie, as she helped clear the table, and put every thing in Pimlico order.

She was curious to know, and when Mrs. Sterling said: "Now, my dear, I am going to take my nap, and thee can help David if thee likes," she was quite ready to try the new work.

She would have been more than woman if she had not first slipped upstairs to smooth her hair, put on a fresh collar, and a black silk apron with certain effective frills and pockets, while a scarlet rigolette replaced the hood, and lent a little color to her pale cheeks.

"I am a poor ghost of what I was," she thought; "but that's no matter: few can be pretty, any one can be neat, and that is more than ever necessary here."

Then she went away to the conservatory, feeling rather oppressed with the pity and sympathy, for which there was no call, and fervently wishing that David would not be so comfortable, for he ate a hearty dinner, laughed four times, and whistled as no heart-broken man would dream of doing.

No one was visible as she went in, and walking slowly down the green aisle, she gave herself up to the enjoyment of the lovely place. The damp, sweet air made summer there, and a group of slender, oriental trees whispered in the breath of wind that blew in from an open sash. Strange vines and flowers hung overhead; banks of azaleas, ruddy, white, and purple, bloomed in one place; roses of every hue turned their lovely faces to the sun; ranks of delicate ferns, and heaths with their waxen bells, were close by; glowing geraniums and stately lilies side by side; savage-looking scarlet flowers with purple hearts, or orange spikes rising from leaves mottled with strange colors; dusky passion-flowers, and gay nasturtiums climbing to the roof. All manner of beautiful and curious plants were there; and Christie walked among them, as happy as a child who finds its playmates again.

Coming to a bed of pansies she sat down on a rustic chair, and, leaning forward, feasted her eyes on these her favorites. Her face grew young as she looked, her hands touched them with a lingering tenderness as if to her they were half human, and her own eyes were so busy enjoying the gold and purple spread before her, that she did not see another pair peering at her over an unneighborly old cactus, all prickles, and queer knobs. Presently a voice said at her elbow:

"You look as if you saw something beside pansies there."

David spoke so quietly that it did not startle her, and she answered before she had time to feel ashamed of her fancy.

"I do; for, ever since I was a child, I always see a little face when I look at this flower. Sometimes it is a sad one, sometimes it's merry, often roguish, but al-

ways a dear little face; and when I see so many together, it 's like a flock of children, all nodding and smiling at me at once."

"So it is!" and David nodded, and smiled himself,
as he handed her two or three of the finest, as if it was
as natural a thing as to put a sprig of mignonette in
his own button-hole.

Christie thanked him, and then jumped up, remembering that she came there to work, not to dream. He
seemed to understand, and went into a little room near
by, saying, as he pointed to a heap of gay flowers on
the table :

"These are to be made into little bouquets for a
'German' to-night. It is pretty work, and better fitted
for a woman's fingers than a man's. This is all you
have to do, and you can use your taste as to colors."

While he spoke David laid a red and white carnation on a bit of smilax, tied them together, twisted a
morsel of silver foil about the stems, and laid it before
Christie as a sample.

"Yes, I can do that, and shall like it very much," she
said, burying her nose in the mass of sweetness before
her, and feeling as if her new situation grew pleasanter
every minute.

"Here is the apron my mother uses, that bit of silk
will soon be spoilt, for the flowers are wet," and David
gravely offered her a large checked pinafore.

Christie could not help laughing as she put it on :
all this was so different from the imaginary picture she
had made. She was disappointed, and yet she began
to feel as if the simple truth was better than the sentimental fiction ; and glanced up at David involuntarily

to see if there were any traces of interesting woe about him.

But he was looking at her with the steady, straightforward look which she liked so much, yet could not meet just yet; and all she saw was that he was smiling also with an indulgent expression as if she was a little girl whom he was trying to amuse.

" Make a few, and I 'll be back directly when I have attended to another order," and he went away thinking Christie's face was very like the pansies they had been talking about, — one of the sombre ones with a bright touch of gold deep down in the heart, for thin and pale as the face was, it lighted up at a kind word, and all the sadness vanished out of the anxious eyes when the frank laugh came.

Christie fell to work with a woman's interest in such a pleasant task, and soon tied and twisted skilfully, exercising all her taste in contrasts, and the pretty little conceits flower-lovers can produce. She was so interested that presently she began to hum half unconsciously, as she was apt to do when happily employed :

> " Welcome, maids of honor,
>> You do bring
>> In the spring,
> And wait upon her.
> She has virgins many,
>> Fresh and fair,
>> Yet you are
> More sweet than any."

There she stopped, for David's step drew near, and she remembered where she was.

" The last verse is the best in that little poem. Have

you forgotten it?" he said, pleased and surprised to find the new-comer singing Herrick's lines "To Violets."

"Almost; my father used to say that when we went looking for early violets, and these lovely ones reminded me of it," explained Christie, rather abashed.

DAVID AND CHRISTIE IN THE GREENHOUSE.

As if to put her at ease David added, as he laid another handful of double-violets on the table:

> " ' Y' are the maiden posies,
>   And so graced,
>   To be placed
>   Fore damask roses.
>   Yet, though thus respected,
>   By and by
>   Ye do lie,
>   Poor girls, neglected.'

"I always think of them as pretty, modest maids after that, and can't bear to throw them away, even when faded."

Christie hoped he did not think her sentimental, and changed the conversation by pointing to her work, and saying, in a business-like way:

"Will these do? I have varied the posies as much as possible, so that they may suit all sorts of tastes and whims. I never went to a 'German' myself; but I have looked on, and remember hearing the young people say the little bouquets didn't mean any thing, so I tried to make these expressive."

"Well, I should think you had succeeded excellently, and it is a very pretty fancy. Tell me what some of them mean: will you?"

"You should know better than I, being a florist," said Christie, glad to see he approved of her work.

"I can grow the flowers, but not read them," and David looked rather depressed by his own ignorance of those delicate matters.

Still with the business-like air, Christie held up one

after another of the little knots, saying soberly, though her eyes smiled:

"This white one might be given to a newly engaged girl, as suggestive of the coming bridal. That half-blown bud would say a great deal from a lover to his idol; and this heliotrope be most encouraging to a timid swain. Here is a rosy daisy for some merry little damsel; there is a scarlet posy for a soldier; this delicate azalea and fern for some lovely creature just out; and there is a bunch of sober pansies for a spinster, if spinsters go to 'Germans.' Heath, scentless but pretty, would do for many; these Parma violets for one with a sorrow; and this curious purple flower with arrow-shaped stamens would just suit a handsome, sharp-tongued woman, if any partner dared give it to her."

David laughed, as his eye went from the flowers to Christie's face, and when she laid down the last breast-knot, looking as if she would like the chance of presenting it to some one she knew, he seemed much amused.

"If the beaux and belles at this party have the wit to read your posies, my fortune will be made, and you will have your hands full supplying compliments, declarations, rebukes, and criticisms for the fashionable butterflies. I wish I could put consolation, hope, and submission into *my* work as easily, but I am afraid I can't," he added a moment afterward with a changed face, as he began to lay the loveliest white flowers into a box.

"Those are not for a wedding, then?"

"For a dead baby; and I can't seem to find any white and sweet enough."

"You know the people?" asked Christie, with the sympathetic tone in her voice.

"Never saw or heard of them till to-day. Isn't it enough to know that 'baby's dead,' as the poor man said, to make one feel for them?"

"Of course it is; only you seemed so interested in arranging the flowers, I naturally thought it was for some friend," Christie answered hastily, for David looked half indignant at her question.

"I want them to look lovely and comforting when the mother opens the box, and I don't seem to have the right flowers. Will you give it a touch? women have a tender way of doing such things that we can never learn."

"I don't think I can improve it, unless I add another sort of flower that seems appropriate: may I?"

"Any thing you can find."

Christie waited for no more, but ran out of the greenhouse to David's great surprise, and presently came hurrying back with a handful of snow-drops.

"Those are just what I wanted, but I didn't know the little dears were up yet! You shall put them in, and I know they will suggest what you hope to these poor people," he said approvingly, as he placed the box before her, and stood by watching her adjust the little sheaf of pale flowers tied up with a blade of grass. She added a frail fern or two, and did give just the graceful touch here and there which would speak to the mother's sore heart of the tender thought some one had taken for her dead darling.

The box was sent away, and Christie went on with her work, but that little task performed together seemed to have made them friends; and, while David tied up several grand bouquets at the same table, they talked as if the strangeness was fast melting away from their short acquaintance.

Christie's own manners were so simple that simplicity in others always put her at her ease: kindness soon banished her reserve, and the desire to show that she was grateful for it helped her to please. David's bluntness was of such a gentle sort that she soon got used to it, and found it a pleasant contrast to the polite insincerity so common. He was as frank and friendly as a boy, yet had a certain paternal way with him which rather annoyed her at first, and made her feel as if he thought her a mere girl, while she was very sure he could not be but a year or two older than herself.

"I'd rather he'd be masterful, and order me about," she thought, still rather regretting the "blighted being" she had not found.

In spite of this she spent a pleasant afternoon, sitting in that sunny place, handling flowers, asking questions about them, and getting the sort of answers she liked; not dry botanical names and facts, but all the delicate traits, curious habits, and poetical romances of the sweet things, as if the speaker knew and loved them as friends, not merely valued them as merchandise.

They had just finished when the great dog came bouncing in with a basket in his mouth.

"Mother wants eggs: will you come to the barn and get them? Hay is wholesome, and you can feed the doves if you like," said David, leading the way with Bran rioting about him.

"Why don't he offer to put up a swing for me, or get me a doll? It's the pinafore that deceives him. Never mind: I rather like it after all," thought Christie;

but she left the apron behind her, and followed with the most dignified air.

It did not last long, however, for the sights and sounds that greeted her, carried her back to the days of egg-hunting in Uncle Enos's big barn; and, before she knew it, she was rustling through the hay mows, talking to the cow and receiving the attentions of Bran with a satisfaction it was impossible to conceal.

The hens gathered about her feet cocking their expectant eyes at her; the doves came circling round her head; the cow stared placidly, and the inquisitive horse responded affably when she offered him a handful of hay.

"How tame they all are! I like animals, they are so contented and intelligent," she said, as a plump dove lit on her shoulder with an impatient coo.

"That was Kitty's pet, she always fed the fowls. Would you like to do it?" and David offered a little measure of oats.

"Very much;" and Christie began to scatter the grain, wondering who "Kitty" was.

As if he saw the wish in her face, David added, while he shelled corn for the hens:

"She was the little girl who was with us last. Her father kept her in a factory, and took all her wages, barely giving her clothes and food enough to keep her alive. The poor child ran away, and was trying to hide when Mr. Power found and sent her here to be cared for."

"As he did me?" said Christie quickly.

"Yes, that's a way he has."

"A very kind and Christian way. Why didn't she stay?"

"Well, it was rather quiet for the lively little thing, and rather too near the city, so we got a good place up in the country where she could go to school and learn housework. The mill had left her no time for these things, and at fifteen she was as ignorant as a child."

"You must miss her."

"I do very much."

"Was she pretty?"

"She looked like a little rose sometimes," and David smiled to himself as he fed the gray hens.

Christie immediately made a picture of the "lively little thing" with a face "like a rose," and was uncomfortably conscious that she did not look half as well feeding doves as Kitty must have done.

Just then David handed her the basket, saying in the paternal way that half amused, half piqued her: "It is getting too chilly for you here: take these in please, and I'll bring the milk directly."

In spite of herself she smiled, as a sudden vision of the elegant Mr. Fletcher, devotedly carrying her book or beach-basket, passed through her mind; then hastened to explain the smile, for David lifted his brows inquiringly, and glanced about him to see what amused her.

"I beg your pardon: I've lived alone so much that it seems a little odd to be told to do things, even if they are as easy and pleasant as this."

"I am so used to taking care of people, and directing, that I do so without thinking. I won't if you don't like it," and he put out his hand to take back the basket with a grave, apologetic air.

"But I do like it; only it amused me to be treated like a little girl again, when I am nearly thirty, and feel seventy at least, life has been so hard to me lately."

Her face sobered at the last words, and David's instantly grew so pitiful she could not keep her eyes on it lest they should fill, so suddenly did the memory of past troubles overcome her.

" I know," he said in a tone that warmed her heart, " I know, but we are going to try, and make life easier for you now, and you must feel that this is home and we are friends."

" I do! " and Christie flushed with grateful feeling and a little shame, as she went in, thinking to herself: " How silly I was to say that! I may have spoilt the simple friendliness that was so pleasant, and have made him think me a foolish stuck-up old creature."

Whatever he might have thought, David's manner was unchanged when he came in and found her busy with the table.

" It 's pleasant to see thee resting, mother, and every thing going on so well," he said, glancing about the room, where the old lady sat, and nodding toward the kitchen, where Christie was toasting bread in her neatest manner.

" Yes, Davy, it was about time I had a helper for thy sake, at least; and this is a great improvement upon heedless Kitty, I am inclined to think."

Mrs. Sterling dropped her voice over that last sentence; but Christie heard it, and was pleased. A moment or two later, David came toward her with a glass in his hand, saying as if rather doubtful of his reception:

" New milk is part of the cure: will you try it? "

For the first time, Christie looked straight up in the honest eyes that seemed to demand honesty in others, and took the glass, answering heartily:

"Yes, thank you; I drink good health to you, and better manners to me."

The newly lighted lamp shone full in her face, and though it was neither young nor blooming, it showed something better than youth and bloom to one who could read the subtle language of character as David could. He nodded as he took the glass, and went away saying quietly:

"We are plain people here, and you won't find it hard to get on with us, I think."

But he liked the candid look, and thought about it, as he chopped kindlings, whistling with a vigor which caused Christie to smile as she strained the milk.

After tea a spider-legged table was drawn out toward the hearth, where an open fire burned cheerily, and puss purred on the rug, with Bran near by. David unfolded his newspapers, Mrs. Sterling pinned on her knitting-sheath, and Christie sat a moment enjoying the comfortable little scene. She sighed without knowing it, and Mrs. Sterling asked quickly:

"Is thee tired, my dear?"

"Oh, no! only happy."

"I am glad of that: I was afraid thee would find it dull."

"It's beautiful!" then Christie checked herself, feeling that these outbursts would not suit such quiet people; and, half ashamed of showing how much she felt, she added soberly, "If you will give me something to do I shall be quite contented."

" Sewing is not good for thee. If thee likes to knit I'll set up a sock for thee to-morrow," said the old lady well pleased at the industrious turn of her new handmaid.

" I like to darn, and I see some to be done in this basket. May I do it?" and Christie laid hold of the weekly job which even the best housewives are apt to set aside for pleasanter tasks.

" As thee likes, my dear. My eyes will not let me sew much in the evening, else I should have finished that batch to-night. Thee will find the yarn and needles in the little bag."

So Christie fell to work on gray socks, and neat lavender-colored hose, while the old lady knit swiftly, and David read aloud. Christie thought she was listening to the report of a fine lecture; but her ear only caught the words, for her mind wandered away into a region of its own, and lived there till her task was done. Then she laid the tidy pile in the basket, drew her chair to a corner of the hearth, and quietly enjoyed herself.

The cat, feeling sure of a welcome, got up into her lap, and went to sleep in a cosy bunch; Bran laid his nose across her feet, and blinked at her with sleepy good-will, while her eyes wandered round the room, from its quaint furniture and the dreaming flowers in the windows, to the faces of its occupants, and lingered there.

The plain border of a Quaker cap encircled that mild old face, with bands of silver hair parted on a forehead marked with many lines. But the eyes were clear and sweet; winter roses bloomed in the cheeks, and an exquisite neatness pervaded the small figure, from the trim feet on the stool, to the soft shawl folded about the shoulders, as only a Quakeress can fold one. In Mrs. Sterling, piety and peace made old age lovely, and the mere presence of this tranquil soul seemed to fill the room with a reposeful charm none could resist.

The other face possessed no striking comeliness of shape or color; but the brown, becoming beard made it manly, and the broad arch of a benevolent brow added nobility to features otherwise not beautiful, — a face plainly expressing resolution and rectitude, inspiring respect .as naturally as a certain protective kindliness of manner won confidence. Even in repose wearing a vigilant look as if some hidden pain or passion lay in wait to surprise and conquer the sober cheerfulness that softened the lines of the firm-set lips, and warmed the glance of the thoughtful eyes.

Christie fancied she possessed the key to this, and longed to know all the story of the cross which Mr. Power said David had learned to bear so well. Then she began to wonder if they could like and keep her, to hope so, and to feel that here at last she was at home with friends. But the old sadness crept over her, as she remembered how often she had thought this before, and how soon the dream ended, the ties were broken, and she adrift again.

"Ah well," she said within herself, "I won't think of the morrow, but take the good that comes and enjoy it while I may. I must not disappoint Rachel, since she kept her word so nobly to me. Dear soul, when shall I see her again?"

The thought of Rachel always touched her heart,

more now than ever; and, as she leaned back in her chair with closed eyes and idle hands, these tender memories made her unconscious face most eloquent. The eyes peering over the spectacles telegraphed a meaning message to the other eyes glancing over the paper now and then; and both these friends in deed as well as name felt assured that this woman needed all the comfort they could give her. But the busy needles never stopped their click, and the sonorous voice read on without a pause, so Christie never knew what mute confidences passed between mother and son, or what helpful confessions her traitorous face had made for her.

The clock struck nine, and these primitive people prepared for rest; for their day began at dawn, and much wholesome work made sleep a luxury.

" Davy will tap at thy door as he goes down in the morning, and I will soon follow to show thee about matters. Good-night, and good rest, my child."

So speaking, the little lady gave Christie a maternal kiss; David shook hands; and then she went away, wondering why service was so lightened by such little kindnesses.

As she lay in her narrow white bed, with the "pale light of stars" filling the quiet, cell-like room, and some one playing softly on a flute overhead, she felt as if she had left the troublous world behind her, and shutting out want, solitude, and despair, had come into some safe, secluded spot full of flowers and sunshine, kind hearts, and charitable deeds.

CHAPTER XI.

FROM that day a new life began for Christie, a happy, quiet, useful life, utterly unlike any of the brilliant futures she had planned for herself; yet indescribably pleasant to her now, for past experience had taught her its worth, and made her ready to enjoy it.

Never had spring seemed so early or so fair, never had such a crop of hopeful thoughts and happy feelings sprung up in her heart as now; and nowhere was there a brighter face, a blither voice, or more willing hands than Christie's when the apple blossoms came.

This was what she needed, the protection of a home, wholesome cares and duties; and, best of all, friends to live and labor for, loving and beloved. Her whole soul was in her work now, and as health returned, much of the old energy and cheerfulness came with it, a little sobered, but more sweet and earnest than ever. No task was too hard or humble; no day long enough to do all she longed to do; and no sacrifice would have seemed too great for those whom she regarded with steadily increasing love and gratitude.

Up at dawn, the dewy freshness of the hour, the

morning rapture of the birds, the daily miracle of sunrise, set her heart in tune, and gave her Nature's most
healing balm. She kept the little house in order, with
Mrs. Sterling to direct and share the labor so pleasantly,
that mistress and maid soon felt like mother and
daughter, and Christie often said she did not care for
any other wages.

The house-work of this small family was soon done,
and then Christie went to tasks that she liked better.
Much out-of-door life was good for her, and in garden
and green-house there was plenty of light labor she
could do. So she grubbed contentedly in the wholesome earth, weeding and potting, learning to prune
and bud, and finding Mrs. Wilkins was quite right in
her opinion of the sanitary virtues of dirt.

Trips to town to see the good woman and carry
country gifts to the little folks; afternoon drives with
Mrs. Sterling in the old-fashioned chaise, drawn by the
Roman-nosed horse, and Sunday pilgrimages to church
to be "righted up" by one of Mr. Power's stirring sermons, were among her new pleasures. But, on the
whole, the evenings were her happiest times: for then
David read aloud while she worked; she sung to the
old piano tuned for her use; or, better still, as spring
came on, they sat in the porch, and talked as people
only do talk when twilight, veiling the outer world,
seems to lift the curtains of that inner world where
minds go exploring, hearts learn to know one another,
and souls walk together in the cool of the day.

At such times Christie seemed to catch glimpses of
another David than the busy, cheerful man apparently contented with the humdrum duties of an ob-

scure, laborious life, and the few unexciting pleasures
afforded by books, music, and much silent thought.
She sometimes felt with a woman's instinct that under
this composed, commonplace existence another life
went on; for, now and then, in the interest of conversation, or the involuntary yielding to a confidential
impulse, a word, a look, a gesture, betrayed an unexpected power and passion, a secret unrest, a bitter
memory that would not be ignored.

Only at rare moments did she catch these glimpses,
and so brief, so indistinct, were they that she half
believed her own lively fancy created them. She longed
to know more; but "David's trouble" made him sacred
in her eyes from any prying curiosity, and always after
one of these twilight betrayals Christie found him so
like his unromantic self next day, that she laughed and
said:

"I never shall outgrow my foolish way of trying to
make people other than they are. Gods are gone,
heroes hard to find, and one should be contented with
good men, even if they do wear old clothes, lead prosaic
lives, and have no accomplishments but gardening,
playing the flute, and keeping their temper."

She felt the influences of that friendly place at once;
but for a time she wondered at the natural way in
which kind things were done, the protective care extended over her, and the confiding air with which these
people treated her. They asked no questions, demanded
no explanations, seemed unconscious of conferring
favors, and took her into their life so readily that she
marvelled, even while she rejoiced, at the good fortune
which led her there.

She understood this better when she discovered, what Mr. Power had not mentioned, that the little cottage was a sort of refuge for many women like herself; a half-way house where they could rest and recover themselves after the wrongs, defeats, and weariness that come to such in the battle of life.

With a chivalry older and finer than any Spenser sung, Mr. Power befriended these forlorn souls, and David was his faithful squire. Whoever knocked at that low door was welcomed, warmed, and fed; comforted, and set on their way, cheered and strengthened by the sweet good-will that made charity no burden, and restored to the more desperate and despairing their faith in human nature and God's love.

There are many such green spots in this world of ours, which often seems so bad that a second Deluge could hardly wash it clean again; and these beneficent, unostentatious asylums are the salvation of more troubled souls than many a great institution gilded all over with the rich bequests of men who find themselves too heavily laden to enter in at the narrow gate of heaven.

Happy the foot-sore, heart-weary traveller who turns from the crowded, dusty highway down the green lane that leads to these humble inns, where the sign of the Good Samaritan is written on the face of whomsoever opens to the stranger, and refreshment for soul and body is freely given in the name of Him who loved the poor.

Mr. Power came now and then, for his large parish left him but little time to visit any but the needy. Christie enjoyed these brief visits heartily, for her new

friends soon felt that she was one of them, and cordially took her into the large circle of workers and
believers to which they belonged.

Mr. Power's heart was truly an orphan asylum, and
every lonely creature found a welcome there. He
could rebuke sin sternly, yet comfort and uplift the
sinner with fatherly compassion; righteous wrath would
flash from his eyes at injustice, and contempt sharpen
his voice as he denounced hypocrisy: yet the eyes
that lightened would dim with pity for a woman's
wrong, a child's small sorrow; and the voice that
thundered would whisper consolation like a mother, or
give counsel with a wisdom books cannot teach.

He was a Moses in his day and generation, born to
lead his people out of the bondage of dead supersti-
tions, and go before them through a Red Sea of persecution into the larger liberty and love all souls hunger
for, and many are just beginning to find as they come
doubting, yet desiring, into the goodly land such pioneers as he have planted in the wilderness.

He was like a tonic to weak natures and wavering
wills; and Christie felt a general revival going on within
herself as her knowledge, honor, and affection for him
grew. His strength seemed to uphold her; his integrity to rebuke all unworthiness in her own life; and the
magic of his generous, genial spirit to make the hard
places smooth, the bitter things sweet, and the world
seem a happier, honester place than she had ever
thought it since her father died.

Mr. Power had been interested in her from the first;
had watched her through other eyes, and tried her by
various unsuspected tests. She stood them well;

showed her faults as frankly as her virtues, and tried to deserve their esteem by copying the excellencies she admired in them.

" She is made of the right stuff, and we must keep her among us; for she must not be lost or wasted by being left to drift about the world with no ties to make her safe and happy. She is doing so well here, let her stay till the restless spirit begins to stir again; then she shall come to me and learn contentment by seeing greater troubles than her own."

Mr. Power said this one day as he rose to go, after sitting an hour with Mrs. Sterling, and hearing from her a good report of his new *protégée.* The young people were out at work, and had not been called in to see him, for the interview had been a confidential one. But as he stood at the gate he saw Christie in the strawberry bed, and went toward her, glad to see how well and happy she looked.

Her hat was hanging on her shoulders, and the sun giving her cheeks a healthy color; she was humming to herself like a bee as her fingers flew, and once she paused, shaded her eyes with her hand, and took a long look at a figure down in the meadow; then she worked on silent and smiling, — a pleasant creature to see, though her hair was ruffled by the wind; her gingham gown pinned up; and her fingers deeply stained with the blood of many berries.

" I wonder if that means any thing? " thought Mr. Power, with a keen glance from the distant man to the busy woman close at hand. " It might be a helpful, happy thing for both, if poor David only could forget."

He had time for no more castle-building, for a startled

robin flew away with a shrill chirp, and Christie looked up.

"Oh, I 'm so glad!" she said, rising quickly. "I was picking a special box for you, and now you can have a feast beside, just as you like it, fresh from the vines. Sit here, please, and I 'll hull faster than you can eat."

"This *is* luxury!" and Mr. Power sat down on the three-legged stool offered him, with a rhubarb leaf on his knee which Christie kept supplying with delicious mouthfuls.

MR. POWER AND CHRISTIE IN THE STRAWBERRY BED.

"Well, and how goes it? Are we still happy and contented here?" he asked.

"I feel as if I had been born again; as if this was a new heaven and a new earth, and every thing was as it should be," answered Christie, with a look of perfect satisfaction in her face.

"That's a pleasant hearing. Mrs. Sterling has been praising you, but I wanted to be sure you were as satisfied as she. And how does David wear? well, I hope."

"Oh, yes, he is very good to me, and is teaching me to be a gardener, so that I needn't kill myself with sewing any more. Much of this is fine work for women, and *so* healthy. Don't I look a different creature from the ghost that came here three or four months ago?" and she turned her face for inspection like a child.

"Yes, David is a good gardener. I often send my sort of plants here, and he always makes them grow and blossom sooner or later," answered Mr. Power, regarding her like a beneficent genie on a three-legged stool.

"You are the fresh air, and Mrs. Sterling is the quiet sunshine that does the work, I fancy. David only digs about the roots."

"Thank you for my share of the compliment; but why say 'only digs'? That is a most important part of the work: I'm afraid you don't appreciate David."

"Oh, yes, I do; but he rather aggravates me sometimes," said Christie, laughing, as she put a particularly big berry in the green plate to atone for her frankness.

"How?" asked Mr. Power, interested in these little revelations.

"Well, he *won't* be ambitious. I try to stir him up,

for he has talents; I've found that out: but he won't seem to care for any thing but watching over his mother, reading his old books, and making flowers bloom double when they ought to be single."

"There are worse ambitions than those, Christie. I know many a man who would be far better employed in cherishing a sweet old woman, studying Plato, and doubling the beauty of a flower, than in selling principles for money, building up a cheap reputation that dies with him, or chasing pleasures that turn to ashes in his mouth."

"Yes, sir; but isn't it natural for a young man to have some personal aim or aspiration to live for? If David was a weak or dull man I could understand it; but I seem to feel a power, a possibility for something higher and better than any thing I see, and this frets me. He is so good, I want him to be great also in some way."

"A wise man says, 'The essence of greatness is the perception that virtue is enough.' *I* think David one of the most ambitious men I ever knew, because at thirty he has discovered this truth, and taken it to heart. Many men can be what the world calls great: very few men are what God calls good. This is the harder task to choose, yet the only success that satisfies, the only honor that outlives death. These faithful lives, whether seen of men or hidden in corners, are the salvation of the world, and few of us fail to acknowledge it in the hours when we are brought close to the heart of things, and see a little as God sees."

Christie did not speak for a moment: Mr. Power's voice had been so grave, and his words so earnest that she could not answer lightly, but sat turning over the new thoughts in her mind. Presently she said, in a penitent but not quite satisfied tone:

"Of course you are right, sir. I'll try not to care for the outward and visible signs of these hidden virtues; but I'm afraid I still shall have a hankering for the worldly honors that are so valued by most people."

"'Success and glory are the children of hard work and God's favor,' according to Æschylus, and you will find he was right. David got a heavy blow some years ago as I told you, I think; and he took it hard, but it did not spoil him: it made a man of him; and, if I am not much mistaken, he will yet do something to be proud of, though the world may never hear of it."

"I hope so!" and Christie's face brightened at the thought.

"Nevertheless you look as if you doubted it, O you of little faith. Every one has two sides to his nature: David has shown you the least interesting one, and you judge accordingly. I think he will show you the other side some day, — for you are one of the women who win confidence without trying, — and then you will know the real David. Don't expect too much, or quarrel with the imperfections that make him human; but take him for what he is worth, and help him if you can to make his life a brave and good one."

"I will, sir," answered Christie so meekly that Mr. Power laughed; for this confessional in the strawberry bed amused him very much.

"You are a hero-worshipper, my dear; and if people don't come up to the mark you are so disappointed that you fail to see the fine reality which remains when the

pretty romance ends. Saints walk about the world to-
day as much as ever, but instead of haircloth and halos
they now wear" —

"Broadcloth and wide-brimmed hats," added Christie, looking up as if she had already found a better
St. Thomas than any the church ever canonized.

He thanked her with a smile, and went on with a
glance toward the meadow.

"And knights go crusading as gallantly as ever
against the giants and the dragons, though you don't
discover it, because, instead of banner, lance, and shield
they carry" —

"Bushel-baskets, spades, and sweet-flag for their
mothers," put in Christie again, as David came up the
path with the loam he had been digging.

Both began to laugh, and he joined in the merriment
without knowing why, as he put down his load, took off
his hat, and shook hands with his honored guest.

"What's the joke?" he asked, refreshing himself
with the handful of berries Christie offered him.

"Don't tell," she whispered, looking dismayed at the
idea of letting him know what she had said of him.

But Mr. Power answered tranquilly:

"We were talking about coins, and Christie was expressing her opinion of one I showed her. The face
and date she understands; but the motto puzzles her,
and she has not seen the reverse side yet, so does
not know its value. She will some day; and then she
will agree with me, I think, that it is *sterling* gold."

The emphasis on the last words enlightened David:
his sunburnt cheek reddened, but he only shook his
head, saying: "She will find a brass farthing I'm afraid,

sir," and began to crumble a handful of loam about the roots of a carnation that seemed to have sprung up by chance at the foot of the apple-tree.

"How did that get there?" asked Christie, with sudden interest in the flower.

"It dropped when I was setting out the others, took root, and looked so pretty and comfortable that I left it. These waifs sometimes do better than the most carefully tended ones: I only dig round them a bit and leave them to sun and air."

Mr. Power looked at Christie with so much meaning in his face that it was her turn to color now. But with feminine perversity she would not own herself mistaken, and answered with eyes as full of meaning as his own:

"I like the single ones best: double-carnations are so untidy, all bursting out of the calyx as if the petals had quarrelled and could not live together."

"The single ones are seldom perfect, and look poor and incomplete with little scent or beauty," said unconscious David propping up the thin-leaved flower, that looked like a pale solitary maiden, beside the great crimson and white carnations near by, filling the air with spicy odor.

"I suspect you will change your mind by and by, Christie, as your taste improves, and you will learn to think the double ones the handsomest," added Mr. Power, wondering in his benevolent heart if he would ever be the gardener to mix the colors of the two human plants before him.

"I must go," and David shouldered his basket as if he felt he might be in the way.

"So must I, or they will be waiting for me at the

hospital. Give me a handful of flowers, David : they often do the poor souls more good than my prayers or preaching."

Then they went away, and left Christie sitting in the strawberry bed, thinking that David looked less than ever like a hero with his blue shirt, rough straw hat, and big boots; also wondering if he *would* ever show her his best side, and if she would like it when she saw it.

CHAPTER XII.

ON the fourth of September, Christie woke up, saying to herself: "It is my birthday, but no one knows it, so I shall get no presents. Ah, well, I'm too old for that now, I suppose;" but she sighed as she said it, for well she knew one never is too old to be remembered and beloved.

Just then the door opened, and Mrs. Sterling entered, carrying what looked very like a pile of snow-flakes in her arms. Laying this upon the bed, she kissed Christie, saying with a tone and gesture that made the words a benediction:

"A happy birthday, and God bless thee, my daughter!"

Before Christie could do more than hug both gift and giver, a great bouquet came flying in at the open window, aimed with such skill that it fell upon the bed, while David's voice called out from below: "A happy birthday, Christie, and many of them!"

" How sweet, how kind of you, this is! I didn't dream you knew about to-day, and never thought of such a beautiful surprise," cried Christie, touched and charmed by this unexpected celebration.

"Thee mentioned it once long ago, and we remembered. They are very humble gifts, my dear; but we could not let the day pass without some token of the thanks we owe thee for these months of faithful service and affectionate companionship."

Christie had no answer to this little address, and was about to cry as the only adequate expression of her feelings, when a hearty "Hear! Hear!" from below made her laugh, and call out:

"You conspirators! how dare you lay plots, and then exult over me when I can't find words to thank you? I always did think you were a set of angels, and now I'm quite sure of it."

"Thee may be right about Davy, but *I* am only a prudent old woman, and have taken much pleasure in privately knitting this light wrap to wear when thee sits in the porch, for the evenings will soon grow chilly. My son did not know what to get, and finally decided that flowers would suit thee best; so he made a bunch of those thee loves, and would toss it in as if he was a boy."

"I like that way, and both my presents suit me exactly," said Christie, wrapping the fleecy shawl about her, and admiring the nosegay in which her quick eye saw all her favorites, even to a plumy spray of the little wild asters which she loved so much.

"Now, child, I will step down, and see about breakfast. Take thy time; for this is to be a holiday, and we mean to make it a happy one if we can."

With that the old lady went away, and Christie soon followed, looking very fresh and blithe as she ran down smiling behind her great bouquet. David was in the porch, training up the morning-glories that bloomed late and lovely in that sheltered spot. He turned as she approached, held out his hand, and bent a little as if he was moved to add a tenderer greeting. But he did not, only held the hand she gave him for a moment, as he said with the paternal expression unusually visible:

"I wished you many happy birthdays; and, if you go on getting younger every year like this, you will surely have them."

It was the first compliment he had ever paid her, and she liked it, though she shook her head as if disclaiming it, and answered brightly:

"I used to think many years would be burdensome, and just before I came here I felt as if I could not bear another one. But now I like to live, and hope I shall a long, long time."

"I'm glad of that; and how do you mean to spend these long years of yours?" asked David, brushing back the lock of hair that was always falling into his eyes, as if he wanted to see more clearly the hopeful face before him.

"In doing what your morning-glories do, — climb up as far and as fast as I can before the frost comes," answered Christie, looking at the pretty symbols she had chosen.

"You have got on a good way already then," began David, smiling at her fancy.

"Oh no, I haven't!" she said quickly. "I'm only about half way up. See here: I'll tell how it is;" and, pointing to the different parts of the flowery wall, she added in her earnest way: "I've watched these grow, and had many thoughts about them, as I sit sewing in the porch. These variegated ones down low are my childish fancies; most of them gone to seed you see. These lovely blue ones of all shades are my girlish dreams and hopes and plans. Poor things! some are dead, some torn by the wind, and only a few pale ones left quite perfect. Here you observe they grow sombre with a tinge of purple; that means pain and gloom, and there is where I was when I came here. Now they turn from those sad colors to crimson, rose, and soft pink. That's the happiness and health I found here. You and your dear mother planted them, and you see how strong and bright they are."

She lifted up her hand, and gathering one of the great rosy cups offered it to him, as if it were brimful of the thanks she could not utter. He comprehended, took it with a quiet "Thank you," and stood looking at it for a moment, as if her little compliment pleased him very much.

"And these?" he said presently, pointing to the delicate violet bells that grew next the crimson ones.

The color deepened a shade in Christie's cheek, but she went on with no other sign of shyness; for with David she always spoke out frankly, because she could not help it.

"Those mean love to me, not passion: the deep red ones half hidden under the leaves mean that. My violet flowers are the best and purest love we can know: the sort that makes life beautiful and lasts for ever. The white ones that come next are tinged with that soft color here and there, and they mean holiness. I know there will be love in heaven; so, whether I ever find it here or not, I am sure I shall not miss it wholly."

Then, as if glad to leave the theme that never can be touched without reverent emotion by a true woman, she added, looking up to where a few spotless blossoms shone like silver in the light:

"Far away there in the sunshine are my highest aspirations. I cannot reach them: but I can look up, and see their beauty; believe in them, and try to follow where they lead; remember that frost comes latest to those that bloom the highest; and keep my beautiful white flowers as long as I can."

"The mush is ready; come to breakfast, children," called Mrs. Sterling, as she crossed the hall with a tea-pot in her hand.

Christie's face fell, then she exclaimed laughing: "That's always the way; I never take a poetic flight but in comes the mush, and spoils it all."

"Not a bit; and that's where women are mistaken. Souls and bodies should go on together; and you will find that a hearty breakfast won't spoil the little hymn the morning-glories sung;" and David set her a good example by eating two bowls of hasty-pudding and milk, with the lovely flower in his button-hole.

"Now, what are we to do next?" asked Christie, when the usual morning work was finished.

"In about ten minutes thee will see, I think," answered Mrs. Sterling, glancing at the clock, and smiling at the bright expectant look in the younger woman's eyes.

She did see; for in less than ten minutes the rumble of an omnibus was heard, a sound of many voices, and then the whole Wilkins brood came whooping down the lane. It was good to see Ma Wilkins jog ponderously after in full state and festival array; her bonnet trembling with bows, red roses all over her gown, and a parasol of uncommon brilliancy brandished joyfully in her hand. It was better still to see her hug Christie, when the latter emerged, flushed and breathless, from the chaos of arms, legs, and chubby faces in which she was lost for several tumultuous moments; and it was best of all to see the good woman place her cherished " bunnit " in the middle of the parlor table as a choice and lovely ornament, administer the family pocket-handkerchief all round, and then settle down with a hearty :

" Wal, now, Mis Sterlin', you've no idee how tickled we all was when Mr. David came, and told us you was goin' to have a galy here to-day. It was so kind of providential, for 'Lisha was invited out to a day's pleasurin', so I could leave jest as wal as not. The childern 's ben hankerin' to come the wust kind, and go plummin' as they did last month, though I told 'em berries was gone weeks ago. I reely thought I 'd never get 'em here whole, they trained so in that bus. Wash would go on the step, and kep fallin' off; Gusty's hat blew out a winder; them two bad boys tumbled round loose; and dear little Victory set like a lady, only I found she 'd got both feet in the basket right atop of the birthday cake, I made a puppose for Christie."

" It hasn't hurt it a bit; there was a cloth over it, and I like it all the better for the marks of Totty's little feet, bless 'em ! " and Christie cuddled the culprit with one hand while she revealed the damaged delicacy with the other, wondering inwardly what evil star was always in the ascendant when Mrs. Wilkins made cake.

" Now, my dear, you jest go and have a good frolic with them childern, I 'm a goin' to git dinner, and you a goin' to play ; so we don't want to see no more of you till the bell rings," said Mrs. Wilkins pinning up her gown, and " shooing" her brood out of the room, which they entirely filled.

Catching up her hat Christie obeyed, feeling as much like a child as any of the excited six. The revels that followed no pen can justly record, for Goths and Vandals on the rampage but feebly describes the youthful Wilkinses when their spirits effervesced after a month's bottling up in close home quarters.

David locked the greenhouse door the instant he saw them ; and pervaded the premises generally like a most affable but very watchful policeman, for the ravages those innocents committed much afflicted him. Yet he never had the heart to say a word of reproof, when he saw their raptures over dandelions, the relish with which they devoured fruit, and the good it did the little souls and bodies to enjoy unlimited liberty, green grass, and country air, even for a day.

Christie usually got them into the big meadow as soon as possible, and there let them gambol at will ; while she sat on the broken bough of an apple-tree, and watched her flock like an old-fashioned shepherdess. To-day she did so ; and when the children were happily sailing boats, tearing to and fro like wild colts, or discovering the rustic treasures Nurse Nature lays ready to gladden little hearts and hands, Christie sat idly making a garland of green brakes, and ruddy sumach leaves ripened before the early frosts had come.

David saw her there, and, feeling that he might come off guard for a time, went strolling down to lean upon the wall, and chat in the friendly fashion that had naturally grown up between these fellow-workers. She was waiting for the new supply of ferns little Adelaide was getting for her by the wall; and while she waited she

A FRIENDLY CHAT.

sat resting her cheek upon her hand, and smiling to herself, as if she saw some pleasant picture in the green grass at her feet.

"Now I wonder what she's thinking about," said David's voice close by, and Christie straightway answered:

"Philip Fletcher."

"And who is he?" asked David, settling his elbow in a comfortable niche between the mossy stones, so that he could "lean and loaf" at his ease.

"The brother of the lady whose children I took care of;" and Christie wished she had thought before she answered that first question, for in telling her adventures at different times she had omitted all mention of this gentleman.

"Tell about him, as the children say: your experiences are always interesting, and you look as if this man was uncommonly entertaining in some way," said David, indolently inclined to be amused.

"Oh, dear no, not at all entertaining! invalids seldom are, and he was sick and lazy, conceited and very cross sometimes." Christie's heart rather smote her as she said this, remembering the last look poor Fletcher gave her.

"A nice man to be sure; but I don't see any thing to smile about," persisted David, who liked reasons for things; a masculine trait often very trying to feminine minds.

"I was thinking of a little quarrel we once had. He found out that I had been an actress; for I basely did not mention that fact when I took the place, and so got properly punished for my deceit. I thought he'd tell his sister of course, so I did it myself, and retired from the situation as much disgusted with Christie Devon as you are.".

"Perhaps I ought to be, but I don't find that I am. Do you know I think that old Fletcher was a sneak?" and David looked as if he would rather like to mention his opinion to that gentleman.

"He probably thought he was doing his duty to the children: few people would approve of an actress for a teacher you know. He had seen me play, and remembered it all of a sudden, and told me of it: that was the way it came about," said Christie hastily, feeling that she must get out of the scrape as soon as possible, or she would be driven to tell every thing in justice to Mr. Fletcher.

"I should like to see you act."

"You a Quaker, and express such a worldly and dreadful wish?" cried Christie, much amused, and very grateful that his thoughts had taken a new direction.

"I'm not, and never have been. Mother married out of the sect, and, though she keeps many of her old ways, always left me free to believe what I chose. I wear drab because I like it, and say 'thee' to her because she likes it, and it is pleasant to have a little word all our own. I've been to theatres, but I don't care much for them. Perhaps I should if I'd had Fletcher's luck in seeing *you* play."

"You didn't lose much: I was not a good actress; though now and then when I liked my part I did pretty well they said," answered Christie, modestly.

"Why didn't you go back after the accident?" asked David, who had heard that part of the story.

"I felt that it was bad for me, and so retired to private life."

"Do you ever regret it?"

"Sometimes when the restless fit is on me: but not so often now as I used to do; for on the whole I'd rather *be* a woman than *act* a queen."

"Good!" said David, and then added persuasively: "But you *will* play for me some time: won't you? I've a curious desire to see you do it."

"Perhaps I'll try," replied Christie, flattered by his interest, and not unwilling to display her little talent.

"Who are you making that for? it's very pretty," asked David, who seemed to be in an inquiring frame of mind that day.

"Any one who wants it. I only do it for the pleasure: I always liked pretty things; but, since I have lived among flowers and natural people, I seem to care more than ever for beauty of all kinds, and love to make it if I can without stopping for any reason but the satisfaction."

"'Tell them, dear, that if eyes were made for seeing,
"'Then beauty is its own excuse for being,'"

observed David, who had a weakness for poetry, and, finding she liked his sort, quoted to Christie almost as freely as to himself.

"Exactly, so look at that and enjoy it," and she pointed to the child standing knee-deep in graceful ferns, looking as if she grew there, a living buttercup, with her buff frock off at one plump shoulder and her bright hair shining in the sun.

Before David could express his admiration, the little picture was spoilt; for Christie called out, "Come, Vic, bring me some more pretties!" startling baby so that she lost her balance, and disappeared with a muffled

cry, leaving nothing to be seen but a pair of small con-
vulsive shoes, soles uppermost, among the brakes.   David took a leap, reversed Vic, and then let her compose
her little feelings by sticking bits of green in all the
button-holes of his coat, as he sat on the wall while she
stood beside him in the safe shelter of his arm.

"You are very like an Englishman," said Christie,
after watching the pair for a few minutes.

"How do you know?" asked David, looking surprised.

"There were several in our company, and I found
them very much alike.   Blunt and honest, domestic and
kind; hard to get at, but true as steel when once won;
not so brilliant and original as Americans, perhaps, but
more solid and steadfast.   On the whole, I think them
the manliest men in the world," answered Christie, in
the decided way young people have of expressing their
opinions.

"You speak as if you had known and studied a great
variety of men," said David, feeling that he need not
resent the comparison she had made.

"I have, and it has done me good.   Women who
stand alone in the world, and have their own way to
make, have a better chance to know men truly than
those who sit safe at home and only see one side of
mankind.   We lose something; but I think we gain a
great deal that is more valuable than admiration, flattery, and the superficial service most men give to our
sex.   Some one says, 'Companionship teaches men and
women to know, judge, and treat one another justly.'
I believe it; for we who are compelled to be fellow-
workers with men understand and value them more
truly than many a belle who has a dozen lovers sigh-

ing at her feet. I see their faults and follies; but I also see so much to honor, love, and trust, that I feel as if the world was full of brothers. Yes, as a general rule, men have been kinder to me than women; and if I wanted a staunch friend I'd choose a man, for they wear better than women, who ask too much, and cannot see that friendship lasts longer if a little respect and reserve go with the love and confidence."

Christie had spoken soberly, with no thought of flattery or effect; for the memory of many kindnesses bestowed on her by many men, from rough Joe Butterfield to Mr. Power, gave warmth and emphasis to her words.

The man sitting on the wall appreciated the compliment to his sex, and proved that he deserved his share of it by taking it exactly as she meant it, and saying heartily:

" I like that, Christie, and wish more women thought and spoke as you do."

" If they had had my experience they would, and not be ashamed of it. I am so old now I can say these things and not be misjudged; for even some sensible people think this honest sort of fellowship impossible if not improper. I don't, and I never shall, so if I can ever do any thing for you, David, forget that I am a woman and tell me as freely as if I was a younger brother."

" I wish you were! "

" So do I; you'd make a splendid elder brother."

" No, a very bad one."

There was a sudden sharpness in David's voice that jarred on Christie's ear and made her look up quickly. She only caught a glimpse of his face, and saw that it was strangely troubled, as he swung himself over the wall with little Vic on his arm and went toward the house, saying abruptly:

"Baby's sleepy: she must go in."

Christie sat some time longer, wondering what she had said to disturb him, and when the bell rang went in still perplexed. But David looked as usual, and the only trace of disquiet was an occasional hasty shaking back of the troublesome lock, and a slight knitting of the brows; two tokens, as she had learned to know, of impatience or pain.

She was soon so absorbed in feeding the children, hungry and clamorous as young birds for their food, that she forgot every thing else. When dinner was done and cleared away, she devoted herself to Mrs. Wilkins for an hour or two, while Mrs. Sterling took her nap, the infants played riotously in the lane, and David was busy with orders.

The arrival of Mr. Power drew every one to the porch to welcome him. As he handed Christie a book, he asked with a significant smile:

"Have you found him yet?"

She glanced at the title of the new gift, read "Heroes and Hero-worship," and answered merrily:

"No, sir, but I'm looking hard."

"Success to your search," and Mr. Power turned to greet David, who approached.

"Now, what shall we play?" asked Christie, as the children gathered about her demanding to be amused.

George Washington suggested leap-frog, and the others added equally impracticable requests; but Mrs. Wilkins settled the matter by saying:

"Let's have some play-actin', Christie. That used to tickle the children amazin'ly, and I was never tired of hearin' them pieces, specially the solemn ones."

"Yes, yes! do the funny girl with the baby, and the old woman, and the lady that took pison and had fits!" shouted the children, charmed with the idea.

Christie felt ready for any thing just then, and gave them Tilly Slowboy, Miss Miggs, and Mrs. Gummage, in her best style, while the young folks rolled on the grass in ecstasies, and Mrs. Wilkins laughed till she cried.

"Now a touch of tragedy!" said Mr. Power, who sat under the elm, with David leaning on the back of his chair, both applauding heartily.

"You insatiable people! do you expect me to give you low comedy and heavy tragedy all alone? I'm equal to melodrama I think, and I'll give you Miss St. Clair as Juliet, if you wait a moment."

Christie stepped into the house, and soon reappeared with a white table-cloth draped about her, two dishevelled locks of hair on her shoulders, and the vinegar cruet in her hand, that being the first bottle she could find. She meant to burlesque the poison scene, and began in the usual ranting way; but she soon forgot St. Clair in poor Juliet, and did it as she had often longed to do it, with all the power and passion she possessed. Very faulty was her rendering, but the earnestness she put into it made it most effective to her uncritical audience, who "brought down the house," when she fell upon the grass with her best stage drop, and lay there getting her breath after the mouthful of vinegar she had taken in the excitement of the moment.

She was up again directly, and, inspired by this superb success, ran in and presently reappeared as Lady Macbeth with Mrs. Wilkins's scarlet shawl for royal robes, and the leafy chaplet of the morning for a crown. She took the stage with some difficulty, for the unevenness of the turf impaired the majesty of her tragic stride, and fixing her eyes on an invisible Thane (who cut his part shamefully, and spoke in the gruffest of gruff voices) she gave them the dagger scene.

David as the orchestra, had been performing a drum solo on the back of a chair with two of the corn-cobs Victoria had been building houses with; but, when Lady Macbeth said, "Give *me* the daggers," Christie plucked the cobs suddenly from his hands, looking so fiercely scornful, and lowering upon him so wrathfully with her corked brows that he ejaculated an involuntary, "Bless me!" as he stepped back quite daunted.

Being in the spirit of her part, Christie closed with the sleep-walking scene, using the table-cloth again, while a towel composed the tragic nightcap of her ladyship. This was an imitation, and having a fine model and being a good mimic, she did well; for the children sat staring with round eyes, the gentlemen watched the woful face and gestures intently, and Mrs. Wilkins took a long breath at the end, exclaiming: "I never did see the beat of that for gastliness! My sister Clarissy used to walk in her sleep, but she warn't half so kind of dreadful."

"If she had had the murder of a few friends on her conscience, I dare say she would have been," said Christie, going in to make herself tidy.

"Well, how do you like her as an actress?" asked

Mr. Power of David, who stood looking, as if he still saw and heard the haunted lady.

"Very much; but better as a woman. I'd no idea she had it in her," answered David, in a wonder-stricken tone.

"Plenty of tragedy and comedy in all of us," began Mr. Power; but David said hastily:

"Yes, but few of us have passion and imagination enough to act Shakspeare in that way."

"Very true: Christie herself could not give a whole character in that style, and would not think of trying."

"*I* think she could; and I'd like to see her try it," said David, much impressed by the dramatic ability which Christie's usual quietude had most effectually hidden.

He was still thinking about it, when she came out again. Mr. Power beckoned to her, saying, as she came and stood before him, flushed and kindled with her efforts:

"Now, you must give me a bit from the 'Merchant of Venice.' Portia is a favorite character of mine, and I want to see if you can do any thing with it."

"No, sir, I cannot. I used to study it, but it was too sober to suit me. I am not a judicial woman, so I gave it up," answered Christie, much flattered by his request, and amused at the respectful way in which David looked at her. Then, as if it just occurred to her, she added, "I remember one little speech that I can say to *you*, sir, with great truth, and I will, since you like that play."

Still standing before him, she bent her head a little, and with a graceful gesture of the hands, as if offering something, she delivered with heartfelt emphasis the first part of Portia's pretty speech to her fortunate suitor :

" You see me, Lord Bassanio, where I stand,
   Such as I am : though, for myself alone,
   I would not be ambitious in my wish,
   To wish myself much better ; yet for you,
   I would be trebled twenty times myself ;
   A thousand times more fair, ten thousand times more rich ;
   That, only to stand high in your account,
   I might in virtues, beauties, livings, friends,
   Exceed account : but the full sum of me
   Is sum of something ; which, to term in gross,
   Is an unlesson'd girl, unschool'd, unpractis'd : —
   Happy in this, she is not yet so old
   But she may learn ; happier than this,
   She is not bred so dull but she can learn ;
   Happiest of all, is that her willing spirit
   Commits itself to yours to be directed,
   As from her lord, her governor, her king."

David applauded vigorously ; but Mr. Power rose silently, looking both touched and surprised ; and, drawing Christie's hand through his arm, led her away into the garden for one of the quiet talks that were so much to her.

When they returned, the Wilkinses were preparing to depart ; and, after repeated leave-takings, finally got under way, were packed into the omnibus, and rumbled off with hats, hands, and handkerchiefs waving from every window. Mr. Power soon followed, and peace returned to the little house in the lane.

Later in the evening, when Mrs. Sterling was engaged with a neighbor, who had come to confide some affliction to the good lady, Christie went into the porch, and found David sitting on the step, enjoying the mellow moonlight and the balmy air. As he did not speak, she sat down silently, folded her hands in her lap, and began to enjoy the beauty of the night in her own way. Presently she became conscious that David's eyes had turned from the moon to her own face. He sat in the shade, she in the light, and he was looking at her with the new expression which amused her.

" Well, what is it? You look as if you never saw me before," she said, smiling.

" I feel as if I never had," he answered, still regarding her as if she had been a picture.

" What do I look like?"

" A peaceful, pious nun, just now."

" Oh! that is owing to my pretty shawl. I put it on in honor of the day, though it is a trifle warm, I confess." And Christie stroked the soft folds about her shoulders, and settled the corner that lay lightly on her hair. " I do feel peaceful to-night, but not pious. I am afraid I never shall do that," she added soberly.

" Why not?"

" Well, it does not seem to be my nature, and I don't know how to change it. I want something to keep me steady, but I can't find it. So I whiffle about this way and that, and sometimes think I am a most degenerate creature."

" That is only human nature, so don't be troubled. We are all compasses pointing due north. We get shaken often, and the needle varies in spite of us; but the minute we are quiet, it points right, and we have only to follow it."

" The keeping quiet is just what I cannot do. Your mother shows me how lovely it is, and I try to imitate it; but this restless soul of mine will ask questions and doubt and fear, and worry me in many ways. What shall I do to keep it still? " asked Christie, smiling, yet earnest.

" Let it alone: you cannot force these things, and the best way is to wait till the attraction is strong enough to keep the needle steady. Some people get their ballast slowly, some don't need much, and some have to work hard for theirs."

" Did you? " asked Christie; for David's voice fell a little, as he uttered the last words.

" I have not got much yet."

" I think you have. Why, David, you are always cheerful and contented, good and generous. If that is not true piety, what is? "

" You are very much deceived, and I am sorry for it," said David, with the impatient gesture of the head, and a troubled look.

"Prove it! " And Christie looked at him with such sincere respect and regard, that his honest nature would not let him accept it, though it gratified him much.

He made no answer for a minute. Then he said slowly, as if feeling a modest man's hesitation to speak of himself, yet urged to it by some irresistible impulse:

" I *will* prove it if you won't mind the unavoidable egotism; for I cannot let you think me so much better than I am. Outwardly I seem to you 'cheerful, contented, generous, and good.' In reality I am sad, dissatisfied, bad, and selfish : see if I 'm not. I often tire of this quiet life, hate my work, and long to break away, and follow my own wild and wilful impulses, no matter where they lead. Nothing keeps me at such times but my mother and God's patience."

David began quietly ; but the latter part of this confession was made with a sudden impetuosity that startled Christie, so utterly unlike his usual self-control was it. She could only look at him with the surprise she felt. His face was in the shadow; but she saw that it was flushed, his eyes excited, and in his voice she heard an undertone that made it sternly self-accusing.

" I am not a hypocrite," he went on rapidly, as if driven to speak in spite of himself. " I try to be what I seem, but it is too hard sometimes and I despair. Especially hard is it to feel that I have learned to feign happiness so well that others are entirely deceived. Mr. Power and mother know me as I am : other friends I have not, unless you will let me call you one. Whether you do or not after this, I respect you too much to let you delude yourself about my virtues, so I tell you the truth and abide the consequences."

He looked up at her as he paused, with a curious mixture of pride and humility in his face, and squared his broad shoulders as if he had thrown off a burden that had much oppressed him.

Christie offered him her hand, saying in a tone that did his heart good : " The consequences are that I respect, admire, and trust you more than ever, and feel proud to be your friend."

David gave the hand a strong and grateful pressure, said, " Thank you," in a moved tone, and then leaned back into the shadow, as if trying to recover from this unusual burst of confidence, won from him by the soft magic of time, place, and companionship.

Fearing he would regret the glimpse he had given her, and anxious to show how much she liked it, Christie talked on to give him time to regain composure.

" I always thought in reading the lives of saints or good men of any time, that their struggles were the most interesting and helpful things recorded. Human imperfection only seems to make real piety more possible, and to me more beautiful; for where others have conquered I can conquer, having suffered as they suffer, and seen their hard-won success. That is the sort of religion I want; something to hold by, live in, and enjoy, if I can only get it."

" I know you will." He said it heartily, and seemed quite calm again; so Christie obeyed the instinct which told her that questions would be good for David, and that he was in the mood for answering them.

" May I ask you something," she began a little timidly.

" Any thing, Christie," he answered instantly.

" That is a rash promise: I am a woman, and therefore curious; what shall you do if I take advantage of the privilege ? "

" Try and see."

" I will be discreet, and only ask one thing," she replied, charmed with her success. " You said just now that you had learned to feign happiness. I wish you would tell me how you do it, for it is such an excellent imitation I shall be quite content with it till I can learn the genuine thing."

David fingered the troublesome forelock thoughtfully for a moment, then said, with something of the former impetuosity coming back into his voice and manner:

"I will tell you all about it; that's the best way: I know I shall some day because I can't help it; so I may as well have done with it now, since I have begun. It is not interesting, mind you, — only a grim little history of one man's fight with the world, the flesh, and the devil: will you have it?"

"Oh, yes!" answered Christie, so eagerly that David laughed, in spite of the bitter memories stirring at his heart.

"So like a woman, always ready to hear and forgive sinners," he said, then took a long breath, and added rapidly :

"I'll put it in as few words as possible and much good may it do you. Some years ago I was desperately miserable; never mind why: I dare say I shall tell you all about it some day if I go on at this rate. Well, being miserable, as I say, every thing looked black and bad to me: I hated all men, distrusted all women, doubted the existence of God, and was a forlorn wretch generally. Why I did not go to the devil I can't say : I did start once or twice; but the thought of that dear old woman in there sitting all alone and waiting for me dragged me back, and kept me here till the first recklessness was over. People talk about duty being sweet; I have not found it so, but there it was : I should have been a brute to shirk it; so I took it up, and held on desperately till it grew bearable."

"It *has* grown sweet now, David, I am sure," said Christie, very low.

"No, not yet," he answered with the stern honesty that would not let him deceive himself or others, cost what it might to be true. "There is a certain solid satisfaction in it that I did not use to find. It is not a mere dogged persistence now, as it once was, and that is a step towards loving it perhaps."

He spoke half to himself, and sat leaning his head on both hands propped on his knees, looking down as if the weight of the old trouble bent his shoulders again.

"What more, David?" said Christie.

"Only this. When I found I had got to live, and live manfully, I said to myself, 'I must have help or I cannot do it.' To no living soul could I tell my grief, not even to my mother, for she had her own to bear: no human being could help me, yet I *must* have help or give up shamefully. Then I did what others do when all else fails to sustain them; I turned to God: not humbly, not devoutly or trustfully, but doubtfully, bitterly, and rebelliously; for I said in my despairing heart, 'If there *is* a God, let Him help me, and I will believe.' He did help me, and I kept my word."

"Oh, David, how?" whispered Christie after a moment's silence, for the last words were solemn in their earnestness.

"The help did not come at once. No miracle answered me, and I thought my cry had not been heard. But it had, and slowly something like submission came to me. It was not cheerful nor pious: it was only a dumb, sad sort of patience without hope or faith. It was better than desperation; so I accepted it, and bore the inevitable as well as I could. Presently, courage seemed to spring up again : I was ashamed to be beaten in the first battle, and some sort of blind instinct made me long to break away from the past and begin again. My father was dead; mother left all to me, and followed where I led. I sold the old place, bought this, and, shutting out the world as much as I could, I fell to work as if my life depended on it. That was five or six years ago : and for a long time I delved away without interest or pleasure, merely as a safety-valve for my energies, and a means of living; for I gave up all my earlier hopes and plans when the trouble came.

" I did not love my work; but it was good for me, and helped cure my sick soul. I never guessed why I felt better, but dug on with indifference first, then felt pride in my garden, then interest in the plants I tended, and by and by I saw what they had done for me, and loved them like true friends."

A broad woodbine leaf had been fluttering against David's head, as he leaned on the slender pillar of the porch where it grew. Now, as if involuntarily, he laid his cheek against it with a caressing gesture, and sat looking over the garden lying dewy and still in the moonlight, with the grateful look of a man who has learned the healing miracles of Nature and how near she is to God.

" Mr. Power helped you : didn't he ? " said Christie, longing to hear more.

" So much ! I never can tell you what he was to me, nor how I thank him. To him, and to my work I owe the little I have won in the way of strength and comfort after years of effort. I see now the compensation that comes out of trouble, the lovely possibilities that exist for all of us, and the infinite patience of God, which is to me one of the greatest of His divine attributes. I have only got so far, but things grow easier as one goes on; and if I keep tugging I may yet *be* the cheerful, contented man I seem. That is all, Christie, and a longer story than I meant to tell."

"Not long enough : some time you will tell me more perhaps, since you have once begun. It seems quite natural now, and I am so pleased and honored by your confidence. But I cannot help wondering what made you do it all at once," said Christie presently, after they had listened to a whippoorwill, and watched the flight of a downy owl.

"I do not think I quite know myself, unless it was because I have been on my good behavior since you came, and, being a humbug, as I tell you, was forced to unmask in spite of myself. There are limits to human endurance, and the proudest man longs to unpack his woes before a sympathizing friend now and then. I have been longing to do this for some time; but I never like to disturb mother's peace, or take Mr. Power from those who need him more. So to-day, when you so sweetly offered to help me if you could, it quite went to my heart, and seemed so friendly and comfortable, I could not resist trying it to-night, when you began about my imaginary virtues. That is the truth, I believe : now, what shall we do about it?"

"Just go on, and do it again whenever you feel like it. I know what loneliness is, and how telling worries often cures them. I meant every word I said this morning, and will prove it by doing any thing in the world I can for you. Believe this, and let me be your friend."

They had risen, as a stir within told them the guest was going; and as Christie spoke she was looking up with the moonlight full upon her face.

If there had been any hidden purpose in her mind, any false sentiment, or trace of coquetry in her manner, it would have spoiled that hearty little speech of hers.

But in her heart was nothing but a sincere desire to prove gratitude and offer sympathy; in her manner the gentle frankness of a woman speaking to a brother; and in her face the earnestness of one who felt the value of friendship, and did not ask or give it lightly.

"I will," was David's emphatic answer, and then, as if to seal the bargain, he stooped down, and gravely kissed her on the forehead.

Christie was a little startled, but neither offended nor confused; for there was no love in that quiet kiss, — only respect, affection, and much gratitude; an involuntary demonstration from the lonely man to the true-hearted woman who had dared to come and comfort him.

Out trotted neighbor Miller, and that was the end of confidences in the porch ; but David played melodiously on his flute that night, and Christie fell asleep saying happily to herself:

"Now we are all right, friends for ever, and every thing will go beautifully."

CHAPTER XIII.

WAKING UP.

KITTY.

EVERY thing *did* "go beautifully" for a time; so much so, that Christie began to think she really *had* "got religion." A delightful peace pervaded her soul, a new interest made the dullest task agreeable, and life grew so inexpressibly sweet that she felt as if she could forgive all her enemies, love her friends more than ever, and do any thing great, good, or glorious.

She had known such moods before, but they had never lasted long, and were not so intense as this; therefore, she was sure some blessed power had come to uphold and cheer her. She sang like a lark as she swept and dusted; thought high and happy thoughts among the pots and kettles, and, when she sat sewing, smiled unconsciously as if some deep satisfaction made sunshine from within. Heart and soul seemed to wake up and rejoice as naturally and beautifully as flowers in the spring. A soft brightness shone in her eyes, a fuller tone sounded in her voice, and her face grew young and blooming with the happiness that transfigures all it touches.

" Christie's growing handsome," David would say to his mother, as if she was a flower in which he took pride.

" Thee is a good gardener, Davy," the old lady would reply, and when he was busy would watch him with a tender sort of anxiety, as if to discover a like change in him.

But no alteration appeared, except more cheerfulness and less silence; for now there was no need to hide his real self, and all the social virtues in him came out delightfully after their long solitude.

In her present uplifted state, Christie could no more help regarding David as a martyr and admiring him for it, than she could help mixing sentiment with her sympathy. By the light of the late confessions, his life and character looked very different to her now. His apparent contentment was resignation; his cheerfulness, a manly contempt for complaint; his reserve, the modest reticence of one who, having done a hard duty well, desires no praise for it. Like all enthusiastic persons, Christie had a hearty admiration for self-sacrifice and self-control; and, while she learned to see David's virtues, she also exaggerated them, and could not do enough to show the daily increasing esteem and respect she felt for him, and to atone for the injustice she once did him.

She grubbed in the garden and green-house, and learned hard botanical names that she might be able to talk intelligently upon subjects that interested her comrade. Then, as autumn ended out-of-door work, she tried to make home more comfortable and attractive than ever.

David's room was her especial care ; for now to her there was something pathetic in the place and its poor furnishing. He had fought many a silent battle there ; won many a secret victory ; and tried to cheer his solitude with the best thoughts the minds of the bravest, wisest men could give him.

She did not smile at the dilapidated idols now, but touched them tenderly, and let no dust obscure their well-beloved faces. She set the books in order daily, taking many a sip of refreshment from them by the way, and respectfully regarded those in unknown tongues, full of admiration for David's learning. She covered the irruptive sofa neatly ; saw that the little vase was always clear and freshly filled ; cared for the nursery in the gable-window ; and preserved an exquisite neatness everywhere, which delighted the soul of the room's order-loving occupant.

She also — alas, for romance ! — cooked the dishes David loved, and liked to see him enjoy them with the appetite which once had shocked her so. She watched over his buttons with a vigilance that would have softened the heart of the crustiest bachelor : she even gave herself the complexion of a lemon by wearing blue, because David liked the pretty contrast with his mother's drabs.

After recording that last fact, it is unnecessary to explain what was the matter with Christie. She honestly thought she had got religion; but it was piety's twin-sister, who produced this wonderful revival in her soul; and though she began in all good faith she presently discovered that she was

> "Not the first maiden
> Who came but for friendship,
> And took away love."

After the birthnight confessions, David found it easier to go on with the humdrum life he had chosen from a sense of duty; for now he felt as if he had not only a fellow-worker, but a comrade and friend who understood, sympathized with, and encouraged him by an interest and good-will inexpressibly comfortable and inspiring. Nothing disturbed the charm of the new league in those early days; for Christie was thoroughly simple and sincere, and did her womanly work with no thought of reward or love or admiration.

David saw this, and felt it more attractive than any gift of beauty or fascination of manner would have been. He had no desire to be a lover, having forbidden himself that hope; but he found it so easy and pleasant to be a friend that he reproached himself for not trying it before; and explained his neglect by the fact that Christie was not an ordinary woman, since none of all the many he had known and helped, had ever been any thing to him but objects of pity and protection.

Mrs. Sterling saw these changes with her wise,

motherly eyes, but said nothing; for she influenced others by the silent power of character. Speaking little, and unusually gifted with the meditative habits of age, she seemed to live in a more peaceful world than this. As George MacDonald somewhere says, "Her soul seemed to sit apart in a sunny little room, safe from dust and noise, serenely regarding passers-by through the clear muslin curtains of her window."

Yet, she was neither cold nor careless, stern nor selfish, but ready to share all the joys and sorrows of those about her; and when advice was asked she gave it gladly. Christie had won her heart long ago, and now was as devoted as a daughter to her; lightening her cares so skilfully that many of them slipped naturally on to the young shoulders, and left the old lady much time for rest, or the lighter tasks fitted for feeble hands. Christie often called her "Mother," and felt herself rewarded for the hardest, humblest job she ever did when the sweet old voice said gratefully, "I thank thee, daughter."

Things were in this prosperous, not to say paradisiacal, state, when one member of the family began to make discoveries of an alarming nature. The first was that the Sunday pilgrimages to church were seasons of great refreshment to soul and body when David went also, and utter failures if he did not. Next, that the restless ambitions of all sorts were quite gone; for now Christie's mission seemed to be sitting in a quiet corner and making shirts in the most exquisite manner, while thinking about — well, say botany, or any kindred subject. Thirdly, that home was woman's sphere after all, and the perfect roasting of beef, brewing of tea, and concocting of delectable puddings, an end worth living for if masculine commendation rewarded the labor.

Fourthly, and worst of all, she discovered that she was not satisfied with half confidences, and quite pined to know all about " David's trouble." The little needle-book with the faded " Letty" on it haunted her; and when, after a pleasant evening below, she heard him pace his room for hours, or play melancholy airs upon the flute, she was jealous of that unknown woman who had such power to disturb his peace, and felt a strong desire to smash the musical confidante into whose responsive breast he poured his woe.

At this point Christie paused; and, after evading any explanation of these phenomena in the most skilful manner for a time, suddenly faced the fact, saying to herself with great candor and decision:

" I know what all this means: I'm beginning to like David more than is good for me. I see this clearly, and won't dodge any longer, but put a stop to it at once. Of course I can if I choose, and now is the time to do it; for I understand myself perfectly, and if I reach a certain point it is all over with me. That point I will *not* reach: David's heart is in that Letty's grave, and he only cares for me as a friend. I promised to be one to him, and I'll keep my word like an honest woman. It may not be easy; but all the sacrifices shall not be his, and I won't be a fool."

With praiseworthy resolution Christie set about the reformation without delay; not an easy task and one that taxed all her wit and wisdom to execute without betraying the motive for it. She decided that Mrs. Sterling must not be left alone on Sunday, so the young people took turns to go to church, and such dismal trips Christie had never known; for all her Sundays were bad weather, and Mr. Power seemed to hit on unusually uninteresting texts.

She talked while she sewed instead of indulging in dangerous thoughts, and Mrs. Sterling was surprised and entertained by this new loquacity. In the evening she read and studied with a diligence that amazed and rather disgusted David; since she kept all her lively chat for his mother, and pored over her books when he wanted her for other things.

"I 'm trying to brighten up my wits," she said, and went on trying to stifle her affections.

But though "the absurdity," as she called the new revelation, was stopped externally, it continued with redoubled vigor internally. Each night she said, "this *must* be conquered," yet each morning it rose fair and strong to make the light and beauty of her day, and conquer her again. She did her best and bravest, but was forced at last to own that she could not "put a stop to it," because she had already reached the point where "it was all over with her."

Just at this critical moment an event occurred which completed Christie's defeat, and made her feel that her only safety lay in flight.

One evening she sat studying ferns, and heroically saying over and over, "Andiantum, Aspidium, and Asplenium, Trichomanes," while longing to go and talk delightfully to David, who sat musing by the fire.

"I can't go on so much longer," she thought despairingly. "Polypodium aureum, a native of Florida," is all very interesting in its place; but it doesn't help me to gain self-control a bit, and I shall disgrace myself if something doesn't happen very soon."

Something did happen almost instantly; for as she shut the cover sharply on the poor Polypods, a knock was heard, and before David could answer it the door flew open and a girl ran in. Straight to him she went, and clinging to his arm said excitedly:

"Oh, do take care of me: I've run away again!"

"Why, Kitty, what's the matter now?" asked David, putting back her hood, and looking down at her with the paternal expression Christie had not seen for a long time, and missed very much.

"Father found me, and took me home, and wanted me to marry a dreadful man, and I wouldn't, so I ran away to you. He didn't know I came here before, and I'm safe if you'll let me stay," cried Kitty, still clinging and imploring.

"Of course I will, and glad to see you back again," answered David, adding pitifully, as he put her in his easy-chair, took her cloak and hood off and stood stroking her curly hair: "Poor little girl! it is hard to have to run away so much: isn't it?"

"Not if I come here; it's so pleasant I'd like to stay all my life," and Kitty took a long breath, as if her troubles were over now. "Who's that?" she asked suddenly, as her eye fell on Christie, who sat watching her with interest:

"That is our good friend Miss Devon. She came to take your place, and we got so fond of her we could not let her go," answered David with a gesture of introduction, quite unconscious that his position just then was about as safe and pleasant as that of

a man between a lighted candle and an open powder barrel.

The two young women nodded to each other, took
a swift survey, and made up their minds before David
had poked the fire. Christie saw a pretty face with
rosy cheeks, blue eyes, and brown rings of hair lying
on the smooth, low forehead; a young face, but not
childlike, for it was conscious of its own prettiness, and
betrayed the fact by little airs and graces that reminded
one of a coquettish kitten. Short and slender, she
looked more youthful than she was; while a gay dress,
with gilt ear-rings, locket at the throat, and a cherry
ribbon in her hair made her a bright little figure in that
plain room.

Christie suddenly felt as if ten years had been added
to her age, as she eyed the new-comer, who leaned back
in the great chair talking to David, who stood on the
rug, evidently finding it pleasanter to look at the vi-
vacious face before him than at the fire.

"Just the pretty, lively sort of girl sensible men
often marry, and then discover how silly they are,"
thought Christie, taking up her work and assuming an
indifferent air.

"She's a lady and nice looking, but I know I shan't
like her," was Kitty's decision, as she turned away and
devoted herself to David, hoping he would perceive
how much she had improved and admire her accordingly.

"So you don't want to marry this Miles because he
is not handsome. You'd better think again before you
make up your mind. He is respectable, well off, and
fond of you, it seems. Why not try it, Kitty? You

need some one to take care of you sadly," David said, when her story had been told.

"If father plagues me much I may take the man; but I'd rather have the other one if he wasn't poor," answered Kitty with a side-long glance of the blue eyes, and a conscious smile on the red lips.

"Oh, there's another lover, is there?"

"Lots of 'em."

David laughed and looked at Christie as if inviting her to be amused with the freaks and prattle of a child. But Christie sewed away without a sign of interest.

"That won't do, Kitty: you are too young for much of such nonsense. I shall keep you here a while, and see if we can't settle matters both wisely and pleasantly," he said, shaking his head as sagely as a grandfather.

"I'm sure I wish you would: I love to stay here, you are always so good to me. I'm in no hurry to be married; and you won't make me: will you?"

Kitty rose as she spoke, and stood before him with a beseeching little gesture, and a confiding air quite captivating to behold.

Christie was suddenly seized with a strong desire to shake the girl and call her an "artful little hussy," but crushed this unaccountable impulse, and hemmed a pocket-handkerchief with reckless rapidity, while she stole covert glances at the *tableau* by the fire.

David put his finger under Kitty's round chin, and lifting her face looked into it, trying to discover if she really cared for this suitor who seemed so providentially provided for her. Kitty smiled and blushed, and dimpled under that grave look so prettily that it soon changed, and David let her go, saying indulgently:

"You shall not be troubled, for you are only a child after all. Let the lovers go, and stay and play with me, for I've been rather lonely lately."

"That's a reproach for me," thought Christie, longing to cry out: "No, no; send the girl away and let *me* be all in all to you." But she only turned up the lamp and pretended to be looking for a spool, while her heart ached and her eyes were too dim for seeing.

"I'm too old to play, but I'll stay and tease you as I used to, if Miles don't come and carry me off as he said he would," answered Kitty, with a toss of the head which showed she was not so childlike as David fancied. But the next minute she was sitting on a stool at his feet petting the cat, while she told her adventures with girlish volubility.

Christie could not bear to sit and look on any longer, so she left the room, saying she would see if Mrs. Sterling wanted any thing, for the old lady kept her room with a touch of rheumatism. As she shut the door, Christie heard Kitty say softly:

"Now we'll be comfortable as we used to be: won't we?"

What David answered Christie did not stay to hear, but went into the kitchen, and had her first pang of jealousy out alone, while she beat up the buckwheats for breakfast with an energy that made them miracles of lightness on the morrow.

When she told Mrs. Sterling of the new arrival, the placid little lady gave a cluck of regret and said with unusual emphasis:

" I 'm sorry for it."

" Why ? " asked Christie, feeling as if she could embrace the speaker for the words.

" She is a giddy little thing, and much care to whoever befriends her." Mrs. Sterling would say no more, but, as Christie bade her good-night, she held her hand, saying with a kiss :

" No one will take thy place with *me*, my daughter."

For a week Christie suffered constant pin-pricks of jealousy, despising herself all the time, and trying to be friendly with the disturber of her peace. As if prompted by an evil spirit, Kitty unconsciously tried and tormented her from morning to night, and no one saw or guessed it unless Mrs. Sterling's motherly heart divined the truth. David seemed to enjoy the girl's lively chat, her openly expressed affection, and the fresh young face that always brightened when he came.

Presently, however, Christie saw a change in him, and suspected that he had discovered that Kitty was a child no longer, but a young girl with her head full of love and lovers. The blue eyes grew shy, the pretty face grew eloquent with blushes now and then, as he looked at it, and the lively tongue faltered sometimes in speaking to him. A thousand little coquetries were played off for his benefit, and frequent appeals for advice in her heart affairs kept tender subjects uppermost in their conversations.

At first all this seemed to amuse David as much as if Kitty were a small child playing at sweethearts ; but soon his manner changed, growing respectful, and a little cool when Kitty was most confiding. He no longer laughed about Miles, stopped calling her " little

girl," and dropped his paternal ways as he had done
with Christie. By many indescribable but significant
signs he showed that he considered Kitty a woman
now and treated her as such, being all the more scru-
pulous in the respect he paid her, because she was so
unprotected, and so wanting in the natural dignity and
refinement which are a woman's best protection.

Christie admired him for this, but saw in it the
beginning of a tenderer feeling than pity, and felt each
day that she was one too many now.

Kitty was puzzled and piqued by these changes, and
being a born flirt tried all her powers on David, veiled
under guileless girlishness. She was very pretty, very
charming, and at times most lovable and sweet when
all that was best in her shallow little heart was touched.
But it was evident to all that her early acquaintance
with the hard and sordid side of life had brushed the
bloom from her nature, and filled her mind with
thoughts and feelings unfitted to her years.

Mrs. Sterling was very kind to her, but never treated
her as she did Christie; and though not a word was
spoken between them the elder women knew that they
quite agreed in their opinion of Kitty. She evidently
was rather afraid of the old lady, who said so little and
saw so much. Christie also she shunned without ap-
pearing to do so, and when alone with her put on airs
that half amused, half irritated the other.

"David is my friend, and I don't care for any one
else," her manner said as plainly as words; and to him
she devoted herself so entirely, and apparently so successfully, that Christie made up her mind he had at
last begun to forget his Letty, and think of filling the
void her loss had left.

A few words which she accidentally overheard confirmed this idea, and showed her what she must do. As she came quietly in one evening from a stroll in the lane, and stood taking off cloak and hood, she caught a glimpse through the half-open parlor door of David pacing to and fro with a curiously excited expression on his face, and heard Mrs. Sterling say with unusual warmth :

" Thee is too hard upon thyself, Davy. Forget the past and be happy as other men are. Thee has atoned for thy fault long ago, so let me see thee at peace before I die, my son."

" Not yet, mother, not yet. I have no right to hope or ask for any woman's love till I am worthier of it," answered David in a tone that thrilled Christie's heart : it was so full of love and longing.

Here Kitty came running in from the green-house with her hands full of flowers, and passing Christie, who was fumbling among the cloaks in the passage, she went to show David some new blossom.

He had no time to alter the expression of his face for its usual grave serenity : Kitty saw the change at once, and spoke of it with her accustomed want of tact.

" How handsome you look ! What *are* you thinking about ? " she said, gazing up at him with her own eyes bright with wonder, and her cheeks glowing with the delicate carmine of the frosty air.

" I am thinking that you look more like a rose than ever," answered David turning her attention from himself by a compliment, and beginning to admire the flowers, still with that flushed and kindled look on his own face.

Christie crept upstairs, and, sitting in the dark, decided with the firmness of despair to go away, lest she should betray the secret that possessed her, a dead hope now, but still too dear to be concealed.

" Mr. Power told me to come to him when I got tired of this. I 'll say I *am* tired and try something else, no matter what: I can bear any thing, but to stand quietly by and see David marry that empty-hearted girl, who dares to show that she desires to win him. Out of sight of all this, I can conquer my love, at least hide it; but if I stay I know I shall betray myself in some bitter minute, and I 'd rather die than do that."

Armed with this resolution, Christie went the next day to Mr. Power, and simply said : " I am not needed at the Sterlings any more : can you give me other work to do ? "

Mr. Power's keen eye searched her face for a moment, as if to discover the real motive for her wish. But Christie had nerved herself to bear that look, and showed no sign of her real trouble, unless the set expression of her lips, and the unnatural steadiness of her eyes betrayed it to that experienced reader of human hearts.

Whatever he suspected or saw, Mr. Power kept to himself, and answered in his cordial way :

" Well, I 've been expecting you would tire of that quiet life, and have plenty of work ready for you. One of my good Dorcases is tired out and must rest; so you shall take her place and visit my poor, report their needs, and supply them as fast as we can. Does that suit you ? "

" Entirely, sir. Where shall I live ? " asked Christie, with an expression of relief that said much.

" Here for the present. I want a secretary to put my papers in order, write some of my letters, and do a thousand things to help a busy man. My old house-keeper likes you, and will let you take a duster now and then if you don't find enough other work to do. When can you come ? "

Christie answered with a long breath of satisfaction : " To-morrow, if you like."

" I do : can you be spared so soon ? "

" Oh, yes ! they don't want me now at all, or I would not leave them. Kitty can take my place : she needs protection more than I ; and there is not room for two." She checked herself there, conscious that a tone of bitterness had crept into her voice. Then quite steadily she added :

" Will you be kind enough to write, and ask Mrs. Sterling if she can spare me? I shall find it hard to tell her myself, for I fear she may think me ungrateful after all her kindness."

" No : she is used to parting with those whom she has helped, and is always glad to set them on their way toward better things. I will write to-morrow, and you can come whenever you will, sure of a welcome, my child."

Something in the tone of those last words, and the pressure of the strong, kind hand, touched Christie's sore heart, and made it impossible for her to hide the truth entirely.

She only said : " Thank you, sir. I shall be very glad to come ; " but her eyes were full, and she held his hand an instant, as if she clung to it sure of succor and support.

Then she went home so pale and quiet; so helpful, patient, and affectionate, that Mrs. Sterling watched her anxiously; David looked amazed; and, even self-absorbed Kitty saw the change, and was touched by it.

On the morrow, Mr. Power's note came, and Christie fled upstairs while it was read and discussed.

"If I get through this parting without disgracing myself, I don't care what happens to me afterward," she said; and, in order that she might do so, she assumed a cheerful air, and determined to depart with all the honors of war, if she died in the attempt.

So, when Mrs. Sterling called her down, she went humming into the parlor, smiled as she read the note silently given her, and then said with an effort greater than any she had ever made in her most arduous part on the stage:

"Yes, I did say to Mr. Power that I thought I'd better be moving on. I'm a restless creature as you know; and, now that you don't need me, I've a fancy to see more of the world. If you want me back again in the spring, I'll come."

"I *shall* want thee, my dear, but will not say a word to keep thee now, for thee does need a change, and Mr. Power can give thee work better suited to thy taste than any here. We shall see thee sometimes, and spring will make thee long for the flowers, I hope," was Mrs. Sterling's answer, as Christie gave back the note at the end of her difficult speech.

"Don't think me ungrateful. I have been very

happy here, and never shall forget how motherly kind you have been to me. You will believe this and love me still, though I go away and leave you for a little while ? " prayed Christie, with a face full of treacherous emotion.

Mrs. Sterling laid her hand on Christie's head, as she knelt down impulsively before her, and with a soft solemnity that made the words both an assurance and a blessing, she said :

" I believe and love and honor thee, my child. My heart warmed to thee from the first : it has taken thee to itself now ; and nothing can ever come between us, unless thee wills it. Remember that, and go in peace with an old friend's thanks, and good wishes in return for faithful service, which no money can repay."

Christie laid her cheek against that wrinkled one, and, for a moment, was held close to that peaceful old heart which felt so tenderly for her, yet never wounded her by a word of pity. Infinitely comforting was that little instant of time, when the venerable woman consoled the young one with a touch, and strengthened her by the mute eloquence of sympathy.

This made the hardest task of all easier to perform ; and, when David met her in the evening, Christie was ready to play out her part, feeling that Mrs. Sterling would help her, if need be. But David took it very quietly ; at least, he showed no very poignant regret at her departure, though he lamented it, and hoped it would not be a very long absence. This wounded Christie terribly ; for all of a sudden a barrier seemed to rise between them, and the old friendliness grew chilled.

"He thinks I am ungrateful, and is offended," she said to herself. "Well, I can bear coldness better than kindness now, and it will make it easier to go."

Kitty was pleased at the prospect of reigning alone, and did not disguise her satisfaction; so Christie's last day was any thing but pleasant. Mr. Power would send for her on the morrow, and she busied herself in packing her own possessions, setting every thing in order, and making various little arrangements for Mrs. Sterling's comfort, as Kitty was a heedless creature; willing enough, but very forgetful. In the evening some neighbors came in; so that dangerous time was safely passed, and Christie escaped to her own room with her usual quiet good-night all round.

"We won't have any sentimental demonstrations; no wailing, or tender adieux. If I'm weak enough to break my heart, no one need know it, — least of all, that little fool," thought Christie, grimly, as she burnt up several long-cherished relics of her love.

She was up early, and went about her usual work with the sad pleasure with which one performs a task for the last time. Lazy little Kitty never appeared till the bell rang; and Christie was fond of that early hour, busy though it was, for David was always before her with blazing fires; and, while she got breakfast, he came and went with wood and water, milk and marketing; often stopping to talk, and always in his happiest mood.

The first snow-fall had made the world wonderfully lovely that morning; and Christie stood at the window admiring the bridal look of the earth, as it lay dazzlingly white in the early sunshine. The little parlor was fresh and clean, with no speck of dust anywhere; the fire burned on the bright andirons; the flowers were rejoicing in their morning bath; and the table was set out with dainty care. So homelike, so pleasant, so very dear to her, that Christie yearned to stay, yet dared not, and had barely time to steady face and voice, when David came in with the little posies he always had ready for his mother and Christie at breakfast time. Only a flower by their plates; but it meant much to them: for, in these lives of ours, tender little acts do more to bind hearts together than great deeds or heroic words; since the first are like the dear daily bread that none can live without; the latter but occasional feasts, beautiful and memorable, but not possible to all.

This morning David laid a sprig of sweet-scented balm at his mother's place, two or three rosy daisies at Kitty's, and a bunch of Christie's favorite violets at hers. She smiled as her eye went from the scentless daisies, so pertly pretty, to her own posy full of perfume, and the half sad, half sweet associations that haunt these blue-eyed flowers.

" I wanted pansies for you, but not one would bloom; so I did the next best, since you don't like roses," said David, as Christie stood looking at the violets with a thoughtful face, for something in the peculiarly graceful arrangement of the heart-shaped leaves recalled another nosegay to her mind.

" I like these very much, because they came to me in the beginning of this, the happiest year of my life;" and scarcely knowing why, except that it was very sweet to talk with David in the early sunshine, she told about the flowers some one had given her at church. As she finished she looked up at him; and, though his face was perfectly grave, his eyes laughed, and with a sudden conviction of the truth, Christie exclaimed!

" David, I do believe it was you ! "

" I couldn't help it: you seemed so touched and troubled. I longed to speak to you, but didn't dare, so dropped the flowers and got away as fast as possible. Did you think it very rude ? "

" I thought it the sweetest thing that ever happened to me. That was my first step along a road that you have strewn with flowers ever since. I can't thank you, but I never shall forget it." Christie spoke out fervently, and for an instant her heart shone in her face. Then she checked herself, and, fearing she had said too much, fell to slicing bread with an energetic rapidity which resulted in a cut finger. Dropping the knife, she tried to get her handkerchief, but the blood flowed fast, and the pain of a deep gash made her a little faint. David sprung to help her, tied up the wound, put her in the big chair, held water to her lips, and bathed her temples with a wet napkin; silently, but so tenderly, that it was almost too much for poor Christie.

For one happy moment her head lay on his arm, and his hand brushed back her hair with a touch that was a caress: she heard his heart beat fast with anxiety; felt his breath on her cheek, and wished that she might die then and there, though a bread-knife was not a romantic weapon, nor a cut finger as interesting as a broken heart. Kitty's voice made her start up, and the blissful vision of life, with David in the little house alone, vanished like a bright bubble, leaving the hard reality to be lived out with nothing but a woman's pride to conceal a woman's most passionate pain.

"It's nothing: I'm all right now. Don't say any thing to worry your mother; I'll put on a bit of court-plaster, and no one will be the wiser," she said, hastily removing all traces of the accident but her own pale face.

"Poor Christie, it's hard that you should go away

"ONE HAPPY MOMENT."

with a wound like this on the hand that has done so much for us," said David, as he carefully adjusted the black strip on that forefinger, roughened by many stitches set for him.

" I loved to do it," was all Christie trusted herself to say.

" I know you did; and in your own words I can only answer: 'I don't know how to thank you, but I never shall forget it.'" And David kissed the wounded hand as gratefully and reverently as if its palm was not hardened by the humblest tasks.

If he had only known — ah, if he had only known! — how easily he might repay that debt, and heal the deeper wound in Christie's heart. As it was, she could only say, " You are too kind," and begin to shovel tea into the pot, as Kitty came in, as rosy and fresh as the daisies she put in her hair.

" Ain't they becoming?" she asked, turning to David for admiration.

" No, thank you," he answered absently, looking out over her head, as he stood upon the rug in the attitude which the best men *will* assume in the bosoms of their families.

Kitty looked offended, and turned to the mirror for comfort; while Christie went on shovelling tea, quite unconscious what she was about till David said gravely:

" Won't that be rather strong?"

" How stupid of me! I always forget that Kitty does not drink tea," and Christie rectified her mistake with all speed.

Kitty laughed, and said in her pert little way:

" Getting up early don't seem to agree with either

of you this morning: I wonder what you've been doing?"

"Your work. Suppose you bring in the kettle: Christie has hurt her hand."

David spoke quietly; but Kitty looked as much surprised as if he had boxed her ears, for he had never used that tone to her before. She meekly obeyed; and David added with a smile to Christie:

"Mother is coming down, and you'll have to get more color into your cheeks if you mean to hide your accident from her."

"That is easily done;" and Christie rubbed her pale cheeks till they rivalled Kitty's in their bloom.

"How well you women know how to conceal your wounds," said David, half to himself.

"It is an invaluable accomplishment for us sometimes: you forget that I have been an actress," answered Christie, with a bitter sort of smile.

"I wish I could forget what *I* have been!" muttered David, turning his back to her and kicking a log that had rolled out of place.

In came Mrs. Sterling, and every one brightened up to meet her. Kitty was silent, and wore an injured air which nobody minded; Christie was very lively; and David did his best to help her through that last meal, which was a hard one to three out of the four.

At noon a carriage came for Christie, and she said good-by, as she had drilled herself to say it, cheerfully and steadily.

"It is only for a time, else I couldn't let thee go, my dear," said Mrs. Sterling, with a close embrace.

"I shall see you at church, and Tuesday evenings,

even if you don't find time to come to us, so I shall not
say good-by at all;" and David shook hands warmly,
as he put her into the carriage.

"I 'll invite you to my wedding when I make up my
mind," said Kitty, with feminine malice; for in her eyes
Christie was an old maid who doubtless envied her her
"lots of lovers."

"I hope you will be very happy.   In the mean time
try to save dear Mrs. Sterling all you can, and let her
make you worthy a good husband," was Christie's answer to a speech she was too noble to resent by a sharp
word, or even a contemptuous look.

Then she drove away, smiling and waving her hand
to the old lady at her window; but the last thing she
saw as she left the well-beloved lane, was David going
slowly up the path, with Kitty close beside him, talking
busily.   If she had heard the short dialogue between
them, the sight would have been less bitter, for Kitty
said:

"She 's dreadful good; but I'm glad she 's gone: ain't
you ?"

"No."

"Had you rather have her here than me?"

"Yes."

"Then why don't you ask her to come back."

"I would if I could!"

"I never did see any thing like it; every one is so
queer and cross to-day I get snubbed all round. If
folks ain't good to me, I 'll go and marry Miles! I declare I will."

"You 'd better," and with that David left her frown-
ing and pouting in the porch, and went to shovelling
snow with unusual vigor.

CHAPTER XIV.

WHICH?

DAVID.

MR. POWER received Christie so hospitably that she felt at home at once, and took up her new duties with the energy of one anxious to repay a favor. Her friend knew well the saving power of work, and gave her plenty of it; but it was a sort that at once interested and absorbed her, so that she had little time for dangerous thoughts or vain regrets. As he once said, Mr. Power made her own troubles seem light by showing her others so terribly real and great that she was ashamed to repine at her own lot.

Her gift of sympathy served her well, past experience gave her a quick eye to read the truth in others, and the earnest desire to help and comfort made her an excellent almoner for the rich, a welcome friend to the poor. She was in just the right mood to give herself gladly to any sort of sacrifice, and labored with a quiet energy, painful to witness had any one known the hidden suffering that would not let her rest.

If she had been a regular novel heroine at this crisis, she would have grown gray in a single night, had a dangerous illness, gone mad, or at least taken to pervading the house at unseasonable hours with her back hair down and much wringing of the hands. Being only a commonplace woman she did nothing so romantic, but instinctively tried to sustain and comfort herself with the humble, wholesome duties and affections which seldom fail to keep heads sane and hearts safe. Yet, though her days seemed to pass so busily and cheerfully, it must be confessed that there were lonely vigils in the night; and sometimes in the morning Christie's eyes were very heavy, Christie's pillow wet with tears.

But life never is all work or sorrow; and happy hours, helpful pleasures, are mercifully given like wayside springs to pilgrims trudging wearily along. Mr. Power showed Christie many such, and silently provided her with better consolation than pity or advice.

"Deeds not words," was his motto; and he lived it out most faithfully. "Books and work" he gave his new charge; and then followed up that prescription with "healthful play" of a sort she liked, and had longed for all her life. Sitting at his table Christie saw the best and bravest men and women of our times; for Mr. Power was a magnet that drew them from all parts of the world. She saw and heard, admired and loved them; felt her soul kindle with the desire to follow in their steps, share their great tasks, know their difficulties and dangers, and in the end taste the immortal satisfactions given to those who live and labor for their fellow-men. In such society all other aims seemed poor and petty; for they appeared to live in a nobler world than any she had known, and she felt as if they belonged to another race; not men nor angels, but a delightful mixture of the two; more as she imagined the gods and heroes of old; not perfect, but wonderfully strong and brave and good; each gifted with a separate virtue, and each bent on a mission that should benefit mankind.

Nor was this the only pleasure given her. One evening of each week was set apart by Mr. Power for the reception of whomsoever chose to visit him; for his parish was a large one, and his house a safe haunt for refugees from all countries, all oppressions.

Christie enjoyed these evenings heartily, for there was no ceremony; each comer brought his mission, idea, or need, and genuine hospitality made the visit profitable or memorable to all, for entire freedom prevailed, and there was stabling for every one's hobby.

Christie felt that she was now receiving the best culture, acquiring the polish that society gives, and makes truly admirable when character adds warmth and power to its charm. The presence of her bosom-care calmed the old unrest, softened her manners, and at times touched her face with an expression more beautiful than beauty. She was quite unconscious of the changes passing over her; and if any one had told her she was fast becoming a most attractive woman, she would have been utterly incredulous. But others saw and felt the new charm; for no deep experience bravely borne can fail to leave its mark, often giving power in return for patience, and lending a subtle loveliness to faces whose bloom it has destroyed.

This fact was made apparent to Christie one evening when she went down to the weekly gathering in one of the melancholy moods which sometimes oppressed her. She felt dissatisfied with herself because her interest in all things began to flag, and a restless longing for some new. excitement to break up the monotonous pain of her inner life possessed her. Being still a little shy in company, she slipped quietly into a recess which commanded a view of both rooms, and sat looking listlessly about her while waiting for David, who seldom failed to come.

A curious collection of fellow-beings was before her, and at another time she would have found much to interest and amuse her. In one corner a newly imported German with an Orson-like head, thumb-ring, and the fragrance of many meerschaums still hovering about him, was hammering away upon some disputed point with a scientific Frenchman, whose national politeness was only equalled by his national volubility. A prominent statesman was talking with a fugitive slave; a young poet getting inspiration from the face and voice of a handsome girl who had earned the right to put M. D. to her name. An old philosopher was calming the ardor of several rampant radicals, and a famous singer was comforting the heart of an Italian exile by talking politics in his own melodious tongue.

There were plenty of reformers: some as truculent as Martin Luther; others as beaming and benevolent as if the pelting of the world had only mellowed them, and no amount of denunciatory thunder could sour the milk of human kindness creaming in their happy hearts. There were eager women just beginning their protest against the wrongs that had wrecked their peace; subdued women who had been worsted in the unequal conflict and given it up; resolute women with "No surrender" written all over their strong-minded countenances; and sweet, hopeful women, whose faith in God and man nothing could shake or sadden.

But to Christie there was only one face worth looking at till David came, and that was Mr. Power's; for he was a perfect host, and pervaded the rooms like a genial atmosphere, using the welcome of eye and hand which needs no language to interpret it, giving to each guest the intellectual fare he loved, and making their enjoyment his own.

"Bless the dear man! what should we all do without him?" thought Christie, following him with grateful eyes, as he led an awkward youth in rusty black to the statesman whom it had been the desire of his ambitious soul to meet.

The next minute she proved that *she* at least could do without the "dear man;" for David entered the room, and she forgot all about him. Here and at church were the only places where the friends had met during these months, except one or two short visits to the little house in the lane when Christie devoted herself to Mrs. Sterling.

David was quite unchanged, though once or twice Christie fancied he seemed ill at ease with her, and immediately tormented herself with the idea that some alteration in her own manner had perplexed or offended him. She did her best to be as frank and cordial as in the happy old days; but it was impossible, and she soon gave it up, assuming in the place of that former friendliness, a grave and quiet manner which would have led a wiser man than David to believe her busied with her own affairs and rather indifferent to every thing else.

If he had known how her heart danced in her bosom, her eyes brightened, and all the world became endurable, the moment he appeared, he would not have been so long in joining her, nor have doubted what welcome awaited him.

As it was, he stopped to speak to his host; and, before he reappeared, Christie had found the excitement she had been longing for.

"Now some bore will keep him an hour, and the evening is *so* short," she thought, with a pang of disappointment; and, turning her eyes away from the crowd which had swallowed up her heart's desire, they fell upon a gentleman just entering, and remained fixed with an expression of unutterable surprise; for there, elegant, calm, and cool as ever, stood Mr. Fletcher.

"How came he here?" was her first question; "How will he behave to me?" her second. As she could answer neither, she composed herself as fast as possible, resolving to let matters take their own course, and feeling in the mood for an encounter with a discarded lover, as she took a womanish satisfaction in remembering that the very personable gentleman before her had once been.

Mr. Fletcher and his companion passed on to find their host; and, with a glance at the mirror opposite, which showed her that the surprise of the moment had given her the color she lacked before, Christie occupied herself with a portfolio of engravings, feeling very much as she used to feel when waiting at a side scene for her cue.

She had not long to wait before Mr. Power came up, and presented the stranger; for such he fancied him, never having heard a certain episode in Christie's life. Mr. Fletcher bowed, with no sign of recognition in his face, and began to talk in the smooth, low voice she remembered so well. For the moment, through sheer surprise, Christie listened and replied as any young lady might have done to a new-made acquaintance. But very soon she felt sure that Mr. Fletcher intended to ignore the past ; and, finding her on a higher round of the social ladder, to accept the fact and begin again.

At first she was angry, then amused, then interested in the somewhat dramatic turn affairs were taking, and very wisely decided to meet him on his own ground, and see what came of it.

In the midst of an apparently absorbing discussion of one of Raphael's most insipid Madonnas, she was conscious that David had approached, paused, and was scrutinizing her companion with unusual interest. Seized with a sudden desire to see the two men together, Christie beckoned ; and when he obeyed, she introduced him, drew him into the conversation, and then left him in the lurch by falling silent and taking notes while they talked.

If she wished to wean her heart from David by seeing him at a disadvantage, she could have devised no better way; for, though a very feminine test, it answered the purpose excellently.

Mr. Fletcher was a handsome man, and just then looked his best. Improved health gave energy and color to his formerly sallow, listless face: the cold eyes were softer, the hard mouth suave and smiling, and about the whole man there was that indescribable something which often proves more attractive than worth or wisdom to keener-sighted women than Christie. Never had he talked better; for, as if he suspected what was in the mind of one hearer, he exerted himself to be as brilliant as possible, and succeeded admirably.

David never appeared so ill, for he had no clew to the little comedy being played before him; and long seclusion and natural reserve unfitted him to shine beside a man of the world like Mr. Fletcher. His simple English sounded harsh, after the foreign phrases that slipped so easily over the other's tongue. He had visited no galleries, seen few of the world's wonders, and could only listen when they were discussed. More than once he was right, but failed to prove it, for Mr. Fletcher skilfully changed the subject or quenched him with a politely incredulous shrug.

Even in the matter of costume, poor David was worsted; for, in a woman's eyes, dress has wonderful significance. Christie used to think his suit of sober gray the most becoming man could wear; but now it looked shapeless and shabby, beside garments which bore the stamp of Paris in the gloss and grace of broadcloth and fine linen. David wore no gloves: Mr. Fletcher's were immaculate. David's tie was so plain no one observed it: Mr. Fletcher's, elegant and faultless enough for a modern Beau Brummel. David's handkerchief was of the commonest sort (she knew that, for she hemmed it herself): Mr. Fletcher's was the finest cambric, and a delicate breath of perfume refreshed the aristocratic nose to which the article belonged.

Christie despised herself as she made these comparisons, and felt how superficial they were; but, having resolved to exalt one man at the expense of the other for her own good, she did not relent till David took advantage of a pause, and left them with a reproachful look that made her wish Mr. Fletcher at the bottom of the sea.

When they were alone a subtle change in his face and manner convinced her that he also had been taking notes, and had arrived at a favorable decision regarding herself. Women are quick at making such discoveries; and, even while she talked with him as a stranger, she felt assured that, if she chose, she might make him again her lover.

Here was a temptation! She had longed for some new excitement, and fate seemed to have put one of the most dangerous within her reach. It was natural to find comfort in the knowledge that somebody loved her, and to take pride in her power over one man, because another did not own it. In spite of her better self she felt the fascination of the hour, and yielded to it, half unconsciously assuming something of the " dash and daring" which Mr. Fletcher had once confessed to finding so captivating in the demure governess. He evidently thought so still, and played his part with spirit; for, while apparently enjoying a conversation which contained no allusion to the past, the memory of it gave piquancy to that long *tête-à-tête.*

As the first guests began to go, Mr. Fletcher's friend beckoned to him; and he rose, saying with an accent of regret which changed to one of entreaty, as he put his question:

"I, too, must go. May I come again, Miss Devon?"

"I am scarcely more than a guest myself; but Mr. Power is always glad to see whoever cares to come," replied Christie rather primly, though her eyes were dancing with amusement at the recollection of those love passages upon the beach.

"Next time, I shall come not as a stranger, but as a former — may I say friend?" he added quickly, as if emboldened by the mirthful eyes that so belied the demure lips.

"Now you forget your part," and Christie's primness vanished in a laugh. "I am glad of it, for I want to ask about Mrs. Saltonstall and the children. I've often thought of the little dears, and longed to see them."

"They are in Paris with their father."

"Mrs. Saltonstall is well, I hope?"

"She died six months ago."

An expression of genuine sorrow came over Mr. Fletcher's face as he spoke; and, remembering that the silly little woman was his sister, Christie put out her hand with a look and gesture so full of sympathy that words were unnecessary. Taking advantage of this propitious moment, he said, with an expressive glance and effective tone : "I am all alone now. You *will* let me come again ? "

"Certainly, if it can give you pleasure," she answered heartily, forgetting herself in pity for his sorrow.

Mr. Fletcher pressed her hand with a grateful, "Thank you ! " and wisely went away at once, leaving compassion to plead for him better than he could have done it for himself.

Leaning back in her chair, Christie was thinking over this interview so intently that she started when David's voice said close beside her :

"Shall I disturb you if I say, ' Good-night ' ? "

"I thought you were not going to say it at all," she answered rather sharply.

"I've been looking for a chance ; but you were so absorbed with that man I had to wait."

"Considering the elegance of 'that man,' you don't treat him with much respect."

"I don't feel much. What brought him here, I wonder. A French *salon* is more in his line."

"He came to see Mr. Power, as every one else does, of course."

"Don't dodge, Christie : you know he came to see you."

"How do you like him ? " she asked, with treacherous abruptness.

"Not particularly, so far. But if I knew him, I dare say I should find many good traits in him."

"I know you would ! " said Christie, warmly, not thinking of Fletcher, but of David's kindly way of finding good in every one.

"He must have improved since you saw him last; for then, if I remember rightly, you found him 'lazy, cross, selfish, and conceited.'"

"Now, David, I never said any thing of the sort," began Christie, wondering what possessed him to be so satirical and short with her.

"Yes, you did, last September, sitting on the old apple-tree the morning of your birthday."

"What an inconvenient memory you have! Well, he *was* all that then; but he is not an invalid now, and so we see his real self."

"I also remember that you gave me the impression that he was an elderly man."

"Isn't forty elderly?"

"He wasn't forty when you taught his sister's children."

"No; but he looked older than he does now, being so ill. I used to think he would be very handsome with good health; and now I see I was right," said Christie, with feigned enthusiasm; for it was a new thing to tease David, and she liked it.

But she got no more of it; for, just then, the singer began to sing to the select few who remained, and every one was silent. Leaning on the high back of Christie's chair, David watched the reflection of her face in the long mirror; for she listened to the music with downcast eyes, unconscious what eloquent expressions were passing over her countenance. She seemed a new Christie to David, in that excited mood; and, as he watched her, he thought:

"She loved this man once, or he loved her; and to-night it all comes back to her. How will it end?"

So earnestly did he try to read that altered face that Christie felt the intentness of his gaze, looked up suddenly, and met his eyes in the glass. Something in the expression of those usually serene eyes, now darkened and dilated with the intensity of that long scrutiny, surprised and troubled her; and, scarcely knowing what she said, she asked quickly:

"Who are you admiring?"

"Not myself."

"I wonder if you'd think me vain if I asked you something that I want to know?" she said, obeying a sudden impulse.

"Ask it, and I'll tell you."

"Am I much changed since you first knew me?"

"Very much."

"For the better or the worse?"

"The better, decidedly."

"Thank you, I hoped so; but one never knows how one seems to other people. I was wondering what you saw in the glass."

"A good and lovely woman, Christie."

How sweet it sounded to hear David say that! so simply and sincerely that it was far more than a mere compliment. She did not thank him, but said softly as if to herself:

"So let me seem until I be"

— and then sat silent, so full of satisfaction in the thought that David found her "good and lovely," she could not resist stealing a glance at the tell-tale mirror to see if she might believe him.

She forgot herself, however; for he was off guard now, and stood looking away with brows knit, lips tightly set, and eyes fixed, yet full of fire; his whole attitude and expression that of a man intent on subduing some strong impulse by a yet stronger will.

It startled Christie; and she leaned forward, watching him with breathless interest till the song ceased, and, with the old impatient gesture, David seemed to relapse into his accustomed quietude.

"It was the wonderful music that excited him: that was all;" thought Christie; yet, when he came round to say good-night, the strange expression was not gone, and his manner was not his own.

"Shall *I* ask if I may come again," he said, imitating Mr. Fletcher's graceful bow with an odd smile.

"I let him come because he has lost his sister, and is lonely," began Christie, but got no further, for David said, "Good-night!" abruptly, and was gone without a word to Mr. Power.

"He's in a hurry to get back to his Kitty," she thought, tormenting herself with feminine skill. "Never mind," she added, with a defiant sort of smile; "*I 've* got my Philip, handsomer and more in love than ever, if I 'm not deceived. I wonder if he *will* come again?"

Mr. Fletcher did come again, and with flattering regularity, for several weeks, evidently finding something very attractive in those novel gatherings. Mr. Power soon saw why he came; and, as Christie seemed to enjoy his presence, the good man said nothing to disturb her, though he sometimes cast an anxious glance toward the recess where the two usually sat, apparently busy with books or pictures; yet, by their faces, showing that an under current of deeper interest than art or literature flowed through their intercourse.

Christie had not deceived herself, and it was evident that her old lover meant to try his fate again, if she continued to smile upon him as she had done of late. He showed her his sunny side now, and very pleasant she found it. The loss of his sister had touched his heart, and made him long to fill the place her death left vacant. Better health sweetened his temper, and woke the desire to do something worth the doing; and the sight of the only woman he had ever really loved, reawakened the sentiment that had not died, and made it doubly sweet.

Why he cared for Christie he could not tell, but he never had forgotten her; and, when he met her again with that new beauty in her face, he felt that time had only ripened the blithe girl into a deep-hearted woman, and he loved her with a better love than before. His whole manner showed this; for the half-careless, half-condescending air of former times was replaced by the most courteous respect, a sincere desire to win her favor, and at times the tender sort of devotion women find so charming.

Christie felt all this, enjoyed it, and tried to be grateful for it in the way he wished, thinking that hearts could be managed like children, and when one toy is unattainable, be appeased by a bigger or a brighter one of another sort.

" I must love some one," she said, as she leaned over a basket of magnificent flowers just left for her by Mr. Fletcher's servant, a thing which often happened now. " Philip has loved me with a fidelity that ought to touch my heart. Why not accept him, and enjoy a new life of luxury, novelty, and pleasure? All these things he can give me: all these things are valued, admired, and sought for; and who would appreciate them more than I? I could travel, cultivate myself in many delightful ways, and do so much good. No matter if I was not very happy: I should make Philip so, and have it in my power to comfort many poor souls. That ought to satisfy me; for what is nobler than to live for others?"

This idea attracted her, as it does all generous natures; she became enamoured of self-sacrifice, and almost persuaded herself that it was her duty to marry Mr. Fletcher, whether she loved him or not, in order that she might dedicate her life to the service of poorer, sadder creatures than herself.

But in spite of this amiable delusion, in spite of the desire to forget the love she would have in the love she might have, and in spite of the great improvement in her faithful Philip, Christie could not blind herself to the fact that her head, rather than her heart, advised the match; she could not conquer a suspicion that, however much Mr. Fletcher might love his wife, he would be something of a tyrant, and she was very sure she never would make a good slave. In her cooler moments she remembered that men are not puppets, to be moved as a woman's will commands, and the uncertainty of being able to carry out her charitable plans made her pause to consider whether she would not be selling her liberty too cheaply, if in return she got only dependence and bondage along with fortune and a home.

So tempted and perplexed, self-deluded and self-warned, attracted and repelled, was poor Christie, that she began to feel as if she had got into a labyrinth without any clew to bring her safely out. She longed to ask advice of some one, but could not turn to Mrs. Sterling; and what other woman friend had she except Rachel, from whom she had not heard for months?

As she asked herself this question one day, feeling sure that Mr. Fletcher would come in the evening, and would soon put his fortune to the touch again, the thought of Mrs. Wilkins seemed to answer her.

"Why not?" said Christie: "she is sensible, kind, and discreet; she may put me right, for I'm all in a tangle now with doubts and fears, feelings and fancies. I'll go and see her: that will do me good, even if I don't say a word about my 'werryments,' as the dear soul would call them."

Away she went, and fortunately found her friend alone in the "settin'-room," darning away at a perfect stack of socks, as she creaked comfortably to and fro in her old rocking-chair.

"I was jest wishin' somebody would drop in: it's so kinder lonesome with the children to school and Adelaide asleep. How be you, dear?" said Mrs. Wilkins, with a hospitable hug and a beaming smile.

"I'm worried in my mind, so I came to see you," answered Christie, sitting down with a sigh.

"Bless your dear heart, what *is* to pay. Free your mind, and I'll do my best to lend a hand."

The mere sound of that hearty voice comforted Christie, and gave her courage to introduce the little fiction under which she had decided to defraud Mrs. Wilkins of her advice. So she helped herself to a very fragmentary blue sock and a big needle, that she might have employment for her eyes, as they were not so obedient as her tongue, and then began in as easy a tone as she could assume.

"Well, you see a friend of mine wants my advice on a very serious matter, and I really don't know what to give her. It is strictly confidential, you know, so I won't mention any names, but just set the case before you and get your opinion, for I've great faith in your sensible way of looking at things."

"Thanky, dear, you'r welcome to my 'pinion ef it's wuth any thing. Be these folks you tell of young?" asked Mrs. Wilkins, with evident relish for the mystery.

"No, the woman is past thirty, and the man 'most forty, I believe," said Christie, darning away in some trepidation at having taken the first plunge.

"My patience! ain't the creater old enough to know her own mind? for I s'pose she's the one in the quanderry?" exclaimed Mrs. Wilkins, looking over her spectacles with dangerously keen eyes.

"The case is this," said Christie, in guilty haste. "The 'creature' is poor and nobody, the man rich and of good family, so you see it's rather hard for her to decide."

"No, I don't see nothin' of the sort," returned blunt Mrs. Wilkins. "Ef she loves the man, take him: ef she don't, give him the mittin and done with it. Money and friends and family ain't much to do with the matter accordin' to my view. It's jest a plain question betwixt them two. Ef it takes much settlin' they'd better let it alone."

"She doesn't love him as much as she might, I fancy, but she is tired of grubbing along alone. He is very fond of her, and very rich; and it would be a fine thing for her in a worldly way, I'm sure."

"Oh, she's goin' to marry for a livin' is she? Wal, now I'd ruther one of my girls should grub the wust kind all their days than do that. Hows'ever, it may suit some folks ef they ain't got much heart, and is contented with fine clothes, nice vittles, and handsome furnitoor. Selfish, cold, silly kinder women might git on, I dare say; but I shouldn't think any friend of your'n would be one of that sort."

"But she might do a great deal of good, and make others happy even if she was not so herself."

"She might, but I doubt it, for money got that way wouldn't prosper wal. Mis'able folks ain't half so charitable as happy ones; and I don't believe five dollars from one of 'em would go half so fur, or be half so comfortin' as a kind word straight out of a cheerful heart. I know some thinks that is a dreadful smart thing to do; but *I* don't, and ef any one wants to go a sacrificin' herself for the good of others, there's better ways of doin' it than startin' with a lie in her mouth."

Mrs. Wilkins spoke warmly; for Christie's face made her fiction perfectly transparent, though the good woman with true delicacy showed no sign of intelligence on that point.

"Then you wouldn't advise my friend to say yes?"

"Sakes alive, no! I'd say to her as I did to my younger sisters when their courtin' time come: 'Jest be sure you're right as to there bein' love enough, then go ahead, and the Lord will bless you.'"

"Did they follow your advice?"

"They did, and both is prosperin' in different ways.

Gusty, she found she was well on't for love, so she married, though Samuel Buck was poor, and they 're happy as can be a workin' up together, same as Lisha and me did. Addy, she calc'lated she wan't satisfied somehow, so she *didn't* marry, though James Miller was wal off; and she 's kep stiddy to her trade, and ain't never repented. There 's a sight said and writ about such things," continued Mrs. Wilkins, rambling on to give Christie time to think; "but I 've an idee that women's hearts is to be trusted ef they ain't been taught all wrong. Jest let 'em remember that they take a husband for wuss as well as better (and there 's a sight of wuss in this tryin' world for some on us), and be ready to do their part patient and faithful, and I ain't a grain afraid but what they 'll be fetched through, always pervidin' they love the man and not his money."

There was a pause after that last speech, and Christie felt as if her perplexity was clearing away very fast; for Mrs. Wilkins's plain talk seemed to show her things in their true light, with all the illusions of false sentiment and false reasoning stripped away. She felt clearer and stronger already, and as if she could make up her mind very soon when one other point had been discussed.

"I fancy my friend is somewhat influenced by the fact that this man loved and asked her to marry him some years ago. He has not forgotten her, and this touches her heart more than any thing else. It seems as if his love must be genuine to last so long, and not to mind her poverty, want of beauty, and accomplishments; for he is a proud and fastidious man."

"I think wal of him for that!" said Mrs. Wilkins,

approvingly ; " but I guess she's wuth all he gives her, for there must be somethin' pretty gennywin' in her to make him overlook her lacks and hold on so stiddy. It don't alter *her* side of the case one mite though ; for love is love, and ef she ain't got it, he'd better not take gratitude instid, but sheer off and leave her for somebody else."

" Nobody else wants her ! " broke from Christie like an involuntary cry of pain ; then she hid her face by stooping to gather up the avalanche of hosiery which fell from her lap to the floor.

" She can't be sure of that," said Mrs. Wilkins cheerily, though her spectacles were dim with sudden mist. " I know there's a mate for her somewheres, so she'd better wait a spell and trust in Providence. It wouldn't be so pleasant to see the right one come along after she'd went and took the wrong one in a hurry : would it ? Waitin' is always safe, and time needn't be wasted in frettin' or bewailin' ; for the Lord knows there's a sight of good works sufferin' to be done, and single women has the best chance at 'em."

" I've accomplished one good work at any rate ; and, small as it is, I feel better for it. Give this sock to your husband, and tell him his wife sets a good example both by precept and practice to other women, married or single. Thank you very much, both for myself and my friend, who shall profit by your advice," said Christie, feeling that she had better go before she told every thing.

" I hope she will," returned Mrs. Wilkins, as her guest went away with a much happier face than the one she brought. " And ef I know her, which I think

I do, she'll find that Cinthy Wilkins ain't fur from right, ef her experience is good for any thing," added the matron with a sigh, and a glance at a dingy photograph of her Lisha on the wall, a sigh that seemed to say there had been a good deal of " *wuss* " in her bargain, though she was too loyal to confess it.

Something in Christie's face struck Mr. Fletcher at once when he appeared that evening. He had sometimes found her cold and quiet, often gay and capricious, usually earnest and cordial, with a wistful look that searched his face and both won and checked him by its mute appeal, seeming to say, " Wait a little till I have taught my heart to answer as you wish."

To-night her eyes shunned his, and when he caught a glimpse of them they were full of a soft trouble ; her manner was kinder than ever before, and yet it made him anxious, for there was a resolute expression about her lips even when she smiled, and though he ventured upon allusions·to the past hitherto tacitly avoided, she listened as if it had no tender charm for her.

Being thoroughly in earnest now, Mr. Fletcher resolved to ask the momentous question again without delay. David was not there, and had not been for several weeks, another thorn in Christie's heart, though she showed no sign of regret, and said to herself, " It is better so." His absence left Fletcher master of the field, and he seized the propitious moment.

" Will you show me the new picture ? Mr. Power spoke of it, but I do not like to trouble him."

" With pleasure," and Christie led the way to a little room where the newly arrived gift was placed.

She knew what was coming, but was ready, and felt a tragic sort of satisfaction in the thought of all she was relinquishing for love of David.

No one was in the room, but a fine copy of Michael Angelo's Fates hung on the wall, looking down at them with weird significance.

" They look as if they would give a stern answer to any questioning of ours," Mr. Fletcher said, after a glance of affected interest.

" They would give a true one I fancy," answered Christie, shading her eyes as if to see the better.

" I'd rather question a younger, fairer Fate, hoping that she will give me an answer both true and kind. May I, Christie?"

" I will be true but — I cannot be kind." It cost her much to say that; yet she did it steadily, though he held her hand in both his own, and waited for her words with ardent expectation.

" Not yet perhaps, — but in time, when I have proved how sincere my love is, how entire my repentance for the ungenerous words you have not forgotten. I wanted you then for my own sake, now I want you for yourself, because I love and honor you above all women. I tried to forget you, but I could not; and all these years have carried in my heart a very tender memory of the girl who dared to tell me that all I could offer her was not worth her love."

" I was mistaken," began Christie, finding this wooing much harder to withstand than the other.

" No, you were right: I felt it then and resented it, but I owned it later, and regretted it more bitterly than I can tell. I'm not worthy of you; I never shall be : but

I've loved you for five years without hope, and I'll
wait five more if in the end you will come to me.
Christie, I need you very much!"

If Mr. Fletcher had gone down upon his knees and
poured out the most ardent protestations that ever left
a lover's lips, it would not have touched her as did that
last little appeal, uttered with a break in the voice that
once was so proud and was so humble now.

"Forgive me!" she cried, looking up at him with
real respect in her face, and real remorse smiting her
conscience. "Forgive me! I have misled you and myself. I tried to love you: I was grateful for your regard,
touched by your fidelity, and I hoped I might repay it;
but I cannot! I cannot!"

"Why?"

Such a hard question! She owed him all the truth,
yet how could she tell it? She could not in words,
but her face did, for the color rose and burned on
cheeks and forehead with painful fervor; her eyes
fell, and her lips trembled as if endeavoring to keep
down the secret that was escaping against her will.
A moment of silence as Mr. Fletcher searched for
the truth and found it; then he said with such sharp
pain in his voice that Christie's heart ached at the
sound:

"I see: I am too late?"

"Yes."

"And there is no hope?"

"None."

"Then there is nothing more for me to say but
good-by. May you be happy."

"I shall not be;—I have no hope;—I only try to be

true to you and to myself. Oh, believe it, and pity me
as I do you!"

As the words broke from Christie, she covered up
her face, bowed down with the weight of remorse
that made her long to atone for what she had done
by any self-humiliation.

Mr. Fletcher was at his best at that moment; for
real love ennobles the worst and weakest while it
lasts: but he could not resist the temptation that confession offered him. He tried to be generous, but the
genuine virtue was not in him; he did want Christie
very much, and the knowledge of a rival in her heart
only made her the dearer.

"I'm not content with your pity, sweet as it is: I
want your love, and I believe that I might earn it
if you would let me try. You are all alone, and life is
hard to you: come to me and let me make it happier.
I'll be satisfied with friendship till you can give me
more."

He said this very tenderly, caressing the bent head
while he spoke, and trying to express by tone and
gesture how eagerly he longed to receive and cherish
what that other man neglected.

Christie felt this to her heart's core, and for a moment
longed to end the struggle, say, "Take me," and accept
the shadow for the substance. But those last words of
his vividly recalled the compact made with David that
happy birthday night. How could she be his friend if
she was Mr. Fletcher's wife? She knew she could not
be true to both, while her heart reversed the sentiment
she then would owe them: David's friendship was
dearer than Philip's love, and she would keep it at all

costs. These thoughts flashed through her mind in the drawing of a breath, and she looked up, saying steadily in spite of wet eyes and still burning cheeks :

"Hope nothing; wait for nothing from me. I will have no more delusions for either of us : it is weak and wicked, for I know I shall not change. Some time we may venture to be friends perhaps, but not now. Forgive me, and be sure I shall suffer more than you for this mistake of mine."

When she had denied his suit before he had been ungenerous and angry; for his pride was hurt and his will thwarted : now his heart bled and hope died hard ; but all that was manliest in him rose to help him bear the loss, for *this* love was genuine, and made him both just and kind. His face was pale with the pain of that fruitless passion, and his voice betrayed how hard he strove for self-control, as he said hurriedly :

"*You* need not suffer : this mistake has given me the happiest hours of my life, and I am better for having known so sweet and true a woman. God bless you, Christie!" and with a quick embrace that startled her by its suddenness and strength he left her, standing there alone before the three grim Fates.

CHAPTER XV.

"NOW it is all over. I shall never have another chance like that, and must make up my mind to be a lonely and laborious spinster all my life. Youth is going fast, and I have little in myself to attract or win, though David did call me 'good and lovely.' Ah, well, I 'll try to deserve his praise, and not let disappointment sour or sadden me. Better to hope and wait all my life than marry without love."

Christie often said this to herself during the hard days that followed Mr. Fletcher's disappearance; a disappearance, by the way, which caused Mr. Power much satisfaction, though he only betrayed it by added kindness to Christie, and in his manner an increased respect very comforting to her.

But she missed her lover, for nothing now broke up the monotony of a useful life. She had enjoyed that little episode; for it had lent romance to every thing while it lasted, even the charity basket with which she went her rounds; for Mr. Fletcher often met her by accident apparently, and carried it as if to prove the sincerity of his devotion. No bouquets came now; no graceful little notes with books or invitations to some coveted pleasure; no dangerously delightful evenings in the recess, where, for a time, she felt and used the power which to a woman is so full of subtle satisfaction; no bitter-sweet hopes; no exciting dreams of what might be with the utterance of a word; no soft uncertainty to give a charm to every hour that passed. Nothing but daily duties, a little leisure that hung heavy on her hands with no hope to stimulate, no lover to lighten it, and a sore, sad heart that would clamor for its right; and even when pride silenced it ached on with the dull pain which only time and patience have the power to heal.

But as those weeks went slowly by, she began to discover some of the miracles true love can work. She thought she had laid it in its grave; but an angel rolled the stone away, and the lost passion rose stronger, purer, and more beautiful than when she buried it with bitter tears. A spirit now, fed by no hope, warmed by no tenderness, clothed in no fond delusion; the vital soul of love which outlives the fairest, noblest form humanity can give it, and sits among the ruins singing the immortal hymn of consolation the Great Musician taught.

Christie felt this strange comfort resting like a baby in her lonely bosom, cherished and blessed it; wondering while she rejoiced, and soon perceiving with the swift instinct of a woman, that this was a lesson, hard to learn, but infinitely precious, helpful, and sustaining when once gained. She was not happy, only patient; not hopeful, but trusting; and when life looked dark and barren without, she went away into that inner world of deep feeling, high thought, and earnest aspiration; which is a never-failing refuge to those whose experience has built within them

" The nunnery of a chaste heart and quiet mind."

Some women live fast; and Christie fought her battle, won her victory, and found peace declared during that winter: for her loyalty to love brought its own reward in time, giving her the tranquil steadfastness which comes to those who submit and ask nothing but fortitude.

She had seen little of David, except at church, and began to regard him almost as one might a statue on a tomb, the marble effigy of the beloved dead below; for the sweet old friendship was only a pale shadow now. He always found her out, gave her the posy she best liked, said cheerfully, " How goes it, Christie ? " and she always answered, " Good-morning, David. I am well and busy, thank you." Then they sat together listening to Mr. Power, sung from the same book, walked a little way together, and parted for another week with a hand-shake for good-by.

Christie often wondered what prayers David prayed when he sat so still with his face hidden by his hand, and looked up with such a clear and steady look when he had done. She tried to do the same; but her thoughts would wander to the motionless gray figure beside her, and she felt as if peace and strength unconsciously flowed from it to sustain and comfort her. Some of her happiest moments were those she spent sitting there, pale and silent, with absent eyes, and lips that trembled now and then, hidden by the flowers held before them, kissed covertly, and kept like relics long after they were dead.

One bitter drop always marred the pleasure of that

hour; for when she had asked for Mrs. Sterling, and sent her love, she forced herself to say kindly:

"And Kitty, is she doing well?"

"Capitally; come and see how she has improved; we are quite proud of her."

"I will if I can find time. It's a hard winter and we have so much to do," she would answer smiling, and then go home to struggle back into the patient mood she tried to make habitual.

But she seldom made time to go and see Kitty's improvement; and, when she did run out for an hour she failed to discover any thing, except that the girl was prettier and more coquettish than ever, and assumed airs of superiority that tried Christie very much.

"I am ready for any thing," she always said with a resolute air after one of these visits; but, when the time seemed to have come she was not so ready as she fancied.

Passing out of a store one day, she saw Kitty all in her best, buying white gloves with a most important air. "That looks suspicious," she thought, and could not resist speaking.

"All well at home?" she asked.

"Grandma and I have been alone for nearly a week; David went off on business; but he's back now and — oh, my goodness! I forgot: I'm not to tell a soul yet;" and Kitty pursed up her lips, looking quite oppressed with some great secret.

"Bless me, how mysterious! Well, I won't ask any dangerous questions, only tell me if the dear old lady is well," said Christie, desperately curious, but too proud to show it.

"She's well, but dreadfully upset by what's happened; well she may be." And Kitty shook her head with a look of mingled mystery and malicious merriment.

"Mr. Sterling is all right I hope?" Christie never called him David to Kitty; so that impertinent little person took especial pains to speak familiarly, sometimes even fondly of him to Christie.

"Dear fellow! he's so happy he don't know what to do with himself. I just wish you could see him go round smiling, and singing, and looking as if he'd like to dance."

"That looks as if he was going to get a chance to do it," said Christie, with a glance at the gloves, as Kitty turned from the counter.

"So he is!" laughed Kitty, patting the little parcel with a joyful face.

"I do believe you are going to be married:" exclaimed Christie, half distracted with curiosity.

"I am, but not to Miles. Now don't you say another word, for I'm dying to tell, and I promised I wouldn't. David wants to do it himself. By-by." And Kitty hurried away, leaving Christie as pale as if she had seen a ghost at noonday.

She had; for the thought of David's marrying Kitty had haunted her all those months, and now she was quite sure the blow had come.

"If she was only a nobler woman I could bear it better; but I am sure he will regret it when the first illusion is past. I fancy she reminds him of his lost Letty, and so he thinks he loves her. I pray he may be happy, and I hope it will be over soon," thought

Christie, with a groan, as she trudged away to carry comfort to those whose woes could be relieved by tea and sugar, flannel petticoats, and orders for a ton of coal.

It *was* over soon, but not as Christie had expected.

That evening Mr. Power was called away, and she sat alone, bravely trying to forget suspense and grief in copying the record of her last month's labor. But she made sad work of it; for her mind was full of David and his wife, so happy in the little home which had grown doubly dear to her since she left it. No wonder then that she put down "two dozen children" to Mrs. Flanagan, and "four knit hoods" with the measles; or that a great blot fell upon "twenty yards red flannel," as the pen dropped from the hands she clasped together; saying with all the fervor of true self-abnegation: "I hope he will be happy; oh, I hope he will be happy!"

If ever woman deserved reward for patient endeavor, hard-won submission, and unselfish love, Christie did then. And she received it in full measure; for the dear Lord requites some faithful hearts, blesses some lives that seem set apart for silent pain and solitary labor.

Snow was falling fast, and a bitter wind moaned without; the house was very still, and nothing stirred in the room but the flames dancing on the hearth, and the thin hand moving to and fro among the records of a useful life.

Suddenly the bell rang loudly and repeatedly, as if the new-comer was impatient of delay. Christie paused to listen. It was not Mr. Power's ring, not his voice in the hall below, not his step that came leaping up the stairs, nor his hand that threw wide the door. She knew them all, and her heart stood still an instant; then she gathered up her strength, said low to herself, "Now it is coming," and was ready for the truth, with a colorless face; eyes unnaturally bright and fixed; and one hand on her breast, as if to hold in check the rebellious heart that would throb so fast.

It was David who came in with such impetuosity. Snow-flakes shone in his hair; the glow of the keen wind was on his cheek, a smile on his lips, and in his eyes an expression she had never seen before. Happiness, touched with the shadow of some past pain; doubt and desire; gratitude and love, — all seemed to meet and mingle in it; while, about the whole man, was the free and ardent air of one relieved from some heavy burden, released from some long captivity.

"O David, what is it?" cried Christie, as he stood looking at her with this strange look.

"News, Christie! such happy news I can't find words to tell them," he answered, coming nearer, but too absorbed in his own emotion to heed hers.

She drew a long breath and pressed her hand a little heavier on her breast, as she said, with the ghost of a smile, more pathetic than the saddest tears:

"I guess it, David."

"How?" he demanded, as if defrauded of a joy he had set his heart upon.

"I met Kitty, — she told me nothing, — but her face betrayed what I have long suspected."

David laughed, such a glad yet scornful laugh, and, snatching a little miniature from his pocket, offered it, saying, with the new impetuosity that changed him so :

" *That* is the daughter I have found for my mother. You know her, — you love her; and you will not be ashamed to welcome her, I think."

Christie took it; saw a faded, time-worn likeness of a young girl's happy face; a face strangely familiar, yet, for a moment, she groped to find the name belonging to it. Then memory helped her; and she said, half incredulously, half joyfully :

" Is it my Rachel ? "

" It is *my* Letty ! " cried David, with an accent of such mingled love and sorrow, remorse and joy, that Christie seemed to hear in it the death-knell of her faith in him. The picture fell from the hands she put up, as if to ward off some heavy blow, and her voice was sharp with reproachful anguish, as she cried :

" O David, David, any thing but that ! "

An instant he seemed bewildered, then the meaning of the grief in her face flashed on him, and his own grew white with indignant repudiation of the thought that daunted her; but he only said with the stern brevity of truth :

" Letty is my sister."

" Forgive me, — how could I know ? Oh, thank God ! thank God ! " and, dropping down upon a chair, Christie broke into a passion of the happiest tears she ever shed.

David stood beside her silent, till the first irrepressible paroxysm was over; then, while she sat weeping softly, quite bowed down by emotion, he said, sadly now, not sternly :

"You could *not* know, because we hid the truth so carefully. I have no right to resent that belief of yours, for I did wrong my poor Letty, almost as much as that lover of hers, who, being dead, I do not curse. Let me tell you every thing, Christie, before I ask your respect and confidence again. I never deserved them, but I tried to; for they were very precious to me."

He paused a moment, then went on rapidly, as if anxious to accomplish a hard task; and Christie forgot to weep while listening breathlessly.

"Letty was the pride of my heart; and I loved her very dearly, for she was all I had. Such a pretty child; such a gay, sweet girl; how could I help it, when she was so fond of me? We were poor then, — poorer than now, — and she grew restless; tired of hard work; longed for a little pleasure, and could not bear to waste her youth and beauty in that dull town. I did not blame my little girl; but I could not help her, for I was tugging away to fill father's place, he being broken down and helpless. She wanted to go away and support herself. *You* know the feeling; and I need not tell you how the proud, high-hearted creature hated dependence, even on a brother who would have worked his soul out for her. She *would* go, and we had faith in her. For a time she did bravely; but life was too hard for her; pleasure too alluring, and, when temptation came in the guise of love, she could not resist. One dreadful day, news came that she was gone, never to come back, my innocent little Letty, any more."

His voice failed there, and he walked fast through the room, as if the memory of that bitter day was still unbearable. Christie could not speak for very pity;

and he soon continued, pacing restlessly before her, as he had often done when she sat by, wondering what unquiet spirit drove him to and fro:

"That was the beginning of my trouble; but not the worst of it: God forgive me, not the worst! Father was very feeble, and the shock killed him; mother's heart was nearly broken, and all the happiness was taken out of life for me. But I could bear it, heavy as the blow was, for I had no part in that sin and sorrow. A year later, there came a letter from Letty, — a penitent, imploring, little letter, asking to be forgiven and taken home, for her lover was dead, and she alone in a foreign land. How would you answer such a letter, Christie?"

"As you did; saying: 'Come home and let us comfort you.'"

"I said: 'You have killed your father; broken your mother's heart; ruined your brother's hopes, and disgraced your family. You no longer have a home with us; and we never want to see your face again.'"

"O David, that was cruel!"

"I said you did not know me; now you see how deceived you have been. A stern, resentful devil possessed me then, and I obeyed it. I was very proud; full of ambitious plans and jealous love for the few I took into my heart. Letty had brought a stain upon our honest name that time could never wash away; had quenched my hopes in despair and shame; had made home desolate, and destroyed my faith in every thing; for whom could I trust, when she, the nearest and dearest creature in the world, deceived and deserted me. I could *not* forgive; wrath burned hot within me, and the desire for retribution would not be appeased till those cruel words were said. The retribution and remorse came swift and sure; but they came most heavily to me."

Still standing where he had paused abruptly as he asked his question, David wrung his strong hands together with a gesture of passionate regret, while his face grew sharp with the remembered suffering of the years he had given to the atonement of that wrong.

Christie put her own hand on those clenched ones, and whispered softly:

" Don't tell me any more now: I can wait."

" I *must*, and you must listen! I 've longed to tell you, but I was afraid; now, you shall know every thing, and then decide if you can forgive me for Letty's sake," he said, so resolutely that she listened with a face full of mute compassion.

" That little letter came to me; I never told my mother, but answered it, and kept silent till news arrived that the ship in which Letty had taken passage was lost. Remorse had been tugging at my heart; and, when I knew that she was dead, I forgave her with a vain forgiveness, and mourned for my darling, as if she had never left me. I told my mother then, and she did not utter one reproach; but age seemed to fall upon her all at once, and the pathetic quietude you see.

" Then, but for her, I should have been desperate; for day and night Letty's face haunted me; Letty's voice cried: 'Take me home!' and every word of that imploring letter burned, before my eyes as if written in fire. Do you wonder now that I hid myself;

that I had no heart to try for any honorable place in the world, and only struggled to forget, only hoped to expiate my sin ? "

With his head bowed down upon his breast, David stood silent, asking himself if he had even now done enough to win the reward he coveted. Christie's voice seemed to answer him; for she said, with heartfelt gratitude and respect :

" Surely you have atoned for that harshness to one woman by years of devotion to many. Was it this that made you 'a brother of girls,' as Mr. Power once called you ? And, when I asked what he meant, he said the Arabs call a man that who has ' a clean heart to love all women as his sisters, and strength and courage to fight for their protection !' "

She hoped to lighten his trouble a little, and spoke with a smile that was like cordial to poor David.

" Yes," he said, lifting his head again. " I tried to be that, and, for Letty's sake, had pity on the most forlorn, patience with the most abandoned; always remembering that she might have been what they were, if death had not been more merciful than I."

" But she was *not* dead : she was alive and working as bravely as you. Ah, how little I thought, when I loved Rachel, and she loved me, that we should ever meet so happily as we soon shall. Tell me how you found her ? Does she know I am the woman she once saved ? Tell me all about her; and tell it fast," prayed Christie, getting excited, as she more fully grasped the happy fact that Rachel and Letty were one.

David came nearer, and his face kindled as he spoke.

" The ship sailed without her; she came later; and,

finding that her name was among the lost, she did not deny it, for she *was* dead to us, and decided to remain so till she had earned the right to be forgiven. You know how she lived and worked, stood firm with no one to befriend her till you came, and, by years of patient well-doing, washed away her single sin. If any one dares think I am ashamed to own her now, let him know what cause I have to be proud of her; let him come and see how tenderly I love her; how devoutly I thank God for permitting me to find and bring my little Letty home."

Only the snow-flakes drifting against the window-pane, and the wailing of the wind, was heard for a moment; then David added, with brightening eyes and a glad voice:

" I went into a hospital while away, to look after one of my poor girls who had been doing well till illness brought her there. As I was passing out I saw a sleeping face, and stopped involuntarily : it was so like Letty's. I never doubted she was dead; the name over the bed was not hers; the face was sadly altered from the happy, rosy one I knew, but it held me fast; and as I paused the eyes opened, — Letty's own soft eyes, — they saw me, and, as if I was the figure of a dream, she smiled, put up her arms and said, just as she used to say, a child, when I woke her in her little bed — ' Why, Davy!' — I can't tell any more, — only that when I brought her home and put her in mother's arms, I felt as if I was forgiven at last."

He broke down there, and went and stood behind the window curtains, letting no one see the grateful tears that washed away the bitterness of those long years.

Christie had taken up the miniature and was looking at it, while her heart sang for joy that the lost was found, when David came back to her, wearing the same look she had seen the night she listened among the cloaks. Moved and happy, with eager eyes and ardent manner, yet behind it all a pale expectancy as if some great crisis was at hand:

" Christie, I never can forget that when all others, even I, cast Letty off, you comforted and saved her. What can I do to thank you for it?"

" Be my friend, and let me be hers again," she answered, too deeply moved to think of any private hope or pain.

" Then the past, now that you know it all, does not change your heart to us?"

" It only makes you dearer."

" And if I asked you to come back to the home that has been desolate since you went, would you come?"

" Gladly, David."

" And if I dared to say I loved you?"

She only looked at him with a quick rising light and warmth over her whole face; he stretched both arms to her, and, going to him, Christie gave her answer silently.

Lovers usually ascend straight into the seventh heaven for a time: unfortunately they cannot stay long; the air is too rarefied, the light too brilliant, the fare too ethereal, and they are forced to come down to mundane things, as larks drop from heaven's gate into their grassy nests. David was summoned from that blissful region, after a brief enjoyment of its divine delights, by Christie, who looked up from her new refuge with the abrupt question:

" What becomes of Kitty ? "

He regarded her with a dazed expression for an instant, for she had been speaking the delightful language of lips and eyes that lovers use, and the old tongue sounded harsh to him.

" She is safe with her father, and is to marry the ' other one' next week."

" Heaven be praised ! " ejaculated Christie, so fervently that David looked suddenly enlightened and much amused, as he said quickly :

" What becomes of Fletcher ? "

" He 's safely out of the way, and I sincerely hope *he* will marry some ' other one' as soon as possible."

" Christie, you were jealous of that girl."

" David, you were jealous of that man."

Then they both burst out laughing like two children, for heavy burdens had been lifted off their hearts and they were bubbling over with happiness.

" But truly, David, weren't you a little jealous of P. F. ? " persisted Christie, feeling an intense desire to ask all manner of harassing questions, with the agreeable certainty that they would be fully answered.

" Desperately jealous. You were so kind, so gay, so altogether charming when with him, that I could not stand by and see it, so I kept away. Why were you never so to me ? "

" Because you never showed that you cared for me, and *he* did. But it was wrong in me to do it, and I repent of it heartily ; for it hurt him more than I thought it would when the experiment failed. I truly tried to love him, but I couldn't."

" Yet he had so much to offer, and could give you all

you most enjoy. It is very singular that you failed to care for him, and preferred a poor old fellow like me," said David, beaming at her like a beatified man.

"I do love luxury and pleasure, but I love independence more. I'm happier poking in the dirt with you than I should be driving in a fine carriage with 'that piece of elegance' as Mr. Power called him; prouder of being your wife than his; and none of the costly things he offered me were half so precious in my sight as your little nosegays, now mouldering away in my treasure-box upstairs. Why, Davy, I've longed more intensely for the right to push up the curly lock that is always tumbling into your eyes, than for Philip's whole fortune. *May* I do it now?"

"You may," and Christie did it with a tender satisfaction that made David love her the more, though he laughed like a boy at the womanly whim.

"And so you thought I cared for Kitty?" he said presently, taking his turn at the new game.

"How could I help it when she was so young and pretty and fond of you?"

"Was she?" innocently.

"Didn't you see it? How blind men are!"

"Not always."

"David, did you see that *I* cared for you?" asked Christie, turning crimson under the significant glance he gave her.

"I wish I had; I confess I once or twice fancied that I caught glimpses of bliss round the corner, as it were; but, before I could decide, the glimpses vanished, and I was very sure I was a conceited coxcomb to think it for a moment. It was very hard, and yet I was glad."

" Glad ! "

" Yes, because I had made a sort of vow that I 'd
never love or marry as a punishment for my cruelty to
Letty."

" That was wrong, David."

" I see it now ; but it was not hard to keep that foolish vow till you came ; and you see I 've broken it
without a shadow of regret to-night."

" You might have done it months ago and saved me
so much woe if you had not been a dear, modest, mor-
bidly conscientious bat," sighed Christie, pleased and
proud to learn her power, yet sorry for the long
delay.

" Thank you, love. You see I didn't find out why
I liked my friend so well till I lost her. I had just
begun to feel that you were very dear, — for after the
birthday you were like an angel in the house, Christie,
— when you changed all at once, and I thought you suspected me, and didn't like it. Your running away when
Kitty came confirmed my fear ; then in came that —
would you mind if I said — confounded Fletcher ? "

" Not in the least."

" Well, as he didn't win, I won't be hard on him ;
but I gave up then and had a tough time of it ; especially that first night when this splendid lover appeared
and received such a kind welcome."

Christie saw the strong hand that lay on David's
knee clenched slowly, as he knit his brows with a grim
look, plainly showing that he was not what she was
inclined to think him, a perfect saint.

" Oh, my heart ! and there I was loving you so dearly
all the time, and you wouldn't see or speak or under-

stand, but went away, left me to torment all three of us," cried Christie with a tragic gesture.

"My dearest girl, did you ever know a man in love do, say, or think the right thing at the right time? *I* never did," said David, so penitently that she forgave him on the spot.

"Never mind, dear. It has taught us the worth of love, and perhaps we are the better for the seeming waste of precious time. Now I've not only got you but Letty also, and your mother is mine in very truth. Ah, how rich I am!"

"But I thought it was all over with me when I found Letty, because, seeing no more of Fletcher, I had begun to hope again, and when she came back to me I knew my home must be hers, yet feared you would refuse to share it if you knew all. You are very proud, and the purest-hearted woman I ever knew."

"And if I *had* refused, you would have let me go and held fast to Letty?"

"Yes, for I owe her every thing."

"You should have known me better, David. But I don't refuse, and there is no need to choose between us."

"No, thank heaven, and you, my Christie! Imagine what I felt when Letty told me all you had been to her. If any thing *could* make me love you more than I now do, it would be that! No, don't hide your face; I like to see it blush and smile and turn to me confidingly, as it has not done all these long months."

"Did Letty tell you what she had done for me?" asked Christie, looking more like a rose than ever Kitty did.

"She told me every thing, and wished me to tell you all her story, even the saddest part of it. I'd better do it now before you meet again."

He paused as if the tale was hard to tell; but Christie put her hand on his lips saying softly :

"Never tell it; let her past be as sacred as if she were dead. She was my friend when I had no other : she is my dear sister now, and nothing can ever change the love between us."

If she had thought David's face beautiful with gratitude when he told the happier portions of that history, she found it doubly so when she spared him the recital of its darkest chapter, and bade him "leave the rest to silence."

"Now you will come home ? Mother wants you, Letty longs for you, and I have got and mean to keep you all my life, God willing ! "

" I 'd better die to-night and make a blessed end, for so much happiness is hardly possible in a world of woe," answered Christie to that fervent invitation.

"We shall be married very soon, take a wedding trip to any part of the world you like, and our honeymoon will last for ever, Mrs. Sterling, Jr.," said David, soaring away into the future with sublime disregard of obstacles.

Before Christie could get her breath after that somewhat startling announcement, Mr. Power appeared, took in the situation at a glance, gave them a smile that was a benediction, and said heartily as he offered a hand to each :

"Now I 'm satisfied; I 've watched and waited patiently, and after many tribulations you have found each other in good time;" then with a meaning look at Christie he added slyly: "But David is 'no hero' you know."

She remembered the chat in the strawberry bed, laughed, and colored brightly, as she answered with her hand trustfully in David's, her eyes full of loving pride and reverence lifted to his face:

"I've seen both sides of the medal now, and found it 'sterling gold.' Hero or not I'm content; for, though he 'loves his mother much,' there is room in his heart for me too; his 'old books' have given him something better than learning, and he has convinced me that 'double flowers' *are* loveliest and best."

CHAPTER XVI.

CHRISTIE'S return was a very happy one, and could not well be otherwise with a mother, sister, and lover to welcome her back. Her meeting with Letty was indescribably tender, and the days that followed were pretty equally divided between her and her brother, in nursing the one and loving the other. There was no cloud now in Christie's sky, and all the world seemed in bloom. But even while she enjoyed every hour of life, and begrudged the time given to sleep, she felt as if the dream was too beautiful to last, and often said:

"Something will happen: such perfect happiness is not possible in this world."

"Then let us make the most of it," David would reply, wisely bent on getting his honey while he could, and not borrowing trouble for the morrow.

So Christie turned a deaf ear to her "prophetic soul," and gave herself up to the blissful holiday that had come at last. Even while March winds were howling outside, she blissfully "poked in the dirt" with David in the green-house, put up the curly lock as often as she liked, and told him she loved him a dozen times a day, not in words, but in silent ways, that touched him to the heart, and made his future look so bright he hardly dared believe in it.

A happier man it would have been difficult to find just then; all his burdens seemed to have fallen off, and his spirits rose again with an elasticity which surprised even those who knew him best. Christie often stopped to watch and wonder if the blithe young man who went whistling and singing about the house, often stopping to kiss somebody, to joke, or to exclaim with a beaming face like a child at a party: "Isn't every thing beautiful?" could be the sober, steady David, who used to plod to and fro with his shoulders a little bent, and the absent look in his eyes that told of thoughts above or beyond the daily task.

It was good to see his mother rejoice over him with an exceeding great joy; it was better still to see Letty's eyes follow him with unspeakable love and gratitude in their soft depths; but it was best of all to see Christie marvel and exult over the discoveries she made: for, though she had known David for a year, she had never seen the real man till now.

"Davy, you are a humbug," she said one day when they were making up a bridal order in the green-house.

"I told you so, but you wouldn't believe it," he answered, using long stemmed rose-buds with as prodigal a hand as if the wedding was to be his own.

"I thought I was going to marry a quiet, studious, steady-going man; and here I find myself engaged to a romantic youth who flies about in the most undignified manner, embraces people behind doors, sings opera airs, — very much out of tune by the way, — and conducts himself more like an infatuated Claude Melnotte, than a respectable gentleman on the awful verge of matrimony. Nothing can surprise me now: I'm prepared for any thing, even the sight of my Quakerish lover dancing a jig."

"Just what I've been longing to do! Come and take a turn: it will do you good;" and, to Christie's utter amazement, David caught her round the waist and waltzed her down the boarded walk with a speed and skill that caused less havoc among the flower-pots than one would imagine, and seemed to delight the plants, who rustled and nodded as if applauding the dance of the finest double flower that had ever blossomed in their midst.

"I can't help it, Christie," he said, when he had landed her breathless and laughing at the other end. "I feel like a boy out of school, or rather a man out of prison, and *must* enjoy my liberty in some way. I'm not a talker, you know; and, as the laws of gravitation forbid my soaring aloft anywhere, I can only express my joyfully uplifted state of mind by 'prancing,' as you call it. Never mind dignity: let's be happy, and by and by I'll sober down."

"I don't want you to; I love to see you so young and happy, only you are not the old David, and I've got to get acquainted with the new one."

"I hope you'll like him better than the frost-bitten 'old David' you first knew and were kind enough to love. Mother says I've gone back to the time before we lost Letty, and I sometimes feel as if I had. In that case you will find me a proud, impetuous, ambitious fellow, Christie, and how will that suit?"

"Excellently; I like pride of your sort; impetuosity becomes you, for you have learned to control it if need be; and the ambition is best of all. I always wondered at your want of it, and longed to stir you up; for you did not seem the sort of man to be contented with mere creature comforts when there are so many fine things men may do. What shall you choose, Davy?"

"I shall wait for time to show. The sap is all astir in me, and I'm ready for my chance. I don't know what it is, but I feel very sure that some work will be given me into which I can put my whole heart and soul and strength. I spoilt my first chance; but I know I shall have another, and, whatever it is, I am ready to do my best, and live or die for it as God wills."

"So am I," answered Christie, with a voice as earnest and a face as full of hopeful resolution as his own.

Then they went back to their work, little dreaming as they tied roses and twined smilax wreaths, how near that other chance was; how soon they were to be called upon to keep their promise, and how well each was to perform the part given them in life and death.

The gun fired one April morning at Fort Sumter told many men like David what their work was to be, and showed many women like Christie a new right to claim and bravely prove their fitness to possess.

No need to repeat the story of the war begun that day; it has been so often told that it will only be touched upon here as one of the experiences of Christie's life, an experience which did for her what it did for all who took a share in it, and loyally acted their part.

The North woke up from its prosperous lethargy, and began to stir with the ominous hum of bees when rude hands shake the hive. Rich and poor were proud to prove that they loved their liberty better than their money or their lives, and the descendants of the brave old Puritans were worthy of their race. Many said: "It will soon be over;" but the wise men, who had warned in vain, shook their heads, as that first disastrous summer showed that the time for compromise was past, and the stern reckoning day of eternal justice was at hand.

To no home in the land did the great trouble bring a more sudden change than the little cottage in the lane. All its happy peace was broken; excitement and anxiety, grief and indignation, banished the sweet home joys and darkened the future that had seemed so clear. David was sober enough now, and went about his work with a grim set to his lips, and a spark in his eyes that made the three women look at one another pale with unspoken apprehension. As they sat together, picking lint or rolling bandages while David read aloud some dismal tale of a lost battle that chilled their blood and made their hearts ache with pity, each woman, listening to the voice that stirred her like martial music, said within herself: "Sooner or later he will go, and I have no right to keep him." Each tried to be ready to make her sacrifice bravely when the time came, and each prayed that it might not be required of her.

David said little, but they knew by the way he neglected his garden and worked for the soldiers, that his heart was in the war. Day after day he left Christie and his sister to fill the orders that came so often now for flowers to lay on the grave of some dear, dead boy brought home to his mother in a shroud. Day after day he hurried away to help Mr. Power in the sanitary work that soon claimed all hearts and hands; and, day after day, he came home with what Christie called the "heroic look" more plainly written on his face. All that first summer, so short and strange; all that first winter, so long and hard to those who went and those who stayed, David worked and waited, and the women waxed strong in the new atmosphere of self-sacrifice which pervaded the air, bringing out the sturdy virtues of the North.

"How terrible! Oh, when will it be over!" sighed Letty one day, after hearing a long list of the dead and wounded in one of the great battles of that second summer.

"Never till we have beaten!" cried David, throwing down the paper and walking about the room with his head up like a war-horse who smells powder. "It *is* terrible and yet glorious. I thank heaven I live to see this great wrong righted, and only wish I could do my share like a man."

"That is natural; but there are plenty of men who have fewer ties than you, who can fight better, and whose places are easier to fill than yours if they die," said Christie, hastily.

"But the men who have most to lose fight best they say; and to my thinking a soldier needs a principle as well as a weapon, if he is to do real service."

"As the only son of a widow, you can't be drafted: that's one comfort," said Letty, who could not bear to give up the brother lost to her for so many years.

"I should not wait for that, and I know mother would give her widow's mite if she saw that it was needed."

"Yes, Davy." The soft, old voice answered steadily; but the feeble hand closed instinctively on the arm of this only son, who was so dear to her. David held it close in both of his, saying gratefully: "Thank you, mother;" then, fixing his eyes on the younger yet not dearer women, he added with a ring in his voice that made their hearts answer with a prompt "Ay, ay!" in spite of love or fear:

"Now listen, you dear souls, and understand that, if I do this thing, I shall not do it hastily, nor without counting well the cost. My first and most natural impulse was to go in the beginning; but I stayed for your sakes. I saw I was not really needed: I thought the war would soon be over, and those who went then could do the work. You see how mistaken we were, and God only knows when the end will come. The boys — bless their brave hearts! — have done nobly, but older men are needed now. We cannot sacrifice all the gallant lads; and we who have more to lose than they must take our turn and try to do as well. You own this; I see it in your faces: then don't hold me back when the time comes for me to go. I *must* do my part, however small it is, or I shall never feel as if I deserved the love you give me. You will let me go, I am sure, and not regret that I did what seemed to me a solemn duty, leaving the consequences to the Lord!"

"Yes, David," sister and sweetheart answered,

bravely forgetting in the fervor of the moment what heavy consequences God might see fit to send.

"Good! I knew my Spartans would be ready, and I won't disgrace them. I've waited more than a year, and done what I could. But all the while I felt that I was going to get a chance at the hard work, and I've been preparing for it. Bennet will take the garden and green-house off my hands this autumn for a year or longer, if I like. He's a kind, neighborly man, and his boy will take my place about the house and protect you faithfully. Mr. Power cannot be spared to go as chaplain, though he longs to desperately; so he is near in case of need, and with your two devoted daughters by you, mother, I surely can be spared for a little while."

"Only one daughter near her, David: I shall enlist when you do," said Christie, resolutely.

"You mean it?"

"I mean it as honestly as you do. I knew you would go: I saw you getting ready, and I made up my mind to follow. I, too, have prepared for it, and even spoken to Mrs. Amory. She has gone as matron of a hospital, and promised to find a place for me when I was ready. The day you enlist I shall write and tell her I *am* ready."

There was fire in Christie's eyes and a flush on her cheek now, as she stood up with the look of a woman bent on doing well her part. David caught her hands in his, regardless of the ominous bandages they held, and said, with tender admiration and reproach in his voice:

"You wouldn't marry me when I asked you this

summer, fearing you would be a burden to me; but now you want to share hardship and danger with me, and support me by the knowledge of your nearness. Dear, ought I to let you do it?"

"You *will* let me do it, and in return I will marry you whenever you ask me," answered Christie, sealing the promise with a kiss that silenced him.

He had been anxious to be married long ago, but when he asked Mr. Power to make him happy, a month after his engagement, that wise friend said to them:

"I don't advise it yet. You have tried and proved one another as friends, now try and prove one another as lovers; then, if you feel that all is safe and happy, you will be ready for the greatest of the three experiments, and then in God's name marry."

"We will," they said, and for a year had been content, studying one another, finding much to love, and something to learn in the art of bearing and forbearing.

David had begun to think they had waited long enough, but Christie still delayed, fearing she was not worthy, and secretly afflicted by the thought of her poverty. She had so little to give in return for all she received that it troubled her, and she was sometimes tempted to ask Uncle Enos for a modest marriage portion. She never had yet, and now resolved to ask nothing, but to earn her blessing by doing her share in the great work.

"I shall remember that," was all David answered to that last promise of hers, and three months later he took her at her word.

For a week or two they went on in the old way; Christie did her housework with her head full of new plans, read books on nursing, made gruel, plasters, and poultices, till Mrs. Sterling pronounced her perfect; and dreamed dreams of a happy time to come when peace had returned, and David was safe at home with all the stars and bars a man could win without dying for them.

David set things in order, conferred with Bennet, petted his womankind, and then hurried away to pack boxes of stores, visit camps, and watch departing regiments with a daily increasing certainty that his time had come.

One September day he went slowly home, and, seeing Christie in the garden, joined her, helped her finish matting up some delicate shrubs, put by the tools, and when all was done said with unusual gentleness:

"Come and walk a little in the lane."

She put her arm in his, and answered quickly:

"You've something to tell me: I see it in your face."

"Dear, I must go."

"Yes, David."

"And you?"

"I go too."

"Yes, Christie."

That was all: she did not offer to detain him now; he did not deny her right to follow. They looked each other bravely in the face a moment, seeing, acknowledging the duty and the danger, yet ready to do the one and dare the other, since they went together. Then shoulder to shoulder, as if already mustered in, these faithful comrades marched to and fro, planning their campaign.

Next evening, as Mrs. Sterling sat alone in the twilight, a tall man in army blue entered quietly, stood watching the tranquil figure for a moment, then went and knelt down beside it, saying, with a most unsoldierly choke in the voice:

"I've done it, mother: tell me you're not sorry."

But the little Quaker cap went down on the broad shoulder, and the only answer he heard was a sob that stirred the soft folds over the tender old heart that clung so closely to the son who had lived for her so long. What happened in the twilight no one ever knew; but David received promotion for bravery in a harder battle than any he was going to, and from his mother's breast a decoration more precious to him than the cross of the Legion of Honor from a royal hand.

When Mr. Power presently came in, followed by the others, they found their soldier standing very erect in his old place on the rug, with the firelight gleaming on his bright buttons, and Bran staring at him with a perplexed aspect; for the uniform, shorn hair, trimmed beard, and a certain lofty carriage of the head so changed his master that the sagacious beast was disturbed.

Letty smiled at him approvingly, then went to comfort her mother who could not recover her tranquillity so soon. But Christie stood aloof, looking at her lover with something more than admiration in the face that kindled beautifully as she exclaimed:

"O David, you are splendid! Once I was so blind I thought you plain; but now my 'boy in blue' is the noblest looking man I ever saw. Yes, Mr. Power, I've found my hero at last! Here he is, my knight without reproach or fear, going out to take his part in the grandest battle ever fought. I wouldn't keep him if I could; I 'm glad and proud to have him go; and if he never should come back to me I can bear it better for knowing that he dutifully did his best, and left the consequences to the Lord."

Then, having poured out the love and pride and confidence that enriched her sacrifice, she broke down and clung to him, weeping as so many clung and wept in those hard days when men and women gave their dearest, and those who prayed and waited suffered almost as much as those who fought and died.

When the deed was once done, it was astonishing what satisfaction they all took in it, how soon they got accustomed to the change, and what pride they felt in "our soldier." The loyal frenzy fell upon the three quiet women, and they could not do too much for their country. Mrs. Sterling cut up her treasured old linen without a murmur; Letty made " comfort bags " by the dozen, put up jelly, and sewed on blue jackets with tireless industry; while Christie proclaimed that if she had twenty lovers she would send them all; and then made preparations enough to nurse the entire party.

David meantime was in camp, getting his first taste of martial life, and not liking it any better than he thought he should; but no one heard a complaint, and he never regretted his "love among the roses," for he was one of the men who had a "principle as well as a weapon," and meant to do good service with both.

It would have taken many knapsacks to hold all the gifts showered upon him by his friends and neighbors. He accepted all that came, and furnished forth those of his company who were less favored. Among these was Elisha Wilkins, and how he got there should be told.

Elisha had not the slightest intention of enlisting, but Mrs. Wilkins was a loyal soul, and could not rest till she had sent a substitute, since she could not go herself. Finding that Lisha showed little enthusiasm on the subject, she tried to rouse him by patriotic appeals of various sorts. She read stirring accounts of battles, carefully omitting the dead and wounded ; she turned out, baby and all if possible, to cheer every regiment that left ; and was never tired of telling Wash how she wished she could add ten years to his age and send him off to fight for his country like a man.

But nothing seemed to rouse the supine Elisha, who chewed his quid like a placid beast of the field, and showed no sign of a proper spirit.

" Very well," said Mrs. Wilkins resolutely to herself, " ef I can't make no impression on his soul I will on his stommick, and see how that 'll work."

Which threat she carried out with such skill and force that Lisha was effectually waked up, for he *was* " partial to good vittles," and Cynthy was a capital cook. Poor rations did not suit him, and he demanded why his favorite dishes were not forthcoming.

" We can't afford no nice vittles now when our men are sufferin' so. I should be ashamed to cook 'em, and expect to choke tryin' to eat 'em. Every one is sacri-ficin' somethin', and we mustn't be slack in doin' our part, — the Lord knows it 's precious little, — and there won't be no stuffin' in this house for a consid'able spell. Ef I *could* save up enough to send a man to do my share of the fightin', I should be proud to do it. Any-way I shall stint the family and send them dear brave fellers every cent I can git without starvin' the chil-dren."

"Now, Cynthy, don't be ferce. Things will come out all right, and it ain't no use upsettin' every thing and bein' so darned uncomfortable," answered Mr. Wilkins with unusual energy.

"Yes it is, Lisha. No one has a right to be comfortable in such times as these, and *this* family ain't goin' to be ef I can help it," and Mrs. Wilkins set down her flat-iron with a slam which plainly told her Lisha war was declared.

He said no more but fell a thinking. He was not as unmoved as he seemed by the general excitement, and had felt sundry manly impulses to "up and at 'em," when his comrades in the shop discussed the crisis with ireful brandishing of awls, and vengeful pounding of sole leather, as if the rebels were under the hammer. But the selfish, slothful little man could not make up his mind to brave hardship and danger, and fell back on his duty to his family as a reason for keeping safe at home.

But now that home was no longer comfortable, now that Cynthy had sharpened her tongue, and turned "ferce," and now — hardest blow of all — that he was kept on short commons, he began to think he might as well be on the tented field, and get a little glory along with the discomfort if that was inevitable. Nature abhors a vacuum, and when food fell short patriotism had a chance to fill the aching void. Lisha had about made up his mind, for he knew the value of peace and quietness; and, though his wife was no scold, she was the ruling power, and in his secret soul he considered her a very remarkable woman. He knew what she wanted, but was not going to be hurried for anybody;

so he still kept silent, and Mrs. Wilkins began to think she must give it up. An unexpected ally appeared however, and the good woman took advantage of it to strike one last blow.

Lisha sat eating a late breakfast one morning, with a small son at either elbow, waiting for stray mouthfuls and committing petty larcenies right and left, for Pa was in a brown study. Mrs. Wilkins was frying flap-jacks, and though this is not considered an heroical em-ployment she made it so that day. This was a favorite dish of Lisha's, and she had prepared it as a bait for this cautious fish. To say that the fish rose at once and swallowed the bait, hook and all, but feebly ex-presses the justice done to the cakes by that long-suffer-ing man. Waiting till he had a tempting pile of the lightest, brownest flapjacks ever seen upon his plate, and was watching an extra big bit of butter melt luxu-riously into the warm bosom of the upper one, with a face as benign as if some of the molasses he was trick-ling over them had been absorbed into his nature, Mrs. Wilkins seized the propitious moment to say im-pressively:

"David Sterlin' has enlisted!"

"Sho! has he, though?"

"Of course he has! any man with the spirit of a muskeeter would."

"Well, he ain't got a family, you see."

"He's got his old mother, that sister home from furrin' parts somewheres, and Christie just going to be married. I should like to know who's got a harder family to leave than that?"

"Six young children is harder: ef I went fifin' and

drummin' off, who'd take care of them I'd like to know?"

" I guess *I* could support the family ef I give my mind to it; " and Mrs. Wilkins turned a flapjack with an emphasis that caused her lord to bolt a hot triangle with dangerous rapidity; for well he knew very little of *his* money went into the common purse. She never reproached him, but the fact nettled him now; and something in the tone of her voice made that sweet morsel hard to swallow.

"'Pears to me you're in ruther a hurry to be a widder, Cynthy, shovin' me off to git shot in this kind of a way," growled Lisha, ill at ease.

" I'd ruther be a brave man's widder than a coward's wife, any day ! " cried the rebellious Cynthy: then she relented, and softly slid two hot cakes into his plate; adding, with her hand upon his shoulder, " Lisha, dear, I want to be proud of my husband as other women be of theirs. Every one gives somethin', I've only got you, and I want to do my share, and do it hearty."

She went back to her work, and Mr. Wilkins sat thoughtfully stroking the curly heads beside him, while the boys ravaged his plate, with no reproof, but a half audible, " My little chaps, my little chaps! "

She thought she had got him, and smiled to herself, even while a great tear sputtered on the griddle at those last words of his.

Imagine her dismay, when, having consumed the bait, her fish gave signs of breaking the line, and escaping after all; for Mr. Wilkins pushed back his chair, and said slowly, as he filled his pipe:

" I'm blest ef I can see the sense of a lot of decent

men going off to be froze, and starved, and blowed up jest for them confounded niggers."

He got no further, for his wife's patience gave out; and, leaving her cakes to burn black, she turned to him with a face glowing like her stove, and cried out:

"Lisha, ain't you got no heart? can you remember what Hepsey told us, and call them poor, long-sufferin' creeters names? Can you think of them wretched wives sold from their husbands; them children as dear as ourn tore from their mothers; and old folks kep slavin eighty long, hard years with no pay, no help, no pity, when they git past work? Lisha Wilkins, look at *that*, and say no ef you darst!"

Mrs. Wilkins was a homely woman in an old calico gown, but her face, her voice, her attitude were grand, as she flung wide the door of the little back bedroom, and pointed with her tin spatula to the sight beyond.

Only Hepsey sitting by a bed where lay what looked more like a shrivelled mummy than a woman. Ah! but it was that old mother worked and waited for so long: blind now, and deaf; childish, and half dead with many hardships, but safe and free at last; and Hepsey's black face was full of a pride, a peace, and happiness more eloquent and touching than any speech or sermon ever uttered.

Mr. Wilkins had heard her story, and been more affected by it than he would confess: now it came home to him with sudden force; the thought of his own mother, wife, or babies torn from him stirred him to the heart, and the manliest emotion he had ever known caused him to cast his pipe at his feet, put on his hat with an energetic slap, and walk out of the house, wearing an expression on his usually wooden face that caused his wife to clap her hands and cry exultingly:

"I thought that would fetch him!"

Then she fell to work like an inspired woman; and at noon a sumptuous dinner "smoked upon the board;" the children were scrubbed till their faces shone; and the room was as fresh and neat as any apartment could be with the penetrating perfume of burnt flapjacks still pervading the air, and three dozen ruffled nightcaps decorating the clothes-lines overhead.

"Tell me the instant minute you see Pa a comin', and I'll dish up the gravy," was Mrs. Wilkins's command, as she stepped in with a cup of tea for old "Marm," as she called Hepsey's mother.

"He's a comin', Ma!" called Gusty, presently.

"No, he ain't: it's a trainer," added Ann Lizy.

"Yes, 'tis Pa! oh, my eye! ain't he stunnin'!" cried Wash, stricken for the first time with admiration of his sire.

Before Mrs. Wilkins could reply to these conflicting rumors her husband walked in, looking as martial as his hollow chest and thin legs permitted, and, turning his cap nervously in his hands, said half-proudly, half-reproachfully:

"Now, Cynthy, *be* you satisfied?"

"Oh, my Lisha! I be, I be!" and the inconsistent woman fell upon his buttony breast weeping copiously.

If ever a man was praised and petted, admired and caressed, it was Elisha Wilkins that day. His wife fed him with the fat of the land, regardless of conse-

quences; his children revolved about him with tireless
curiosity and wonder; his neighbórs flocked in to ap-
plaud, advise, and admire; every one treated him with
a respect most grateful to his feelings; he was an object
of interest, and with every hour his importance increased, so that by night he felt like a Commander-in-
Chief, and bore himself accordingly. He had enlisted
in David's regiment, which was a great comfort to his
wife; for though her stout heart never failed her, it grew
very heavy at times; and when Lisha was gone, she
often dropped a private tear over the broken pipe that
always lay in its old place, and vented her emotions by
sending baskets of nourishment to Private Wilkins,
which caused that bandy-legged warrior to be much
envied and cherished by his mates.

"I 'm glad I done it; for it will make a man of
Lisha; and, if I 've sent him to his death, God knows
he 'll be fitter to die than if he stayed here idlin' his life
away."

Then the good soul openly shouldered the burden
she had borne so long in secret, and bravely trudged
on alone.

"Another great battle!" screamed the excited news-
boys in the streets. "Another great battle!" read
Letty in the cottage parlor. "Another great battle!"
cried David, coming in with the war-horse expression
on his face a month or two after he enlisted.

The women dropped their work to look and listen;
for his visits were few and short, and every instant was
precious. When the first greetings were over, David
stood silent an instant, and a sudden mist came over his
eyes as he glanced from one beloved face to another;

then he threw back his head with the old impatient gesture, squared his shoulders, and said in a loud, cheerful voice, with a suspicious undertone of emotion in it, however:

"My precious people, I've got something to tell you: are you ready?"

They knew what it was without a word. Mrs. Sterling clasped her hands and bowed her head. Letty turned pale and dropped her work; but Christie's eyes kindled, as she answered with a salute:

"Ready, my General."

"We are ordered off at once, and go at four this afternoon. I've got a three hours' leave to say goodby in. Now, let's be brave and enjoy every minute of it."

"We will: what can I do for you, Davy?" asked Christie, wonderfully supported by the thought that she was going too.

"Keep your promise, dear," he answered, while the warlike expression changed to one of infinite tenderness.

"What promise?"

"This;" and he held out his hand with a little paper in it. She saw it was a marriage license, and on it lay a wedding-ring. She did not hesitate an instant, but laid her own hand in his, and answered with her heart in her face:

"I'll keep it, David."

"I knew you would!" then holding her close he said in a tone that made it very hard for her to keep steady, as she had vowed she would do to the last: "I know it is much to ask, but I want to feel that you are mine

before I go. Not only that, but it will be a help and
protection to you, dear, when you follow. As a married
woman you will get on better, as my wife you will be
allowed to come to me if I need you, and as my " —
he stopped there, for he could not add — " as my widow
you will have my pension to support you."

She understood, put both arms about his neck as if
to keep him safe, and whispered fervently :

" Nothing can part us any more, not even death; for
love like ours will last for ever."

" Then you are quite willing to try the third great
experiment ? "

" Glad and proud to do it."

" With no doubt, no fear, to mar your consent."

" Not one, David."

" That 's true love, Christie ! "

Then they stood quite still for a time, and in the
silence the two hearts talked together in the sweet
language no tongue can utter. Presently David said
regretfully :

" I meant it should be so different. I always planned
that we 'd be married some bright summer day, with
many friends about us ; then take a happy little journey
somewhere together, and come back to settle down at
home in the dear old way. Now it 's all so hurried,
sorrowful, and strange. A dull November day; no
friends but Mr. Power, who will be here soon ; no journey but my march to Washington alone ; and no happy
coming home together in this world perhaps. Can you
bear it, love ? "

" Have no fear for me : I feel as if I could bear any
thing just now; for I 've got into a heroic mood and I

mean to keep so as long as I can. I've always wanted to live in stirring times, to have a part in great deeds, to sacrifice and suffer something for a principle or a person; and now I have my wish. I like it, David: it's a grand time to live, a splendid chance to do and suffer; and I want to be in it heart and soul, and earn a little of the glory or the martyrdom that will come in the end. Surely I shall if I give you and myself to the cause; and I do it gladly, though I know that my heart has got to ache as it never has ached yet, when my courage fails, as it will by and by, and my selfish soul counts the cost of my offering after the excitement is over. Help me to be brave and strong, David: don't let me complain or regret, but show me what lies beyond, and teach me to believe that simply doing the right is reward and happiness enough."

Christie was lifted out of herself for the moment, and looked inspired by the high mood which was but the beginning of a nobler life for her. David caught the exaltation, and gave no further thought to any thing but the duty of the hour, finding himself stronger and braver for that long look into the illuminated face of the woman he loved.

" I'll try," was all his answer to her appeal; then proved that he meant it by adding, with his lips against her cheek: " I must go to mother and Letty. We leave them behind, and they must be comforted."

He went, and Christie vanished to make ready for her wedding, conscious, in spite of her exalted state of mind, that every thing *was* very hurried, sad, and strange, and very different from the happy day she had so often planned.

"No matter, we are 'well on't for love,' and that is all we really need," she thought, recalling with a smile Mrs. Wilkins's advice.

"David sends you these, dear. Can I help in any way?" asked Letty, coming with a cluster of lovely white roses in her hand, and a world of affection in her eyes.

"I thought he'd give me violets," and a shadow came over Christie's face.

"But they are mourning flowers, you know."

"Not to me. The roses are, for they remind me of poor Helen, and the first work I did with David was arranging flowers like these for a dead baby's little coffin."

"My dearest Christie, don't be superstitious: all brides wear roses, and Davy thought you'd like them," said Letty, troubled at her words.

"Then I'll wear them, and I won't have fancies if I can help it. But I think few brides dress with a braver, happier heart than mine, though I do choose a sober wedding-gown," answered Christie, smiling again, as she took from a half-packed trunk her new hospital suit of soft, gray, woollen stuff.

"Won't you wear the pretty silvery silk we like so well?" asked Letty timidly, for something in Christie's face and manner impressed her very much.

"No, I will be married in my uniform as David is," she answered with a look Letty long remembered.

"Mr. Power has come," she said softly a few minutes later, with an anxious glance at the clock.

"Go dear, I'll come directly. But first" — and Christie held her friend close a moment, kissed her tenderly, and whispered in a broken voice: "Remember, I don't take his heart from you, I only share it with my sister and my mother."

"I'm glad to give him to you, Christie; for now I feel as if I had partly paid the great debt I've owed so long," answered Letty through her tears.

Then she went away, and Christie soon followed, looking very like a Quaker bride in her gray gown with no ornament but delicate frills at neck and wrist, and the roses in her bosom.

"No bridal white, dear?" said David, going to her.

"Only this," and she touched the flowers, adding with her hand on the blue coat sleeve that embraced her: "I want to consecrate my uniform as you do yours by being married in it. Isn't it fitter for a soldier's wife than lace and silk at such a time as this?"

"Much fitter: I like it; and I find you beautiful, my Christie," whispered David, as she put one of her roses in his button-hole.

"Then I'm satisfied."

"Mr. Power is waiting: are you ready, love?"

"Quite ready."

Then they were married, with Letty and her mother standing beside them, Bennet and his wife dimly visible in the door-way, and poor Bran at his master's feet, looking up with wistful eyes, half human in the anxious affection they expressed.

Christie never forgot that service, so simple, sweet, and solemn; nor the look her husband gave her at the end, when he kissed her on lips and forehead, saying fervently, "God bless my wife!"

A tender little scene followed that can better be

imagined than described; then Mr. Power said cheerily.

"One hour more is all you have, so make the most of it, dearly beloved. You young folks take a wedding-trip to the green-house, while we see how well we can get on without you."

David and Christie went smiling away together, and

"THEN THEY WERE MARRIED."

if they shed any tears over the brief happiness no one saw them but the flowers, and they loyally kept the secret folded up in their tender hearts.

Mr. Power cheered the old lady, while Letty, always glad to serve, made ready the last meal David might ever take at home.

A very simple little marriage feast, but more love, good-will, and tender wishes adorned the plain table than is often found at wedding breakfasts; and better than any speech or song was Letty's broken whisper, as she folded her arms round David's empty chair when no one saw her, "Heaven bless and keep and bring him back to us."

How time went that day! The inexorable clock *would* strike twelve so soon, and then the minutes flew till one was at hand, and the last words were still half said, the last good-byes still unuttered.

" I *must* go ! " cried David with a sort of desperation, as Letty clung to one arm, Christie to the other.

" I shall see you soon: good-by, my husband," whispered Christie, setting him free.

" Give the last kiss to mother," added Letty, following her example, and in another minute David was gone.

At the turn of the lane, he looked back and swung his cap; all waved their hands to him; and then he marched away to the great work before him, leaving those loving hearts to ask the unanswerable question: " How will he come home ? "

Christie was going to town to see the regiment off, and soon followed with Mr. Power. They went early to a certain favorable spot, and there found Mrs. Wilkins, with her entire family perched upon a fence, on the spikes of which they impaled themselves at intervals, and had to be plucked off by the stout girl en- gaged to assist in this memorable expedition.

" Yes, Lisha's goin', and I was bound he should see every one of his blessed children the last thing, ef I took 'em all on my back. He knows where to look, and he's a goin' to see seven cheerful faces as he goes by. Time enough to cry byme by; so set stiddy, boys, and cheer loud when you see Pa," said Mrs. Wilkins, fanning her hot face, and utterly forgetting her cherished bonnet in the excitement of the moment.

" I hear drums! They're comin'!" cried Wash, after a long half hour's waiting had nearly driven him frantic.

The two younger boys immediately tumbled off the fence, and were with difficulty restored to their perches. Gusty began to cry, Ann Elizy to wave a minute red cotton handkerchief, and Adelaide to kick delightedly in her mother's arms.

" Jane Carter, take this child for massy sake: my legs do tremble so I can't h'ist her another minute. Hold on to me behind, somebody, for I *must* see ef I do pitch into the gutter," cried Mrs. Wilkins, with a gasp, as she wiped her eyes on her shawl, clutched the railing, and stood ready to cheer bravely when her conquering hero came.

Wash had heard drums every five minutes since he arrived, but this time he was right, and began to cheer the instant a red cockade appeared at the other end of the long street.

It was a different scene now than in the first en- thusiastic, hopeful days. Young men and ardent boys

filled the ranks then, brave by instinct, burning with
loyal zeal, and blissfully ignorant of all that lay before
them.

Now the blue coats were worn by mature men,
some gray, all grave and resolute ; husbands and fathers
with the memory of wives and children tugging at
their heart-strings; homes left desolate behind them,
and before them the grim certainty of danger, hardship, and perhaps a captivity worse than death. Little
of the glamour of romance about the war now : they
saw what it was, a long, hard task; and here were
the men to do it well.

Even the lookers-on were different. Once all was
wild enthusiasm and glad uproar; now men's lips were
set, and women's smileless even as they cheered;
fewer handkerchiefs whitened the air, for wet eyes
needed them ; and sudden lulls, almost solemn in their
stillness, followed the acclamations of the crowd. All
watched with quickened breath and proud souls that
living wave, blue below, and bright with a steely
glitter above, as it flowed down the street and away
to join the sea of dauntless hearts that for months
had rolled up against the South, and ebbed back reddened with the blood of men like these.

As the inspiring music, the grand tramp drew near,
Christie felt the old thrill and longed to fall in and
follow the flag anywhere. Then she saw David, and
the regiment became one man to her. He was pale,
but his eyes shone, and his whole face expressed that
two of the best and bravest emotions of a man, love
and loyalty, were at their height as he gave his new-
made wife a long, lingering look that seemed to say :

" I could not love thee, dear, so much,
    Loved I not honor more."

Christie smiled and waved her hand to him, showed
him his wedding roses still on her breast, and bore
up as gallantly as he, resolved that his last impression
of her should be a cheerful one. But when it was
all over, and nothing remained but the trampled street,
the hurrying crowd, the bleak November sky, when
Mrs. Wilkins sat sobbing on the steps like Niobe with
her children scattered about her, then Christie's heart
gave way, and she hid her face on Mr. Power's shoulder
for a moment, all her ardor quenched in tears as she
cried within herself:

" No, I could *not* bear it if I was not going too ! "

CHAPTER XVII.

THE COLONEL.

TEN years earlier Christie made her *début* as an
Amazon, now she had a braver part to play on a
larger stage, with a nation for audience, martial music
and the boom of cannon for orchestra; the glare of
battle-fields was the "red light;" danger, disease, and
death, the foes she was to contend against; and the
troupe she joined, not timid girls, but high-hearted
women, who fought gallantly till the "demon" lay
dead, and sang their song of exultation with bleeding
hearts, for this great spectacle was a dire tragedy to
them.

Christie followed David in a week, and soon proved
herself so capable that Mrs. Amory rapidly promoted
her from one important post to another, and bestowed
upon her the only honors left the women, hard work,
responsibility, and the gratitude of many men.

"You are a treasure, my dear, for you can turn your
hand to any thing and do well whatever you undertake. So many come with plenty of good-will, but not
a particle of practical ability, and are offended because
I decline their help. The boys don't want to be cried
over, or have their brows 'everlastingly swabbed,' as
old Watkins calls it: they want to be well fed and

nursed, and cheered up with creature comforts. Your nice beef-tea and cheery ways are worth oceans of tears and cart-loads of tracts."

Mrs. Amory said this, as Christie stood waiting while she wrote an order for some extra delicacy for a very sick patient. Mrs. Sterling, Jr., certainly did look like an efficient nurse, who thought more of " the boys " than of herself; for one hand bore a pitcher of gruel, the other a bag of oranges, clean shirts hung over the right arm, a rubber cushion under the left, and every pocket in the big apron was full of bottles and bandages, papers and letters.

" I never discovered what an accomplished woman I was till I came here," answered Christie, laughing. " I 'm getting vain with so much praise, but I like it immensely, and never was so pleased in my life as I was yesterday when Dr. Harvey came for me to take care of poor Dunbar, because no one else could manage him."

" It 's your firm yet pitiful way the men like so well. I can't describe it better than in big Ben's words : ' Mis Sterlin' is the nuss for me, marm. She takes care of me as ef she was my own mother, and it 's a comfort jest to see her round.' It 's a gift, my dear, and you may thank heaven you have got it, for it works wonders in a place like this."

" I only treat the poor fellows as I would have other women treat my David if he should be in their care. He may be any hour, you know."

" And my boys, God keep them ! "

The pen lay idle, and the gruel cooled, as young wife and gray-haired mother forgot their duty for a moment in tender thoughts of the absent. Only a moment, for in came an attendant with a troubled face, and an important young surgeon with the well-worn little case under his arm.

"Bartlett's dying, marm: could you come and see to him?" says the man to Mrs. Amory.

"We have got to amputate Porter's arm this morning, and he won't consent unless you are with him. You will come, of course?" added the surgeon to Christie, having tried and found her a woman with no "confounded nerves" to impair her usefulness.

So matron and nurse go back to their duty, and dying Bartlett and suffering Porter are all the more tenderly served for that wasted minute.

Like David, Christie had enlisted for the war, and in the two years that followed, she saw all sorts of service; for Mrs. Amory had influence, and her right-hand woman, after a few months' apprenticeship, was ready for any post. The gray gown and comforting face were known in many hospitals, seen on crowded transports, among the ambulances at the front, invalid cars, relief tents, and food depots up and down the land, and many men went out of life like tired children holding the hand that did its work so well.

David meanwhile was doing his part manfully, not only in some of the great battles of those years, but among the hardships, temptations, and sacrifices of a soldiers' life. Spite of his Quaker ancestors, he was a good fighter, and, better still, a magnanimous enemy, hating slavery, but not the slave-holder, and often spared the master while he saved the chattel. He was soon promoted, and might have risen rapidly, but was content to remain as captain of his company; for his men loved him, and he was prouder of his influence over them than of any decoration he could win.

His was the sort of courage that keeps a man faithful to death, and though he made no brilliant charge, uttered few protestations of loyalty, and was never heard to "damn the rebs," his comrades felt that his brave example had often kept them steady till a forlorn hope turned into a victory, knew that all the wealth of the world could not bribe him from his duty, and learned of him to treat with respect an enemy as brave and less fortunate than themselves. A noble nature soon takes its proper rank and exerts its purifying influence, and Private Sterling won confidence, affection, and respect, long before promotion came; for, though he had tended his flowers like a woman and loved his books like a student, he now proved that he could also do his duty and keep his honor stainless as a soldier and a gentleman.

He and Christie met as often as the one could get a brief furlough, or the other be spared from hospital duty; but when these meetings did come, they were wonderfully beautiful and rich, for into them was distilled a concentration of the love, happiness, and communion which many men and women only know through years of wedded life.

Christie liked romance, and now she had it, with a very sombre reality to give it an added charm. No Juliet ever welcomed her Romeo more joyfully than she welcomed David when he paid her a flying visit unexpectedly; no Bayard ever had a more devoted lady in his tent than David, when his wife came through every obstacle to bring him comforts or to nurse the few wounds he received. Love-letters, written beside watch-fires and sick-beds, flew to and fro like carrier-doves with wondrous speed; and nowhere in all the brave and busy land was there a fonder pair than this, although their honeymoon was spent apart in camp and hospital, and well they knew that there might never be for them a happy going home together.

In her wanderings to and fro, Christie not only made many new friends, but met some old ones; and among these one whose unexpected appearance much surprised and touched her.

She was "scrabbling" eggs in a tin basin on board a crowded transport, going up the river with the echoes of a battle dying away behind her, and before her the prospect of passing the next day on a wharf serving out food to the wounded in an easterly storm.

"O Mrs. Sterling, do go up and see what's to be done! We are all full below, and more poor fellows are lying about on deck in a dreadful state. I'll take your place here, but I can't stand that any longer," said one of her aids, coming in heart-sick and exhausted by the ghastly sights and terrible confusion of the day.

"I'll go: keep scrabbling while the eggs last, then knock out the head of that barrel and make gruel till I pass the word to stop."

Forgetting her bonnet, and tying the ends of her shawl behind her, Christie caught up a bottle of brandy and a canteen of water, and ran on deck. There a sight to daunt most any woman, met her eyes; for all about her, so thick that she could hardly step without treading on them, lay the sad wrecks of men: some moaning for help ; some silent, with set, white faces turned up to the gray sky ; all shelterless from the cold wind that blew, and the fog rising from the river. Surgeons and nurses were doing their best; but the boat was loaded, and greater suffering reigned below.

" Heaven help us all ! " sighed Christie, and then she fell to work.

Bottle and canteen were both nearly empty by the time she came to the end of the long line, where lay a silent figure with a hidden face. "Poor fellow, is he dead ? " she said, kneeling down to lift a corner of the blanket lent by a neighbor.

A familiar face looked up at her, and a well remembered voice said courteously, but feebly :

" Thanks, not yet. Excuse my left hand. I'm very glad to see you."

" Mr. Fletcher, can it be you ! " she cried, looking at him with pitiful amazement. Well she might ask, for any thing more unlike his former self can hardly be imagined. Unshaven, haggard, and begrimed with powder, mud to the knees, coat half on, and, worst of all, the right arm gone, there lay the " piece of elegance " she had known, and answered with a smile she never saw before :

" All that's left of me, and very much at your service. I must apologize for the dirt, but I've laid in a mud-puddle for two days; and, though it was much easier than a board, it doesn't improve one's appearance."

" What can I do for you? Where can I put you? I can't bear to see you here ! " said Christie, much afflicted by the spectacle before her.

" Why not? we are all alike when it comes to this pass. I shall do very well if I might trouble you for a draught of water."

She poured her last drop into his parched mouth and hurried off for more. She was detained by the way, and, when she returned, fancied he was asleep, but soon discovered that he had fainted quietly away, utterly spent with two days of hunger, suffering, and exposure. He was himself again directly, and lay contentedly looking up at her as she fed him with hot soup, longing to talk, but refusing to listen to a word till he was refreshed.

" That's very nice," he said gratefully, as he finished, adding with a pathetic sort of gayety, as he groped about with his one hand: " I don't expect napkins, but I *should* like a handkerchief. They took my coat off when they did my arm, and the gentleman who kindly lent me this doesn't seem to have possessed such an article."

Christie wiped his lips with the clean towel at her side, and smiled as she did it, at the idea of Mr. Fletcher's praising burnt soup, and her feeding him like a baby out of a tin cup.

"I think it would comfort you if I washed your face: can you bear to have it done?" she asked.

" If you can bear to do it," he answered, with an apologetic look, evidently troubled at receiving such services from her.

Yet as her hands moved gently about his face, he shut his eyes, and there was a little quiver of the lips now and then, as if he was remembering a time when he had hoped to have her near him in a tenderer capacity

than that of nurse. She guessed the thought, and tried
to banish it by saying cheerfully as she finished:

"There, you look more like yourself after that. Now
the hands."

"Fortunately for you, there is but one," and he
rather reluctantly surrendered a very dirty member.

"Forgive me, I forgot. It is a brave hand, and I
am proud to wash it!"

"How do you know that?" he asked, surprised at
her little burst of enthusiasm, for as she spoke she
pressed the grimy hand in both her own.

"While I was recovering you from your faint, that
man over there informed me that you were his Colonel;
that you 'fit like a tiger,' and when your right arm was
disabled, you took your sword in the left and cheered
them on as if you 'were bound to beat the whole rebel
army.'"

"That's Drake's story," and Mr. Fletcher tried to
give the old shrug, but gave an irrepressible groan
instead, then endeavored to cover it, by saying in a
careless tone, "I thought I might get a little excitement out of it, so I went soldiering like all the rest of
you. I'm not good for much, but I *can* lead the way
for the brave fellows who do the work. Officers make
good targets, and a rebel bullet would cause no sorrow
in taking me out of the world."

"Don't say that! *I* should grieve sincerely; and
yet I'm very glad you came, for it will always be a
satisfaction to you in spite of your great loss."

"There are greater losses than right arms," muttered
Mr. Fletcher gloomily, then checked himself, and added
with a pleasant change in voice and face, as he glanced
at the wedding-ring she wore:

"This is not exactly the place for congratulations, but I can't help offering mine; for if I'm not mistaken *your* left hand also has grown doubly precious since we met?"

Christie had been wondering if he knew, and was much relieved to find he took it so well. Her face said more than her words, as she answered briefly:

"Thank you. Yes, we were married the day David left, and have both been in the ranks ever since."

"Not wounded yet? your husband, I mean," he said, getting over the hard words bravely.

"Three times, but not badly. I think a special angel stands before him with a shield;" and Christie smiled as she spoke.

"I think a special angel stands behind him with prayers that avail much," added Mr. Fletcher, looking up at her with an expression of reverence that touched her heart.

"Now I must go to my work, and you to sleep: you need all the rest you can get before you have to knock about in the ambulances again," she said, marking the feverish color in his face, and knowing well that excitement was his only strength.

"How can I sleep in such an *Inferno* as this?"

"Try, you are so weak, you'll soon drop off;" and, laying the cool tips of her fingers on his eyelids, she kept them shut till he yielded with a long sigh of mingled weariness and pleasure, and was asleep before he knew it.

When he woke it was late at night; but little of night's blessed rest was known on board that boat laden with a freight of suffering. Cries still came up from below, and moans of pain still sounded from the deck, where shadowy figures with lanterns went to and fro among the beds that in the darkness looked like graves.

Weak with pain and fever, the poor man gazed about him half bewildered, and, conscious only of one desire, feebly called " Christie! "

" Here I am ;" and the dull light of a lantern showed him her face very worn and tired, but full of friendliest compassion.

" What can I do for you? " she asked, as he clutched her gown, and peered up at her with mingled doubt and satisfaction in his haggard eyes.

" Just speak to me; let me touch you: I thought it was a dream; thank God it isn't. How much longer will this last?" he added, falling back on the softest pillows she could find for him.

" We shall soon land now; I believe there is an officers' hospital in the town, and you will be quite comfortable there."

" I want to go to your hospital: where is it?"

" I have none ; and, unless the old hotel is ready, I shall stay on the wharf with the boys until it is."

" Then I shall stay also. Don't send me away, Christie: I shall not be a trouble long; surely David will let you help me die?" and poor Fletcher stretched his one hand imploringly to her in the first terror of the delirium that was coming on.

" I will not leave you: I 'll take care of you, and no one can forbid it. Drink this, Philip, and trust to Christie."

He obeyed like a child, and soon fell again into a

troubled sleep while she sat by him thinking about David.

The old hotel *was* ready; but by the time he got there Mr. Fletcher was past caring where he went, and for a week was too ill to know any thing, except that Christie nursed him. Then he turned the corner and began to recover. She wanted him to go into more comfortable quarters; but he would not stir as long as she remained; so she put him in a little room by himself, got a man to wait on him, and gave him as much of her care and time as she could spare from her many duties. He was not an agreeable patient, I regret to say; he tried to bear his woes heroically, but did not succeed very well, not being used to any exertion of that sort; and, though in Christie's presence he did his best, his man confided to her that the Colonel was "as fractious as a teething baby, and the domineeringest party he ever nussed."

Some of Mr. Fletcher's attempts were comical, and some pathetic, for though the sacred circle of her wedding-ring was an effectual barrier against a look or word of love, Christie knew that the old affection was not dead, and it showed itself in his desire to win her respect by all sorts of small sacrifices and efforts at self-control. He would not use many of the comforts sent him, but insisted on wearing an army dressing-gown, and slippers that cost him a secret pang every time his eye was affronted by their ugliness. Always after an angry scene with his servant, he would be found going round among the men bestowing little luxuries and kind words; not condescendingly, but humbly, as if it was an atonement for his own shortcomings, and a tribute due to the brave fellows who bore their pains with a fortitude he could not imitate.

"Poor Philip, he tries so hard I must pity, not despise him; for he was never taught the manly virtues that make David what he is," thought Christie, as she went to him one day with an unusually happy heart.

She found him sitting with a newly opened package before him, and a gloomy look upon his face.

"See what rubbish one of my men has sent me, thinking I might value it," he said, pointing to a broken sword-hilt and offering her a badly written letter.

She read it, and was touched by its affectionate respect and manly sympathy; for the good fellow had been one of those who saved the Colonel when he fell, and had kept the broken sword as a trophy of his bravery, "thinking it might be precious in the eyes of them that loved him."

"Poor Burny might have spared himself the trouble, for I've no one to give it to, and in my eyes it's nothing but a bit of old metal," said Fletcher, pushing the parcel away with a half-irritated, half-melancholy look.

"Give it to me as a parting keepsake. I have a fine collection of relics of the brave men I have known; and this shall have a high place in my museum when I go home," said Christie, taking up the "bit of old metal" with more interest than she had ever felt in the brightest blade.

"Parting keepsake! are you going away?" asked Fletcher, catching at the words in anxious haste, yet looking pleased at her desire to keep the relic.

"Yes, I'm ordered to report in Washington, and start to-morrow."

" Then I 'll go as escort. The doctor has been wanting me to leave for a week, and now I 've no desire to
stay," he said eagerly.

But Christie shook her head, and began to fold up
paper and string with nervous industry as she answered :

" I am not going directly to Washington : I have a
week's furlough first."

" And what is to become of me ? " asked Mr. Fletcher,
as fretfully as a sick child ; for he knew where her short
holiday would be passed, and his temper got the upper-
hand for a minute.

" You should go home and be comfortably nursed :
you 'll need care for some time ; and your friends will
be glad of a chance to give it I 've no doubt."

" I have no home, as you know ; and I don't believe
I 've got a friend in the world who cares whether I
live or die."

" This looks as if you were mistaken ; " and Christie
glanced about the little room, which was full of comforts and luxuries accumulated during his stay.

His face changed instantly, and he answered with
the honest look and tone never given to any one but
her.

" I beg your pardon : I 'm an ungrateful brute. But
you see I 'd just made up my mind to do something
worth the doing, and now it is made impossible in
a way that renders it hard to bear. You are very
patient with me, and I owe my life to your care :
I never can thank you for it ; but I will take myself
out of your way as soon as I can, and leave you free
to enjoy your happy holiday. Heaven knows you
have earned it ! "

He said those last words so heartily that all the bitterness went out of his voice, and Christie found it easy to reply with a cordial smile :

" I shall stay and see you comfortably off before I go myself. As for thanks and reward I have had both; for you *have* done something worth the doing, and you give me this."

She took up the broken blade as she spoke, and carried it away, looking proud of her new trophy.

Fletcher left next day, saying, while he pressed her hand as warmly as if the vigor of two had gone into his one :

" You will let me come and see you by and by when you too get your discharge: won't you ? "

" So gladly that you shall never again say you have no home. But you must take care of yourself, or you will get the long discharge, and we can't spare you yet," she answered warmly.

" No danger of that: the worthless ones are too often left to cumber the earth ; it is the precious ones who are taken," he said, thinking of her as he looked into her tired face, and remembered all she had done for him.

Christie shivered involuntarily at those ominous words, but only said, " Good-by, Philip," as he went feebly away, leaning on his servant's arm, while all the men touched their caps and wished the Colonel a pleasant journey.

CHAPTER XVIII.

SUNRISE.

THREE months later the war seemed drawing toward an end, and Christie was dreaming happy dreams of home and rest with David, when, as she sat one day writing a letter full of good news to the wife of a patient, a telegram was handed to her, and tearing it open she read:

"Captain Sterling dangerously wounded. Tell his wife to come at once.   E. WILKINS."

"No bad news I hope, ma'am?" said the young fellow anxiously, as his half-written letter fluttered to the ground, and Christie sat looking at that fateful strip of paper with all the strength and color stricken out of her face by the fear that fell upon her.

"It might be worse. They told me he was dying once, and when I got to him he met me at the door. I'll hope for the best now as I did then, but I never felt like this before," and she hid her face as if daunted by ominous forebodings too strong to be controlled.

In a moment she was up and doing as calm and steady as if her heart was not torn by an anxiety too keen for words. By the time the news had flown through the house, she was ready; and, coming down with no luggage but a basket of comforts on her arm, she found the hall full of wan and crippled creatures gathered there to see her off, for no nurse in the hospital was more-beloved than Mrs. Sterling. Many eyes followed her, — many lips blessed her, many hands were outstretched for a sympathetic grasp: and, as the ambulance went clattering away, many hearts echoed the words of one grateful ghost of a man, "The Lord go with her and stand by her as she's stood by us."

It was not a long journey that lay before her; but to Christie it seemed interminable, for all the way one unanswerable question haunted her, "Surely God will not be so cruel as to take David now when he has done his part so well and the reward is so near."

It was dark when she arrived at the appointed spot; but Elisha Wilkins was there to receive her, and to her first breathless question, "How is David?" answered briskly:

"Asleep and doin' well, ma'am. At least I should say so, and I peeked at him the last thing before I started."

"Where is he?"

"In the little hospital over yonder. Camp warn't no place for him, and I fetched him here as the nighest, and the best thing I could do for him."

"How is he wounded?"

"Shot in the shoulder, side, and arm."

"Dangerously you said?"

"No, ma'am, that warn't and ain't my opinion. The sergeant sent that telegram, and I think he done wrong.

The Captain is hit pretty bad; but it ain't by no means desperate accordin' to my way of thinkin'," replied the hopeful Wilkins, who seemed mercifully gifted with an unusual flow of language.

" Thank heaven! Now go on and tell me all about it as fast as you can," commanded Christie, walking along the rough road so rapidly that Private Wilkins would have been distressed both in wind and limb if discipline and hardship had not done much for him.

" Well, you see we've been skirmishin' round here for a week, for the woods are full of rebs waitin' to surprise some commissary stores that's expected along. Contrabands is always comin' into camp, and we do the best we can for the poor devils, and send 'em along where they'll be safe. Yesterday four women and a boy come: about as desperate a lot as I ever see; for they'd been two days and a night in the big swamp, wadin' up to their waists in mud and water, with nothin' to eat, and babies on their backs all the way. Every woman had a child, one dead, but she'd fetched it, ' so it might be buried free,' the poor soul said."

Mr. Wilkins stopped an instant as if for breath, but the thought of his own " little chaps " filled his heart with pity for that bereaved mother; and he understood now why decent men were willing to be shot and starved for " the confounded niggers," as he once called them.

" Go on," said Christie, and he made haste to tell the little story that was so full of intense interest to his listener.

" I never saw the Captain so worked up as he was by the sight of them wretched women. He fed and warmed 'em, comforted their poor scared souls, give what clothes we could find, buried the dead baby with his own hands, and nussed the other little creeters as if they were his own. It warn't safe to keep 'em more 'n a day, so when night come the Captain got 'em off down the river as quiet as he could. Me and another man helped him, for he wouldn't trust no one but himself to boss the job. A boat was ready, — blest if I know how he got it, — and about midnight we led them women down to it. The boy was a strong lad, and any of 'em could help row, for the current would take 'em along rapid. This way, ma'am; be we goin' too fast for you?"

" Not fast enough. Finish quick."

" We got down the bank all right, the Captain standing in the little path that led to the river to keep guard, while Bates held the boat stiddy and I put the women in. Things was goin' lovely when the poor gal who 'd lost her baby must needs jump out and run up to thank the Captain agin for all he 'd done for her. Some of them sly rascals was watchin' the river: they see her, heard Bates call out, ' Come back, wench; come back!' and they fired. She did come back like a shot, and we give that boat a push that sent it into the middle of the stream. Then we run along below the bank, and come out further down to draw off the rebs. Some followed us and we give it to 'em handsome. But some warn't deceived, and we heard 'em firin' away at the Captain; so we got back to him as fast as we could, but it warn't soon enough. — Take my arm, Mis' Sterlin' : it 's kinder rough here."

" And you found him ? " —

" Lyin' right acrost the path with two dead men in

front of him; for he'd kep 'em off like a lion till the firin' brought up a lot of our fellers and the rebs skedaddled. I thought he was dead, for by the starlight I see he was bleedin' awful, — hold on, my dear, hold on to me, — he warn 't, thank God, and looked up at me and sez, sez he, 'Are they safe?' 'They be, Captain,' sez I. 'Then it's all right,' sez he, smilin' in that bright way of his, and then dropped off as quiet as a lamb. We got him back to camp double quick, and when the surgeon see them three wounds he shook his head, and I mistrusted that it warn't no joke. So when the Captain come to I asked him what I could do or git for him, and he answered in a whisper, 'My wife.' "

For an instant Christie did "hold on" to Mr. Wilkins's arm, for those two words seemed to take all her strength away. Then the thought that David was waiting for her strung her nerves and gave her courage to bear any thing.

" Is he here?" she asked of her guide a moment later, as he stopped before a large, half-ruined house, through whose windows dim lights and figures were seen moving to and fro.

" Yes, ma'am; we 've made a hospital of this; the Captain 's got the best room in it, and now he 's got the best nuss that 's goin' anywheres. Won't you have a drop of something jest as a stand-by before you see him ? "

" Nothing; take me to him at once."

" Here we be then. Still sleepin': that looks well."

Mr. Wilkins softly led the way down a long hall, opened a door, and after one look fell back and saluted as the Captain's wife passed in.

A surgeon was bending over the low bed, and when a hoarse voice at his elbow asked:

" How is he? " The doctor answered without looking up:

" Done for: this shot through the lungs will finish him before morning I'm afraid."

" Then leave him to me: I am his wife," said the voice, clear and sharp now with the anguish those hard words had brought.

" Good God, why did no one tell me! My dear lady, I thought you were a nurse!" cried the poor surgeon rent with remorse for what now seemed the brutal frankness of his answer, as he saw the white face of the woman at his side, with a look in her eyes harder to see than the bitterest tears that ever fell.

" I *am* a nurse. If you can do nothing, please go and leave him to me the little while he has to live."

Without a word the surgeon vanished, and Christie was alone with David.

The instant she saw him she felt that there was no hope, for she had seen too many faces wear the look his wore to be deceived even by her love. Lying with closed eyes already sunken by keen suffering, hair damp with the cold dew on his forehead, a scarlet spot on either cheek, gray lines about the mouth, and pale lips parted by the painful breaths that came in heavy gasps or fluttered fitfully. This was what Christie saw, and after that long look she knew the truth, and sunk down beside the bed, crying with an exceeding bitter cry:

" O David, O my husband, must I give you up so soon ? "

His eyes opened then, and he turned his cheek to hers, whispering with a look that tried to be a smile, but ended in a sigh of satisfaction:

"I knew you'd come;" then, as a tearless sob shook her from head to foot, he added steadily, though each breath cost a pang, "Yes, dear, I must go first, but it won't be hard with you to help me do it bravely."

In that supremely bitter moment there returned to Christie's memory certain words of the marriage service that had seemed so beautiful when she took part in it: "For better for worse, till death us do part." She had known the better, so short, so sweet! This was the worse, and till death came she must keep faithfully the promise made with such a happy heart. The thought brought with it unexpected strength, and gave her courage to crush down her grief, seal up her tears, and show a brave and tender face as she took that feeble hand in hers ready to help her husband die.

He saw and thanked her for the effort, felt the sustaining power of a true wife's heart, and seemed to have no other care, since she was by him steadfast to the end. He lay looking at her with such serene and happy eyes that she would not let a tear, a murmur, mar his peace; and for a little while she felt as if she had gone out of this turbulent world into a heavenly one, where love reigned supreme.

But such hours are as brief as beautiful, and at midnight mortal suffering proved that immortal joy had not yet begun.

Christie had sat by many death-beds, but never one like this; for, through all the bitter pangs that tried his flesh, David's soul remained patient and strong, upheld by the faith that conquers pain and makes even Death a friend. In the quiet time that went before, he had told his last wishes, given his last messages of love, and now had but one desire, — to go soon that Christie might be spared the trial of seeing suffering she could neither lighten nor share.

"Go and rest, dear; go and rest," he whispered more than once. "Let Wilkins come: this is too much for you. I thought it would be easier, but I am so strong life fights for me inch by inch."

But Christie would not go, and for her sake David made haste to die.

Hour after hour the tide ebbed fast, hour after hour the man's patient soul sat waiting for release, and hour after hour the woman's passionate heart clung to the love that seemed drifting away leaving her alone upon the shore. Once or twice she could not bear it, and cried out in her despair:

"No, it is not just that you should suffer this for a creature whose whole life is not worth a day of your brave, useful, precious one! Why did you pay such a price for that girl's liberty?" she said, as the thought of her own wrecked future fell upon her dark and heavy.

"Because I owed it; — she suffered more than this seeing her baby die; — I thought of *you* in her place, and I could not help doing it."

The broken answer, the reproachful look, wrung Christie's heart, and she was silent: for, in all the knightly tales she loved so well, what Sir Galahad had rescued a more wretched, wronged, and helpless woman than the poor soul whose dead baby David buried tenderly before he bought the mother's freedom with his life?

Only one regret escaped him as the end drew very

near, and mortal weakness brought relief from mortal pain. The first red streaks of dawn shone in the east, and his dim eyes brightened at the sight;

"Such a beautiful world!" he whispered with the ghost of a smile, "and so much good work to do in it, I wish I could stay and help a little longer," he added, while the shadow deepened on his face. But soon he said, trying to press Christie's hand, still holding his: "You will do my part, and do it better than I could. Don't mourn, dear heart, but work; and by and by you will be comforted."

"I will try; but I think I shall soon follow you, and need no comfort here," answered Christie, already finding consolation in the thought. "What is it,

" DON'T MOURN, DEAR HEART. BUT WORK.

David ?" she asked a little later, as she saw his eyes turn wistfully toward the window where the rosy glow was slowly creeping up the sky.

"I want to see the sun rise;—that used to be our happy time;—turn my face toward the light, Christie, and we'll wait for it together."

An hour later when the first pale ray crept in at the low window, two faces lay upon the pillow; one full of the despairing grief for which there seems no balm; the other with lips and eyes of solemn peace, and that mysterious expression, lovelier than any smile, which death leaves as a tender token that all is well with the new-born soul.

To Christie that was the darkest hour of the dawn, but for David sunrise had already come.

CHAPTER XIX.

LITTLE HEART'S-EASE.

WHEN it was all over, the long journey home, the quiet funeral, the first sad excitement, then came the bitter moment when life says to the bereaved: "Take up your burden and go on alone." Christie's had been the still, tearless grief hardest to bear, most impossible to comfort; and, while Mrs. Sterling bore her loss with the sweet patience of a pious heart, and Letty mourned her brother with the tender sorrow that finds relief in natural ways, the widow sat among them as tranquil, colorless, and mute, as if her soul had followed David, leaving the shadow of her former self behind.

"He will not come to me, but I shall go to him," seemed to be the thought that sustained her, and those who loved her said despairingly to one another: "Her heart is broken: she will not linger long."

But one woman wise in her own motherliness always answered hopefully: "Don't you be troubled; Nater knows what's good for us, and works in her own way. Hearts like this don't break, and sorrer only makes 'em stronger. You mark my words: the blessed baby that's a comin' in the summer will work a merrycle, and you'll see this poor dear a happy woman yet."

Few believed in the prophecy; but Mrs. Wilkins stoutly repeated it and watched over Christie like a mother; often trudging up the lane in spite of wind or weather to bring some dainty mess, some remarkable puzzle in red or yellow calico to be used as a pattern for the little garments the three women sewed with such tender interest, consecrated with such tender tears; or news of the war fresh from Lisha who " was goin' to see it through ef he come home without a leg to stand on." A cheery, hopeful, wholesome influence she brought with her, and all the house seemed to brighten as she sat there freeing her mind upon every subject that came up, from the delicate little shirts Mrs. Sterling knit in spite of failing eyesight, to the fall of Richmond, which, the prophetic spirit being strong within her, Mrs. Wilkins foretold with sibylline precision.

She alone could win a faint smile from Christie with some odd saying, some shrewd opinion, and she alone brought tears to the melancholy eyes that sorely needed such healing dew; for she carried little Adelaide, and without a word put her into Christie's arms, there to cling and smile and babble till she had soothed the bitter pain and hunger of a suffering heart.

She and Mr. Power held Christie up through that hard time, ministering to soul and body with their hope and faith till life grew possible again, and from the dust of a great affliction rose the sustaining power she had sought so long.

As spring came on, and victory after victory proclaimed that the war was drawing to an end, Christie's sad resignation was broken by gusts of grief so stormy, so inconsolable, that those about her trembled for her life. It was so hard to see the regiments come home proudly bearing the torn battle-flags, weary, wounded, but victorious, to be rapturously welcomed, thanked, and honored by the grateful country they had served so well; to see all this and think of David in his grave unknown, unrewarded, and forgotten by all but a faithful few.

"I used to dream of a time like this, to hope and plan for it, and cheer myself with the assurance that, after all our hard work, our long separation, and the dangers we had faced, David would get some honor, receive some reward, at least be kept for me to love and serve and live with for a little while. But these men who have merely saved a banner, led a charge, or lost an arm, get all the glory, while he gave his life so nobly; yet few know it, no one thanked him, and I am left desolate when so many useless ones might have been taken in his place. Oh, it is not just! I cannot forgive God for robbing him of all his honors, and me of all my happiness."

So lamented Christie with the rebellious protest of a strong nature learning submission through the stern discipline of grief. In vain Mr. Power told her that David *had* received a better reward than any human hand could give him, in the gratitude of many women, the respect of many men. That to do bravely the daily duties of an upright life was more heroic in God's sight, than to achieve in an enthusiastic moment a single deed that won the world's applause; and that the seeming incompleteness of his life was beautifully rounded by the act that caused his death, although no eulogy recorded it, no song embalmed it, and few knew it but those he saved, those he loved, and the Great Commander who promoted him to the higher rank he had won.

Christie could not be content with this invisible, intangible recompense for her hero : she wanted to see, to know beyond a doubt, that justice had been done ; and beat herself against the barrier that baffles bereaved humanity till impatient despair was wearied out, and passionate heart gave up the struggle.

Then, when no help seemed possible, she found it where she least expected it, in herself. Searching for religion, she had found love : now seeking to follow love she found religion. The desire for it had never left her, and, while serving others, she was earning this reward ; for when her life seemed to lie in ashes, from their midst, this slender spire of flame, purifying while it burned, rose trembling toward heaven ; showing her how great sacrifices turn to greater compensations ; giving her light, warmth, and consolation, and teaching her the lesson all must learn.

God was very patient with her, sending much help, and letting her climb up to Him by all the tender ways in which aspiring souls can lead unhappy hearts.

David's room had been her refuge when those dark hours came, and sitting there one day trying to understand the great mystery that parted her from David, she seemed to receive an answer to her many prayers for some sign that death had not estranged them. The house was very still, the window open, and a soft south wind was wandering through the room with hints of May-flowers on its wings. Suddenly a breath of music startled her, so airy, sweet, and short-lived that no human voice or hand could have produced it. Again and again it came, a fitful and melodious sigh, that to one made superstitious by much sorrow, seemed like a spirit's voice delivering some message from another world.

Christie looked and listened with hushed breath and expectant heart, believing that some special answer was to be given her. But in a moment she saw it was no supernatural sound, only the south wind whispering in David's flute that hung beside the window. Disappointment came first, then warm over her sore heart flowed the tender recollection that she used to call the old flute "David's voice," for into it he poured the joy and sorrow, unrest and pain, he told no living soul. How often it had been her lullaby, before she learned to read its language; how gaily it had piped for others; how plaintively it had sung for him, alone and in the night; and now how full of pathetic music was that hymn of consolation fitfully whispered by the wind's soft breath.

Ah, yes! this was a better answer than any supernatural voice could have given her; a more helpful sign than any phantom face or hand; a surer confirmation of her hope than subtle argument or sacred promise: for it brought back the memory of the living, loving man so vividly, so tenderly, that Christie felt as if the barrier was down, and welcomed a new sense of David's nearness with the softest tears that had flowed since she closed the serene eyes whose last look had been for her.

After that hour she spent the long spring days lying

on the old couch in his room, reading his books, thinking of his love and life, and listening to "David's voice." She always heard it now, whether the wind touched the flute with airy fingers or it hung mute; and it sung to her songs of patience, hope, and cheer, till a mysterious peace came to her, and she discovered in herself the strength she had asked, yet never thought to find. Under the snow, herbs of grace had been growing silently; and, when the heavy rains had melted all the frost away, they sprung up to blossom beautifully in the sun that shines for every spire of grass, and makes it perfect in its time and place.

Mrs. Wilkins was right; for one June morning, when she laid "that blessed baby" in its mother's arms, Christie's first words were:

"Don't let me die: I must live for baby now," and gathered David's little daughter to her breast, as if the soft touch of the fumbling hands had healed every wound and brightened all the world.

"I told you so; God bless 'em both!" and Mrs. Wilkins retired precipitately to the hall, where she sat down upon the stairs and cried most comfortable tears; for her maternal heart was full of a thanksgiving too deep for words.

A sweet, secluded time to Christie, as she brooded over her little treasure and forgot there was a world outside. A fond and jealous mother, but a very happy one, for after the bitterest came the tenderest experience of her life. She felt its sacredness, its beauty, and its high responsibilities; accepted them prayerfully, and found unspeakable delight in fitting herself to bear them worthily, always remembering that she had a double duty to perform toward the fatherless little creature given to her care.

It is hardly necessary to mention the changes one small individual made in that feminine household. The purring and clucking that went on; the panics over a pin-prick; the consultations over a pellet of chamomilla; the raptures at the dawn of a first smile; the solemn prophecies of future beauty, wit, and wisdom in the bud of a woman; the general adoration of the entire family at the wicker shrine wherein lay the idol, a mass of flannel and cambric with a bald head at one end, and a pair of microscopic blue socks at the other. Mysterious little porringers sat unreproved upon the parlor fire, small garments aired at every window, lights burned at unholy hours, and three agitated nightcaps congregated at the faintest chirp of the restless bird in the maternal nest.

Of course Grandma grew young again, and produced nursery reminiscences on every occasion; Aunt Letty trotted day and night to gratify the imaginary wants of the idol, and Christie was so entirely absorbed that the whole South might have been swallowed up by an earthquake without causing her as much consternation as the appearance of a slight rash upon the baby.

No flower in David's garden throve like his little June rose, for no wind was allowed to visit her too roughly; and when rain fell without, she took her daily airing in the green-house, where from her mother's arms she soon regarded the gay sight with such sprightly satisfaction that she seemed a little flower herself dancing on its stem.

She was named Ruth for grandma, but Christie

always called her "Little Heart's-ease," or "Pansy," and
those who smiled at first at the mother's fancy, came in
time to see that there was an unusual fitness in the
name. All the bitterness seemed taken out of Christie's sorrow by the soft magic of the child : there was
so much to live for now she spoke no more of dying;
and, holding that little hand in hers, it grew easier to
go on along the way that led to David.

A prouder mother never lived ; and, as baby waxed
in beauty and in strength, Christie longed for all the
world to see her. A sweet, peculiar, little face she had,
sunny and fair; but, under the broad forehead where
the bright hair fell as David's used to do, there shone
a pair of dark and solemn eyes, so large, so deep, and
often so unchildlike, that her mother wondered where
she got them. Even when she smiled the shadow lingered in these eyes, and when she wept they filled and
overflowed with great, quiet tears like flowers too full
of dew. Christie often said remorsefully :

"My little Pansy! I put my own sorrow into your
baby soul, and now it looks back at me with this
strange wistfulness, and these great drops are the unsubmissive tears I locked up in my heart because I
would not be grateful for the good gift God gave me,
even while he took that other one away. O Baby,
forgive your mother; and don't let her find that she
has given you clouds instead of sunshine."

This fear helped Christie to keep her own face cheerful, her own heart tranquil, her own life as sunny,
healthful, and hopeful as she wished her child's to be.
For this reason she took garden and green-house into
her own hands when Bennet gave them up, and, with a

stout lad to help her, did well this part of the work
that David bequeathed to her. It was a pretty sight
to see the mother with her year-old daughter out
among the fresh, green things : the little golden head
bobbing here and there like a stray sunbeam; the baby
voice telling sweet, unintelligible stories to bird and
bee and butterfly; or the small creature fast asleep in
a basket under a rose-bush, swinging in a hammock
from a tree, or in Bran's keeping, rosy, vigorous, and
sweet with sun and air, and the wholesome influence
of a wise and tender love.

While Christie worked she planned her daughter's
future, as mothers will, and had but one care concern-
ing it. She did not fear poverty, but the thought of
being straitened for the means of educating little
Ruth afflicted her. She meant to teach her to labor
heartily and see no degradation in it, but she could not
bear to feel that her child should be denied the harm-
less pleasures that make youth sweet, the opportunities
that educate, the society that ripens character and
gives a rank which money cannot buy. A little sum to
put away for Baby, safe from all risk, ready to draw
from as each need came, and sacredly devoted to this
end, was now Christie's sole ambition.

With this purpose at her heart, she watched her
fruit and nursed her flowers; found no task too hard,
no sun too hot, no weed too unconquerable; and soon
the garden David planted when his life seemed barren,
yielded lovely harvests to swell his little daughter's
portion.

One day Christie received a letter from Uncle Enos
expressing 'a wish to see her if she cared to come so

far and "stop a spell." It both surprised and pleased her, and she resolved to go, glad that the old man remembered her, and proud to show him the great success of her life, as she considered Baby.

So she went, was hospitably received by the ancient cousin five times removed who kept house, and greeted with as much cordiality as Uncle Enos ever showed to any one. He looked askance at Baby, as if he had not bargained for the honor of her presence; but he said nothing, and Christie wisely refrained from mentioning that Ruth was the most remarkable child ever born.

She soon felt at home, and went about the old house visiting familiar nooks with the bitter, sweet satisfaction of such returns. It was sad to miss Aunt Betsey in the big kitchen, strange to see Uncle Enos sit all day in his arm-chair too helpless now to plod about the farm and carry terror to the souls of those who served him. He was still a crabbed, gruff, old man; but the narrow, hard, old heart was a little softer than it used to be; and he sometimes betrayed the longing for his kindred that the aged often feel when infirmity makes them desire tenderer props than any they can hire.

Christie saw this wish, and tried to gratify it with a dutiful affection which could not fail to win its way. Baby unconsciously lent a hand, for Uncle Enos could not long withstand the sweet enticements of this little kinswoman. He did not own the conquest in words, but was seen to cuddle his small captivator in private; allowed all sorts of liberties with his spectacles, his pockets, and bald pate; and never seemed more comfortable than when she confiscated his newspaper, and sitting on his knee read it to him in a pretty language of her own.

"She's a good little gal; looks consid'able like you; but you warn't never such a quiet puss as she is," he said one day, as the child was toddling about the room with an old doll of her mother's lately disinterred from its tomb in the garret.

"She is like her father in that. But I get quieter as I grow old, uncle," answered Christie, who sat sewing near him.

"You be growing old, that's a fact; but somehow it's kind of becomin'. I never thought you'd be so much of a lady, and look so well after all you've ben through," added Uncle Enos, vainly trying to discover what made Christie's manners so agreeable in spite of her plain dress, and her face so pleasant in spite of the gray hair at her temples and the lines about her mouth.

It grew still pleasanter to see as she smiled and looked up at him with the soft yet bright expression that always made him think of her mother.

"I'm glad you don't consider me an entire failure, uncle. You know you predicted it. But though I have gone through a good deal, I don't regret my attempt, and when I look at Pansy I feel as if I'd made a grand success."

"You haven't made much money, I guess. If you don't mind tellin', what *have* you got to live on?' asked the old man, unwilling to acknowledge any life a success, if dollars and cents were left out of it.

"Only David's pension and what I can make by my garden."

"The old lady has to have some on't, don't she?"

"She has a little money of her own; but I see that she and Letty have two-thirds of all I make."

"That ain't a fair bargain if you do all the work."

"Ah, but we don't make bargains, sir: we work for one another and share every thing together."

"So like women!" grumbled Uncle Enos, longing to see that "the property was fixed up square."

"She's a good little gal; looks consid'able like you."

"How are you goin' to eddicate the little gal? I s'pose you think as much of culter and so on as ever you did," he presently added with a gruff laugh.

"More," answered Christie, smiling too, as she remembered the old quarrels. "I shall earn the money, sir. If the garden fails I can teach, nurse, sew, write, cook even, for I've half a dozen useful accomplishments at my fingers' ends, thanks to the education you and dear Aunt Betsey gave me, and I may have to use them all for Pansy's sake."

Pleased by the compliment, yet a little conscience-stricken at the small share he deserved of it, Uncle Enos sat rubbing up his glasses a minute, before he led to the subject he had in his mind.

"Ef you fall sick or die, what then?"

"I've thought of that," and Christie caught up the child as if her love could keep even death at bay. But Pansy soon struggled down again, for the dirty-faced doll was taking a walk and could not be detained. "If I am taken from her, then my little girl must do as her mother did. God has orphans in His special care, and He won't forget her I am sure."

Uncle Enos had a coughing spell just then; and, when he got over it, he said with an effort, for even to talk of giving away his substance cost him a pang:

"I'm gettin' into years now, and it's about time I fixed up matters in case I'm took suddin'. I always meant to give you a little suthing, but as you didn't ask for 't, I took good care on 't, and it ain't none the worse for waitin' a spell. I jest speak on 't, so you needn't be anxious about the little gal. It ain't mucb, but it will make things easy I reckon."

"You are very kind, uncle; and I am more grateful than I can tell. I don't want a penny for myself, but I should love to know that my daughter was to have an easier life than mine."

"I s'pose you thought of that when you come so quick?" said the old man, with a suspicious look, that made Christie's eyes kindle as they used to years ago, but she answered honestly:

"I did think of it and hope it, yet I should have come quicker if you had been in the poor-house."

Neither spoke for a minute; for, in spite of generosity and gratitude, the two natures struck fire when they met as inevitably as flint and steel.

"What's your opinion of missionaries," asked Uncle Enos, after a spell of meditation.

"If I had any money to leave them, I should bequeath it to those who help the heathen here at home, and should let the innocent Feejee Islanders worship their idols a little longer in benighted peace," answered Christie, in her usual decided way.

"That's my idee exactly; but it's uncommon hard to settle *which* of them that stays at home you'll trust your money to. You see Betsey was always pesterin' me to give to charity things; but I told her it was better to save up and give it in a handsome lump that looked well, and was a credit to you. When she was dyin' she reminded me on't, and I promised I'd do suthing before I follered. I've been turnin' on't over in my mind for a number of months, and I don't seem to find any thing that's jest right. You've ben round among the charity folks lately accordin' to your tell, now what would you do if you had a tidy little sum to dispose on?"

"Help the Freed people."

The answer came so quick that it nearly took the old gentleman's breath away, and he looked at his niece with his mouth open after an involuntary, "Sho!" had escaped him.

"David helped give them their liberty, and I would so gladly help them to enjoy it!" cried Christie, all the old enthusiasm blazing up, but with a clearer, steadier flame than in the days when she dreamed splendid dreams by the kitchen fire.

"Well, no, that wouldn't meet my views. What else is there?" asked the old man quite unwarmed by her benevolent ardor.

"Wounded soldiers, destitute children, ill-paid women, young people struggling for independence, homes, hospitals, schools, churches, and God's charity all over the world."

"That's the pesky part on 't: there's such a lot to choose from; I don't know much about any of 'em," began Uncle Enos, looking like a perplexed raven with a treasure which it cannot decide where to hide.

"Whose fault is that, sir?"

The question hit the old man full in the conscience, and he winced, remembering how many of Betsey's charitable impulses he had nipped in the bud, and now all the accumulated alms she would have been so glad to scatter weighed upon him heavily. He rubbed his bald head with a yellow bandana, and moved uneasily in his chair, as if he wanted to get up and finish the neglected job that made his helplessness so burdensome.

"I'll ponder on 't a spell, and make up my mind," was all he said, and never renewed the subject again.

But he had very little time to ponder, and he never did make up his mind; for a few months after Christie's long visit ended, Uncle Enos " was took suddin', " and left all he had to her.

Not an immense fortune, but far larger than she expected, and great was her anxiety to use wisely this unlooked-for benefaction. She was very grateful, but she kept nothing for herself, feeling that David's pension was enough, and preferring the small sum he earned so dearly to the thousands the old man had hoarded up for years. A good portion was put by for Ruth, something for "mother and Letty" that want might never touch them, and the rest she kept for David's work, believing that, so spent, the money would be blest.

CHAPTER XX.

AT FORTY.

" NEARLY twenty years since I set out to seek my fortune. It has been a long search, but I think I have found it at last. I only asked to be a useful, happy woman, and my wish is granted: for, I believe I *am* useful; I *know* I am happy."

Christie looked so as she sat alone in the flowery parlor one September afternoon, thinking over her life with a grateful, cheerful spirit. Forty to-day, and pausing at that half-way house between youth and age, she looked back into the past without bitter regret or unsubmissive grief, and forward into the future with courageous patience; for three good angels attended her, and with faith, hope, and charity to brighten life, no woman need lament lost youth or fear approaching age. Christie did not, and though her eyes filled with quiet tears as they were raised to the faded cap and sheathed sword hanging on the wall, none fell; and in a moment tender sorrow changed to still tenderer joy as her glance wandered to rosy little Ruth playing hospital with her dollies in the porch. Then they shone with genuine satisfaction as they went from the letters and papers on her table to the garden, where several young women were at work with a healthful color in the cheeks that had been very pale and thin in the spring.

" I think David is satisfied with me; for I have given all my heart and strength to his work, and it prospers well," she said to herself, and then her face grew thoughtful, as she recalled a late event which seemed to have opened a new field of labor for her if she chose to enter it.

A few evenings before she had gone to one of the many meetings of working-women, which had made some stir of late. Not a first visit, for she was much interested in the subject and full of sympathy for this class of workers.

There were speeches of course, and of the most unparliamentary sort, for the meeting was composed almost entirely of women, each eager to tell her special grievance or theory. Any one who chose got up and spoke; and whether wisely or foolishly each proved how great was the ferment now going on, and how difficult it was for the two classes to meet and help one another in spite of the utmost need on one side and the sincerest good-will on the other. The workers poured out their wrongs and hardships passionately or plaintively, demanding or imploring justice, sympathy, and help; displaying the ignorance, incapacity, and prejudice, which make their need all the more pitiful, their relief all the more imperative.

The ladies did their part with kindliness, patience, and often unconscious condescension, showing in their turn how little they knew of the real trials of the women whom they longed to serve, how very narrow a sphere of usefulness they were fitted for in spite of cult-

ure and intelligence, and how rich they were in generous theories, how poor in practical methods of relief.

One accomplished creature with learning radiating
from every pore, delivered a charming little essay on
the strong-minded women of antiquity; then, taking
labor into the region of art, painted delightful pictures
of the time when all would work harmoniously together
in an Ideal Republic, where each did the task she liked,
and was paid for it in liberty, equality, and fraternity.

Unfortunately she talked over the heads of her audience, and it was like telling fairy tales to hungry children to describe Aspasia discussing Greek politics with
Pericles and Plato reposing upon ivory couches, or
Hypatia modestly delivering philosophical lectures to
young men behind a Tyrian purple curtain; and the
Ideal Republic met with little favor from anxious seam-
stresses, type-setters, and shop-girls, who said ungrate-
fully among themselves, "That's all very pretty, but I
don't see how it's going to better wages among us
now."

Another eloquent sister gave them a political ora-
tion which fired the revolutionary blood in their veins,
and made them eager to rush to the State-house *en
masse*, and demand the ballot before one-half of them
were quite clear what it meant, and the other half were
as unfit for it as any ignorant Patrick bribed with a
dollar and a sup of whiskey.

A third well-wisher quenched their ardor like a wet
blanket, by reading reports of sundry labor reforms in
foreign parts; most interesting, but made entirely futile
by differences of climate, needs, and customs. She
closed with a cheerful budget of statistics, giving the

exact number of needle-women who had starved, gone
mad, or committed suicide during the past year; the
enormous profits wrung by capitalists from the blood
and muscles of their employés; and the alarming increase in the cost of living, which was about to plunge
the nation into debt and famine, if not destruction
generally.

When she sat down despair was visible on many
countenances, and immediate starvation seemed to be
waiting at the door to clutch them as they went out;
for the impressible creatures believed every word and
saw no salvation anywhere.

Christie had listened intently to all this; had admired,
regretted, or condemned as each spoke; and felt a steadily increasing sympathy for all, and a strong desire to
bring the helpers and the helped into truer relations
with each other.

The dear ladies were so earnest, so hopeful, and so
unpractically benevolent, that it grieved her to see so
much breath wasted, so much good-will astray; while
the expectant, despondent, or excited faces of the work-
women touched her heart; for well she knew how much
they needed help, how eager they were for light, how
ready to be led if some one would only show a possible
way.

As the statistical extinguisher retired, beaming with
satisfaction at having added her mite to the good cause,
a sudden and uncontrollable impulse moved Christie to
rise in her place and ask leave to speak. It was readily
granted, and a little stir of interest greeted her; for she
was known to many as Mr. Power's friend, David Sterling's wife, or an army nurse who had done well. Whis-

pers circulated quickly, and faces brightened as they turned toward her; for she had a helpful look, and her first words pleased them. When the president invited her to the platform she paused on the lowest step, saying with an expressive look and gesture :

"I am better here, thank you; for I have been and mean to be a working-woman all my life."

"Hear! hear!" cried a stout matron in a gay bonnet, and the rest indorsed the sentiment with a hearty round. Then they were very still, and then in a clear, steady voice, with the sympathetic undertone to it that is so magical in its effect, Christie made her first speech in public since she left the stage.

That early training stood her in good stead now, giving her self-possession, power of voice, and ease of gesture ; while the purpose at her heart lent her the sort of simple eloquence that touches, persuades, and convinces better than logic, flattery, or oratory.

What she said she hardly knew: words came faster than she could utter them, thoughts pressed upon her, and all the lessons of her life rose vividly before her to give weight to her arguments, value to her counsel, and the force of truth to every sentence she uttered. She had known so many of the same trials, troubles, and temptations that she could speak understandingly of them ; and, better still, she had conquered or outlived so many of them, that she could not only pity but help others to do as she had done. Having found in labor her best teacher, comforter, and friend, she could tell those who listened that, no matter how hard or humble the task at the beginning, if faithfully and bravely performed, it would surely prove a stepping-stone to something better, and with each honest effort they were fitting themselves for the nobler labor, and larger liberty God meant them to enjoy.

The women felt that this speaker was one of them; for the same lines were on her face that they saw on their own, her hands were no fine lady's hands, her dress plainer than some of theirs, her speech simple enough for all to understand; cheerful, comforting, and full of practical suggestion, illustrations out of their own experience, and a spirit of companionship that uplifted their despondent hearts.

Yet more impressive than any thing she said was the subtle magnetism of character, for that has a universal language which all can understand. They saw and felt that a genuine woman stood down there among them like a sister, ready with head, heart, and hand to help them help themselves; not offering pity as an alms, but justice as a right. Hardship and sorrow, long effort and late-won reward had been hers they knew; wife-hood, motherhood, and widowhood brought her very near to them; and behind her was the background of an earnest life, against which this figure with health on the cheeks, hope in the eyes, courage on the lips, and the ardor of a wide benevolence warming the whole countenance stood out full of unconscious dignity and beauty; an example to comfort, touch, and inspire them.

It was not a long speech, and in it there was no learning, no statistics, and no politics; yet it was the speech of the evening, and when it was over no one else seemed to have any thing to say. As the meeting broke up Christie's hand was shaken by many rough-

ened by the needle, stained with printer's ink, or hard
with humbler toil; many faces smiled gratefully at her,
and many voices thanked her heartily. But sweeter
than any applause were the words of one woman who
grasped her hand, and whispered with wet eyes:

" I knew your blessed husband; he was very good to
me, and I 've been thanking the Lord he had such a
wife for his reward! "

Christie was thinking of all this as she sat alone that
day, and asking herself if she should go on; for the
ladies had been as grateful as the women; had begged
her to come and speak again, saying they needed just
such a mediator to bridge across the space that now
divided them from those they wished to serve. She
certainly seemed fitted to act as interpreter between
the two classes; for, from the gentleman her father she
had inherited the fine instincts, gracious manners, and
unblemished name of an old and honorable race; from
the farmer's daughter, her mother, came the equally
valuable dower of practical virtues, a sturdy love of
independence, and great respect for the skill and courage that can win it.

Such women were much needed and are not always
easy to find; for even in democratic America the hand
that earns its daily bread must wear some talent, name,
or honor as an ornament, before it is very cordially
shaken by those that wear white gloves.

" Perhaps this is the task my life has been fitting me
for," she said. " A great and noble one which I should
be proud to accept and help accomplish if I can. Others
have finished the emancipation work and done it splendidly, even at the cost of all this blood and sorrow. I

came too late to do any thing but give my husband and behold the glorious end. This new task seems to offer me the chance of being among the pioneers, to do the hard work, share the persecution, and help lay the foundation of a new emancipation whose happy success I may never see. Yet I had rather be remembered as those brave beginners are, though many of them missed the triumph, than as the late comers will be, who only beat the drums and wave the banners when the victory is won."

Just then the gate creaked on its hinges, a step sounded in the porch, and little Ruth ran in to say in an audible whisper:

"It's a lady, mamma, a very pretty lady: can you see her?"

"Yes, dear, ask her in."

There was a rustle of sweeping silks through the narrow hall, a vision of a very lovely woman in the door-way, and two daintily gloved hands were extended as an eager voice asked: "Dearest Christie, don't you remember Bella Carrol?"

Christie did remember, and had her in her arms directly, utterly regardless of the imminent destruction of a marvellous hat, or the bad effect of tears on violet ribbons. Presently they were sitting close together, talking with April faces, and telling their stories as women must when they meet after the lapse of years. A few letters had passed between them, but Bella had been abroad, and Christie too busy living her life to have much time to write about it.

"Your mother, Bella? how is she, and where?"

"Still with Augustine, and he you know is melan-

choly mad : very quiet, very patient, and very kind
to every one but himself. His penances for the sins
of his race would soon kill him if mother was not
there to watch over him. And her penance is never
to leave him."

"Dear child, don't tell me any more; it is too sad.
Talk of yourself and Harry. Now you smile, so I'm
sure all is well with him."

"Yes, thank heaven! Christie, I do believe fate
means to spare us as dear old Dr. Shirley said. I never
can be gay again, but I keep as cheerful and busy as
I can, for Harry's sake, and he does the same for mine.
We shall always be together, and all in all to one
another, for we can never marry and have homes apart
you know. We have wandered over the face of the
earth for several years, and now we mean to settle
down and be as happy and as useful as we can."

"That's brave! I am so glad· to hear it, and so truly
thankful it is possible. But tell me, Bella, what Harry
means to do? You spoke in one of your first letters
of his being hard at work studying medicine. Is that
to be his profession?"

"Yes; I don't know what made him choose it, unless
it was the hope that he might spare other families from
a curse like ours, or lighten it if it came. After
Helen's death he was a changed creature; no longer a
wild boy, but a man. I told him what you said to me,
and it gave him hope. Dr. Shirley confirmed it as far
as he dared; and Hal resolved to make the most of his
one chance by interesting himself in some absorbing
study, and leaving no room for fear, no time for dangerous recollections. I was so glad, and mother so com-

forted, for we both feared that sad trouble would destroy him. He studied hard, got on splendidly, and then went abroad to finish off. I went with him; for poor August was past hope, and mamma would not let me help her. The doctor said it was best for me to be away, and excellent for Hal to have me with him, to cheer him up, and keep him steady with a little responsibility. We have been happy together in spite of our trouble, he in his profession, and I in him; now he is ready, so we have come home, and now the hardest part begins for me."

"How, Bella?"

"He has his work and loves it: I have nothing after my duty to him is done. I find I've lost my taste for the old pleasures and pursuits, and though I have tried more sober, solid ones, there still remains much time to hang heavy on my hands, and such an empty place in my heart, that even Harry's love cannot fill it. I'm afraid I shall get melancholy, — that is the beginning of the end for us, you know."

As Bella spoke the light died out of her eyes, and they grew despairing with the gloom of a tragic memory. Christie drew the beautiful, pathetic face down upon her bosom, longing to comfort, yet feeling very powerless to lighten Bella's burden.

But Christie's little daughter did it for her. Ruth had been standing near regarding the "pretty lady," with as much wonder and admiration as if she thought her a fairy princess, who might vanish before she got a good look at her. Divining with a child's quick instinct that the princess was in trouble, Ruth flew into the porch, caught up her latest and dearest treasure, and presented it as a sure consolation, with such sweet good-will, that Bella could not refuse, although it was only a fuzzy caterpillar in a little box.

"I give it to you because it is my nicest one and just ready to spin up. Do you like pussy-pillars, and know how they do it?" asked Ruth, emboldened by the kiss she got in return for her offering.

"Tell me all about it, darling," and Bella could not help smiling, as the child fixed her great eyes upon her, and told her little story with such earnestness, that she was breathless by the time she ended.

"At first they are only grubs you know, and stay down in the earth; then they are like this, nice and downy and humpy, when they walk; and when it's time they spin up and go to sleep. It's all dark in their little beds, and they don't know what may happen to 'em; but they are not afraid 'cause God takes care of 'em. So they wait and don't fret, and when it's right for 'em they come out splendid butterflies, all beautiful and shining like your gown. They are happy then, and fly away to eat honey, and live in the air, and never be creeping worms any more."

"That's a pretty lesson for me," said Bella softly, "I accept and thank you for it, little teacher; I'll try to be a patient 'pussy-pillar' though it *is* dark, and I don't know what may happen to me; and I'll wait hopefully till it's time to float away a happy butter-fly."

"Go and get the friend some flowers, the gayest and sweetest you can find, Pansy," said Christie, and, as the child ran off, she added to her friend:

"Now we must think of something pleasant for you

to do. It may take a little time, but I know we shall find your niche if we give our minds to it."

"That's one reason why I came. I heard some friends of mine talking about you yesterday, and they seemed to think you were equal to any thing in the way of good works. Charity is the usual refuge for people like me, so I wish to try it. I don't mind doing or seeing sad or disagreeable things, if it only fills up my life and helps me to forget."

"You will help more by giving of your abundance to those who know how to dispense it wisely, than by trying to do it yourself, my dear. I never advise pretty creatures like you to tuck up their silk gowns and go down into the sloughs with alms for the poor, who don't like it any better than you do, and so much pity and money are wasted in sentimental charity."

"Then what shall I do?"

"If you choose you can find plenty of work in your own class; for, if you will allow me to say it, they need help quite as much as the paupers, though in a very different way."

"Oh, you mean I'm to be strong-minded, to cry aloud and spare not, to denounce their iniquities, and demand their money or their lives?"

"Now, Bella, that's personal; for I made my first speech a night or two ago."

"I know you did, and I wish I'd heard it. I'd make mine to-night if I could do it half as well as I'm told you did," interrupted Bella, clapping her hands with a face full of approval.

But Christie was in earnest, and produced her new project with all speed.

"I want you to try a little experiment for me, and if it succeeds you shall have all the glory; I've been waiting for some one to undertake it, and I fancy you are the woman. Not every one could attempt it; for it needs wealth and position, beauty and accomplishments, much tact, and more than all a heart that has not been spoilt by the world, but taught through sorrow how to value and use life well."

"Christie, what is it? this experiment that needs so much, and yet which you think me capable of trying?" asked Bella, interested and flattered by this opening.

"I want you to set a new fashion: you know you can set almost any you choose in your own circle; for people are very like sheep, and will follow their leader if it happens to be one they fancy. I don't ask you to be a De Staël, and have a brilliant *salon:* I only want you to provide employment and pleasure for others like yourself, who now are dying of frivolity or *ennui.*"

"I should love to do that if I could. Tell me how."

"Well, dear, I want you to make Harry's home as beautiful and attractive as you can; to keep all the elegance and refinement of former times, and to add to it a new charm by setting the fashion of common sense. Invite all the old friends, and as many new ones as you choose; but have it understood that they are to come as intelligent men and women, not as pleasure-hunting beaux and belles; give them conversation instead of gossip; less food for the body and more for the mind; the healthy stimulus of the nobler pleasures they can command, instead of the harmful excitements of present dissipation. In short, show them the sort of society we need more of, and might so easily have if those who possess the means of culture cared for the best sort, and took pride in acquiring it. Do you understand, Bella?"

"Yes, but it's a great undertaking, and you could do it better than I."

"Bless you, no! I haven't a single qualification for it but the will to have it done. I'm 'strong-minded,' a radical, and a reformer. I've done all sorts of dreadful things to get my living, and I have neither youth, beauty, talent, or position to back me up; so I should only be politely ignored if I tried the experiment myself. I don't want you to break out and announce your purpose with a flourish; or try to reform society at large, but I *do* want you to devote yourself and your advantages to quietly insinuating a better state of things into one little circle. The very fact of your own want, your own weariness, proves how much such a reform is needed. There are so many fine young women longing for something to fill up the empty places that come when the first flush of youth is over, and the serious side of life appears; so many promising young men learning to conceal or condemn the high ideals and the noble purposes they started with, because they find no welcome for them. You might help both by simply creating a purer atmosphere for them to breathe, sunshine to foster instead of frost to nip their good aspirations, and so, even if you planted no seed, you might encourage a timid sprout or two that would one day be a lovely flower or a grand tree all would admire and enjoy."

As Christie ended with the figure suggested by her favorite work, Bella said after a thoughtful pause:

"But few of the women I know can talk about any thing but servants, dress, and gossip. Here and there one knows something of music, art, or literature; but the superior ones are not favorites with the larger class of gentlemen."

"Then let the superior women cultivate the smaller class of men who do admire intelligence as well as beauty. There are plenty of them, and you had better introduce a few as samples, though their coats may not be of the finest broadcloth, nor their fathers 'solid men.' Women lead in society, and when men find that they can not only dress with taste, but talk with sense, the lords of creation will be glad to drop mere twaddle and converse as with their equals. Bless my heart!" cried Christie, walking about the room as if she had mounted her hobby, and was off for a canter, "how people can go on in such an idiotic fashion passes my understanding. Why keep up an endless clatter about gowns and dinners, your neighbors' affairs, and your own aches, when there is a world full of grand questions to settle, lovely things to see, wise things to study, and noble things to imitate. Bella, you *must* try the experiment, and be the queen of a better society than any you can reign over now."

"It looks inviting, and I *will* try it with you to help me. I know Harry would like it, and I'll get him to recommend it to his patients. If he is as successful here as elsewhere they will swallow any dose he orders; for he knows how to manage people wonderfully well. He prescribed a silk dress to a despondent, dowdy patient once, telling her the electricity of silk was good for her nerves: she obeyed, and when well dressed felt so much better that she bestirred herself generally and recovered; but to this day she sings the praises of Dr. Carrol's electric cure."

Bella was laughing gaily as she spoke, and so was Christie as she replied:

"That's just what I want you to do with *your* patients. Dress up their minds in their best; get them out into the air; and cure their ills by the magnetism of more active, earnest lives."

They talked over the new plan with increasing interest; for Christie did not mean that Bella should be one of the brilliant women who shine for a little while, and then go out like a firework. And Bella felt as if she had found something to do in her own sphere, a sort of charity she was fitted for, and with it a pleasant sense of power to give it zest.

When Letty and her mother came in, they found a much happier looking guest than the one Christie had welcomed an hour before. Scarcely had she introduced them when voices in the lane made all look up to see old Hepsey and Mrs. Wilkins approaching.

"Two more of my dear friends, Bella: a fugitive slave and a laundress. One has saved scores of her own people, and is my pet heroine. The other has the bravest, cheeriest soul I know, and is my private oracle."

The words were hardly out of Christie's mouth when in they came; Hepsey's black face shining with affection, and Mrs. Wilkins as usual running over with kind words.

"My dear creeter, the best of wishes and no end of happy birthdays. There's a triflin' keepsake; tuck it away, and look at it byme by. Mis' Sterlin', I'm proper glad to see you lookin' so well. Aunt Letty, how's that darlin' child? I ain't the pleasure of your acquaintance, Miss, but I'm pleased to see you. The children all sent love, likewise Lisha, whose bones is better sense I tried the camfire and red flannel."

Then they settled down like a flock of birds of various plumage and power of song, but all amicably disposed, and ready to peck socially at any topic which might turn up.

Mrs. Wilkins started one by exclaiming as she "laid off" her bonnet:

"Sakes alive, there's a new picter! Ain't it beautiful?"

"Colonel Fletcher brought it this morning. A great artist painted it for him, and he gave it to me in a way that added much to its value," answered Christie, with both gratitude and affection in her face; for she was a woman who could change a lover to a friend, and keep him all her life.

It was a quaint and lovely picture of Mr. Greatheart, leading the fugitives from the City of Destruction. A dark wood lay behind; a wide river rolled before; Mercy and Christiana pressed close to their faithful guide, who went down the rough and narrow path bearing a cross-hilted sword in his right hand, and holding a sleeping baby with the left. The sun was just rising, and a long ray made a bright path athwart the river, turned Greatheart's dinted armor to gold, and shone into the brave and tender face that seemed to look beyond the sunrise.

"There's just a hint of Davy in it that is very comforting to me," said Mrs. Sterling, as she laid her old hands softly together, and looked up with her devout eyes full of love.

"Dem women oughter bin black," murmured Hepsey, tearfully; for she considered David worthy of a place with old John Brown and Colonel Shaw.

"The child looks like Pansy, we all think," added Letty, as the little girl brought her nosegay for Aunty to tie up prettily.

Christie said nothing, because she felt too much; and Bella was also silent because she knew too little. But Mrs. Wilkins with her kindly tact changed the subject before it grew painful, and asked with sudden interest:

"When be you a goin' to hold forth agin, Christie? Jest let me know beforehand, and I'll wear my old gloves: I tore my best ones all to rags clappin' of you; it was so extra good."

"I don't deserve any credit for the speech, because it spoke itself, and I couldn't help it. I had no thought of such a thing till it came over me all at once, and I was up before I knew it. I'm truly glad you liked it, but I shall never make another, unless you think I'd better. You know I always ask your advice, and what is more remarkable usually take it," said Christie, glad to consult her oracle.

"Hadn't you better rest a little before you begin any new task, my daughter? You have done so much these last years you must be tired," interrupted Mrs. Sterling, with a look of tender anxiety.

"You know I work for two, mother," answered Christie, with the clear, sweet expression her face always wore when she spoke of David. "I am not tired yet: I hope I never shall be, for without my work I should fall into despair or *ennui.* There is so much to be done, and it is so delightful to help do it, that 1 never mean to fold my hands till they are useless. I owe all I can do, for in labor, and the efforts and experiences that grew out of it, I have found independence, education, happiness, and religion."

"Then, my dear, you are ready to help other folks into the same blessed state, and it's your duty to do it!" cried Mrs. Wilkins, her keen eyes full of sympathy and commendation as they rested on Christie's cheerful, earnest face. "Ef the sperrit moves you to speak, up and do it without no misgivin's. *I* think it was a special leadin' that night, and I hope you'll foller, for it ain't every one that can make folks laugh and cry with a few plain words that go right to a body's heart and stop there real comfortable and fillin'. I guess this is your next job, my dear, and you'd better ketch hold and give it the right turn; for it's goin' to take time, and women ain't stood alone for so long they'll need a sight of boostin'."

There was a general laugh at the close of Mrs. Wilkins's remarks; but Christie answered seriously: "I accept the task, and will do my share faithfully with words or work, as shall seem best. We all need much preparation for the good time that is coming to us, and can get it best by trying to know and help, love and educate one another, — as we do here."

With an impulsive gesture Christie stretched her hands to the friends about her, and with one accord they laid theirs on hers, a loving league of sisters, old and young, black and white, rich and poor, each ready to do her part to hasten the coming of the happy end.

"Me too!" cried little Ruth, and spread her chubby hand above the rest: a hopeful omen, seeming to promise that the coming generation of women will not only receive but deserve their liberty, by learning that the greatest of God's gifts to us is the privilege of sharing His great work.

"Each ready to do her part to hasten the coming of the happy end."